The Jerusalem Case: 1

THE

CROWN AND OWN

SALVATION

The Jerusalem Case: I

THE CROWN AND SALVATION

NEIL R. FOX

ISBN: 978-1-4866-2245-0
eBook ISBN: 978-1-4866-2246-7

Word Alive Press
119 De Baets Street Winnipeg, MB R2J 3R9
www.wordalivepress.ca

WORD ALIVE
—P R E S S—

Cataloguing in Publication information can be obtained from Library and Archives Canada.

Dedicated to all my Grandchildren

Foreword

Fly on the wall?

What would it have been like to be a witness to the most momentous event in human history?

To be there as it unfolded, uncertain of what would come next. Fearful for your own safety.

How would you have reacted? The choice would have been yours to make and still is today.

I invite you to come on a journey. A journey of faith.

Prologue

THE YEAR IS 3792 BY THE HEBREW LUNAR CALENDAR.
A.D. 32 BY THE ROMAN SOLAR CALENDAR
THE DATE IS NISSAN 8,[1] FRIDAY APRIL, 4TH[2]

The insurgents had been meticulously planning this for weeks. It was to be a lightning-quick strike that would take place on this Friday afternoon, just before Shabbat, when the streets would be at their busiest.

Over 75 men from cell groups scattered around Jerusalem were now converging on the open square in front of the Antonia Fortress. There had been many successful raids earlier in the year, but this time something felt wrong. Nervous tension spread among them as they began to arrive , each scanning the perimeters, looking for danger.

The rebels came from all different directions, pouring out from the side streets into the square in unison. Armed Roman soldiers were on guard outside the massive fortress, lining the high wall by the main entrance. They stood in the sweltering afternoon sun, fully equipped with armor, sword, spear and shield, ready for action. The Zealots had only stones and daggers. Their intent was to disrupt.

These constant demonstrations of defiance were putting a strain on the Romans, but more importantly, word of the Zealots' simple successes was being spread throughout the land, attracting more young men to their movement. They would swiftly descend on the guards, pummeling them with rocks, causing as much injury as possible, then vanish into the crowded streets of Jerusalem.

These were Zealots. The religious right wing of the Pharisees who staunchly believed God gave the descendants of Abraham this land of Israel, and the Torah, to the Jewish people millennia before. They were to protect both at all costs. The Roman occupation had arrived almost a hundred years earlier, bringing with it pagan idol worship, military rule, corruption and crippling taxes. Rome ruled by brutality, but the Jews of Israel were not to be subdued easily.

Twenty-five years earlier witnessed the birth of the Zealots, the resistance.

---

[1] Biblical days begin at sundown. Nissan is the 1st month of the year.

[2] See appendix for all dates used

Within the first few years, they aggressively launched many assaults on the Romans, attempting to uproot them from Israel, the land of their fathers.

At the height of the rebels' strength years earlier, one such attack was a major advance on Jerusalem, which they nearly won. The Romans brought in the required reinforcements, brutally crushing the rebels, leaving them in total disarray, dispersing them throughout Israel. Now, over the past few years, they had regrouped. With new members enlisting every day, the Zealot movement was gaining strength rapidly, becoming more emboldened. With that came the equivalent response from Rome.

When the Zealots assembled in front of the fortress to begin their assault, the guards made no move to counter. They were expecting an alarm would be sounded immediately with the arrival of so many men simultaneously, but it was not. In front of the fortress the guards stood firm. The men looked at one another, sensing something was amiss. Suddenly, Roman soldiers poured out of the garrison entrance and side streets, swiftly surrounding them, engaging in battle. It was an ambush, a betrayal. It was fight or die.

It all happened so quickly. The whole square erupted into a fierce battle. Cries of injured men filled the air as others were dropping to the ground, dead. The Zealots were higher in numbers, but no contest for the trained and well-equipped soldiers with their heavy armor.

Atara was a new recruit, having just arrived in Jerusalem after a year of training with the Zealots. He immediately found himself face to face with a young Roman soldier brandishing a sword.

Backing away, he fired off as many stones from his pack as he could, the young soldier repelling them just as fast with his shield while moving forward, threatening. Out of stones Atara pulled out his dagger as the soldier lunged toward him. He evaded the thrust of the sword by twisting his body as the freshly honed steel sliced by his side, narrowly missing its mark. Engaging the soldier in a fierce skirmish one on one, they grappled close with each other for their lives. Sweat poured from both their bodies as they intertwined, forcefully wrestling for each other's weapon. Atara knew if they drew apart, he would be no match for the sword. Managing to grip the wrist that wielded the sword high in the air, he struggled to keep it away. The Roman held fast to Atara's wrist grasping the dagger.

It was a standoff, two locking eyes, inches apart. Atara could not hold the sword at bay for much longer. The other man was clearly stronger.

As Atara was about to lose this contest of strength, three of his comrades arrived, immediately pouncing on the soldier. For only a few seconds knives, fists, and sword all flailed in every direction until the young Roman went limp. Then a piercing cry. "Run!"

The Zealots were in retreat, scattering in every direction to the side streets leading away from the square with Roman soldiers hotly in pursuit.

Atara tore off in the direction leading toward the center of Jerusalem, hoping he would find safety there. Looking over his shoulder he could see several soldiers had spotted him, giving chase. Atara was young and fast, but he knew there would be more soldiers ahead stationed throughout the city on full alert. Barreling toward the street ahead, he reached down to sheath his dagger. The sight of crimson caught his eye. 'What have I done?' His only hope now would be to disappear into the crowds that had arrived for Passover.

Over the next few days leading up to Passover, Jews from all over Israel would arrive in Jerusalem, filling the city beyond capacity. Each day the streets would become more and more impenetrable as the multitudes squeezed into its narrow passages. So too would the Roman presence increase.

Atara entered the street leading to the market area at full speed, three soldiers at his heels.

The narrow residential street, with stone homes randomly stacked high one on another, offered no choice but forward. Fortunately, there were few pedestrians, allowing Atara to pull ahead with his youth and speed. The soldiers carried heavy weapons and armor, slowing their progress as they attempted to keep up. They pushed ahead, any person getting in their way being forcefully shoved aside.

One side street went by and then another. No doors or alleys to disappear in. Atara panicked. The streets leading to the market were all too crowded to pass through. With adrenaline pumping and long strides he managed to stay ahead of his pursuers. His sandals beat a soft pulsing sound as they pounded the ancient stones while those close behind clinked with the echo of iron. 'When, Lord? When will you deliver us from this oppression!' His eyes scanning desperately for a way out. 'They knew. They must have been informed. It was a trap.'

The soldiers had descended on them from all directions at the exact time of the uprising. They didn't stand a chance. He saw there was much bloodshed as the Romans outfought the Zealots, arresting many. Those captured would face certain death by crucifixion. The Romans had even overpowered one of their leaders, leaving the rest in chaos. He was a man that men would follow. A man that conveys strength and confidence. He was Jesus Barabbas. As Atara was backing away from the soldier, he saw the Romans take Barabbas, but not without heavy loss.

Never had Jerusalem suffered a time like this. Jerusalem, with its troubled history of wars, occupations and destructions, was under the siege of Rome. The Jews cried out for their messiah as never before. Beatings and crucifixions were a daily occurrence, men were arrested to be taken away as slaves for the ships' galleys for the most minor of offenses, and women were abused. The population lived in fear. The heavy Roman taxation was bleeding the tiny country dry while all resources were sent directly back to Rome. But worst of all was the pagan defilement Rome brought into Israel. Pagan gods of all types were being worshiped on Israel's soil with the influx of so many soldiers, politicians and their families. Israel, the land the one true God gave to Abraham and his offspring, the Jews, to worship Him. Jerusalem, where the Temple of the Lord was first established and the Ark of the Covenant once rested.

Sensing his dilemma Atara realized he would have to make a move. There was only one more market lane ahead before the street opened into a large square where there were certain to be more soldiers on guard. There was no choice. He had to turn into the market to disappear into the crowds. It was a risky move. There were Roman sentries posted at all major intersections while many others patrolled the streets, keeping Jerusalem in check.

'Now!' Atara made a sharp turn to the left, immediately encountering the congested market. Sweat poured down his forehead as he maneuvered his way through the packed street, twisting and turning stealthily around each person in his path. The soldiers made the turn, following him, gaining ground as they shoved marketgoers aside, forcing their way through.

This street was typical of the market area. The market was a labyrinth of narrow laneways and alleys buried deep beneath the shadows of stacked houses. Merchants with colorful wares tightly packed together in small stalls, crying out their special deals of the day. This was Friday afternoon, the busiest day of the week just before Shabbat. People were carrying out their last-minute purchases to take home in preparation for the Shabbat dinner. It was a sea of humanity pressed together, all with a common cause.

Following right after him, the cries of "Halt!" rang out from behind, the soldiers pushing closer. Atara was agile and slender. Bending down, he lowered his profile from their sight as he nimbly slipped through the throngs with little resistance.

The Romans, however, drew much resistance. Most here felt no love for them, making it as difficult as possible for them to pass through. But they did with brute force. Pushing and shoving the human traffic aside, they made progress toward their prey.

Not certain if they could still see him, Atara made a sudden turn to the right up a short alley to the next market street. Before turning again on the next street, he looked over his shoulder only to see his pursuers making the same turn. He had not lost them. Pivoting left on this incline, he bolted upward just as a large group of Pharisees, coming from afternoon prayers at the Temple, were arriving at this same intersection. They parted slightly, enough to allow him to slip through the assemblage unnoticed.

When the Romans arrived, seconds behind, the group instinctively closed ranks, making it as difficult as they could for the soldiers to pass. By the time they were free, Atara was gone.

The soldiers thrust their way through the market crowds, shouting for all to move aside. In frustration and anger, their tactic changed as swords came out, along with much cursing, making it clear they had had enough from the locals. They would deal mercilessly with anyone obstructing their way. Precious moments had been lost in their pursuit as they attempted to march up the incline, through the mass, hunting for the one eluding them. Ahead, by a couple of alleys, there were sentries stationed at their post now alerted to the search, closing off his only means of escape. They knew the rebel was near and they would ferret him out.

After making that turn, then through the group of Pharisees, Atara had stopped, desperately looking around to determine where to go. Fear was taking hold of him. He realized how impossible his situation had become. He was trapped.

Glancing to his left, he locked eyes with a fish merchant who motioned just perceivably with a slight shift in his gaze for Atara to take refuge behind his stall. With no time to think, he dove around the stall, tucking himself out of sight underneath the counter. The fishmonger, not missing a beat nor looking down, used his leg to slide over a barrel of smelly tilapia, covering Atara's position just as the Romans turned the corner, freeing themselves from the entanglement of the Pharisees.

They were now searching. The sentries up ahead were working their way down while his pursuers began searches through each small shop. Between a tiny crack Atara saw a pair of feet wearing the sandals of a Roman soldier stopping in front of the fishmonger's stall.

Another soldier could be heard pushing his way past the fishmonger into the booth, commenting on the foul odor, positioning himself only inches from Atara.

He could hear the inquisition.

Tucked in this tiny enclave, fear crept over him like a thousand spiders. There were informants everywhere. His life was at the mercy of those around. 'Would one of the marketgoers or merchants turn me in for a reward? Would the fishmonger lose his nerve and give me away? The penalty for harboring a fugitive would be severe. This man was risking his life.'

With the stench of fish all around him, Atara closed his eyes in fear, daring not move a muscle. As the soldier moved even closer, Atara silently held his breath.

Part I

A.D. 30

ISRAEL[3]

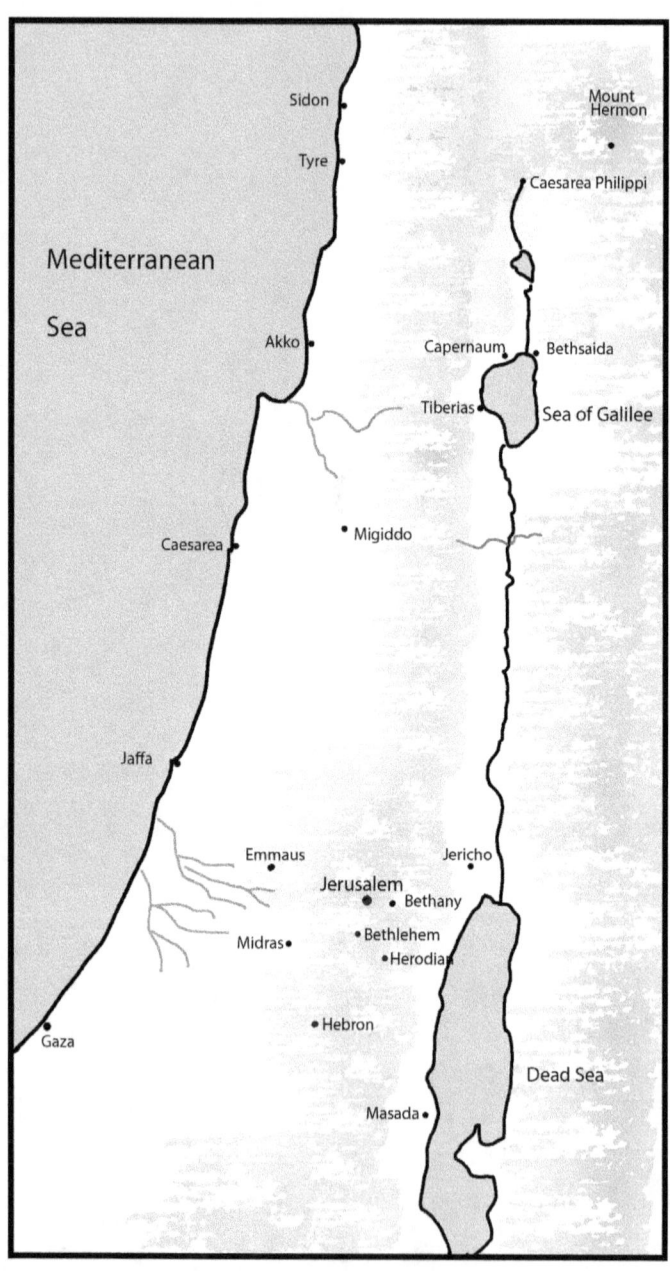

Sidon

Tyre

Mount Hermon

Caesarea Philippi

Mediterranean

Sea

Akko

Capernaum

Bethsaida

Tiberias

Sea of Galilee

Migiddo

Caesarea

Jaffa

Emmaus

Jericho

Jerusalem

Bethany

Bethlehem

Midras

Herodian

Hebron

Gaza

Dead Sea

Masada

---

[3] For information on Maps see Appendix

Chapter 1

THE PORT CITY OF SIDON: A.D. 30

A tara grew up in Sidon on the coast of the Mediterranean Sea. The family business was there. He loved standing on the pier with his father's hand in his, waving to his older brothers returning home from their first adventure at sea. His mother's embrace. Atara was young when she died and his memories of her were vague, but he could still remember her warmth, the sense of feeling secure.

His grandfather had come from Jerusalem to start this business as a result of the contacts he had procured in the court of Herod the Great. It was a prosperous time for anyone supplying materials for the king. Throughout his reign Herod engaged in many enormous building projects, creating a legacy for himself. He oversaw the creation of palaces and fortresses in Jerusalem along with water supply systems throughout the city. An entire mountain, the highest in all Judea, had been raised to construct a fortress palace south of Bethlehem, which he named after himself – Herodion. Masada was forged atop a massive butte by the Dead Sea as an impenetrable fortress. But Herod's rebuilding of the Great Temple of Jerusalem was the greatest achievement for the Jews. Royalty required the royal color. Purple dye was worth more in weight than gold. This is what drew Atara's grandfather to Sidon.

The royal dye was secreted from sea snails harvested from the Mediterranean Sea. The region of Sidon and Tyre along the coast had long been famous for the production of this rare color, now supplying the insatiable appetite of Rome. His grandfather moved the family business there many years before to act as agents of dye for Herod's projects. The business was tremendously successful. For the many years Herod reigned, there was no end to the continuous demand for their product. They even had the great honor of supplying dyes for the new Jerusalem Temple. Atara's father, Josiah BenAsher, followed successfully in his father's footsteps.

This was a time of good fortune for the BenAsher family. They lived well in Sidon, in a large mansion they had built by the sea with gardens and servants to look after them. Atara could remember the beautiful clothes his mother would wear of the finest materials, and could still smell the expensive fragrance that adorned her. With his brothers Reuben and Nathan he would play for hours in the garden, looking out to sea, breathing in the warm salt air, dreaming of adventure.

It wasn't long after Josiah BenAsher inherited the business that Herod the Great died. The family's business continued to thrive for many years, but eventually began to taper off with the number of projects from Jerusalem diminishing. Atara could remember his father sitting in his study, brow furrowed, looking over the books. Misfortune struck when his mother took ill. It was a painful illness of several months that eventually took her life. The loss of his wife changed Atara's father. He had been a good father and businessman, but to Atara he seemed like a different man afterward, losing the enthusiasm he once felt for life.

Josiah had the three boys tutored in their schooling. As the years progressed it was obvious the two older brothers were better suited for the outdoors, the physical life. Mayhem always reigned in the home when the brothers were around. Their poor tutor threw up his hands many a time in exasperation. Being quite a bit older than Atara, Reuben and Nathan finished their basic schooling long before him, both eager to get on with life, to begin working in the family business. Reuben had grown very tall as a young adult, robust and muscular. Nathan was only a little shorter, but made up for it with his broad shoulders and strength.

Atara was different. He loved the studies, proving to be a very talented student. Learning came easily as he studied hard, devouring books relentlessly, the Torah being his favorite subject. Their father made sure the boys had good religious training as they grew up – all holidays fully observed, the synagogue visited weekly, prayers said daily and Shabbat strictly adhered to. By the time Atara turned 13, Josiah decided it would serve the boy best to be sent to a good yeshiva for training to become a rabbi. Allowing his son to study would be a great sacrifice for him, as the family business needed all the help it could get, but it would be an honor to have a son as a rabbi.

Calling Atara into his study one day, Josiah addressed his son. "Atara, I have given a great deal of thought to your future."

This, not being a subject Atara had discussed with his father before, brought great apprehension as he stood nervously waiting. The family business did not capture his interest like it had his brothers. Atara was afraid his schooling would be over now, that he would be told tomorrow would be his first day in a career of dye marketing. "Yes," was all he could think of saying while awaiting the verdict.

"You have excelled in all of your studies and shown a great interest in the Torah. I believe you will someday make a great and learned rabbi. I would like to send you to the yeshiva in Sidon for further instruction."

Before his father could finish, Atara was already shouting with joy. This was a dream come true. "Thank you, Father! This is good news for me! I have wanted to continue learning and to be a rabbi as long as I can remember!"

"You will have to live at the yeshiva, coming home each week for Shabbat and all holidays. I will expect to hear that you are doing well, if you wish to continue."

"I will make you proud, Father."

Around the family table that night, Josiah announced the news to Atara's brothers.

"So the bookworm is getting out of the family business," chided Reuben.

"Choosing the easy life, eh Atara?" was Nathan's response as he playfully punched Atara in the arm.

Being only 13 Atara wasn't certain how to take these reproaches, but soon realized Reuben and Nathan were only teasing. They assured him how proud they would be of their little brother, the rabbi.

What Atara didn't know was that underneath the jesting the brothers were well aware of the difficulties that lay ahead.

Atara experienced little of Sidon in his formative years. Most of his upbringing was on their estate, remote from the realities of this famous port town. He had heard rumors spoken in their home, or when visiting Father's business, but was naïve to the ways of the city himself. Since his mother had passed away, the family kept very much to themselves.

Sidon was a Roman seaport. It was an international population comprised mostly of Phoenicians and Romans with roots going all the way back to the Canaanites. The Romans and Phoenicians brought their many pagan practises and gods with them to Sidon, constructing Temples everywhere throughout the city to these gods.

Being a port town immorality and debauchery of all kinds were accepted, even inspired by their gods. This was abhorrent to the minority Jewish population that lived and worked there. Roman coins had images of Caesar imprinted on them, graven images to the Jews. Rome demanded complete allegiance to Caesar, who they had recently elevated to the status of a god. When greeted by a Roman, there would be a pronouncement of "Hail Caesar!" If an equal response of "Hail Caesar," "Hail Caesar, son of god" or "Caesar is lord" was not forthcoming, it was treasonous. This was something the Jews of Sidon would not, could not, utter. It was a defilement of the one true God of Abraham.

For decades the Jews of Sidon managed to work in coexistence with their Roman neighbors with reasonable success. That was until Rome appointed a new governor to the province of Phoenicia in recent years. Atara was young then, but could still remember the hushed talk around the table of the persecution and restrictions under this militant new governor – a governor with no love for the Jews, also allowing much corruption to flourish under his authority.

However, the real trials for the BenAsher family still lay ahead. Taxes were being raised every year to support Rome's exorbitant expenses, crippling Jewish businesses in the region. As a result of Jewish problems intensifying in Jerusalem, the governor decided Rome would not purchase produce from Jewish businesses in Sidon, reducing the orders to a mere trickle. The final blow occurred when a new legion commander arrived – Lucius.

Lucius was appointed to Sidon just after Atara had left for the start of his yeshiva studies. Lucius hated the Jews. It was not long after his arrival in Sidon that he spotted the beautiful BenAsher mansion. Asking after it, he discovered it was owned by a Jewish merchant struggling with his business.

Commander Lucius paid Josiah BenAsher a visit shortly afterward at his office in the port district. He was an imposing man, tall and broad chested, immaculately dressed in full legionnaire uniform. After initial introductions he got right to the point. "I understand the estate on the town limits belongs to you. I would like to purchase it." This did not come across as a question.

Josiah BenAsher's response was swift. "It is not for sale."

"You would be wise to sell while the offer is fair," came the curt reply. "I understand your business is not doing well, that you are in arrears with your taxes. Do not wait for the inevitable."

There was a long pause in the room as the two men eyed each other, calculating their next move. Josiah would not sell to the Roman. But to defy the legion commander outright would be very dangerous. He needed to proceed cautiously.

"It is true, the business has had some minor setbacks. However, we are on the verge of turning our fortunes around with some lucrative contracts. Perhaps we could talk about this again in the future?"

This, of course, was not true. Their contracts had been slowly drying up over the years between Jerusalem and Rome. With new laws, taxes and restrictions being added each year, the situation was becoming impossible for the family business. But he would not sell to this Roman.

That was the only time the commander spoke with Josiah BenAsher.

The officer in charge of the port area had just been newly appointed by Commander Lucius. He was a centurion who was known by the name of Gallus. Gallus was a crude man. A professional soldier who took his orders seriously, relishing any opportunity for conflict he could take the pleasure of engaging in. Stocky, with many battle scars lacing his arms and face, Gallus brought fear to those he was ordered to deal with. His new assignment was simple – put Josiah BenAsher out of business, acquiring the estate for his commander.

The next four years would prove very difficult for the BenAsher family.

There were Roman laws in force. Rome had the authority to confiscate property for treason or unpaid taxes, but these cases could always be appealed and brought to trial. This is not what Lucius intended. It began with visits from

Gallus, always amply backed by a handful of armed soldiers, applying pressure for the heavy taxes owed. Each month the interest would increase with the payments crippling the business further. Then the isolation. Word traveled around the port that it would not be wise to do business with the BenAsher family. The fishermen avoided selling to them, the dock workers shunned the work and eventually the buyers evaporated into thin air. It was a desperate time for the family.

During this period Reuben and Nathan did all they could to support their father. The young men worked hard in the warehouse, went out to sea with local fishermen in search of the mollusks, doing what they could to maintain or find new accounts. But month by month the noose tightened. There was hardly ever a dinner hour where an argument or complaining did not take place, most of which centered around their increasing hatred of the Romans. By the end of the four years no servants were left in the household to care for it, and the business appeared to be beyond salvation.

Atara continued with his studies during this time. As a young teenager Josiah felt it would be better for Atara to complete his studies for his future. Initially Josiah and the brothers agreed it best not to involve Atara with the business problems so he would not feel obligated to return to the family to help out. They were proud of his achievements. But over the years the constant talk of the Roman oppression eventually led Atara to the revelation of the state of affairs. Atara knew. He saw the change in his brothers and father – the frustration, the anger.

While Atara was at the yeshiva, he thrived. He loved the study of the Torah and had a mind that was capable of remembering everything he read. The yeshiva he attended interpreted the Laws of the Torah very strictly, teaching Atara to love the order God instilled through them. As he grew, he learned more about the pagan ways of the Romans in Sidon as he and the other boys would huddle around each other, revealing all they had heard or seen. Corruption, false gods, slavery, Temple prostitutes, all within a thin veneer of a highly sophisticated society. But underneath it all was a brutal regime. The seeds of hatred and disdain that had been sown gradually grew within him.

It was in the summer of his 17th year that this would all change for Atara. At that time he still had two years left of yeshiva training to be completed. Atara was now well aware of the affairs of his family's business. One afternoon Josiah had called him home to discuss the future of his studies. The brothers were out to sea, so Josiah felt it would be a good time to speak with Atara privately about their state of affairs. There was no more money. The yeshiva had been gracious to the family regarding tuition, as Atara was a gifted student, but now a future plan would have to be worked out. He was a young man now, full grown, lean and studious. It was that fateful day when the pounding on the mansion's door interrupted their conversation, changing Atara's life forever.

There was no waiting for anyone to answer. Centurion Gallus entered the estate forthright, followed by four of his men. Josiah had made it as far as the study door, Atara at his side, when he came face to face with Gallus.

Standing squarely in front of Josiah, he commanded, "Josiah BenAsher, you are under arrest for the nonpayment of taxes and will be taken to Sidon prison to await trail." Seizing Josiah firmly by the arm, Gallus pulled him from the doorway into the hall.

In the split second Atara saw his aging father being manhandled, he pushed his way between Gallus and his father. Gallus was caught off balance, stepping back to regain his stance. Drawing his sword his eyes flashed with anger as he made a move toward Atara. Josiah, fearing his son would be killed, grabbed Gallus' arm, causing him to spin around in a furor, placing the blade deep between Josiah's ribs. The soldiers were already on Atara, firmly restraining him.

"No, stop!" he cried, as he watched his father crumple to the floor in a pool of blood.

Atara struggled with the soldiers, doubling over as they laid heavy blows to his side and head, beating him until he was almost unconscious.

"We will take this one to the prison," muttered Gallus coldly, more aggravated by the nuisance than anything else. "Commander Lucius can decide his fate there."

Two of the soldiers dragged the semiconscious Atara out of the house, tethering him to one of the horses waiting outside, to be forced to walk behind or be dragged. They had brought no arresting cart. There had never been any intention of bringing Josiah BenAsher out alive.

Further back from the gate stood a gleaming silver chariot with Legion Commander Lucius watching over the proceedings, waiting to enter his new home.

Chapter 3

Pulling up to the shore, all six men nimbly hopped from the craft to pull it firmly onto the beach. Reuben and Nathan were about to help with the catch when another fisherman coming from further up the beach approached them, slyly whispering something in Reuben's ear, then continuing down the beach without looking back.

The two brothers moved close together, whispering to each other for a moment. Looking in the direction the fisherman had come from they saw a Roman patrol questioning each boat as they arrived. They knew the soldiers were searching for them.

Without speaking a word the young men picked up their belongings, headed along the beach away from the patrol, then over the break wall out of sight.

By good fortune the crew of the boat had beached it farthest from the city port. If they had been any closer, the brothers would have had to pass through a Roman checkpoint to leave the port area. From here though, all they had to do was walk up from the beach into the city, keeping a watchful eye for any patrols. They headed directly to the home of family friends to find out what had occurred. Levi and Talia had watched these boys grow up and quickly ushered them into their home.

"What has happened?" questioned Nathan. "When we returned from sea, we were tipped off that the Romans had a warrant for our arrest!"

"It is true," replied Levi as he bid them to sit in the front room. "Word is that earlier today Centurion Gallus," at which point he spit on the floor, showing his disdain, "entered your family home with an order to arrest your father. It appears some sort of altercation took place. I am sorry to tell you, my dear boys, that your father was killed. He was murdered by that Roman. Talia and I were just about to go to the local station to see about your poor father's body for a proper burial."

The brothers sank back in their chairs in disbelief, trying desperately to process this information. "How could this happen?"

"There is more. Apparently Atara was home at that exact time with your father. I don't know all that happened, but they have beaten and arrested him. At this moment they are combing the city for you two. It is no secret among our community that Commander Lucius has wanted your family estate for some time and now he has it after sending his thug Gallus to do his dirty work. Your father had been warned of the risk by a number of us, but wrongly felt Roman law would prevail. Sadly, it didn't. I am so sorry."

"Roman law!" seethed Reuben, up and pacing. "There is no law for us here! The Romans take what they want from us and leave us with nothing!" He sank back into his chair with his head between his hands. "What will we do now? What about Atara?"

Nathan just sat looking at the floor, fist clenched, jaws grinding with anger.

"We will have to see what can be done about him. It will likely take some time for a trial to take place. Our community will do all we can to help with that. As for you both you need to get far away from here. We have friends in Tiberius, by the Sea of Galilee. They will help you."

"What about Father? How will we bury him?" asked Reuben. "We must be here to see that he has a proper burial!"

"You can't stay here. The Romans have spies everywhere who will be watching for you. If you try to attend your father's funeral, they will arrest you. You are wanted on charges of tax evasion, but these are fraudulent. Lucius wants you out of the way so no protest can be made over his illegal acquisition of your father's estate. You must flee. The Romans are looking for strong men like you to send to the galleys and quarries. You would never return."

Levi stepped out of the room. The boys sat in silence, stunned and seething with anger. The tears would come later. The shock was too great.

After a while Levi returned with two packs. "Here are some supplies. This should help with your travels in the next few days. Also," pulling a small pouch out from the pack, "your father did anticipate that there would be trouble ahead, so he left some money here for you just in case. Take it now, the address you need is in there. Go with God's speed. You dare not stay here any longer, but you must be vigilant in avoiding any Roman patrols you see."

"But Atara!" protested Nathan. "We can't abandon him!"

"You must, otherwise you will only join him. We will do all that we can for him here. I will send word to Tiberias of any news. Now go!"

The young men stood to embrace their friends, Talia with tears in her eyes. Reuben and Nathan turned away, bolting out the front door into the yard. In anger and despair, Nathan landed a hard blow with his fist while passing the large tree in the center of the garden, mixing flesh with bark. They disappeared down the path out of sight.

Chapter 4

Atara had no memory of the past hour. In a daze, half walking and half being dragged behind the centurion's horse, they had brought him into the Sidon Fortress. The soldiers then stripped and flogged him before taking him to a cell, which was standard Roman procedure to ensure there would be little resistance from the prisoner. He was thrown to the ground as the iron gate slammed behind him.

His cell was deep under the fortress. Atara's eyes strained to see, but could make out nothing in this tiny dungeon. 'Am I blind?' he thought as he lay on the cold stone ground in the blackness. After some time his eyes were still attempting to adjust to the single ray of light emanating from the tiny opening near the ceiling, allowing him to see ever so slightly – nothing. Just a block room, not even large enough to lie down in, with only a tiny hole in one corner for sewage. Other sounds could be heard echoing off the stone, but they seemed abstract, miles away. The place reeked of urine. Atara curled up with his knees to his chest and wept.

'Was Father really dead? How could this have happened?'

The pain was overwhelming. The beating and flogging were now taking full effect. Bruises to his sides, chest and face were now beginning to swell, tightening the skin, intensifying his misery as it did. The lashes were moist with blood, burning as if hot coals had been poured onto his back. The agony subsided only when he finally passed out.

When he woke he had no idea how long he had been in this tiny cell. Hours? Days? At first he had trouble opening his eyes as they were caked together so badly. Pushing himself to sit up, Atara surveyed his surroundings, his eyes now fully adjusted to the darkness. Just stone walls with an iron gate were all this prison offered. A small pan sat on the floor in front of him that had been slid under the gate. All that was left were a few crumbs the vermin had missed.

Forcing himself to stand Atara moved closer to the iron gate to find out what he could see. With his face against the bars he saw a long corridor to the left with iron gates lining both sides. His cell was at the end, far away from the others. The faint sounds of prisoners drifted through the tunnel toward him from a distance, but no one spoke. He knew where he was.

He sat back down on the hard floor. It seemed as if it was just minutes ago he was in the study talking with his father. Slowly, the realization of his situation began to sink in. 'What will happen to me? Did they arrest Reuben and Nathan? What charges will be laid? When will there be a trial?' Questions played over and over in his mind as he tried desperately to find answers. But there were none. He mourned for his father, blaming himself for his death, not knowing Commander Lucius had ordered Gallus to be certain Josiah did not come out of the house alive.

The first few days went by much the same. He would sit on the stone floor, rocking back and forth, mourning his father, uncertain of his brothers' fate and his own desperate situation. Night and day fought with each other as Atara slipped in and out of consciousness while his body wrestled with its wounds, fever burning inside and out. The small tray left each day was untouched till the vermin found their way. Vague memories haunted his sleep of strange sensations moving up a leg or across his body until he shook them off. 'Am I in hell?'

By the fourth day the fever broke, allowing Atara to begin thinking much clearer. The swelling from the bruising had gone down and the flesh wounds to his back had begun to heal, but now a different type of torture awaited. The light through the tiny window, if you could call it that, had just begun to show itself, so Atara figured it was now morning. He wasn't sure how many days he had already been here, but knew he had had nothing to eat for days. He heard the noises and voices of other prisoners as the jailer worked his way down the dim corridor.

When he arrived at the end, Atara's cell, Atara stood, demanding answers. "Where is my counsel? How long am I to be held here? Are my brothers here?"

In the dim light the jailer just gave Atara a vacant look, then bent over abruptly, sliding the final pan of bread under the door.

"Why won't you answer me? Can you help me? I have injuries!" Atara persisted, anger growing stronger.

It was some time later he discovered his jailer had no tongue.

Each day was the same. The mute man arrived with a small amount of food, then would later work his way down the subterranean tunnel with water to fill the small pans. Never, of course, a word spoken. The daily food was mostly a piece of stale bread. Atara quickly learned that every third day or so there would be some sort of rancid stew mix added to the plate. At first, he balked at the horrid mix, but soon realized this only form of nourishment was badly needed, so he ate. From time to time he would hear voices, sometimes other prisoners talking with each other, but most of the time it would be soldiers either bringing in a new prisoner or taking one out. This confused him. The prison seemed to be a very busy place with prisoners coming and going. 'Why haven't they come to take me to trial?'

The days turned into weeks. Whenever soldiers arrived escorting a prisoner, Atara would shout down the hall, begging for someone to speak with him, tell him what was happening. But no one ever did. He was left very much alone.

For the first two weeks, he spent long days and nights questioning God. 'Why? Why has this happened? I didn't deserve this! Haven't I been an outstanding student and observant Jew, abiding by God's Laws faithfully? Studying the Torah?' Following this was always the denial and blame. 'Why, God? Why would you do this to me?'

Slowly, through all his misery, he began to listen to a voice. It was his own. It was his own. Complaining, whining, lamenting. It was his own arrogant voice blaming God for his situation. Atara had been a privileged child. He knew nothing of suffering or sacrifice growing up. Day by day he began to realize his own sense of self-importance as he sat on the cell floor, truly hearing himself for the first time ever. He did not like what he heard.

One day a scripture came to him – Job 13:15: *"Though he slay me, yet will I hope in him.* Hope? Is that what it takes? Hope in what?'

Isaiah 40:30–31 also flashed through his mind. *'Even youths grow tired and weary, and young men stumble and fall; but those who hope in the Lord will renew their strength, they will soar on wings like eagles; they will run and not grow weary, they will walk and not be faint.* Yes, there is hope! God has promised us the messiah. That is our hope! With the messiah we'll defeat the Romans to be free to worship God once again. Hope.'

From that day forward scriptures flowed into Atara's mind, filling his days. His mind was such that all of what he had read in the yeshiva over the years he found he was able to recall, verse by verse, chapter by chapter. Atara vowed to survive this with God's help, believing in the hope of the coming messiah. 'Wasn't it supposed to be soon?'

He made a plan for each day, creating a routine he would meticulously follow. Recite scriptures, meditate on them, pacing his tiny enclosure to condition his legs, exercising in any imaginative way he could think of to build his body up. Atara found what must have been at least a hundred creative ways to use the cell's bars as a tool for exercise. So he filled his days in this tiny, clammy cell. Day after day with no word, hoping and praying for the messiah to come.

Night brought with it a different underbelly of trials. Atara found his mood would shift as he lay on the damp stone, trying desperately to shut out this horrible little world that had been thrust on him. Scenes of his father's death would come to him, the Roman sword piercing the flesh. The expression of surprise on his father's face as he fell to the ground stayed frozen in his mind. The anguish of not knowing about his brothers, or his own fate, played over and over, anger boiling within him. It was the Romans. These defiled people who bring with them persecution and cruelty. He recalled every discussion at the yeshiva, and at home, of Roman profanity. His hatred began to cut deeply as he lay awake at night, haunted by the demons of despair feeding on his seething anger. And the fear, unexplainable fear that would consume him through the night.

As the days passed life became a little more tolerable. Atara disciplined himself to say the morning and evening prayers. For every pittance of food he received, he made certain a blessing was said over it. In the first months he had suffered from food poisoning twice, leaving him crippled in agony, lying on the cell floor for days. Since blessing the food he had been fine.

He did not know what day it was, but wanting to observe Shabbat he made his own schedule to be observant of God's command. Atara believed the way to God was through His Laws, that those obedient to the Laws would be in God's favor, which he needed desperately. But how to atone for his sins? This fear and anger that was gripping his soul?

It might have been around nine months — he had lost track of time — that early one morning Atara opened his eyes, sensing a cloaked presence standing in front of the iron bars.

Startled, he jumped to his feet. He had seen no other man, other than the mute jailer, the whole time of his incarceration. Occasionally, when a prisoner was being escorted to or from a nearby cell, if he pressed his face against the bars, he could see the motion of a figure being shoved into a cell, but otherwise, no one. Atara approached the bars as the man lowered his hood.

It was Levi.

Levi recoiled from the sight. Even in this dimness, Atara's stench and appearance caused him to step back from the bars.

"Ssshh, we must be very quiet. I am so sorry it has taken this long, Atara," began Levi while covering his nose with a cloth. "It was months before we found out where they had taken you. We first assumed they had transferred you to the ships' galleys or quarries, but eventually tracked you down here."

"Reuben and Nathan? Where are they?"

"They are fine. When they returned from fishing that day, the Romans were searching for them. They managed to escape successfully to the Galilee area. Your brothers have now joined the Zealots."

"The Zealots. Yes, yes, that is the way to fight the Romans! Why am I here? Why has there been no trial? Why are they just leaving me to rot in this dungeon?"

"We think that is exactly what Lucius wants. He has taken your family property illegally and can have no witnesses. You were not expected to be there that day at the house. Gallus had been ordered to kill your father, making it look like he resisted arrest, but you have posed an obstacle. You can't go to trial, so Lucius has made certain you have been hidden away at the back of this dungeon with instructions that no one might see or know about you."

The realization his father's death had been prearranged lifted an enormous weight off his shoulders, even as he stood listening to Levi. "You mean it wasn't my fault? I'm not to blame?"

"No, my dear boy. His death had nothing to do with you."

Atara felt the tears welling, but blinked them back. So many questions remained.

"So many prisoners pass through here. Where do they go?"

"You are in the Sidon prison. It is just holding cells for accused convicts until their trial. The Romans have no intention of feeding prisoners any longer than they have to, so the trials are quick. The condemned are taken directly to row in the galleys of the navy's ships, or to the quarries. Either way, no man survives. If a prisoner is condemned to death, it is to the courtyard to be lashed, then to a cross for public crucifixion. You have just been hidden away, as if you don't exist."

Atara's head bowed low. 'Don't exist.'

«What news is there from outside?"

"The situation for we Jews here is still the same. Though last week there was a visit of a man from the Galilee who they say is a prophet, some even say he is the messiah. He spoke of love and forgiveness, healing many and casting out demons. I did not see him, but there was much talk at the synagogue about this man."

"The messiah? Did he talk of defeating the Romans? Will he unite an army?"

"That, I cannot say. Only time will reveal an answer to that. And I have little time today," added Levi with a sense of urgency. "We are trying to work out a plan to get you out of here. It is very difficult and dangerous, taking a great deal of strategy. No one has ever escaped from here before. I finally was able to bribe my way in today, but I don't think I will be able to do that again, so you will have to be patient. Here, I have brought some clothes and food, there is a blanket in there as well." Levi pushed the bulky package under the cell door. "I have to go now, but I want you to know that there is hope, that we are doing all that we can."

Atara nodded in appreciation. He desperately did not want Levi to go. This was the first human contact he'd had in over nine months. "What about father, did he have a proper burial?" he asked, holding on to every second.

"Yes, we gave your father a good burial, observing all our traditions. I must go now." Levi moved away from the bars.

"Levi," Atara whispered.

"Yes?"

"What day is it?"

"It is Shabbat."

Levi turned, groping his way down the dark corridor of human misery, disappearing out of sight.

Atara stepped back and smiled. Shabbat. God had given him the correct day to choose as his Shabbat.

The visit gave him a renewed sense of hope. For days he basked in the knowledge he had not been forgotten, that Reuben and Nathan were safe and that there was hope for his release. And a messiah? Perhaps there was cause for hope. He rationed the fresh food Levi had brought, savoring every bite, defending it from the vermin that stalked his cell. He cherished the clean clothing, vowing to take a small amount of his daily water to cleanse himself. The old clothing was compacted into a pillow. But the blanket! The luxury of a warm blanket on the cold, damp stones restored his spirit.

As the days turned into weeks the hope remained, but the excitement and certainty eventually began to diminish. When the weeks turned into months, the night demons eventually returned, torturing him once again.

Chapter 5

It was midday when Atara heard the familiar sounds of steel armor and weapons clanging down the long corridor, searching for their prisoner. But this time it continued farther, stopping directly in front of his cell. He had been sitting with his back to the iron bars reciting scriptures, imagining the single tiny ray of light coming through the hole in the wall was bathing him in warmth. He spun his head around to see the glimmer reflecting off the breastplates of two tall Roman soldiers positioned in front of his bars.

'Is this it? Am I to be finally taken away to be crucified?'

One soldier motioned for him to approach the bars. As Atara stood, straining his eyes after looking up at the little daylight, he suddenly recognized the faces.

"Reuben! Nathan!"

Their fingers went immediately to their lips, motioning for him to be quiet. Both brothers looked carefully at Atara in the darkness, barely recognizing him. He had lost so much weight, his arms so thin, they could put their thumb and forefinger around the whole diameter. He had a long, scraggly beard with hair that ran down his back, all twisted and matted. Atara could see the shock in their eyes.

To him they looked like gleaming angels. Tall and full figures with muscles that rippled through their arms as they spoke. 'They look just like Roman soldiers.' He fought the tears as he looked into his brothers' eyes.

"We must be quiet and quick," said Reuben. "There is no time to talk now. This is very dangerous what we are about to do, so you need to listen to everything we have to say. Can you do that?"

Atara nodded.

Nathan slipped back down the corridor to fetch the jailkeeper.

Reuben continued, "We will take you out as a prisoner. You must allow us to drag you and abuse you as a Roman soldier would. We will pass through the courtyard to the front gate. There we will show the soldiers on guard the forged papers we have, ordering us to take you to the quarries for work. Don't worry, we are certainly not going there. The centurion in charge right at this moment has agreed to help us. If he keeps his word, we will pass out of here to make our escape. It will be a long, hard journey, and by the looks of you this will be very difficult. Do you understand?"

"Yes, but where did you get the uniforms?"

Reuben only gave a slight smile as Nathan returned.

This rescue attempt had taken months to plan. There wasn't any question of successfully having Atara released legally. Lucius had made certain of that. The only option was escape, but no one had ever escaped from this fortress. It was surrounded on four sides by the Mediterranean Sea with a single rampart leading from the main gate to the shore, a long walk that would expose any enemy or those trying to escape. By sea seemed impossible because you would have to lower yourself 150 feet by rope without being spotted by tower guards. The only option turned out to be a bold attempt right under their noses.

The key problem they had to solve was how to get past the guards at the main gate. With uniforms and forged papers, the rest would be simple enough as long as no one suspected. But they needed to be certain they would be let through the gate. The brothers kept a very low profile while in Sidon because they were wanted men, but with the help of the local community they made a possible contact that offered a solution.

There was an apparent rivalry between two officers in the forces. Two centurions. One was Gallus and the other a soldier named Quintus. Rumor had it Centurion Quintus was a decent man, sympathetic to the plight of the local Jews, quite unlike Gallus, who was no more than a thug. Approaching the man would be very risky as he could decide to arrest them at any time. Through mutual friends the contact was made and a meeting arranged. It was agreed only one brother would go, just in case something went awry.

On the day of the meeting, Reuben walked along the path with a great deal of apprehension to a local restaurant where the meeting was to take place. He carefully surveyed the surrounding alleys and buildings to be sure he was not walking into a trap. Once convinced it was safe, he entered the courtyard of the restaurant to find a lone soldier in full centurion uniform sitting at the far table, very much alone as the restaurant had not yet opened for the day.

Introducing himself he sat in front of Centurion Quintus, nervously eyeing the Roman. Reuben laid out the entire story of Commander Lucius' plot to seize the BenAsher estate, strangling the family business, leading to the murder of his father. He told Quintus of Atara's misfortune of being there at the wrong time, how he has been imprisoned with no trial for over a year. All the time Quintus sat without a word, listening.

"What is it you want me to do?" asked Quintus when Reuben was finished.

Reuben took the biggest gamble of his life. "I believe the only way to get Atara out is for my brother and I to walk in and escort him out."

Quintus scoffed. "How could you possibly do that? No one has ever escaped from the fortress!"

"And no one will," answered Reuben. By your own Roman ledgers, Atara is not even there, so there is no risk to anyone. Only Gallus and Lucius know. Lucius would not dare expose his own crimes, so an alarm might never even be raised!"

Now Quintus leaned forward, listening more attentively. "But how would you expect to walk right by the Roman guard?"

"In Roman uniform," came the reply.

Quintus leaned back and very much to Reuben's great surprise let out a hearty laugh. "Well, I never thought I would see the day when two Jews would be brave enough to walk right into a Roman outpost to pull something like this off!"

To which Reuben thought to himself, 'You have never read our scriptures. The stories of many brave men protected by God to do His will!'

The soldier sat, rubbing his chin while contemplating what he had just been asked to do. He thought of his contempt for unprofessional soldiers like Gallus, who rob and kill whoever they wish. Of greedy commanders of legions, like Lucius, who take want they want, conniving and cheating their way to wealth. To Quintus, this was not what the Roman army stood for. It stood for law and order, and this was neither.

Quintus looked again at Reuben, admiring the strength and conviction of this young man. Good Roman qualities. "I assume you already are aware that I head the squadron twice a week on the gate to the fortress."

Reuben nodded. Quintus smiled.

"And where do you intend to acquire two Roman uniforms? I trust you would not be trying to murder some of my men!"

"No, sir. We were hoping you would be able to loan us those."

"By the gods! Is there anything else you would like? A couple of horses perhaps?" His voice ricocheted off the walls.

Reuben was aghast. He thought he pushed too hard, now endangering himself and his brother.

"Next Wednesday at 1 p.m. I will leave uniforms for you in a shed out back of this courtyard. Pick them up that morning at sunrise and be sure to return them immediately afterward."

Quintus stood, looked Reuben in the eyes, then began to abruptly walk out. Several paces away he paused and looked over his shoulder. "If you fail and are captured, I will personally cut out your tongues so you might never speak of this. You should pray to your God that Gallus does not show that day." He turned away, exiting the small courtyard.

Reuben sat for some time before his shaking legs would lift him to his feet. He realized the forged papers alone would not have escaped the astuteness of this man. They needed his help and must now put their trust in God.

———————————

The door to the cell gave way to the iron key as it slowly squealed open in protest. It had been over a year since it was last used. The brothers immediately began their ruse by seizing Atara roughly by the arms, pulling him from the cell.

"My belongings!" protested Atara.

"You won't be needing them where you are going!" replied Nathan curtly for the benefit of the jailkeeper and prying eyes.

They pushed past the jailkeeper, half dragging Atara as they moved along the narrow dungeon, down a corridor Atara had no memory of. The brothers pulled him up flights of stairs, easing a little as they went, arriving at the door of the central tower. All three brothers looked at one another, and with a quick prayer to God opened the door to the courtyard.

The afternoon sun blazed into their eyes. For the brothers it only took a second to adjust, but for Atara it had been so long since he had been in daylight, the pain seared deeply into his brain. He cried out in his anguish, trying desperately to cover his eyes.

The center of the courtyard was full of soldiers on drill exercises. On the perimeters many were walking to and fro about their duties. Reuben and Nathan dared not hesitate. They pulled Atara forward, mercilessly marching toward the gate. Crossing the perimeter of the courtyard took mere seconds before arriving at the main gate where they found themselves standing at full attention in front of a blockade. Many soldiers milled around with one approaching to demand the papers. He looked the trio over suspiciously, then began to open the seal on the forged orders. Out of the guard tower marched Quintus. "Give me the papers!"

Reuben and Nathan didn't breathe. Atara, still struggling with the light, could barely stand as the two soldiers held him in place. This was it. This is when they would find out if Quintus was going to arrest them or have mercy on them. Their lives were in his hands, surrounded by Roman soldiers, and they were well aware of it.

Quintus examined the documents, paused for what seemed like an eternity, then looked at the three of them, slowly, up and down. 'What kind of love and loyalty would bind these brothers with so much strength?'

"Take your prisoner and follow the orders," was all he barked, loud enough for all to hear as he handed the papers back. "Be on your way."

The boys dragged Atara at a pace faster than he could walk all the way down the long rampart that separated the fortress from land. At the end they had a cart with horse waiting to throw the prisoner in, leading him away from the dungeon.

Several blocks later, when no one was looking, they pulled into a small gated courtyard, shutting the gate behind. They would now get ready to leave Sidon immediately in case an alarm was sounded, resulting in a citywide manhunt they would not likely escape.

But that never happened. Atara became the first man to escape the Sidon Fortress, and no one would ever hear about it.

Chapter 6

When Reuben and Nathan arrived at Levi's home, it was the first opportunity they had to carefully look at Atara. They were horrified by what they saw.

He was still struggling with the bright daylight. He stood before them, shaking from the strain, pale, dirty and scrawny, probably weighing no more than 100 pounds. Sores covered his body from the lack of nutrition, perhaps even from vermin bites. He now had a long, scraggly, unkept beard, matching his lengthy, unwashed hair, along with the stench of one year's worth of grime. But that did not matter. The three boys drew close in a long embrace to celebrate their reunion and success. Tears flowed amid the happiness as they gave thanks to the one true God for their deliverance.

Atara was taken directly inside the home by Levi and Talia. Shortly after, friends arrived to help by returning the armor and uniform back to the shed where Quintus had left them. In no time Atara was back outside, cleaned, fed and trimmed, ready to leave. The brothers knew they could not stay there long, endangering their friends. They must move on.

"He was not able to eat much," Talia informed them, the mother in her coming out as she attempted to instruct the brothers on how to look after him. "All that time in prison must have shrunk his stomach. Forcing him now would just make him sick, so you will have to increase his diet slowly. Also his skin is very pale and the sun will burn it easily. Take this shawl and use it for several days until he adjusts. You should know Atara is very weak. I don't know how he will be able to do this. Perhaps you should stay here for a while, just until he gathers his strength?"

Reuben replied, "That is not an option. You have been so kind to us. May God bless you both."

"I have spent most of my days pacing that small cell," added Atara, hoping to show some confidence. "I will be able to walk."

After Levi spoke a blessing over them, the three brothers left the home, and Sidon, forever.

The journey was a slow one. Atara was indeed weak, taking many rests initially to continue. They avoided main roads and checkpoints, especially the Appian Way, the central Roman corridor that ran directly down the center of Israel to Jerusalem. From Sidon they worked their way into the mountains to the east, then traveled southward at the higher altitudes through the forests toward the Galilee. It was Spring now and the fresh, cool air of the mountains invigorated Atara as he grew stronger.

Initially, the brothers had planned to stop in the Galilee for a while, but soon realized it would not be a good idea. If word was out of an escape, Tiberias would not be a safe place for them. They agreed their eventual destination would be an enclave of Zealots in the foothills southwest of Jerusalem near Midras. Atara had informed them of his decision to join the Zealots in their fight against the Roman army, so to Midras it was.

They continued their journey south, past the Galilee, following the mountain forests toward Jerusalem. To avoid contact with people, when supplies were needed only one brother, Reuben or Nathan, would go into a town to make purchases. Atara discovered Nathan had become quite an adept hunter while with the Zealots. Pheasant and quail frequently supplemented their diet very nicely.

As they neared Jerusalem it was necessary to turn westward into the foothills to avoid the area entirely. Jerusalem had the heaviest concentration of Roman soldiers in all Israel. Skirting around the city was also dangerous, simply because of the higher population of the entire region. However, by this time the trio had become more relaxed as they worked their way toward Midras. Anytime one of them had been in a small town, they inquired about the latest news, but there was never mention of an escape from Sidon Fortress.

A few days later they were in Midras. The entire trip had taken close to a month, three times what it could have taken if they had come directly from Sidon, and if Atara had been in good health. He was much better now as most of his strength had returned. The majority of sores had healed, he was acclimatized to the Mediterranean sun and the haunting memories of his nights were gradually diminishing.

There was no Roman presence in the area of Midras. The village itself was small, in a good farming area of gently rolling hills with good soil. The Zealots had chosen to make their base camp nearby.

The brothers circumvented the village, walking up a dusty path through a field of grain. It was a perfect Spring day, blue sky laced with white cumulus clouds drifting slowly by. When they reached the top of the hill, before them lay a wide open field with many men milling about, some in combat drills, others exercising in the fresh air, even a fire blazing with a lamb roasting above. It surprised Atara to see so many men.

"Welcome to Midras!" Reuben said, putting his arm around Atara's shoulder. "This is where we trained to be Zealots! Now it is your turn, little brother!"

Atara marveled at all the activity, but turned to his brothers. "I don't see any barracks or homes. Where does everyone stay?"

The brothers both laughed. "You will see."

When they reached the bottom of the hill, they were greeted heartily by many men. Micah, Seth, Dov, Daniel – too many names and faces to remember, but already Atara felt the comradeship in this band. Men very much like his brothers and him – young, ambitious, religious, full of a common hatred for the Romans. The greetings went on for the rest of the afternoon as the brothers moved about the grounds reuniting with their comrades.

When the sun was low, Nathan spoke up. "Well, Reuben, do you think it is time to show Atara where he will be staying?"

"Let's go."

They walked with Atara up a nearby hill, then descended through a field of wild grasses and flowers, a blanket of vivid red poppies waving gently in the afternoon breeze like ripples of water over a shallow beach. Reaching the bottom Atara spotted several tombs nearby he thought must serve the local village. The brothers stopped at the first and looked in.

These tombs were large, open rooms cut into the soft earth of the hillside with a stone archway built around the entrance, large enough for a man to enter. A large round stone had been rolled back, leaving the tomb open.

Atara stopped, firmly digging his feet into the ground. "We're not going in there?" was really more of a statement than a question.

"Yes, we will show you."

"But isn't it a defilement of the dead?"

"No," replied Reuben. "These tombs were emptied centuries before. The stone sarcophaguses remain, but that is all. The Romans won't enter a tomb because of their superstitions, so it suits our needs perfectly."

"How can we all fit?" Then, admitting more to the truth of the matter, "I don't think I can go back into a confined space after that prison."

Understanding Atara's hesitation Reuben answered. "You will see. There is plenty of space. Come, we will show you."

The brothers entered the tomb, ducking through the small entrance as they went. Standing for a while to allow their eyes to adjust, they pointed to the three sarcophaguses that lined the wall of the small chamber. Then walking around behind the far sarcophagus, tucked away hidden from view in the tight space between the wall and the sarcophagus, was the opening of a tunnel.

"Each sarcophagus has a tunnel behind," explained Reuben. "Two of the tunnels are false, leading deep into the hillside. The other one leads into our quarters. If we were to be pursued by the Romans, they would have to split up to find us. The tunnels are made very narrow, so a soldier can't enter with his armor, giving us a fighting chance. We are constructing an underground network through this entire region, enabling us to perform raids, then disappear! Can you do this? Can you make it through?"

Atara looked ahead at the tiny hole in the dim light. He could feel the beads of sweat beginning to form on his forehead.

"Yes, I can," he replied, as he steeled himself for what lay ahead. "I'll remember this is freedom, that this will be my revenge for father."

With that said Reuben squeezed between the sarcophagus and the wall, bent over, twisting into the black hole, then disappeared. It was now Atara's turn. Squeezing, bending, peering into the hole, Atara could just barely see Reuben's sandals as they vanished into the dark. He wanted, needed, to be close to him, so he made the move, pushing ahead into the tunnel.

It was only shoulder width. The only way forward was to wiggle through, using his elbows and knees to make progress. Nose to boot, Nathan followed closely behind, talking with Atara the whole time, making sure he was alright. On and on they went, Atara feeling the perspiration dripping into his eyes, not even being able to move his hands to wipe it away.

Finally, when he thought he could see a glimmer of light ahead, Atara moved swiftly to escape this confinement. After Reuben he popped out of the tunnel, rolling onto the ground with Nathan not far behind. Brushing themselves off they were now standing in a room-sized chamber lit by a single torch lamp.

"Is this it? Is this where we're going to stay?" panicked Atara. 'It's larger than my cell, but how could someone live here?'

"No, this is just for the Romans," replied Reuben. "Look, if any Roman soldier is in pursuit, the minute their head pops out of the tunnel, well, let's just say his shoulders would quickly be much lighter. The body would plug the tunnel, giving us more time. Look behind."

Atara turned and now noticed four separate tunnels leading out of the chamber.

"It is a maze," Reuben continued. "Three of the tunnels are false. The Romans won't know which one to take if they break through, once again buying us a great deal of time while they try to find their way. These tunnels go on for quite a distance, twisting and turning. If 20 or so soldiers enter, when they hit a dead end, the only way out is for the long strand of men to wiggle backward! Not an easy feat.

"Look here." Reuben took the light and shone it into the tunnel on the far right. "When you look down this tunnel all you see is a dead end, but it is deceiving. When you arrive there, you discover it takes a sharp turn down, hiding its true nature. Come on, let's continue. Are you okay?"

Atara nodded, but wasn't so sure. He followed Reuben, entering the tunnel, feeling his way along in the blackness. After a short distance the tunnel did in fact drop straight down. He had to bend forward, push with his toes, then slither downward without being able to move his arms ahead to block the fall. Digging his elbows against the sides to act as brakes, upside down, until he finally touched bottom softly with his head, then arching his back to go horizontal once again. For Atara, being so slight, he had plenty of room to maneuver, but by the sounds of his brothers' grunts and groans, they were having a much more difficult time.

This tunnel led to another chamber of mazes, then eventually after yet another tunnel Atara found himself standing in an enormous, well-lit man-made cavern, large enough to hold a hundred men. It had multiple rooms leading off to the sides, even stairs up to second-floor rooms. Atara just stood in amazement.

"What do you think?" asked Nathan. "Enough room here for you?"

Atara didn't quite know what to say as he scanned the premises. "How long has it taken to build this?"

"It has been years in the making," answered Reuben. "There are many more like this and we are digging out more all the time. The Romans have never found us here. It is a closely guarded secret. There are underground pens for the animals, a columbarium for the pigeons we use to send messages. It's like a little city down here. You will have lots of time to explore."

This would be Atara's home for the next year. He was to receive training for basic fighting skills and would help excavate new tunnels. For Atara, this was a time to heal. Each day saw his body grow stronger through combat practise and physical work. In fact, stronger than he had ever been. But it was the religious aspect of the Zealots' daily life that really resonated with him. The Zealots adhered to the strict rule of Jewish Law. Prayers night and day, careful observance of Shabbat, study of the Torah – this is what meant so much to him. Here he found the fellowship of other men who revered the Torah as he did, willing to sacrifice their lives to protect their faith and traditions.

A young man named Benjamin arrived around the same time, the two quick-ly becoming friends. Benjamin was from an upstanding family that farmed in the region not far from Midras. He was a good-natured man, just a year older than Atara, who had a natural inclination for compassion. When he heard of Atara's experiences from the brothers, Benjamin could see the extraordinary pain Atara suffered, so he decided to befriend him. Not long after, the brothers announced they would be going back to join the Zealots in the Galilee, believing Atara was now stable enough for them to leave. Benjamin took their place in Atara's life as the two young men continued their training together.

In the evenings men would assemble in the subterranean halls for political and religious debates under the illumination of many lamps placed throughout. They would gather around in small clusters whenever news arrived, debating wildly with animation any outside news just received.

One day a group had arrived from Jerusalem, telling of this proclaimed messiah teaching the Torah and healing people. A lively debate ensued with the vast majority dismissing this man as a false messiah. The real messiah would come to lead them against the Romans in battle! He would be a king! The talk quickly reverted to what action should be taken against the latest Roman atrocities.

The constant verbal assault about the Roman problem slowly began to grate on Atara. Many of these men had never even had direct contact with Roman sol-diers, or Romans for that matter. To them this was all a theory of right or wrong, of who belongs or who doesn't. For Atara it was different, personal. Some nights he would return to his cell in Sidon, crying out in anger, blaming the Romans for his father's death, for the persecutions and tribulations of the Jews. The hatred was festering underneath the surface, fed by the constant focus on the Romans. 'It's good,' Atara tried to rationalize. 'If I'm to be a fighter, I need this passion burning inside.' But many a night his demons returned, consuming his soul. He would plead with God for help as he struggled to feel His presence, His purpose in all this.

Atara knew it was by the Hand of God he had been rescued from that prison cell. He had to discover why.

———————

The months went by. Men came and went in the camp, following the orders of the leadership. It was almost a year since he had arrived when Atara received his orders to be deployed. He was assigned to a cell group in Jerusalem leaving immediately.

'Jerusalem! The city of King David! Where the Temple sat on Mount Moriah, Abraham offering his son up to God! The Holy of Holies, the dwelling place of the Lord most High!'

Atara had only been to Jerusalem once. His father brought him to the Temple for Passover when he was 12 years old, as was the custom. Atara could remember the enormous wall around the entire city, the massive crowds for Passover, the shofar blowing from high in the Temple. It was intoxicating for a young boy from a Roman town. Now he was to travel there once again for Passover, which was only two weeks away.

Further instructions would be given by his cell commander when he arrived. Atara was excited to learn Reuben and Nathan had also been assigned to Jerusalem.

'Something big must be planned.'

Part II

A.D. 32

JERUSALEM

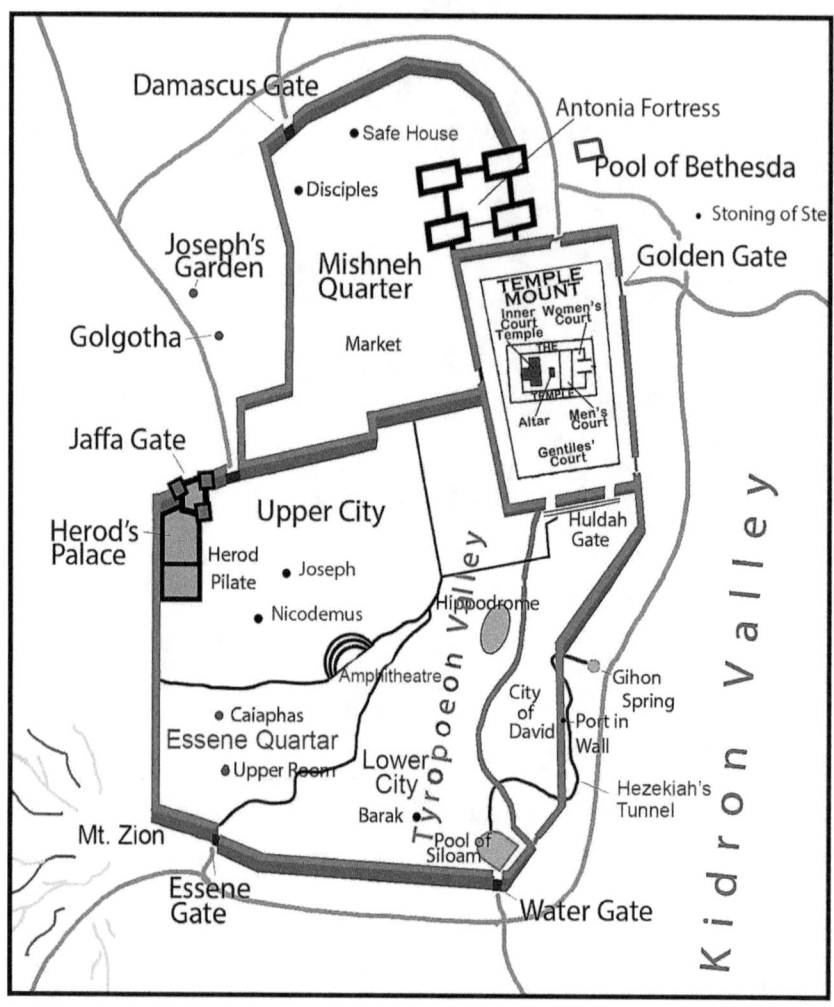

Chapter 7

The Roman soldier wielding his sword pressed in close to the fishmonger, perspiration running down his face. Gripping the man by the tunic, he demanded information about the young man evading capture. Atara could hear the poor man attempting to convince the soldier he had seen nothing, that he didn't know. That a large group of Pharisees had passed by just at that moment, blocking his view. He had been bartering with a customer, so he had not seen this young man they were talking about. The Roman pulled the fishmonger closer to his face, eyeing him suspiciously, searching for the lies.

Atara crouched, slowly becoming more claustrophobic as he curled up tight in his prison, breathing shallow and sporadic. 'Please, God,' he prayed. But no other words came.

The other soldier stood directly in front of the stall, cutting off any hope of escape. Seconds seemed like minutes as Atara waited for the response. The Roman finally grunted. Pushing the fishmonger into some crates, he motioned to the other soldier for them both to move on to the next merchant. After he exited the stall, Atara finally took a breath. But it was not over. If any of the other merchants nearby were to hesitate under questioning, the Romans would arrest them, taking them away. Fear was in the air.

'Would someone betray me? Would anyone break down under interrogation, giving away my location? If they did, the Romans would also arrest the fishmonger who risked his life for me. The consequences would be brutal.'

Now it was a waiting game. The minutes seemed to turn to hours. There was nowhere to go while the sweeps were going on. If the soldiers finished without finding their insurgent, they might decide to circle back for more thorough searches. He would be found. The street was empty of shoppers now as it had been closed by the sentries further up the incline to cut off their prey. All around, the heavy air was still, no one making a sound for fear of what would come next. The heat and foul odor of fish was making Atara nauseous. He needed air.

Slowly, the fish barrel that hid him began to move aside. The merchant motioned to come out of hiding. Farther up the street the soldiers had worked their way to the end. It likely would not be long before they decided to return. Atara crawled out on all fours, peering out of the entrance to survey the situation.

"They will be back, my friend. You must make your move now. I am sorry that I can do no more for you."

"You saved my life," responded Atara. Turning his head toward the fishmonger, he could see the kindness and concern on his face. Then looking around to all the merchants, he added with gratitude, "Everyone has."

"Take the lane to the left, which will take you toward the Upper City where there will be fewer crowds. You will have a better chance of getting away, providing you can avoid the sentries."

Standing now and ready to run, Atara peered out of the stall, once again looking for an opportunity to make his escape. At that moment all the soldiers were either in booths checking or had their backs to him. Seizing the opportunity he bolted out of the booth, adrenaline flowing into his veins. Heading back the way he came, when he reached the laneway Atara made a sharp turn left, catapulting himself at full speed up the narrow passage. He heard the shouts. He had been spotted just as he was making the turn.

Atara had a good head start this time, but the shouts of the soldiers in pursuit would easily alert any others ahead of him. Weaving his way around people, he passed one street, two, then on to the third where he decided to turn left just as his pursuers turned onto the lane below, keeping him in full view. This was risky because it was heading back near where the sentries had earlier joined the search. Atara was hoping the soldiers would not be expecting him to return that way. As he barreled past they were not there. They had joined the chase and were now behind him. Pushing his legs while dodging his way through the crowd, Atara was slightly pulling ahead. He needed them to lose sight of him. It was the only way. One street ahead and he would be out of the market area into the Upper City.

The Upper City was the most affluent quarter of Jerusalem. The privileged and the wealthy made the Upper City their home with large houses on wide streets. It was a labyrinth of lanes and alleys between affluent homes atop Mount Zion. Atara was not familiar with this area of the city, so he wasn't sure which way to proceed. He knew that the main city gate, Jaffa Gate, lay to the right. Beside Jaffa Gate was King Herod's Palace, but otherwise he was lost for direction.

The soldiers were catching up. Atara decided to turn left, weaving and zigzagging at every small intersection, trying to lose them. There was a risk of ending up in a dead end, or turning so many times he would run in a circle right back into them, but there was no other choice. If he continued straight, there were sure to be sentries posted who would stop him. He made his turn.

Then another, another and another, through the narrow streets and lanes of high walls surrounding the homes of the wealthy. He had no idea where he was. Atara could hear the shouts echoing in the distance, searching, but they were not too close yet. He stopped for a moment, bending with his hands on his knees to steady himself, catching his breath. 'What do I do now?'

The voices drew nearer. Pulling himself together he spotted a small lane ahead and made a dash for it.

She was slightly hunched over and unstable as she carefully walked over the ancient cobblestones carrying a large wicker basket.

Coming from the Lower City, the old lady was approaching the door to her residence. In the narrow alley a long stretch of high stone wall on both sides had a singular small door that was barely visible. Vines had long ago overtaken the wall with their sweet blackberries, and with beautiful deep purple blooms of bougainvillea almost covering the entire door, it was nearly invisible.

She pushed the brush aside, then pulled the large iron key from her bag, methodically inserting it into the lock. The approaching commotion from the backstreets alarmed her as it came closer and closer. She nervously quickened her attempt to open the door to disappear before it gave her away.

As the door swung open, a young man rounded the corner at full pace, bolting up the alley at tremendous speed. She froze in place.

Rounding the corner and heading up a small alley at his top speed, Atara spotted an elderly lady by an open door. Sprinting as fast as his exhausted body could manage, without a word spoken, he plunged through the door, carrying the old lady with him.

Both tumbled inside to the ground. He sprung to his feet, slamming the door shut, quickly sliding a large iron bolt in place to secure it. Turning to brace the door with his back, he slipped down to the ground, closing his eyes, leaning with his back against the thin veil of lumber that separated him from freedom or arrest, listening.

The shouts became louder and for a moment the pace slowed. Atara heard footsteps. He could almost feel the hand reaching out to test the lock that separated him from life or death, his hand on his now blood-stained dagger. The door rattled hard, but held firm.

After a moment the soldiers' pace resumed and within seconds faded away into the distance. He breathed a deep sign of relief, then opened his eyes.

There in front of him was the old lady sprawled on the courtyard floor, feet splayed, propping herself up by her hands. A shawl covered her face, but he could clearly see the bewilderment in her eyes.

Realizing what he had done, he bound to his feet, offering his hand of assistance. He braced himself firmly, pulling his savior to her feet, apologizing profusely in very hushed tones in case any soldiers remained outside the wall.

"I'm so sorry, are you hurt?" he said as he pulled her close and steadied her.

"Well, you should be!" she retorted, brushing herself off to inspect the damage. As she did so her scarf fell away from her face.

Startled, he exclaimed, "You're just a girl!"

She glared at him, answering sharply, "Well, you're just a mere boy! What have you done to have the entire Roman army after you? You stink of fish! And by the way, you're welcome!"

She scrutinized him. He was average height, well built but slender, appearing to be around 20 years of age. She instantly judged him to be cocky, overconfident and slightly full of himself, as she felt most young men were prone to be.

The young girl looked all of 18, quite obviously full of independence and vigor. Her pulled-back wavy hair was as rich as ebony, her silky skin a beautiful olive. But it was her eyes that had his full attention. Large, warm brown eyes that held him captive for much too long.

Snapping out of his trance, he responded, "What are you doing out on the streets without an escort? Why are you dressed as an old woman?"

Locked in battle over who would be first to answer, the two simply stared at each other for what seemed like forever until intuitively a truce was reached. With not a word said, both collapsed to the ground. He on the meticulous stone pavement, her to a low marble bench nearby.

The weight of the close encounter with the Romans was finally sinking in. It had been a matter of life or death, which even a 20-year-old will comprehend with some reflection.

He surveyed the courtyard. The wooden door that had saved him was almost completely hidden by the bushes on this side of the wall as well. Turning his head from where he sat he could see an exquisite garden with its enchanting flora and greenery. It was the most beautiful place he had seen in Jerusalem. They were seated in a small alcove by the door to one side of the garden that was hidden on three sides by beautifully manicured bushes. Atara leaned out to look around the shrubs and could see a majestic house standing tall at the end of the garden up a flight of stairs. It was very large by Jerusalem's standards, so it was obvious the owner of this property was wealthy. Taking a deep breath, and with a sigh, his disposition began to mellow.

"My name is Atara BenJosiah. I'm so sorry for pushing you in through the door like that. Are you hurt?"

"No," came the icy reply.

"I come from the north in the area of Sidon. I was studying in yeshiva to become a rabbi. I've seen firsthand what the Romans have done to our people. The taxes, the poverty, the oppression are like never before. I was forced to leave my studies after the Romans took our home and murdered my father. I have come to Jerusalem to fight with the Zealots against the tyranny of the Roman rule!"

Trying desperately to sound very important, he was now standing to add to the effect. "For too long we have suffered, too many have died at their hands while our leaders do nothing! The rebels are gaining strength. Soon we will be in a position to push the tyrants out of our land. My brothers joined the Zealots two years ago and I have recently followed in their footsteps. Our leaders planned an insurrection for today at the Antonia Fortress, but somehow the Romans found out, setting an ambush for us. Many were arrested and I believe some have given their lives. I only managed to escape capture by the grace of God. Roman justice will be swift. Tomorrow we will see many more crucifixions outside the city walls."

With the thought of friends and allies being crucified or sent to the galleys, Atara lowered his eyes, the impact finally catching up with him. "What's your name?" he asked softly to escape the melancholy.

"I'm Shira," she gently responded, sensing the pain he was feeling as he once again took his seat near her on the courtyard floor. "In answer to your question, I was taking food to a poor family who lives in the Lower City. So many families have nothing now. With Passover approaching this week and the city swelling as the pilgrims arrive, the cost of food has become impossible for many. I dress as an old woman for my safety. I sneak away from the house like this because, as you know, being a young woman I'm forbidden out on my own. This way the Romans never stop me and the men just ignore me."

"Where are we? Whose home is this?"

"This is the home of Nicodemus in the Upper City. I'm his daughter."

"Nicodemus the Pharisee? The Sanhedrin?" Atara responded arrogantly. "What are they doing for our people? Never since the time of the Babylonians have we suffered more! Where are our leaders? Why don't they fight the Roman occupation? They give in to all Roman demands while lining their own pockets!" He gestured, looking around the beautiful courtyard and home. "They talk of a messiah, but persecute those willing to stand up to the Romans. Nothing was done when the Romans put an apostate and puppet king on the throne! They did nothing when the Romans hand picked Caiaphas as the high priest in a political move and they do nothing to help the poor! Even the Temple court is filled with thieves and profiteers, especially now at Passover when people need to buy a sacrifice at inflated prices! All they do is talk while every day our people are being crucified and taken into slavery by the Romans! They have their Temple, but where is God in all this?"

"My father is not like that!" Shira responded, lips tightening, eyes beginning to flash. "He's different from most of the Sanhedrin, and there are a few others like him. He sees the suffering and wants to make changes, but it's difficult. Father listens to people. He even had the Galilean to our home one night to hear what he had to say!"

"The Galilean? Jesus?" Atara looked puzzled. "I heard the Pharisees and the Sanhedrin are after him because he criticized their impotence. The Zealots believed when he first came on the scene in the Galilee he might actually be the messiah, but because he refuses to take up arms, they say he can't be. He talks of peace and love at a time when we're being starved and slaughtered! What good is that?"

"There's something about him," Shira responded. "He's different. When Jesus visited I was allowed to sit in the room while Father listened to him. Jesus speaks with an authority I've never heard before. The scriptures seem to come from his mouth as if he wrote them himself. He has so much compassion for those who are suffering. I've heard of many healings, the good work he's doing for the people, that he has many disciples and followers. There are reports that just this past week he raised a man named Lazarus from the dead! Can this be someone not sent by God? Lately I've heard those around him claim he is the messiah, that he's even able to forgive sins! I am afraid the Temple priests will label him a blasphemer, calling for his execution! But he's a good man. The things he says make sense when you listen. He told us we should love those who persecute us."

Atara flared back in anger. "Love our enemies? Those who beat us, persecute us, enslave us, starve us and crucify us? Never! You have no idea what I've been through! Why won't he fight the Romans with us? We need a leader, a messiah, a king. Who is he anyway? A man from Galilee? We all know that according to Torah Micah 5:2–5 that the messiah will be born in Bethlehem, David's home, coming from the line of David, a king in Isaiah 9:7! This man is a Galilean!"

"Well, that's what we thought!" Shira exclaimed. "It turns out he grew up in Nazareth, so when Father had the same question and looked into it, he discovered Jesus' parents were ordered to return to Bethlehem during the Roman census a number of years ago. Bethlehem is in fact where Jesus was born. Both parents are also direct descendants of the line of David!"

"I still don't see how it would be possible that this man could ever be our leader," Atara replied, calming somewhat. "We need a King David, a military commander to save us. Isn't this what a messiah should be? This Jesus has many followers, listening to him, but is that enough? I also heard that the crazy man in the desert who baptizes people, who some believed to be a prophet, has been preaching about the messiah. When he baptized Jesus he ordained this Jesus as *the one*. Who was he to be making those kinds of claims? Look where that got him, his head on a platter in Herod's court!"

"My father is very well connected and understands these things," responded Shira. "I overheard a conversation he was having with another member of the Sanhedrin about John the Baptist. His father was Zechariah, one of the Temple priests, a descendant of Aaron. He was selected by lot one year to enter behind the Temple curtain into the holy of holies, when something happened. Coming out he had been struck mute. He couldn't speak! He and his wife were both older, but at that very time they conceived, having a baby boy they named, against all tradition, John. As soon as the boy's name was given, Zechariah's voice returned and he prophesied about the messiah. They say it was amazing, directly from God!

But this is the point Father made – both John's parents were direct descendants of Aaron. This would mean their son was entitled to be high priest in the priestly order at the Temple by birthright. He was raised to be a priest, leaving the Temple only going to the desert after God had spoken to him. There are very few that meet this criteria for the priesthood. If the messiah was to be ordained, it would have to be by a priest of this lineage. When John baptized Jesus, laying his hand on him to ordain Jesus, he had God's authority to do it!"

"Being a student of a yeshiva, I understand what your father is saying. The messiah must follow the principles laid out by God in the Torah, if he is truly the messiah. God can't work against Himself and His own principles. God has given us the Law and the Temple, for that's God's way. Even so, how could this Jesus accomplish that? He has rejected the rebels' way, seethes against the hypocrisy of the Temple establishment, heals on the Sabbath and ignores the Romans?"

Atara paused for a moment musing, "The people seem to love and listen to him, though. Everywhere you go you hear talk of him. His miracles and compassion seem to speak to all. So how can we tell? He brings signs and wonders, speaks of things some want to hear, but inflame others. But does he fulfill all the prophesies? Does he follow the Laws of God as laid out in the Torah and Temple?"

"Jesus speaks of love and radical change in the heart," answered Shira. "He says he has been sent by the Father to bring us back to God. He spoke to us that night about being born again. My father didn't understand, but I think he was talking about being born spiritually. We follow the Law, but is it in our hearts?"

The young rebel stood, rubbing his temple, trying to respond to her. "I don't understand. Why would a God and a messiah let His people suffer like this at the hands of the Romans? A messiah would put an end to this suffering, wouldn't he?"

"Perhaps he was talking about more than the Romans."

Atara was not keen to hear more of this. His thoughts went back to his own family, the death of his father and his time in prison. He blamed the Romans for all the suffering of his own family and the Jewish nation. In his mind they were the cause. He just could not see the Israelites had hardened their hearts, becoming enslaved in the Law.

Brushing himself off, trying to sound more mature than his age, Atara responded. "I'll ask around. I know many of the Zealots who have had contact with this Jesus and his disciples. They will have heard things. If he is who he claims, there has to be proof! Can I come back sometime to let you know what I found?"

He genuinely wanted to find the truth about this Galilean Jesus. However, being honest with himself, he was more than slightly drawn to the warm, caring personality of his rescuer that day, and of course her radiant beauty.

"Yes, I really want to find out more too. I'll ask my father some more questions about the conversation he had with Jesus. The Sabbath is approaching now, but Sunday is the 10th day of Nissan. On this day we'll travel out of Jerusalem, as is our family tradition, to purchase our Passover lamb. Maybe we could meet after sunset then? I can't be seen with a young man alone, but at that time the gardener will be gone and the rest of the household secure indoors. In fact, you should go now. Shabbat is arriving soon and I must get into the house unnoticed to change before it does."

"Yes, I should go now as it will take me a while to travel to where I'm staying. I pray the Romans have given up their search by now. How will I find you?"

"Knock quietly on this door. I'll be on this side, waiting. This spot is my secret place, well hidden from view of the house. I don't want to be seen talking with a young man. This would not be considered proper by my family."

Opening the old door very carefully, he checked both directions for any remaining soldiers. With the coast clear he slipped silently into the alleyway.

'That was strange. And what a strange young man,' thought Shira as she turned and walked up to the house in her strange attire.

JERUSALEM AND VICINITY

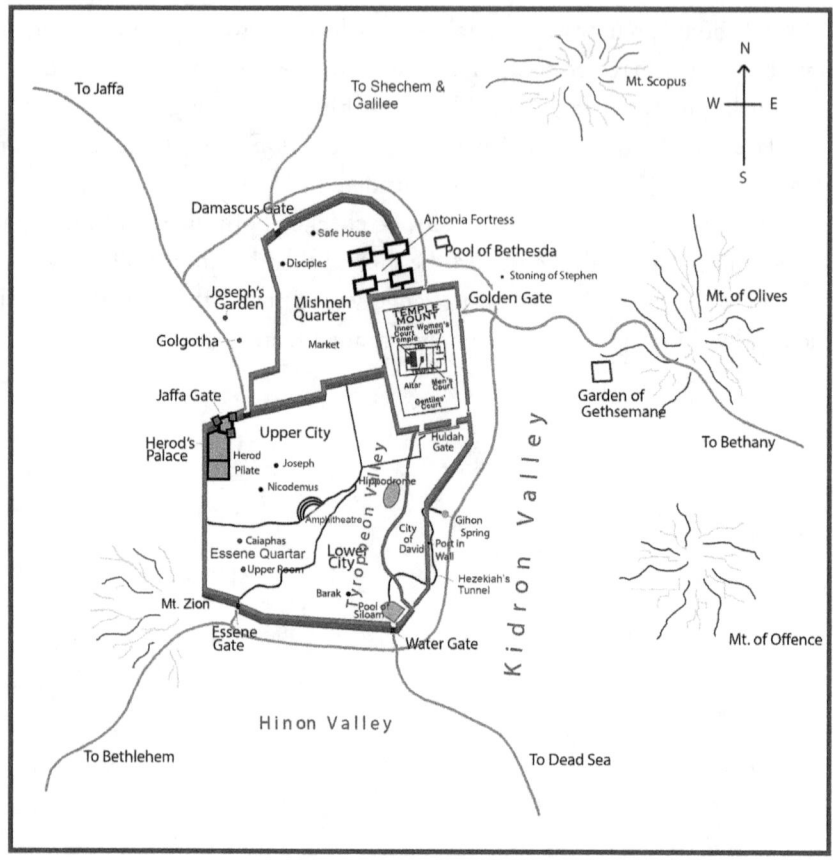

$$\text{Chapter 8}$$

SUNDAY: NISSAN 10 / APRIL 6TH

Shira's two older brothers had just returned from their morning prayers as the April sun rose above the mountains. The household was already abuzz on this first day of the week as preparations were being made for the traditional Passover outing.

Missing was their mother. Three years earlier the wife of Nicodemus had succumbed to a long-standing illness. The family still mourned the loss. Being an affluent merchant the home of Nicodemus was well looked after, but the absence of a mother had left its mark, particularly on Shira. There were two servants and a cook to look after their daily needs, but with the two boys boarding at the yeshiva during the week, the home often felt very empty.

Every family was to bring home a Passover lamb on the 10th of Nissan, as prescribed in Exodus 12:3, in preparation for the Passover. The lamb was to be a one-year-old male with no defects, taken care of until Passover four days later. The lamb represented purity and was a covering of protection. Many children in Jerusalem would fall in love with their stocky lamb as they cared for it for the next four days, finding it very difficult later in the week to hand it over for slaughter.

The celebration of Passover[4] is the first command God gave the Israelites after fleeing Egypt. It was in commemoration of the final plague God sent the Egyptians, forcing them to release the Israelites from their slavery.

God instructed Moses to direct the Israelites to slaughter a perfect lamb at twilight on the 14th of Nissan, placing the blood on their doorposts that very eve. On the night of the 15th of Nissan, about midnight, God promised He would pass over every house in Egypt with the blood of the lamb on the doorpost, sealing it with His protection. Following that, the destroyer[5] sought out all firstborn sons of Egypt without God's covering, bringing death to each family.

The blood of the lamb, (lamb is *taleh* in Hebrew, which also means covering) would be a covering, a protection, for every family who accepted God's command

---

[4] Exodus 11:4–5; Exodus 12:14–28
[5] Exodus 12:23

by placing the lamb's blood on the doorposts. God's Passover is a story of promise, redemption, and freedom at a time when the Jewish people were suffering in slavery at the hands of Pharaoh. When Pharaoh finally relented after that night, the Israelites were released from their slavery, being redeemed by God's promise.

Passover is a time of celebration and thankfulness. Jewish families reunited with Jews from all over Israel, flocking to Jerusalem to be together and offer sacrifices at the Temple. Jerusalem would swell from a normal population of 600,000 to often over 2 million people during the Passover. Today, this 10th day of Nissan, would see over half a million lambs brought back to Jerusalem.

For Passover most families would crowd together in their small apartments throughout the city. Other pilgrims would set up tents for temporary dwellings in, and outside, the city walls, creating small villages throughout the valleys around. It was meant to be an exciting time of reflection and hope. But the foreign occupation in these days of Passover only reminded the Jews of their current bondage under the Roman rule.

With such burgeoning crowds, and a foreboding of rebellion, the Romans would bring in extra troops to manage the huge swell of humanity, given orders to subdue brutally any hint of rebellion or crime. The streets within the city walls at times became impassable with so many people visiting. Throughout this coming week Rome put into place nighttime curfews to maintain control.

The family would have to leave early. Their favorite place to find their perfect lamb was near Bethany. They delighted in their annual excursion together. Shira would remember the many times she would hold her mother's hand as they searched through the lambs, looking for their perfect choice. To reach their destination they would have to walk through the Kidron Valley, then ascend the Mount of Olives to approach Bethany on the other side. On a good day that would only be a walk of slightly over an hour, but at Passover the roads would be very, very crowded with many others taking the same route.

Today it could take them two to three hours to make the trip. There were also many Roman checkpoints along the way during Passover that would slow the progress. If they didn't arrive at Bethany early, there was a chance the lambs would all be sold from their favorite dealer. They would have to find another one, or as a last resort purchase a lamb in the Temple courtyard at an inflated price. Nicodemus refused to buy his lamb there. Most of the Temple priests and Sanhedrin were wealthy enough to purchase their sacrifices and Passover lambs in the Temple court, but Nicodemus would not. He was very aware the market for the Temple sacrifices had become unaffordable for the average person. He felt it was an abuse. Everyone should be able to buy what was needed at the Temple, regardless of their wealth.

It started like this every year, the two brothers Avi and Judah teasing Shira about not yet finding a husband, her feisty response being they would never find a bride. Both boys were rabbinical students, and had inherited their wit and desire to accomplish from their father. Shira, on the other hand, had inherited her mother's zesty spirit, which could sometimes land her in quite a bit of trouble. "Oy," their father would often say, with just a little cynicism in his voice. "God would bless me with such a daughter!"

It did not take long before they had made their way, descending from the Upper City to where they arrived between the Lower City and the Temple Mount. Normally, the quickest route would be to pass through the Temple grounds, but today they would avoid the Temple because there would be so many people in the courtyard, it would be impassible. Instead they would take the main road south down the Tyropoeon Valley, past the Hippodrome, then to the Pool of Siloam to exit through the Water Gate. Once outside the city wall they descended farther into the Kidron Valley, now turning to head north. Walking past the open area of Absalom's Tomb, there were many pilgrims camping out and fellowshiping with one another in the shadow of the great wall. The road was very crowded. Many families had already set out on their journey to find their lamb.

Shira and her family had already passed three Roman checkpoints. At the second, by the Water Gate, there were two crucifixions in progress, casting a somber mood over the travelers as they quietly passed the Roman guards. Shira wondered if these men had taken part in the demonstration two days earlier and shivered at the thought one of them could have been Atara. You could not escape the reality of life in Jerusalem for very long.

By the time they passed through the city, beginning their accent up the Mount of Olives, their family spirit was returning. In troubled times people take what little joy they can have in their festivals and cherish it. Up they went. Past the Garden of Gethsemane, following the long, winding trail to the top. Stopping at the summit to rest, they pulled aside from the crowded road to view Jerusalem from this spectacular viewpoint. What a magnificent vista it was! Jerusalem, the city of God with its beautiful Temple and Golden Gate. Jerusalem, the home of David. The very spot where Abraham was willing to sacrifice his son at the request of God. Then God at the last moment provided a ram caught in thorns as a substitute. A substitute sacrifice.

The view was breathtaking. Every year the family stood here in awe. Soon they decided it was best to move on, once again joining the crowds marching along. It was good they had an early start because from their vantage point they could see the swell of pilgrims now coming out of the city to purchase their lambs.

It wasn't far now. Arriving in Bethany they joined other families. While they roamed through the market, most of the talk of the town was about a man named Lazarus. The townspeople said Jesus was staying there, and that earlier the Galilean had raised Lazarus, who had been entombed for three days, from the dead! This, of course, was not news to Nicodemus. The Sanhedrin had been called together to deal with this rumor, the high priest Caiaphas making his position clear. This Jesus had too great a following and was becoming a threat to the Temple. From that day on the Pharisees were plotting to kill Jesus. This greatly distressed Nicodemus. There were only a few on the council who did not agree with Caiaphas.

There seemed innumerable shepherds selling their lambs throughout the town as markets had sprung up all over for Passover. It was a sea of pure white with the aroma of makeshift kitchens and sounds of bargaining Shira so fondly remembered. The rabbis were there as well to inspect each prospect, blessing the lamb and making sure it was without blemish. The family's favorite dealer was on the far side of Bethany where they normally purchased their yearling. This year it didn't take long.

Shira spotted the lamb immediately. With arms embracing the flawless bundle of white, she had already made up her mind. "Father, I have found the lamb," she gushed as she scooped him up. "He's perfect!"

Nicodemus could not resist Shira's charm, so after the traditional bartering with everyone shaking hands, the deal was made. Afterward, they enjoyed a savory meal in the market. Of course, the brothers were grumbling about coming along since they didn't even have a say in which lamb was chosen, but it was all in good jest.

Little did Shira know this might be the very last Passover the family would be together.

Beginning their return homeward, they found the crowds growing very dense, slowing their pace dramatically. They came across several other families they knew, making the time seem to pass a little easier as they walked slowly together, but when they reached the Mount of Olives they came to a complete standstill. The crowds going either way were not making any progress at all. The sounds of shouting in the distance could be heard. Nicodemus motioned to his family to leave the road to walk farther up to the pinnacle of the Mount of Olives where they had stood alone earlier.

Once at the top, they viewed a spectacle that was completely unexpected. In the distance pilgrims all the way down the Mount of Olives lined the sides of the roadway, cheering and shouting, "Hosannah!", laying palm branches and clothing on the road ahead of a tiny entourage working its way down the mountain road through the valley toward the Temple. The crowds were parting just ahead of this small group. Then closing in as soon as it passed by, shouting, praising God and waving branches.

"It's Jesus!" Shira exclaimed.

Both brothers looked on with disdain, Judah retorting, "What foolishness is this?"

Everyone on the mountaintop stood transfixed as they watched Jesus descending the mountain on the back of a donkey through the thick crowds waving palm branches high above as he passed. Soon rumors were excitedly being passed among the travelers as people watched. "They say it is the messiah." "Who is this?" "Can it be?" "Isn't this the Nazarene, the man from the Galilee?" Soon everyone was talking and questioning, "Could this be the messiah?" The closer Jesus and his followers slowly moved toward the Temple, the larger the crowds grew. Even from this distance you could hear the cries of "Messiah!" "Savior!" "Hosannah!" echoing throughout the valley.

"Isn't that a donkey he's riding on?" asked Shira.

"He is probably trying to fulfill the messianic prophesy of Zechariah 9:9: '*See, your king comes to you, righteous and victorious, lowly and riding on a donkey, on a colt,*'" sneered Avi with almost as much cynicism as Judah.

"I wouldn't be too hasty to judge," interrupted Nicodemus calmly. "There is a lot about this man that is yet to be discovered. I don't quite see how it all fits yet. I know he is a good man, but he has made many enemies. Look at the multitudes that are welcoming him as the messiah! Is this not the time we are expecting the messiah?"

Shira did not fully understand what exactly she was feeling as she watched this procession slowly make its way down the winding mountain road. Excitement and elation seemed to overcome her, but she had no idea why. Was it the immense crowds with their choruses of "Messiah!" and "Hosannah!"? It was like nothing else she had ever seen before. With Jerusalem and the Temple standing behind as the backdrop, the position where they stood high above as the gallery, it was like standing in part of a living theatre. At the same time she felt such a peace. It fell over her like a warm blanket on a cold Jerusalem night. She felt so drawn to this unassuming man she had met only once before. Was he really the messiah? Or, like her brother so quickly pointed out, was this staged by a mad-man, a false prophet who would surely be deserving of death? The conflict within her was too much. She had to find out.

"Look, he's going to enter the Temple Mount through the Golden Gate. The crowds are incredible!" noted Shira.

"Staged," fumed Judah. "This man doesn't even keep the Sabbath and look at the mass of people blindly worshiping him!"

"But if he is the messiah, wouldn't he enter through the Golden Gate, the gate we also call the Messiah's Gate because we have long believed the messiah will enter the Temple here?" she asked.

"Anyone can enter there and claim that."

"What of the good he has been doing? So many reports of compassion, heal-ings and teaching of God?"

Before Judah could respond Nicodemus interjected. "Children, this is a day of celebration. Let us observe what has took place here today and meditate on it before we argue."

In response to Nicodemus' cautioning, the family quietly stood to watch the procession disappear through the gate in the distance. Judah outraged, Avi indignant, Nicodemus pensive and Shira full of hope.

It took quite some time for the crowds to disperse. The family had to wait at the top of the Mount of Olives for the road to clear enough to continue their trip home. Once on the move it still took even longer for them to wind their way slowly back to the city.

When they reached the Water Gate at the southern tip of the city, they found it completely blocked from the dispersing crowds that had earlier lined the Mount of Olives. They decided it would be quickest to continue outside the walls, up to Mount Zion, entering there. There would be less traffic at this little-used gate that led into the much more affluent area of Jerusalem. As they passed by the Water Gate, the site of the earlier crucifixions was different. One cross was now empty and on the other cross the withered man still hung, gasping for air.

Each member of the party seemed a little quieter on this return walk. They were reflecting on what they had seen on the Mount of Olives and its possible significance. Between passing the lamb back and forth, the boys would every so often enter a discussion, but it was mostly to speculate on the outcome of this

Jesus, a charlatan, a false prophet. Since Avi and Judah attended yeshiva during the week, they had not met Jesus in their father's home that night. They had only heard the gossip around the yeshiva.

Nicodemus, normally very talkative, keep to himself, reflecting on his own conversations with the man.

Realizing it was becoming late in the afternoon, Shira remembered she had an appointed time with Atara and was hoping to make it back before the sun set. She couldn't wait to tell him about the events of the day. 'I wonder what Atara found out today or if he was in the crowd on the road?' She would have to hurry to the back gate as soon as she could after supper.

She could not possibly imagine how the events of this next week would unfold.

Chapter 9

SUNDAY EVENING: NISSAN 11 / APRIL 6TH

By the time Nicodemus' family ascended Mount Zion to enter through the Essene Gate, which was the nearest to the Upper City, the sun was getting very low. Once inside the gate the pace quickened as all were eager to return home. Supper would soon be ready. Every day in this wealthy household dinner was prepared shortly following sunset. After a much longer day than anticipated, they were all very hungry.

On arrival Shira took the lamb and made sure it was well settled in its makeshift stable put behind the house for Passover, then rushed upstairs to bathe and change. She was excited about seeing the boy again.

Over supper the men began questioning about the events of the day, in particular who this man from the Galilee was. That in itself was a major stumbling block for them because they, as most Jerusalem Jews, long had the opinion that those from the north were not as educated or sophisticated. Especially Judah. He became angry during the conversation, making it very clear he did not believe this man was the messiah. Seeing the multitudes of Jews worshiping Jesus as he rode through the crowds had infuriated him. The more they talked about this, the angrier he became. Nicodemus tried in vain to moderate the discussion, but by the end of the meal it had become quite an argument. Shira learned nothing new as she listened intently to the deliberations. She hated these confrontations. After the meal was finished, she quietly slipped away, leaving the men to their debate.

The sun had just set below the horizon, wrapping the city in the cool of twilight. Shira covered her head with a beautifully woven scarf of blue and white, then slipped out the back door to hurry down into the garden. Arriving at the hidden gate, she carefully unlatched the ancient lock, pulling the door open a crack to peer out into the alley. There Atara sat with his back to the wall, uneasily looking up the alleyway on guard for any Roman soldiers. With the old wooden door creaking open, he turned his head, staring right in Shira's deep brown eyes. A wide smile beamed from his lips. This took Shira a little aback as she had not yet seen a smile from this strange young man willing to face the Romans (albeit, to outrun them as well). Shira quickly beckoned him through the gate, closing the door quietly behind.

"Not too loud!" she exclaimed in a hushed voice. "My brothers are here. It'll cause quite an uproar if I was to be seen with you without an escort." Atara understood, but he was anxious to talk about the happenings of this first day of the week.

"Did you hear what happened today?" He blurted out. "The talk of this Jesus is all over Jerusalem! They are saying that half of the city witnessed him riding into the Temple Mount on a donkey! I ran to the Temple when I heard what was happening, but the crowds were so thick, I couldn't even get close!"

"We were there! We were on our way back from Bethany after purchasing our lamb. When we reached the top of the Mount of Olives, we saw Jesus and his disciples traveling down the slope."

"What was it like? I heard there were huge crowds, and they all were worshiping him as the messiah!"

"It was amazing! They were shouting hosannahs and praises! People laid palm branches and clothing ahead of him as he approached. It was a massive crowd that lined the road all the way from the top of the mountain down to the Temple. There were so many people, we couldn't even start down the mountainside until well after the procession had ended. Afterward, while walking home, everyone was talking about it. Many say he's the messiah. They have heard of his miracles and the good news he is spreading. People want the messiah and are ready to believe. Others don't believe he is the messiah, saying he's a false prophet. Claiming to be a prophet, let alone the messiah, and being a sham carries the death penalty. Some aren't sure either way and are waiting to see. Father and my brothers are in the house right at this moment, having a heated debate. It has caused division and argument in our household, as I'm sure it has in most."

Atara looked very serious while he listened. "I still don't understand it," he said. "The messiah should enter the city with an army, not on a silly donkey! What possible good can that do? How are we to rid ourselves of this oppression unless we take up arms? I'm sure the Romans are quaking in their sandals now!" He was becoming quite animated. "We need a leader, a king! Someone to oust the Roman occupiers with their false idols and pagan ways, allowing us to worship our God in peace!"

Shira put her finger to her lips to remind Atara they had to be quiet. Atara stopped speaking and they both stared awkwardly at the ground in silence. Once he had calmed down a bit, he beckoned for her to have a seat on the stone bench

– the one where she had sat on their first encounter. He sat gently down beside her.

"I've heard from my friends in the underground that the Romans are very concerned," he admitted. "Any large gathering of Jews puts them on alert, especially with the immense crowds here and more still to arrive for Passover. To them, this man claims to be a leader with many dedicated followers. Yes, the Romans are very interested in this Jesus. They have spies and informants everywhere. Perhaps this is just the beginning? Perhaps this Jesus will now unite the people of Israel and help us defeat the Romans!"

"The Sanhedrin also is becoming very agitated. My brother Judah is in yeshiva with some other boys whose fathers sit on the council. He says he has heard that the majority of the Sanhedrin believe Jesus is a false prophet, making unbelievable claims. They are plotting to label him a blasphemer! I saw my father's face and could tell this was the truth. He isn't one of them, that I know. But I believe my brothers could be."

The mood became melancholy as they sat for a moment, reflecting on the situation. "I'm sure he's not a false prophet," Shira finally spoke again. "He has performed many miracles of healing. Even today in Bethany all the talk was about Jesus raising a man named Lazarus from the dead! He teaches about love, helps the people who are oppressed and sick, and knows the Torah. I have heard him speak. He speaks with authority and knowledge like I have never heard before. How could he be of evil and do all this good?"

"Well, that would seem to be true," responded Atara. "It's just so hard to understand. The scriptures point to a messiah who would be a king. A mighty warrior who will save us from our afflictions. That is what we are looking for during this terrible occupation. Yet prophetic scripture also paints a picture of a suffering messiah. We Jews have not been able to reconcile the two. Are there to be two messiahs? A kingly leader and a suffering servant? Or is there to be only one messiah embodying both qualities?"

Shira gazed at Atara transfixed as he was beginning to sound more like a rabbi than a rebel. "I've heard from Father that a possible explanation for this is that it'll be the same messiah, but he'll be coming twice."

"I've heard that as well, but not given it much thought. It's not taught in yeshiva that way. But still, what we need now is for God to provide us with a leader to remove us from this oppression. With the masses honoring him today, he just could be the messiah. One thing for certain, if this Jesus is to become the messiah, everything that occurs must follow the scriptures. When word came today of what was happening, scriptures keep running through my mind. Things I have not thought about since leaving the yeshiva. The crowds said he was riding a donkey. At first I scoffed, thinking what a ridiculous way to rally the people into a rebellion! But then, the prophetic scriptures came to mind of Zechariah 9:9: *'See your king comes to you, righteous and having salvation, gentle and riding on a donkey, on a colt, the foal of a donkey.'* This sounds so much like what I have heard of this man."

"My brother Judah brought that scripture up as well when we were on the mountain watching," interjected Shira. "But he mocked it, saying anyone who knew scripture could orchestrate that as a show."

"That was my first thought as well. Then, the more I thought about it, the scripture seems to fit this man. He talks about righteousness and salvation, while having a caring and gentle spirit. I think the symbolism might go deeper. When Solomon became king, he rode a donkey to his coronation, as did his father King David. It not only represented humility, but also an ordained succession to the throne of King David. We know scripture prophesied that the messiah would come from the house of David and from Bethlehem. Also, as I thought more about it, I realized there is something further at play here. I have heard when John baptized Jesus he laid his hands on Jesus, ordaining him the Lamb of God.'"

"Yes. I heard that as well."

"So then, this goes much deeper than just an orchestrated show to trick the people into following him. What were you, and everyone returning to Jerusalem, carrying today?"

"Lambs for Passover."

"Perfect lambs. And what does Passover represent?"

"The exodus from Egypt. Freedom and salvation from slavery. God decreed that the blood of the lambs would provide protection."

"Exactly." He was now sounding more like the rabbi he had always wanted to be. "So on this exact day, the same day that all Jews are commanded to bring home a sacrificial lamb, a perfect lamb, this Jesus, who they say is the messiah, rides down the mountain on a prophesied donkey, as the ordained Lamb of God to the Temple, a place of sacrifice!" Atara was on his feet now and pacing back and forth as the significance of what he was saying was starting to sink in.

"And there is more. Where do these lambs come from?"

This was a question Shira was not expecting, taking her a little off guard. She looked puzzled for a second, and then her eyes opened wide as she realized where this was going. "Lambs for the Temple are raised in the fields of Bethlehem, the City of David, the shepherd and king!"

"Yes!" Atara could see the glow in her expression as they both were trying to put this together. "So this man, who had been ordained the Lamb of God by that crazy priest in the desert, enters the Temple, being worshiped as the messiah. On the very same day of Nissan 10 as commanded by God in Exodus. He comes as the Lamb of God, representing freedom from slavery and oppression. He was birthed in the same place as was prophesied and where the lambs for the Temple sacrifices are born! How could this all be coincidence? It must mean more!" Atara collapsed back onto the marble bench.

The two sat silently for a moment, processing.

"I still don't see how it's possible though," changing his tone to dismay. "The Romans have such tight control, with huge armed forces at their disposal, and we barely have any weapons at all. Without an army of men with weapons, how do we stand a chance? The best a rebellion can hope for at this point is to create such a nuisance for Rome that they leave us alone."

"As you said, he does have the support of the people. The Romans might be worried about this. The Sanhedrin is very much against Jesus, but what if he is the messiah? Shouldn't we look into this more deeply? He has done so many miracles and his words have drawn so many to repent."

Atara thought for a moment. He knew he agreed with her. All day he had been thinking about the prophesies of Isaiah 29:18 and 35:5: *'In that day the deaf will hear the words of the scroll, and out of gloom and darkness the eyes of the blind will see / then will the eyes of the blind be opened and the ears of the deaf unstopped.'* These passages are recognized as messianic verses by the rabbis. They clearly fit the miracles of this man, this Jesus.

"You're right, Shira. We need to find out more. We need to know who this man is. If he is the messiah, then all things will come together according to scripture, prophesies and in accordance with God's Temple ordinances."

The two sat for a moment longer, contemplating. The clear night air was cool and refreshing. The bleating of the lamb could be heard in the garden by the bushes around the corner from where they sat. Shira walked over to the temporary pen, struggled to pick the heavy yearling up to comfort it and returned to sit with Atara. High above, the open sky proclaimed the glory of God in the heavens.

"It's late. My father will wonder where I am if I don't return to the house soon. I want to know more. I'm not allowed into the city on my own, of course."

This came with an unmistakable undertone of a slight giggle. "But I know an old lady who can! Tomorrow I have to return to the Lower City with some more food for a family I help. I'll see what else I can find out. I'll also try to talk with Father. He knows so much and is privy to everything the council is planning."

"We'll see what tomorrow brings, then. There were rumors Jesus will be at the Temple. I'll ask around and then go there first thing in the morning. If I can find him, I'll follow the crowds and maybe learn more. He might be planning to make his move. The Passover crowds are here in Jerusalem, putting the Romans at a disadvantage if there is mass disruption. This could be a turning point!" Atara looked into Shira's brown eyes and the hardness of the rebel within seemed to melt away. They agreed to meet tomorrow evening, after the sun had set.

Atara unlocked the heavy wooden door, once again vanishing into the alleyway.

Chapter 10

SUNDAY NIGHT: NISSAN 11 / APRIL 6TH

Atara returned to the home of Barak the potter in the Lower City where he had been assigned to stay with a band of Zealots. He was careful to avoid Roman sentries as he made his way through the twisted lanes down the side of Mount Zion to his place of shelter at the bottom of the city. Several times he had to turn back up a laneway to find another path when he spotted soldiers on their patrols, taking quite a long time for him to navigate around the city.

Finally arriving he stood in a laneway down the street from the house, observing. The weathered apartment was a very modest one, piled underneath two more ancient units of equally nondescript character, jammed between a row of others that looked much the same.

Once certain the lodgings were not being watched, Atara stealthily slipped down the worn stairs to his lair. He announced his arrival with a quiet, patterned knock, signaling to those inside he was not a foe. When the door opened slightly, he skirted past the greeter into a small room where a dozen of his compatriots sat conversing in hushed tones by the light of a single oil lamp around an olive-wood table. This was not a group of men you would expect to find in a lair of rebels. There were no withered faces, crooked noses, blinded eyes or scars. Those before him were much like him, faces of idealist young men, religious in dress and appearance.

Simeon was the oldest, the most experienced fighter of this band, but there were no more than 25 years on him. He joined the Zealots five years before and Atara had met him several times in Midras when he came there to help train recruits. There were numerous disturbances and insurrections Simeon had been involved in over the past several years, many resulting in the death of Roman soldiers. This earned him the respect of the other younger men.

Benjamin was there too. He and Atara were the only new recruits among the Zealots in this safe house.

All heads turned when Simeon greeted Atara with, "Where have you been? We've just learned that the Romans put a price on your head! Soldiers were killed on Friday, so you can be certain the Romans will be out in force, looking for us all!"

With a quick scan of all eyes around the table, Atara understood implicitly he was not the only one on that list.

"Doesn't matter," Atara respond bravely, as any young man would before peers. "The Roman soldiers here don't know what I look like, so as long as I avoid checkpoints I'll be fine." Inside, however, he wasn't so sure. What really hit him was that there had been deaths. This was the first operation Atara had been involved with since joining the Zealots. The scuffle with the Romans had been so confusing, he wasn't sure what really happened. But to take life! Atara could not shake the feeling of guilt.

They all agreed that for the Romans to acquire names, and with the failed protest last week, they knew there must be a traitor in their midst. Perhaps in this room, or perhaps in other cells throughout the city, but someone must have given the names to the Romans. His two brothers left word they had been identified, so they were leaving Jerusalem for the Galilee until things cooled down a bit.

"Your brothers said you should follow to meet them at the safe house in Tiberias," Simeon added.

These few days had not been good for the Zealots. It seemed they were in quite a disarray throughout the city. But Atara had no intention of leaving Jerusalem now. There were too many questions he needed answers to.

The talk around the table quickly reverted to the events of the past few days. When Atara entered the room the main topic of discussion had been about Barabbas. Ezra, an ambitious young man the same age as Atara asked, "What will happen to Barabbas? Will there be a trial? Or will the new Governor Pilate order him executed?"

They all weighed in at once, engaging in a lengthy debate. Simeon eventually had the last word. "At this point, we have to assume Barabbas will not be returning. Immediate execution or trial, it will end up the same. Members from the other cells are trying to find out through connections where he is being held. We will have to see if there is any possibility of rescue or payoff, but for now we will have to wait."

"We should send in our young resident escape artist to free Barabbas!" chided one of the men looking directly at Atara. "We have the only man to ever escape the Sidon Fortress right here in our midst!" All eyes went to Atara.

Atara blushed, looking down. Neither he nor Benjamin had told any of the Zealots of his past, but word spreads quickly among men with common cause.

"It wasn't me," responded Atara. "It was my brothers who saved my life and God who protected us."

"Perhaps God will protect Barabbas too," was the reply.

Several years before the Zealots lost their leader when Judas of Galilee, son of Hezekiah, was executed. At that time the Romans defeated a major uprising, executing thousands of Zealots. Following that, there had been a power struggle among the Zealots. Now, after a time of disbandment, they were attempting to regroup and gain ground. Several leaders emerged in different areas. The most prominent was a proven fighter from the Galilee where the movement had started. But here in Jerusalem their hope was with Jesus Barabbas.

The Zealots believed God would use them to protect the Torah. They believed the Romans, with all their apostate gods, were defiling the Jewish land. That they were called by God to defend the Torah in any way possible, ultimately driving the Romans with all their oppression from Israel. They viewed the Sanhedrin as impotent against the Romans and the Temple priests as greedy, out of touch with the people. King Herod was a Roman-appointed puppet king who did not care for the people. He was not even a Jew!

The Essenes fled to their caves in the desert, which to these young radicals proved them cowardly. The Sadducees' liberal faith, and interpretation of the Torah, was held in disdain among the Zealots, who very much believed in the literal truth of the Torah. That left only the Pharisees. The beliefs of the Pharisees aligned very much with their own, with one exception – the Pharisees would not advocate military action, so most of the people felt they had given in to Rome.

Atara now believed the Zealots held the only true solution. His year in prison had left him searching for meaning in life while still struggling with the bitterness within. He deeply believed in his faith and God's promise to Abraham for the Jewish nation. If the messiah would only come to take the leadership, all would be well. In the Torah David was a king who commanded the armies of the Jewish nation. The messiah was to be a descendent of his, so would it not follow that the messiah would bring salvation to the Jews by military might?

The arrest of Barabbas was a disappointment for the men around the table. They all felt he would have emerged a significant leader in the movement. He was a man who did not hesitate to use violence as a means to an end and was gifted with oratory skills that could rally the men. The past of this large, athletic man was perhaps a bit questionable, but what mattered now was leadership. With his arrest they knew a trial would be imminent. The matter at hand around the table was who would they find in Jerusalem to replace him? Where was the awaited messiah?

This had been the main topic of conversation with this small band since the failed demonstration that ended with the arrest of Jesus Barabbas. Now though, the discussion turned to the events of this past day, the 10th day of Nissan. (This evening was now the 11th day of Nissan as the biblical day begins at sunset.) There had been many discussions in the past about this Jesus from the Galilee. Since many of the new Zealots over the past two years were from the Galilee, several of them had heard Jesus speak. Although everyone who did was very taken by the message, the question still remained. Is this the man of God, the messiah, that would lead them against the Romans?

The Galilean spoke of love, peace, repentance, forgiveness and salvation. He expounded on the Torah as none of them had ever heard before, but also was known to break the Law of the Sabbath, which they held as an absolute. He healed many and drove out demons! Yet, not a word on the Roman occupation, their false gods and defilement of the Jewish land. 'Wouldn't the messiah say something about these things?' thought Atara.

There was a glimmer of hope as the men turned the discussion to the main event of this day – the procession down the Mount of Olives.

Benjamin saw the procession at the time he was scouting out the city walls for possible future attacks on the Roman soldiers. "Is it possible that this could be the messiah?" Benjamin had heard Jesus speak before and like Atara wanted to learn more about this man from Galilee. "But will he bring us victory?" he asked.

Another of them, Uri, was near the Temple Mount when Jesus entered the city with thousands following, but he couldn't get close enough to see or hear. Uri was by far the most skeptical and militant of the group. He had a fierce temper that often got the better of him. "All this talk of repentance! Unless he is prepared to pick up arms with us, I say he is nothing more than a charlatan, a false prophet, misleading our people. How can we secure the future of the Torah and Temple by 'turning the other cheek' as this man advocates? I say we use the unrest he is creating to our advantage, launching an immediate attack!" Mordechai, who often stood close to his friend Uri, was quick to agree.

The two recently made it known they were joining ranks with the feared Sicarii. The Sicarii, which means dagger, were a militant offshoot of the Zealots. Not only did they passionately hate the Romans, but in their view any Jew who was thought to fraternize, in any way, with the Romans should be killed as an example. They would track down a perpetrator, using their daggers to demonstrate the consequence of aiding the Romans. It was a brutal tactic. They were feared throughout Jerusalem.

The news of Lazarus was all over Jerusalem, the whole city was abuzz with talk. Was this the messiah? Word was out that only a few days earlier Jesus raised this man from the dead! One by one each person would account for all the stories they had heard – some confirmed by others, some seemed too fantastic to be true. Who was this man?

Atara was very interested to learn one of Jesus' disciples was one of them, or at least had been, and still had connections with the movement. A man named Simon the Zealot of the Galilee joined with Jesus to be one of his 12 disciples when Jesus was in the Galilee. Perhaps if he could find this man at some point, he would discover the answers he was looking for.

As the night went on, debates raged within this small chamber of rebels. At one point Atara excitedly explained to the men what had been revealed to him and Shira (without, of course, mentioning anything about her) about Jesus. He didn't have to reiterate the significance of this 10th day of Nissan to this deeply religious group. But he went further by demonstrating the significance of Jesus entering Jerusalem on the donkey on this day when lambs were being chosen for sacrifice. The men quieted down as Atara attempted to put all this together, as he and Shira had done, with what he had learned about Jesus. He had to admit, though, he couldn't yet see how this man could be the conquering messiah, their leader, the one to drive away the Romans and restore the glory of Jerusalem. And yet?

The word was that Jesus would be at the Temple in the morning. A few of the men around the table agreed (not Uri and Mordechai) they should be there to see what would happen next. If this Jesus was going to incite the people against Rome, then this would be the perfect time, and they certainly didn't want to miss the opportunity of standing by any man who would speak against Rome.

Discussions trailed off afterward as one by one sleep overcame each man. Atara sat for a while, mulling over the discussions of the day. He felt strangely drawn to this man he had never met. He was determined to find out more.

Chapter 11

MONDAY: NISSAN 11 / APRIL 7TH

The house of Barak awoke with the first break of dawn. The men went about preparing for their daily routine of prayer by washing and dressing first. Ten men were present, enough to create a *minyan* or quorum, so the men donned their *tefillin*[6] and *tallit*,[7] then went directly into prayers of praise and thanksgiving to God. They began by reciting the Sh'ma: '*Hear, O Israel: The Lord our God, the Lord is one. Love the Lord your God with all your heart and with all your soul and with all your strength.* [8]

When prayers finished each of the men took a little of what food there was, silently slipping out through the door up the damp stone stairs into the laneway. They rushed off to their assignments in staggered intervals over a short period to avoid spying eyes. Atara was out early, dodging any assignment for the day. He was eager to arrive at the Temple in case this Jesus did show up, as the rumors had indicated. Once in the narrow alley, he began the ascent northward over the worn cobblestones, through the poorer areas of the Lower City toward the Temple. The morning air was cool and damp. Barak's house was at the bottom of the Tyropoeon Valley, very near the Pool of Siloam, so there was some distance to cover, all uphill.

Atara was careful to stay off the main streets, as there was an increase today of Roman sentries posted on all the main paths. It took some time to wind his way up through the Lower City on a circular route that purposely avoided the Roman Hippodrome where during Passover scores of Roman troops were temporarily being housed. He then crossed eastward over the area that was the original city of King David. As he approached the magnificent Huldah Gate at the south end of the Temple, he could hear a commotion coming from the Temple court on the other side of the gate.

People were running up the imposing stairs into the Temple to see what was

[6] Tefillin: Phylacteries, scripture wrapped around the hand, forearm and forehead, Deuteronomy 6:8

[7] Tallit: Prayer shawl

[8] Deuteronomy 6:4

happening. Others, most notably merchants and money changers, were rapidly fleeing outward. What was happening?

Normally a bustling place, the Court of the Gentiles on the Temple Mount was extremely busy during this Passover week with pilgrims making their daily sacrifices at the Temple. The Court of the Gentiles was a vast area outside the Temple itself where Jews and Gentiles could gather. Over the years it had developed into a vast market area to supply Temple sacrifices. Here vendors brought their animals – doves, lambs, cattle to sell for sacrifices. Many, many stalls with crowded animals and doves filled the immense square on the south side of the court. The Temple and priests took their share of the vendors' profit, becoming quite dependent on the income, which over the years turned this area into one of work rather than worship.

This rampant display of greed in Israel's holiest site disgusted Atara. To make matters worse, and to increase their profits, there was a tendency to cheat pilgrims with inflated prices, particularly at the festival times like Passover. At this time of year, for example, the major sacrifice was, of course, the lambs. These lambs, according to the Torah, must be *taleh*, or without blemish. The priests inspected the lambs. Those sold within the courtyard would be sold as certified, and those being brought in by families would have to be inspected with a much more stringent inspection because there was no profit in this for the Temple. Often a poor family or person would arrive with their very best lamb from their flock, or one they could afford from a purchase outside the Temple, only to find the priest would discover a minor defect, rejecting their offering. Devastating to the family, and with not enough funds to purchase another lamb, they would have to leave in shame.

Atara had seen this for himself. 'Surely God would accept these modest offerings.' He was greatly disturbed at what he had witnessed.

To add to the chaos, there was a need for currency exchange with all this commerce. Many stalls of money changers were there to exchange the numerous types of currencies from pilgrims coming from afar. Again, at inflated exchange rates. Many of these currencies were embossed with graven images that would not be accepted by the Temple, so pilgrims had no choice but to deal with the money changers.

All this had disturbed Atara in the past, but what was this noise coming from the courtyard today? It differed from the normally crowded sounds of people and animals.

Atara quickly increased his pace as he bound up the massive steps leading to the Huldah Gate. Through all the calamity he could see the entire court was packed full of people, all stretching and straining to look in the direction of the commotion. 'Have the other Zealot cells made a move I don't know about? Has there been an attack? Why would they target the Temple court? Have the Romans moved in to take over?' Atara's mind reeled as thoughts raced through his head. He quickly found a young man clinging to the top of a pillar ledge inside the gate. "What is it? What's happening?"

"It is Jesus, the Nazarene!" he exclaimed. "He has toppled tables and beaten off merchants! I can see what looks like a whip flailing! Men are running away!"

Atara had to see for himself. He began pushing through the enormous crowd around the outer edge to get closer. 'Was Jesus finally revealing himself as a warrior? Had the revolution begun? But why here, why the Temple and not the Antonia Fortress? Was he attempting to draw the Romans in?' Confused, but excited, Atara pushed forward until eventually he reached a spot behind a sheep pen on the east wall. Here he could climb the rail for a better view. Then he saw him.

What he witnessed was a man, very ordinary looking in most respects, driving the merchants to the far side of the court in an apparent move to force them out. His anger was clear. Atara had never seen anything like it. It was just one man! The whip flared, tables turned over, men ran for the exit. In a voice of authority clearly heard throughout the court, *"It is written… My house will be a house of prayer; but you have made it a den of robbers!"*[9]

Atara was transfixed. 'Who is this man?' The great strength of a carpenter was clear as he toppled tables one after the other with little effort. Atara could see the Temple priests had retreated up their stairs high into their balconies, looking down and pointing fingers. But they did nothing. Scattered throughout the grounds were numerous Pharisees and Sadducees who had moved to the sides of the court for fear of attack. His disciples stood by as if to ensure his protection, but it appeared very evident he needed none.

'Where are the Zealots?' He had expected with all the commotion that it might involve them, bringing out their concealed weapons. But there was no sign of anyone he knew. Atara recalled from the discussions the night before that one disciple, Simon, was a Zealot, so he tried to discern which one that might be. Maybe he would be able to speak with him.

Atara had arrived at his wooden perch along the side of the wall just as the incident was coming to an end. 'Why are the Temple guards not arresting him? They just stand by the sides and do nothing!'

Most of the merchants had already fled, the last few were hurriedly gathering

[9] Luke 19:46

their flocks and wares. As the commotion died down, Jesus found a place on the stairs near Atara where he could be seen by all. He simply sat down, calmly, as if nothing had happened. It was clear now that the Temple guards had been instructed to stand down for fear of riots. He figured the priests knew if there was rioting on the Temple grounds, the Romans would become involved. They did not want Roman presence defiling the Temple Mount, so they could do nothing. The crowd, which numbered many thousands, quieted. People sat all around the court as Jesus began to speak:

"A man planted a vineyard, rented it to some farmers and went away for a long time."

It astounded Atara that Jesus was speaking in his normal voice. It was piercing, yet compassionate. You would expect that in a court of this magnitude, full of people, that a person would have a hard time being heard to the far corners, even if shouting at full volume. Yet it appeared to him absolutely no one was having difficulty hearing his words.

Jesus continued. *"At harvest time he sent a servant to the tenants so they would give him some of the fruit of the vineyard. But the tenants beat him and sent him away empty-handed. He sent another servant, but that one also they beat and treated shamefully, and sent away empty-handed. He sent a third, and they wounded him and threw him out.*

"Then the owner of the vineyard said, 'What shall I do? I will send my son, whom I love; perhaps they will respect him.'

"But when the tenants saw him, they talked the matter over. 'This is the heir,' they said. 'Let's kill him, and the inheritance will be ours.' So they threw him out of the vineyard and killed him.

"What then will the owner of the vineyard do to them? He will come and kill those tenants and give the vineyard to others."[10]

Jesus looked directly at them and asked, *"Then what is the meaning of that which is written: 'The stone the builders rejected has become the cornerstone'?"*[11]

Atara was familiar with this scripture and knew it was considered a messianic prophesy. Somehow he knew Jesus was addressing the Pharisees and priests. 'Was he claiming to be the cornerstone? Rejected, to be killed as a prophet? Who is this son?' Atara understood the parable was referring to the prophets Israel had beaten and ignored. He could see anger in their eyes. This message was clearly a warning to Israel.

It was more than that, though. Atara felt there was a message here for him.

---

[10] Luke 20:9–15
[11] Luke 20:17

A foreshadowing of something yet to come that would involve him personally, for him to discover as all of this unfolded. He became riveted to every word Jesus spoke.

As Jesus addressed the crowd, there was complete silence. The Pharisees present eventually became emboldened, coming forward to challenge him. One by one they asked questions to entrap him. "On whose authority are you doing these things?" "Is it right to pay the imperial tax to Caesar?" "Whose wife will she be after the resurrection?" "Of all the commandments, which is the most important?" These questions were a trap to find Jesus in error for these were trick questions most rabbis had no definitive answers for. Questions each religious faction present would have a different response to. They were attempting to cause division, thereby discrediting Jesus. But he answered each one definitively, avoiding their snares with an authority Atara had never heard from a rabbi.

To the question of which is the most important commandment, Jesus answered, *"Hear, O Israel: The Lord our God, the Lord is one. Love the Lord your God with all your heart, and with all your soul, and with all your mind and with all your strength. The second is this: Love your neighbor as yourself. There is no commandment greater than these."*[12] The first being the Sh'ma Atara recited every morning, but the second – this was new.

For the rest of the morning, well into the afternoon, the courtyard was a scene of the master teaching the pupils. The crowds grew as word quickly spread throughout the city. By noon there was barely any room left in the entire Temple Mount to sit or stand. Every question the Pharisees brought forward was answered and rebuked. By noon they had left in frustration. It was clear they were very, very angry at this public humiliation. But the crowds listened attentively.

Jesus spoke many parables, stories with deeper meanings, and taught from the Torah as the crowds seemed to hang on every word. Atara listened intently. He felt such a passion within to understand what Jesus was saying, with thoughts and arguments from yeshiva racing through his mind. Yet, strangely enough, he always came out agreeing with what Jesus was saying to be true and righteous. From time to time his mind would slip away to thoughts of Shira. 'What would she think of this? Would she agree?' Or of his fellow compatriots. 'Are they here in this crowd listening? Do they think this man will be our future leader?'

By the middle of the afternoon, the Spring sun was beating down heavily onto the people in the courtyard. After a final discourse, Jesus nodded to his disciples that it was time to leave. They whisked him away through the Golden

---

[12] Mark 12:29–31

Gate to outside the Temple Mount. They moved quickly past Atara, then were out of sight.

The multitudes were still for a while, as if no one wanted to end the moment, meditating on his last words. Atara understood. He too wanted to hear more, to be closer to this man. For some inexplicable reason, he needed to know more. It was as if he sensed this Jesus had answers to the many questions that challenged his young mind.

Then the crowds slowly dispersed, leaving the Temple grounds eerily empty. Atara decided to head out to a private place he had discovered previously on the city wall where he had gone a few times to pray and think. He exited through the Huldah Gate, descending the stairs into the ancient area of the City of David. Following the city walls downward, and avoiding Romans, about halfway down the slope he found his spot in the wall. It was a small port to be used by archers when under attack, about three-quarters of the way up the wall, but for now was left vacant. High above, along the top of the wall, Roman soldiers patrolled with watchful eyes. He climbed the narrow stairs built into the wall, making sure no one was looking, then tucked himself into his little enclave.

Thinking about the morning caused him to re-examine himself, his life, his own righteousness. That led him to consider his ambition and direction in life, the purpose of the Zealots, and then the future of Jerusalem and Israel. From there his thoughts dug even deeper, further into the meaning of a relationship with God and the Torah. Normally, he would be quite content to focus on that type of abstract discussion, but today it was different. The process of thought reversed itself as he found himself challenged personally with his own lack of righteousness. Somehow this Jesus had penetrated deep inside the core of his being like Atara had never experienced before.

The remainder of the afternoon slipped by as he sat ruminating. At one point, looking out through the port in the wall not long after he had arrived in his refuge, he saw a small crowd in the far distance working its way up the Mount of Olives. 'That must be Jesus.' He wished he had followed. The sun was setting now.

Suddenly, he snapped out of his deep thoughts as he became aware of the time, remembering his arranged rendezvous with Shira. The prospect of sharing the day's experience with her sent him excitedly flying out of his sanctum, down the narrow stairs and into the streets toward the Upper City.

Chapter 12

MONDAY EVENING :NISSAN 12 / APRIL 7TH

Shira's brothers were back at the yeshiva full-time, so sitting at the dinner table were just Shira and her father. She took every minute of opportunity with him to ask about what had taken place in the Sanhedrin today. At one point Martha, the head servant in the household who was more like a nanny to Shira, scolded her for pestering her father so much after such a strenuous day. But Nicodemus waved it off, continuing to field her questions. What she learned greatly troubled her.

By the time the conversation finished, the plates had long been cleared away. When Shira realized the time, she became anxious to meet Atara and share what she had just learned. She had been thinking all day of her time later with him. Even the distraction of slipping away from the family home to take some food to the lower valley was not enough to keep her mind from thinking of him.

She learned little during the day about their mutual interest in Jesus. Other than while she was out she heard many rumors about Jesus being at the Temple. Something had happened. The gossip ranged from an outright rebellion to a prophet prophesying on the Temple Mount! Shira was sure the stories must be greatly exaggerated. She was excited, but also worried Atara would somehow be caught up in the trouble. However, what really concerned her was what she had learned from her father. She wanted desperately to talk with Atara.

Shira slipped on a heavy tunic, then silently passed through the back door into the garden.

———————————

Atara worked his way from the Lower City, up past the Essene Quarter, through back roads and alleys. He was becoming quite skilled at navigating the complex maze of Jerusalem.

Being careful to avoid the Roman amphitheater on the edge of the Upper City for fear of Roman soldiers, this route took him closer to the west side of the city, passing right by the high priest Caiaphas' house in the area now known as Mount Zion. Once in the Upper City, the difference was obvious. The laneways were wider and much cleaner than in other sections of Jerusalem. The newer homes were large, towering two or three stories high. They were for single families rather than small units jammed together for multiple families, one on another, as in the Lower City. It was clearly an area for the wealthy.

The sky was dark now. As Atara made his last turn, he found himself standing in front of the familiar wooden door.

When Shira reached the garden door, unbolting it, she found Atara sitting on the pavement outside, much the same as the night before. "How long have you been here?" she asked, then continued before he had a chance to answer. "I'm sorry I'm so late, but there were many questions to ask Father. I had to wait for everyone to go to bed before I could make my escape!"

"That's alright," answered Atara as he brushed closely by her, entering the doorway. Looking momentarily into those deep brown eyes, he doubted anyone could be annoyed with her. "I haven't been here long. I have some incredible news!"

It was clear both were very excited to see one another and anxious to share what they had found out. In their zeal they both began to speak at once, stopped, then apologized to each other, offering for the other to speak, but then both began together again. Laughing now, they finally decided it was best to sit down on the familiar marble bench and take turns.

When they had awkwardly settled into place, Shira calmly glanced at Atara. "You first. What did you find out?"

As he related his story of the day, Shira sat transfixed, listening to every word. Atara did not leave out any details as he told her how Jesus had cleared the Temple courtyard, driving out the merchants and rebuking the leaders. It was very evident to her this act of authority left quite an impression on Atara.

"Finally, this man is revealing himself!" Atara exclaimed, sounding more like the Zealot he aspired to be. "He showed no fear at all! The Temple guards were powerless, just standing in the background watching! The priests and Pharisees ran for shelter as merchants gathered what they could, fleeing his whip. It was amazing! Jesus might actually be the leader we've been looking for to rid us of this oppression! We have been crushed, persecuted by the Greeks, Hasmoneans and now the Romans for centuries. Now is the time to finally free ourselves! Maybe he is a warrior worthy of our following who is ready to make his move." Atara paused. "But I don't understand why he chose the Temple. Why not stand up to the Romans at the Antonia Fortress as they are our enemy?"

After allowing Atara a moment to reflect on what he had just said, Shira responded softly, much as she had done two days ago. "Perhaps it's not why he's here."

"Well, he certainly was directing his messages to our religious leaders. He told a parable of two sons who were asked by their father to work in a vineyard. One said he would not, but changed his mind, going later in the day. The other said he would go, but did not. Jesus then asked the leaders which of the two sons did what the father wanted? The leaders agreed it was the first son, but Jesus turned the story on them saying, '*Truly I tell you, the tax collectors and the prostitutes are entering the Kingdom of God ahead of you*'[13]!

"The Pharisees were furious! Jesus told another story of a landowner and his tenants. This again was directed at all the religious leaders who were there. He seemed to say in this parable that we Jews have rejected every prophet God has sent in the past. He then used the scripture from Psalm 118:22 which is referring to the messiah. Rejected, but becomes the cornerstone? I think he was referring to himself as the messiah and that he would be rejected by the very men present!"

"They will reject him," responded Shira with a melancholy Atara had not heard from her before. "Father was there today. First, you need to know that Father, and a small handful of others on the Sanhedrin, are secret supporters of Jesus. They've heard many of the things he has said and agree. I don't believe many of them are certain he is the messiah, but they've been impressed with what he's been saying. The Sanhedrin and the Temple priests have become very corrupt. Under the leadership of Caiaphas, the corruption has become much worse these past years. When the Pharisees and priests left the Temple today around noon, they were extremely angry, as you saw. They convened a meeting. Father was excluded, but later found out they're plotting to kill Jesus."

"Odd," responded Atara. "That's exactly what Jesus seemed to foretell when he spoke today."

"There is more to it than that," Shira said. "It would seem on the surface Jesus is just another man claiming to be a prophet. That he's simply rebelling against Jewish authority, advocating a return to our values and to God. But it seems to go much deeper. Let me tell you about the first meeting Father had with Jesus two years ago."

---

[13] Matthew 21:31

Shira had Atara's full attention now. He was eager to hear more about what Nicodemus had learned from Jesus. "Father heard Jesus speak during his first trip to Jerusalem from the Galilee. We had all heard of this man before he arrived. The stories of his many miracles, healings and teachings in the synagogues had already reached the ears of most of the religious leaders, as well as the public. After Father listened to him speak one day, he decided he would like to talk with Jesus to learn more. It was very difficult, as there were always crowds of people around, and to be honest he didn't want to be seen by other members of the Sanhedrin. So he waited to approach Jesus until after dark when the crowds had been sent away. They began to talk when Father decided to invite Jesus to come to our home for supper. Father allowed me to sit in the room and listen to the men speak.

"Jesus said some remarkable things. In the discussions he claimed no one could enter the Kingdom of God without being born again, born of water and spirit. He said, *'Flesh gives birth to flesh, but the Spirit gives birth to spirit. You should not be surprised at my saying, "You must be born again!"'* Father didn't understand what he meant by born again, so Jesus continued. *'No one has ever gone into heaven except the one who came from heaven – the Son of Man. Just as Moses lifted up the snake in the wilderness, so the Son of Man must be lifted up, that everyone who believes might have eternal life.'"*[14]

"How can someone be born again?" Atara asked, skeptical.

"Well, that's just it! The answer is right there. Everyone who believes can have eternal life!"

"Believes in what?"

"In the Son of Man. Jesus often is referring to himself as the Son of Man. He has also been heard to claim he's the Son of God. I'm sure he was saying that he has been sent from heaven so we might have eternal life, if we only believe in him."

Shira looked humbly at the ground. She then quietly said, "I don't know how I knew that, but as soon as he spoke those words, I knew this man before me was sent by God. He was saying something so simple that it was profound. Perhaps beyond the reach of those looking for a more complex answer. But more than that, his words seemed to penetrate my soul, speaking directly to me. I just understood. Atara, I don't know why, but I believe Jesus is the messiah. I sat in that room that night with tears in my eyes. I felt so close to this stranger. I'm not sure why he used the example of Moses and the Son of Man being lifted up, but the feeling I have is very dark. A foretelling of something horrible to come."

---

[14] John 3:6–7, 13–15

Atara looked confused. This conversation had taken a turn in a direction he certainly had not expected. It was obvious this Jesus affected Shira very deeply, in a way he could not fully comprehend. His own experience today with Jesus had also made a powerful impression on him, but they were so different. Shira saw Jesus as the messiah, one who has come to capture their hearts by faith, a savior of the soul. Atara saw him as a messiah, a potential leader of military might and spiritual righteousness, who would lead them into freedom. 'Who is this man who affects people like this?'

They both sat for a while without a word being spoken. What could be said? Neither was really certain of what this all meant. How it would all fit together. But they did both agree something significant was about to happen.

Atara leaned toward Shira. "Why don't you come with me tomorrow? Word has spread that Jesus will be back at the Temple. You should hear what he has to say."

"I'm not allowed out on my own. Father will be at the Sanhedrin tomorrow. I'm sure he'll be there defending Jesus."

"I'll be with you."

"But there is no time for me to introduce you properly to Father. Besides, there would still have to be a chaperone."

She thought for a moment. Then the little sparkle in her eyes Atara had seen before returned. "Unless it was my cousin who could take me there," she said coyly. "I'll wait until just before Father is going to prayers first thing in the morning, then tell him Cousin Jonathan, who is very trustworthy, will be taking me out to the market for the day to shop. I don't think he will question that."

Atara looked with amazement at this young woman who seemingly had so much experience in finding her way around Jerusalem, and probably just as much experience in mischief!

They agreed to meet right after morning prayers by the gate, then proceed directly to the Temple Mount.

What Shira shared that day would challenge Atara in the days to come.

Chapter 13

MONDAY NIGHT: NISSAN 12 / APRIL 7TH

Atara sensed the added Roman presence on the streets of Jerusalem. It appeared the Romans were increasing the number of soldiers on patrol significantly as Passover neared. Rather than return to the home of Barak by the route he took the night before, he had heard there was another way. By using rooftops to approach the Lower City, someone could cross most of the way, avoiding Roman patrols.

Once he left the Mount Zion Quarter, he came across a small set of stairs leading upward past a modest apartment three stories up. Quietly passing by their door, the rooftop ahead opened to an expanse high above the city streets. He was merely a silhouette against the dark sky as he began to work his way across. This section of the city took a dramatic downward slope toward the Tyropoeon Valley, leading eventually to the Kidron Valley. He would find steps or crude ladders that would lower him from one rooftop to the next, enabling him to successfully continue. Twice when there were neither stairs nor ladder, he lowered himself over the edge from the higher roof, dropping to the one below. Three times he came to a point where a gap between the roofs over a street passing below blocked his way. He had to find a way back down to the street level to find other paths to the rooftops. Once he did, his journey continued. At one point he stood still for a while, transfixed by the spectacular view.

There was almost a full moon rising from behind the Mount of Olives, bathing Jerusalem in a shimmering blue glow. Off to the left, and much higher now, towered the Temple walls with just the top of the magnificent Temple showing from this angle. The moonlight dancing off the golden trim around the Temple roof was spectacular. 'Surely there could be nothing more breathtaking than this.'

Ahead Atara could make out the Roman Hippodrome where during the day Roman chariots would thunder down the track. To the right the city descended toward the Kidron Valley down to the Pool of Siloam. He knew he shouldn't linger as it would provide more opportunity to be spotted, but what a view! He continued downward and at one point, close to his destination, he seemed to run out of rooftops to find. So the last part of this journey continued at street level through laneways and narrow alleys, leading to his place of refuge.

When he arrived at the home of Barak, he hesitated for a moment farther up the lane, checking to ensure it was safe and not being watched. Certain no one was looking, he made his familiar approach down the tired old stairs, then softly rhymed the code out on the weathered wooden door. The sound of the bolt sliding inside signaled all was well, and the door swung open, allowing him to deftly slip in to greet his comrades.

Food sat on the table and everyone was there except Barak, who had other business to attend to. Greetings aside Atara sat to eat beside his friend Benjamin. He had such an incredible day that he had forgotten how famished he was. It was a simple meal of bread, salted fish and fresh vegetables, but Atara devoured more than his share in very short order. The other Zealots had arrived much earlier and had more time to recount their stories with each other. They were now keen to hear what Atara had learned.

He found out a few of the men had gone to the Temple Mount, witnessing the event. Simeon arrived a little ahead of Atara, just as Jesus made his entrance, so he saw the whole spectacle. He seemed very impressed as Jesus cleared the courtyard, but once Jesus began to speak, he lost interest and left. "We do not need more talk!" he exclaimed, "We need action, and against the Romans – not our fellow Jews!"

Benjamin and Ezra arrived at the Temple much the same time as Atara, also managing to find their way into the courtyard through the crowds. Together they stayed the full day. Both were excited when Jesus drove the merchants out thinking, like Atara, this man might turn out to be a Zealot. But they too felt the words Jesus spoke were truthful and relevant. It was clear to Atara their minds were still open to the subject, to the possibility Jesus was the messiah. "His physical actions at the Temple truly demonstrated the markings of a great leader!" said Benjamin. "I was in awe that one man could wield such authority and power!"

A different story came from Uri and Mordechai. They did not go to the Temple, acting rather disgruntled the others had wasted their time. They both were trying to discover what happened to Barabbas, believing this to be much more important. But all they could find out was that Barabbas was being held prisoner in the Antonia Fortress.

The others would seem to agree on one point or another, then in typical fashion change opinion several times throughout the remaining evening.

After discussing the events of the day, rather more like an animated debate, the group finally settled down. Atara decided to share what Shira told him about the meeting of Jesus and Nicodemus, withholding names, of course. The others tried to get him to reveal his source, but when he made it clear he was standing firm, they agreed to listen. He did say, however, that his source was a very powerful Pharisee in the Sanhedrin and that there were others like him who supported Jesus, adding credibility to what he was about to tell them. He then shared with them Shira's story of being born again.

"It seems this Jesus isn't concerned with the Romans. He showed no interest in the Roman occupation today, but rather our relationship with God as Jews. Over and over he spoke of our corruption, not only in finances and commerce, which was pretty evident today, but also of our faith! I think he's telling us change comes from within ourselves first, that we'll discover the solutions to our other problems as a consequence. It might be what he means by repentance because we have strayed. His reference to being born again might mean we are to look at our spirit, rather than our physical problems?"

Atara couldn't believe what he was saying. Defending Jesus? Offering an explanation? He was not sure what this man stood for and he certainly avoided bringing up the point that this could be achieved by believing in him! Even so, was this not what Jesus was saying?

The reaction from his comrades was swift with Uri taking the most offensive stand. He retorted, his face flushing in anger, "Are you accusing us? Those of us who are willing to put our lives on the line for the Torah, of having the wrong motives? I for one will not stand and do nothing!"

Most of the others seemed to agree. The tempest that followed rivaled any debate they had previously. From time to time Simeon would stand, trying to quiet the raucous down, fearing it might be heard on the street and draw attention to them. As the long evening turned to night, one by one they would tire of the debate, finding places to sleep until there was no one left to argue.

Atara sat for a while longer. He agreed with what most of the men were saying, but somehow he knew there was more to this. To be honest with himself, the words of Jesus today had left a larger impression on him than the driving out of the merchants. This really surprised him. It was something he had not expected. But even more, it was the simple faith and explanation Shira showed that totally confused him. He had to know more.

Chapter 14

The men of the house rose at 6 a.m., just before dawn. As was the tradition every morning they prepared for their morning prayers when they first arose. This morning Atara's prayers went beyond the recited rituals. He found himself attempting to speak with God, like he was actually talking with someone in the room. It differed from anything he had ever experienced before. Atara was asking God to show him the way, to reveal to him the path he should take, the truth behind what he had heard and seen over the past four days.

After sharing their food the men began to leave the home of Barak. A few of them told Atara they were going to the Temple to pray, but really, they were anxious to see if Jesus was going to show up again today, putting on another display of strength and controversy. Perhaps this day his focus would be on the Romans!

Some of the others were going to stay around the Antonia Fortress to see if they could find out what the Romans were going to do with Barabbas. Simeon, Uri and Mordechai were off to another cell in the north end of the city where there was a planning meeting between a number of the Zealot groups. Atara asked Uri if he would ask about his brothers, if there was any word on their safety.

Atara was restless to get moving. He was planning to arrive at the Temple with Shira early, just as the gates were opening at 9 a.m. At precisely that time, which is the third hour of daylight, the shofar would blow and the gates would open. At that time, the first sacrifice would be made according to the Book of Exodus, of a one-year-old lamb. This is a corporate offering for the sins of the people. Afterward, daily offerings would be made by all the people who would be bringing a sacrifice to the Temple for their personal atonement. Atara was hoping Jesus would return today, as rumored.

After scanning the laneway he bound out of the house, up those familiar worn stairs, and headed as quickly as he could toward the Upper City. It was a beautiful morning, cool and fresh, the morning sun just now rising above the Mount of Olives. You could seldom see an early morning sun from Jerusalem, or a late day sun for that matter, for the city is nestled between two mountains hiding the sun until it reveals itself. In early January, when the sun is the farthest south, a person standing on the south walls of the city can view a spectacular sunrise over the Kidron Valley, but now in April it was well hidden behind the Mount of Olives for more than an hour each morning, making the definition of sunrise rather obscure.

Atara was moving rapidly up the back alleys he had traveled before, perhaps not as carefully as previous times because his focus was on his rendezvous with Shira. Fortunately, the Roman presence at this early hour was very light. 'Did Shira manage to convince her father that Cousin Jonathan would be arriving to take her out?'

The streets were becoming exceptionally busy, even at this early hour with the influx of Passover pilgrims slowing down the travel considerably. Many times he was shoulder to shoulder with strangers while working his way up toward Mount Zion. Most of the traffic was in opposition to his route because the majority of those were headed either toward the Temple for prayers, or to the market for shopping.

As he approached the Amphitheater, he noticed many guards were beginning to arrive at their posts. Atara quickly snapped out of his thoughts, realizing he would have to alter his course, being more careful. Finding one of the stairwells he had descended the night before, he decided to try the rooftops once again for the last block before reaching the Upper City.

Atara ascended the steps, passing by a handful of doors where those inside were preparing for the day ahead, then found himself standing in the bright sunlight on the rooftops. He spotted Roman soldiers posted at high places throughout the city, keeping an eye on the Passover crowds, but none close enough to be a threat to him. This being a residential area, it normally would not pose much danger to the Romans. He worked his way across the rooftops, up and down small sets of stairs, passing many women hanging up their fresh laundry in the sun. Dogs barked and roosters crowed as he passed by the numerous homes that had access to the roofs. At the end of the block he easily found the stairwell leading back down, finding himself atop Mount Zion. Not far now through the Upper City to the quiet alley where he anticipated today's meeting with Shira.

When he arrived he found the door slightly ajar behind the wall of bougainvillea. Worried there was something amiss, he slowly pushed on the heavy door until he was able to glimpse into the courtyard. Shira was sitting quietly on the old marble bench. Her face was turned slightly away from him, a look of peaceful reflection about her. She was radiant in the morning light that streamed through the garden, backlighting her ebony hair. Atara stood frozen, not wanting the scene in front of him to ever vanish. Shira sensed his presence and jumped a little as if startled out of deep thought. "Goodness, you came so quietly! I left the door open a little so you'd know I was here."

"I'm sorry if I startled you," he apologized. He almost felt guilty, as if spying on her, but really he would have liked to gaze much longer.

"I was worried maybe something was wrong," he said in his own defense. Deciding it would be best to change the subject, he asked if she would be coming with him today.

"Yes," she answered with much enthusiasm. "Father had no problem with me going out with Cousin Jonathan. In fact, with all that is going on, he felt this was a great idea. Father left very early this morning to meet with the Sanhedrin, looking very worried. Not his normal talkative self. I just have to figure out how to tip my cousin off just in case the families talk!" she said with that familiar coy smile.

They were off with the excitement of youth. Shira had covered her face with her scarf so not to be recognized, and took Atara in her arm. They made a handsome couple no one would question, not even the Romans.

After leaving the small laneway, they talked as they walked through the streets of the Upper City. Atara was much more relaxed now, but still thought it was safest to avoid Roman sentries as much as possible as they headed toward the Temple. They walked as quickly as they could through the thick crowds because it was getting quite close to the opening time of the Temple and they didn't want to miss anything. They traveled right by the Amphitheater, heading farther eastward toward the Temple by backstreets, across the north end of the Lower City, then to the City of David.

They passed numerous beggars on the way. People of misfortune. Widows with no families. The sick and ailing, the blind and lame. These were hard times in Jerusalem, and Atara regretted that he had only a couple of small coins that might be needed that day. Shira, not so familiar with this area of the city, became emotional on passing so many unfortunate people who needed a helping hand. Many times she would travel to the Temple or market with her Father, but that was always on the main streets, which the Romans kept clear of beggars. Even her clandestine trips alone were restricted to the passages well travelled. The maze of back alleys and laneways revealed another side of Jerusalem. It had a very sobering effect on their time together. When they approached the beautiful Huldah Gate to the Temple there were many begging on the steps. The glaring contrast of the Temple and abject poverty greatly troubled Shira.

Ascending the massive steps Atara sensed how different this was from the day before. In fact, different from any normal day at the Temple. It was very quiet. There were the few bleating sounds of lambs, the general hum of crowds, but nowhere near what you would expect for a Tuesday. Certainly different from yesterday with all the action and noise.

When they arrived at the top of the stairs to enter the Temple Mount area, Atara was quite astonished. There were very few vendors and money changers present. A few brave souls had set up on the far outside walls, but only a handful had returned from the day before. Perhaps with the word out that Jesus would be returning, most of the vendors decided it more prudent to stay away.

But it was the crowds that really surprised Atara. They had to push their way up the stairs to get there, and already the entire courtyard of several acres was almost full of people arriving and settling in. Yet there was almost no sound. People were there with purpose, they were there to hear this man from the Galilee who heals the sick and the blind. Who entered the city of Jerusalem from the mountaintop to cries of "Messiah!" The man that closed down the Temple court.

Atara decided to move close to the area where he had been yesterday, guiding Shira through the crowds toward the east wall near the steps of the Temple. Atara was curious as to why the Temple guards had allowed this to happen. When he asked around, he was told the crowds were so enormous when the gates opened this morning, the guards were completely overwhelmed, unable to stop them. And again, the leaders fearing Roman intervention simply did nothing.

Where was this Galilean? Atara and Shira sat down in their chosen place with the others all around, waiting. There was very little conversation among the huge crowd and what little there was, was in anticipation of his arrival.

After about half an hour, the entire court was packed with people, many lining up outside the gates. There were families with their children cheerfully playing with one another, Temple priests and Pharisees standing off to the side, waiting for confrontation, and those with afflictions who had come to be healed. Then word began to spread and all eyes turned toward the Golden Gate on the eastern side of the Temple Mount. The crowds silently parted as Jesus, followed by his disciples, entered through the gate, moving directly to the same steps he had sat on yesterday.

As he approached, Jesus saw a small crowd of Pharisees standing there waiting. He went directly to them and asked, *"What do you think about the Messiah? Whose son is he?"*

"The son of David," they replied.

Then Jesus said to them, *"How is it then that David, speaking by the Spirit, calls him 'Lord'? For he says,*

"'The Lord said to my Lord: Sit at my right hand until I put your enemies under your feet.'

"If then David calls him 'Lord', how can he be his son?" No one could say a word in reply, and from that day on, no one dared ask him any more questions.[15]

After the leaders retreated, Jesus, still standing, proceeded to speak, *"The teachers of the Law and the Pharisees sit in Moses' seat. So you must be careful to do everything they tell you."*

Shira was already stunned by what Jesus had said. It was so different from the time when he had been talking with her father in their home. His voice was so authoritative, he could be heard over the entire courtyard!

"But do not do what they do, for they do not practise what they preach. They tie up heavy, cumbersome loads and put them on other people's shoulders, but they themselves are not willing to lift a finger to move them."[16]

Shira now felt very uncomfortable. He was talking about the leaders, the Sanhedrin, her father! 'Father had said similar things in the past. Father was a good man and didn't agree with many on the council, or their actions. Was Jesus here to cleanse the leadership of those who didn't live by what they preached?'

Jesus continued. *"Everything they do is done for people to see: They make their phylacteries wide and the tassels[17] on their garments long; they love the place of honor at the banquets and the most important seats in the synagogues, they love to be greeted with respect in the marketplaces and to be called Rabbi by others. But you are not to be called Rabbi, for you have one Teacher, and you are all brothers. And do not call anyone on earth father, for you have only one Father, and he is in heaven. Nor are you to be called instructor, for you have only one Instructor, the Messiah. The greatest among you will be your servant. For those who exalt themselves will be humbled, and those who humble themselves will be exalted!"*[18]

Atara flushed as he glanced down to the tzitzit[19] threaded with blue on his own tunic, the long tassels flowing from the four corners. He thought of his quest to become a rabbi. He felt as if Jesus was looking right through him as he realized deep down inside he wanted the position more than the righteousness. In fact, even his turning to the Zealots was deeply motivated by his need to be

---

[15] Matthew 22:41–46; Matthew 23:2,3

[16] Matthew 23:3–4

[17] Tassels, tzitzit in Hebrew. Numbers 15:38–40

[18] Mathew 23:5–12

[19] Tassels, Numbers 15:37

noticed, to do something significant that would make him important. Jesus was not just speaking to the leaders, but his words cut through Atara sharper and more truthful than any sword. 'I'm not humble.'

He glanced sideways at Shira and could see a tear in her eye. Not of joy this time, but the words of Jesus had obviously affected her as well. Atara moved closer to her and as they sat together they listened to him speak.

Jesus continued, listing the sins of the leaders one by one. The crowd sat motionless and stunned. Criticizing the religious leaders was not part of the Jewish culture or tradition. People were raised from childhood with a deep respect for their leaders and were taught obedience. This was radical. Throughout the courtyard many Pharisees, Sadducees and priests cloistered together, plotting. But by the time Jesus had finished, most had disappeared.

"You hypocrites … you blind guides … woe to you, teachers of the Law … whitewashed tombs (clean on the outside, but inside?) … So you testify against yourselves that you are the descendants of those who murdered the prophets. Go ahead then, and complete what your ancestors started!"[20]

'What? Was Jesus baiting them to come after him? Or foretelling what was to come?' Atara was shocked.

"You snakes! You brood of vipers! How will you escape being condemned to hell? Therefore I am sending you prophets and sages and teachers. Some of them you will kill and crucify, others you will flog in your synagogues and pursue from town to town."[21]

'Jesus will be sending others in his footsteps? We, the Jews with our Laws and courts, will kill them? It was true, those who God had sent in the past weren't treated well as they called for the repentance of a nation. They were flogged, beaten, imprisoned, stoned to death, killed by the sword and even sawn in two. Was this any different? Who will he be sending? On what authority?' Atara's mind raced as he tried to process what was really being said here, with such authority! He had the same feeling yesterday that somehow he had a role to play in all this, and he needed to find out what it was.

Shira sat wide-eyed.

Jesus continued with much lament. *"Jerusalem, Jerusalem, you who kill the prophets and stone those sent to you, how often I have longed to gather your children together, as a hen gathers her chicks under her wings, and you were not willing. Look, your house is left to you desolate. For I tell you, you will not see me again until you say, 'Blessed is he who comes in the name of the Lord.'"*[22]

---

[20] Matthew 23:16–32 abridged
[21] Matthew 23:33–34
[22] Matthew 23:37–39

It seemed to Shira Jesus was on the verge of tears. She could feel the longing in his heart for everyone present in this dramatic setting. But she then realized he had just said, *"You will not see me again."*

'What did he mean by this? Is he leaving, quitting? Or worse, is he to be another prophet rejected by the people he loves?'

At this point the crowd began to murmur among themselves. Everyone was asking the same questions, trying to understand what Jesus meant. For those who had heard or followed Jesus before, the message today was so different. Compassion, love, forgiveness had turned to warnings. Yet they were to be heeded. What was clear to most was these words were truthful and powerful, a cry out from this man of Nazareth for the Israelites to change course. To follow the Torah with their hearts, rather than just outward appearances.

Some men began talking with Jesus' disciples and the disciples in turn then spoke with Jesus. After some time he again addressed the multitude. *"The hour has come for the Son of Man to be glorified. Very truly I tell you, unless a kernel of wheat falls to the ground and dies, it remains only a single seed. But if it dies, it produces many seeds. Anyone who loves their life will lose it, while anyone who hates their life in this world will keep it for eternal life. Whoever serves me must follow me; and where I am, my servant also will be. My Father will honor the one who serves me."*

He continued, lifting his eyes. *"Now my soul is troubled and what shall I say? Father, save me from this hour? No. It was for this very reason I came to this hour. Father, glorify your name!"*[23]

This stunned the assembly, but what transpired next was truly shocking. A voice came from above, louder and with even more authority than that of Jesus. The multitude all looked around for the source.

"I have glorified it and will glorify it again."[24]

Was this the voice of another prophet? Some said it was the voice of an angel. Others claimed it was the voice of God Himself!

Jesus addressed them saying, *"This voice was for your benefit, not mine. Now is the time for judgment on this world; now the prince of this world will be driven out. And I, when I am lifted up from the earth, will draw all people to myself."*[25]

After Jesus said this, the people began again to speak among themselves again. Trying to understand they questioned him. "We have heard the messiah

---

[23] John 12:23–28
[24] John 12:28
[25] John 12:30–32

will remain forever, so how can you say, 'The Son of Man must be lifted up?' Who is this son of man?"

Atara immediately thought back to Jesus' reference to Moses from Numbers 21 when Nicodemus and Jesus had spoken. 'Lifted up?'

Jesus finished by saying, *"You are going to have the light just a little while longer. Walk while you have the light before the darkness overtakes you. Whoever walks in the dark does not know where they are going. Believe in the light while you have the light, so that you may become the children of light."*[26]

Atara was listening so intensely that his palms were now becoming sweaty. He realized Jesus was referring to the messianic prophesy of Isaiah 9:2. But there was even more. Atara's mind went back to Genesis 1:3, the beginning of all, where God said, *"Let there be light."* This was The Light before the sun, Light of the world, Light of God, the Messiah Himself. Was Jesus claiming to be this Light?'

Shira and Atara looked at each other. So many questions, so many needed answers. They had to know more. Jesus' warning sounded like the time was imminent and that action was necessary now.

The morning had passed into early afternoon. As Jesus and his disciples began to exit, the crowd parted, allowing them to go back the way they came. This took them right past Atara and Shira. In that instant Atara decided to follow Jesus. When he glanced at her she simply nodded as if knowing what his intentions were, so they quickly followed directly behind and out of the Temple through the Golden Gate.

There was a small crowd following Jesus and the disciples. Atara did not want to presume he was invited. He simply wanted to know more, so they stayed well behind. The crowd picked up a few more people as it progressed. At one point while ascending the winding path up the Mount of Olives, Jesus stopped to address his disciples and the growing number. For the next hour he taught and answered questions, but what really stood out in Atara's and Shira's minds was what he said near the end:

"Whoever believes in me does not believe in me only, but in the one who sent me. The one who looks at me is seeing the one who sent me. I have come into the world as a light, so that no one who believes in me should stay in darkness. If anyone hears my words, but does not keep them, I do not judge that person. For I did not come to judge the world, but to save the world. There is a judge for the one who rejects me and does not accept my words; the very words I have spoken will condemn them at the last day.

---

[26] John12:35–37

For I did not speak on my own, but the Father who sent me commanded me to say all that I have spoken. I know that his command leads to eternal life. So whatever I say is just what the Father has told me to say."²⁷

To Shira this was the Jesus she had heard once before in her father's room. "Whoever believes in me." 'How could someone not?' He spoke to her very soul.

Atara needed to know more. There were simply too many pieces he had to fit together, too many questions, but underlying it all he felt there was a destiny here for him to fulfill.

After Jesus had spoken a small group of children who had been playing nearby rushed over to him. He effortlessly scooped three of them up in his arms, spinning them around, looking high to the heavens with a laugh full of joy. Sitting down with them now gathered by his side, Jesus indicated to those around that he would like to have private time with his future young disciples. This was the last time he would speak in public.

Before Atara would leave he asked around as to which of the disciples was Simon the Zealot. Once the man was pointed out to him, Atara left Shira briefly, approaching Simon to introduce himself as a fellow Zealot.

"Shalom, brother," Simon said. "Are you here to follow?"

"I'm not sure yet," responded Atara. "I need to know more. The truth is I feel the sense of urgency in what Jesus is saying now, and I almost feel that he is talking to me."

"I understand," said Simon. "He has a way of doing that. I have to go now, but next time we cross paths, let us talk. For now I need to be with the Master."

Atara returned to Shira. Taking her by the arm they started to make their way down the mountainside back to the city. There was much to meditate on as they made their way down the winding path on the Mount of Olives.

---

²⁷ John 12:44–50

Chapter 15

TUESDAY AFTERNOON: NISSAN 12 / APRIL 8TH

The cobbled road twisting down the side of the Mount of Olives was bustling with throngs of people going about their business two days before Passover. When Atara and Shira had reached the bottom, he glanced back up the slope and could see the small procession surrounding Jesus had just reached the mountaintop, heading toward Bethany.

Looking ahead, he decided since they were already outside the city walls it would be much safer to walk southward around the city, avoiding the many Roman soldiers inside. The only obstacle would be the checkpoint at the gate of re-entry into the city. The Water Gate down by the Pool of Siloam was probably the least guarded entrance to the city, providing the safest way in.

Atara and Shira left the road leading back to the Golden Gate. Turning southward there was a rugged path leading into the Kidron Valley. Their time together up to this point had been a very quiet one, both of them taking some time to process everything Jesus had said today. Arriving at the valley floor, they passed by the ancient Tomb of Absalom, the rebellious son of King David. Then, for the first time that day, Atara looked up, realizing what a beautiful day it was. The deep blue sky was crystal clear, the afternoon temperature near perfect. He could hear the birds playfully singing in the bushes close to the path and as he glanced up to his right, the towering walls of Jerusalem in front of the Temple Mount appeared impenetrable. It was magnificent.

On his left, Shira walked silently as she contemplated the words of Jesus. Her light blue scarf was loosely wrapped around her face and hair, her feet elegantly crossing the rocky path. Atara gazed at her. She lifted her eyes for a moment, catching the stare, but just as quickly looked back down to the path, a bit embarrassed.

Atara snapped out of his thoughts. "You must be thirsty," he said with concern in his voice. "We're almost at the Gihon Spring where we can rest."

Shira nodded. Then they left the path as they continued the few hundred more yards to the spring. The Gihon Spring was a remarkable place. At the bottom of the Kidron Valley, water gushed from a small underground crevice, filling a pool that had been made to contain it. On the west side of the pool the water flowed into a subterranean tunnel cut through solid rock by King Hezekiah 700 years earlier. The tunnel crossed under the ancient City of David, then reappeared inside the city walls to fill the pool of Siloam.

When they arrived they were greeted by a few other travelers and Passover pilgrims accessing the water from the well. The man in charge was to be paid a coin for his service. Today was a busy day for him. Many of the pilgrims had set up tents in the valley near the spring for Passover, this being the only source of water for quite a distance. After Atara paid the man, they both drank of this pure, cool spring water right from its source.

It was now late in the afternoon. The eastern sun was hidden from view in this deep valley by the high walls of Jerusalem, providing rejuvenating and much-appreciated shade. Cooled and refreshed, Atara suggested they climb to a place with soft grass he had spotted just above the spring to rest for a while.

Once settled they took a moment to soak in the beauty of their surroundings. Across from them to the east towered the Mount of Olives. Beautifully green with olive groves and almond trees filling the landscape, the babbling sound of the spring in the background filled the air with calm. It was Spring. The poppies were in full bloom, blanketing the mountainside in crimson red. Directly behind them rose the majestic wall of Jerusalem. Sitting at the base they had to strain their necks back to view the top. Hiding behind that the Temple of the Lord God. It was exhilarating to Atara. For a moment he forgot about the oppression and grief the Jewish people were suffering under Roman rule.

Shira spoke first, interrupting the stillness that had engulfed them. "I was surprised and troubled at first when Jesus spoke today. It was so different from the time when he visited with Father. But as I have thought about it, many of the things Jesus said about the Jewish leadership were true. Father has been complaining about the corruption in the Temple and Sanhedrin for as long as I can remember. After Mother died, when I was quite young, Father became withdrawn and bitter, always searching for answers. Since he met Jesus he has been different. It's hard to explain, but he appears much more certain about his faith and purpose, more at peace with himself. He also has become braver, more vocal about the abuses he witnesses within the leadership. So I understand now what Jesus was saying. We, as Jews, have been chosen by God to be His representatives on this earth and we have lost our way."

"What about the heathens, the pagans? The murderous Romans who take lives every day, forcing us to live in misery?" responded Atara. Normally a statement such as this would come from him very forcefully, but this time it truly was a question searching for an answer. "Jesus talked only of the sins of our people. What about those who persecute us? Are they not far worse?"

"Yes, maybe they are," she answered. "But isn't it us who know better? Are we not to be held accountable for all God has given us with the Torah?"

This cut into Atara like a knife. He felt so much anger against all Romans that he had lost sight of that simple fact. 'Should it not begin with us? Should our hearts not be right with God first before we can expect God to help us? But how? Through this messiah?' So many questions raced through his mind. He had to admit he was a little confused at how peaceful Shira seemed to be while his own mind was tormented with questions and doubt.

"Well," in an attempt to avoid a direct answer to her question, avoiding any argument with her, "he certainly gave us something to think about at the Temple today! I agree we have a long history as a people of killing the messengers, the prophets of God. When he spoke I could feel the injustice perpetuated by our own people. That message was very clear."

After a moment he added, "What really is hard to understand is what he was saying to us when we followed afterward up the mountainside."

"I'm glad we did follow. He sounded so much more like the man Father has talked about and the man I met. But he seemed very sad."

"What does he mean by 'whoever believes in me'? If he is the messiah, then what would that mean? He doesn't seem to be talking about military might here, not yet at least, but of our belief in him. What would that do?"

"What do you mean?" asked Shira gently.

"I can't understand the purpose behind what he's saying. I understand we're separated from God. That there is a chasm between man and God, a wall of sin from the time of Adam, keeping us apart. God is holy and pure, we can't stand in His presence with our sin. We have been given the sacrifices at the Temple as a way to make atonement for our sins and the Law to guide us. Jesus said today, '*I do not come to judge the world, but to save the world.*' If we believe in him, it would lead to eternal life? What does he mean? We have the Temple and sacrifices. How would believing in him change anything?"

Shira reflected for a moment. "How well has the Law been working for our people? Are we not the ones crying out for the messiah? Jesus said we have killed our prophets and corrupted our faith. Think for a moment of last Sunday when Jesus rode into the city. We both agreed that could have symbolized him entering as a lamb with all the other lambs for Passover, which would mean salvation.

Maybe what he's trying to tell us is he'll bring us salvation somehow. He'll be like the lamb I have at home. I don't understand either, but I think I believe what he's saying."

Shira's confidence and simplicity irritated him. It was like having all the wires in his mind charged at once. 'Lamb! We need a lion, not a lamb! How could she possibly accept this without more proof? How does it all fit with the Torah and God's commands of the Temple? How?'

Atara took a big breath, looking into Shira's brown eyes, and let it go. "I can see what you're saying, but I need to know more. I need proof. I just do. The more I've listened to Jesus, the more confused I seem to be. Everything is upside down from what I would've expected from a messiah, yet there is no doubt he's a powerful and persuasive man. I do know if he is the messiah, however, he must fit all the prophesies and Temple ordinances. That is where we must look if we want the truth. Perhaps in the days to come he'll draw attention to our plight with the Romans as well."

Shira could see he was adamant about his position. He needed to search for answers. Deep inside she felt a yearning for him to see Jesus for who he was, as she did.

They picked themselves up, brushing off the coarse grass from their clothing. Atara explained they would have to stay very close together when entering the city through the gate to avoid Roman scrutiny. It would be unlikely anyone would recognize him, but it would be best to find a crowd to mix in with, just to be sure.

As they approached the lower part of the city, they could see the Water Gate ahead. Fortunately, with the large Passover crowds, also with this being one of the smaller gates, everyone was funneled together as they passed by the weary soldiers. Shira pressed close up against Atara, gripping his arm tightly as one soldier looked her up and down. But no move was made, so they passed through without any trouble.

Once inside the wall Atara was elated to be through, but reluctant to have Shira drop his arm to be on her own. This was a feeling Atara had never experienced before, adding much confusion to his already clouded mind. 'Sentries, messiahs, this woman. A lot for one day.'

Walking by the beautiful Pool of Siloam, Shira said to Atara, "Would you like to visit the family I bring food to? It's not far from here."

"I would," responded Atara, hoping to spend even a little more time with her. They wound their way through a few of the alleys in the Lower City to a very modest apartment on the top of two others. "This is very close to where I've been staying," observed Atara as they climbed the stairs to the apartment.

It was a single room, only a few meters wide. In the corner a small fire was burning with a pot of water over it. On a cot against the wall an old lady, the grandmother, lay in a very fragile state. In the center of the room sitting around the table was the mother with her three children. It was obvious by the state of their attire they had no money and there was not much evidence of food to be seen.

The children looked up from their lessons and on seeing Shira their eyes opened wide as they squealed with delight, running to her open arms for big hugs. Shira greeted the mother with the traditional "Shalom," introducing her to Atara as Naomi. Shira explained she had met Naomi at synagogue shortly after the Romans had taken her husband away. He was unable to pay the tax, so he was arrested. She hadn't heard word of him since. With no income they were in very dire straights, relying on the generosity of others to help see them through.

The mention of the Roman arrest made Atara's blood boil. He could feel his face become flush, but for the sake of the children would try not to allow his anger to show.

For the next hour they visited and played with the children. Shira marveled at how gentle Atara was, how quickly the children took to him. When it was time to leave, Shira promised Naomi she would try to return tomorrow with some more food. She pressed the one coin she had left into Naomi's hand, saying their goodbyes, then descended the stairs into the laneway.

Winding their way upward toward the home of Nicodemus, Atara turned to Shira and said, "This is a good thing you are doing for the family. It's terrible what the Romans have done to her."

Shira blushed a little, then pushed the comment aside as if to say, "I wish I could do more."

As they worked their way to the Upper City they passed some familiar landscapes. Shira knew her way around this part of the city, choosing a route passing by the home of Caiaphas, the high priest, then near the corner of Herod's Fortress. They decided to turn here to elude the fortress as they could see many guards ahead.

The sun was low now with the end of the day rapidly approaching. The two of them felt such excitement from their day. So much had happened in the short time since they had left through the alley gate. Neither wanted this day to end.

When they turned the last corner into the alleyway with the wooden door, Atara was desperately searching for an excuse to see her again.

Chapter 16

Shira pulled the iron key out of the small pouch on her belt. She reached for the old wooden door, inserted the key, fumbling around to turn the old lock. With a metallic thunk the lock gave way, releasing the door as it creaked open a crack, but she stood perfectly still, not wanting to leave Atara. The two of them stood awkwardly, waiting for the other to say something, when a low voice came from inside the door.

"Cousin Jonathan, I presume?"

Nicodemus stepped out of the shade to open the door fully, then added, looking directly at Atara, "Odd, last time I saw you at the Temple today, you were dressed entirely differently."

Atara and Shira stood silently. Neither knew what to say, Nicodemus had taken them so off-guard. Atara cleared his throat and was about to babble some form of explanation, but before he had a chance, Nicodemus added, "You two had both better come into the garden." He turned around and went in.

They looked at each other. Atara could sense the fear… no, not fear, but sadness in Shira's eyes. He realized it was not from being caught, but for disappointing her father. He felt guilty.

They followed him into the middle of the courtyard where he beckoned them to sit. Not where they had both been meeting previously, which was hidden from view, but in the center of the garden where there were several marble benches overlooking the pond. Atara had thought the first time he had viewed the garden on that fateful day just last week, that it was one of the most spectacular gardens he had ever seen. The roses and bougainvillea grew up marble trellises surrounding the pond, and vines lined the garden wall, protecting this enclave from the world. It truly was a secret garden of beauty. He nervously sat down after Shira, and waited.

Nicodemus was looking at them both, examining them with eyes penetrating as only a father's possibly could, while Atara felt the sweat exuding from his pores.

Nicodemus finally spoke, but not in anger. "You two need to give me an explanation," was all he said.

Stunned by the simplicity of his statement, Atara blurted out at exactly the same time as Shira, and it sounded like two schoolchildren in front of the rabbi. Embarrassed, Atara held up his hand. "It's for me to explain, Shira. This is my fault." She knew at this point her father would expect this, so she resigned herself to silence while Atara explained.

After introducing himself Atara told the story from the beginning. Admitting he had joined the Zealots, believing in their cause, running from a foiled uprising attempt with Romans in pursuit, where he ended up inside this courtyard for protection. He left out how that happened, not wanting to reveal Shira's secret excursions, but Nicodemus picked up on that omission immediately, at which point Shira had to explain her purpose for the many trips to the Lower City.

When Atara continued he outlined his return on Sunday night and the discussions they had. He attempted to justify their decision to sneak out today because of the urgency. There wasn't any time to formally meet with him to request an outing, or to arrange a chaperone, so this just seemed like the only choice they had. Atara apologized several times to add emphasis, but it did not look like Nicodemus was accepting the excuses.

He did notice Nicodemus looked over at Shira a few times, rolling his eyes, just perceivably. It would appear he knew his daughter very well. Atara then outlined today's events, but it wasn't until Shira spoke up to recount what Jesus had said that Nicodemus' composure appeared to soften.

"Father, did you hear him today?"

"I did child," he responded in a subdued tone. "But first, let us not change the subject at hand. I can accept you apparently have been running a covert operation to help another family, but why not ask for my help and permission, as it should be? I could help. I am impressed you are willing to help this young man, Shira, even though he was thrust on you, and I am glad you have entered into discussions of the messiah. However, today's decision was a poor one for you both. I am very disheartened you would not confide in me. Both for reasons of tradition and because of my love for you."

Atara and Shira both looked down in shame as Nicodemus spoke. He looked at the two of them, reflecting on what should be said to this young couple while stroking his long, white beard. As a rabbi of yeshiva and judge of the Law, he had long ago learned to examine both sides of a situation.

'They broke with traditions, but on the other hand their motivations and intentions seem to be honorable enough. She has disobeyed my wishes as a father, but on the other hand she is a good daughter who loves her father. What to do! He, well, he is a young man running around Jerusalem with my daughter and no chaperone, and without my permission! But, he seems like a good boy, and searching for the messiah! These are exceptional days for Jerusalem. Who could fault a young man searching for answers? Oh, Lord, such a daughter you have given me! Might I be blessed with old age if I survive this!'

Finally, after what seemed like an eternity, Nicodemus spoke. "It would appear to me that on all accounts, except for one, you had the best of intentions at heart. Your lie about your Cousin Jonathan was wrong, for that you are right to be sorry. But for wanting to learn more from Jesus, I find no fault. We Jews love to learn and the truth is of utmost importance to us. I am afraid some of us have forgotten that. When I first heard Jesus speak, there was an authority and knowledge there that could only have come from God. Perhaps as a learned rabbi, certainly that of a prophet or even the messiah himself. I am still not clear on everything, but I do know he speaks the word of God, which now places him in grave danger."

That last statement startled both Atara and Shira. Forgetting their guilt both looked up at Nicodemus. "What do you mean?" exclaimed Shira. "What's going to happen?"

"I do not know exactly," said Nicodemus. "Because many in the Sanhedrin know that I and a handful of others are sympathetic to Jesus, they exclude us from their secret meetings. I have found out, though, they are planning to label him a blasphemer, which will carry the death penalty. They are plotting how they can arrest him as we speak."

"Father, how can they do this?" Shira cried. "He has done nothing wrong, only good for people!"

"I know, child. He is a good man. But claiming to be a prophet, let alone the messiah, can have grave consequences. The penalty for falsely claiming that is death."

"But how can they prove he isn't'?" she responded. "He has healed many, helped many, taught with wisdom and said prophetic things that can't yet be proven wrong!"

"You have grown beyond your years, my daughter! When did this happen before my very eyes?" Nicodemus sighed with the weight of history before him. He knew that in the days to come something of greatness was about to unfold. "You are correct, and I very much agree with you. However, Jesus' attacks on the Temple leadership have made him a lot of enemies – they plot to kill him. His claims of corruption and hardness of heart within our government are indeed very well founded. Caiaphas was livid with anger today. He is not a man to be crossed! You were there today, you heard what Jesus said."

Shira reflected on this and knew it to be true.

Atara then said, "What's going to happen?"

"I suspect over the next couple of days that will be revealed to us." Nicodemus answered. "I know word has reached Jesus of their plotting, but instead of leaving Jerusalem he runs right into the Temple Mount, making further damning accusations, calling it 'his Father's house'! He either knows what he is doing or he is mad!"

"We both heard him say these things," said Atara. "We followed him out of the Temple today up the Mount of Olives to hear more."

With this news Nicodemus leaned forward with great interest.

"Jesus spoke as if he knew what lay ahead." Atara explained to Nicodemus. He thought of the symbolism when Jesus had entered Jerusalem on Sunday with the lambs, as a lamb.

Shira interjected from time to time with words Jesus had spoken, describing himself as the Lamb of God and several of the prophetic scriptures that fit the situation. Atara admitted that Jesus's lack of interest in the Roman occupation was something he could not understand, but in all other respects he was drawn to this man from the Galilee, wanting to learn more.

There was a moment of silence. It seemed to Nicodemus it was no longer a circle of father, daughter and potential suitor, but of three pilgrims on a search for the messiah. Her mother would be very proud.

"I do not expect you two to be sneaking around behind my back," Nicodemus finally stated. "You need to apprise me of any further decisions or places you have in mind to investigate. This is a very dangerous time. The Romans are on high alert. The Sanhedrin is nervous, consumed with more anger than I have ever seen. We must be careful. I am willing to overlook your indiscretions of the past few days because they have been exceptional days. Also I am willing to let you travel together, if you are searching for the messiah. But you must promise me you will behave appropriately, not dishonoring me." He was looking directly at Atara.

They both agreed, giving their word.

"How can we find out more?" Atara asked. "Perhaps if I can find out what is being plotted, I can warn Jesus or his disciples. I met one of his men called Simon today. I think he'll listen if I bring word."

Nicodemus thought for a moment. "There is a man on the Sanhedrin that is a secret follower of Jesus. He has been included in the Temple meetings because the others are unaware of his association. He will have information for you as this unfolds. I will give you his name, but you must promise to keep it secret." Atara nodded. "His name is Joseph of Arimathea. He is a good man and friend. You can call by his house and tell him I have sent you. He will know. And now, my children, it is time to part for the evening to go our separate ways."

"How can I contact you when I need to talk with you again?" asked Atara, directed at Shira.

"You could throw a pebble to the first window on the second floor," responded Shira. "I will hear and come to open the gate."

"Oy, the things a father has to hear!" muttered Nicodemus as he walked up the path. "For me," he said as he turned back to address Atara, "you can use the front door! Although be careful not to be seen since the Romans, as do the Sanhedrin, have spies and informants everywhere."

Atara exited into the alley with the iron bolt echoing behind him on the solid wood door.

Chapter 17

TUESDAY EVENING: NISSAN 13 / APRIL 8TH

The sun had now set, bathing Jerusalem in the soft azure of twilight. Atara followed the similar path he normally took through the wealthy area of the Upper City to the edge of Mount Zion.

From here the city steeply declines downward toward the Lower City, eventually leading to the Kidron Valley outside the walls. He decided once again to cross the rooftops to avoid traffic and Roman patrols. But really, being of a young age, and of certain disposition, the opportunity to explore is always irresistible.

This time he first worked his way farther south, closer to the city wall where he discovered a stairway that led him up to the rooftops. Once there the whole Lower City lay ahead of him as it descended the mountain slope. An irregular mixture of house on house scattered over the top of the city, plunging downward toward the deep valley below, creating a beautiful mosaic of blocks backlit by the partial moonlight which was yet to fully rise. Ahead lay one rooftop after another with small stone steps and ladders leading down from one to another.

Occasionally there were no stairs to be found, forcing Atara to leap over a balcony to the next roof below. Several times the roof would come to an end high above a street or alley. The gap, too wide to leap over, would cause him to find a way down to the ground level, then another way up on the other side.

On one such detour, arriving at the street level, he quickly retreated into the stairwell. He had descended just as a small patrol of sentries making their rounds passed by. Waiting in the shadows until they were out of sight, he crossed over the street to find the next path to the rooftops. Eventually he worked his way to the valley below, coming close to the home of Barak the potter. Atara was very pleased with this new route he had discovered, wondering if it would prove useful in the future.

When he arrived at the street corner leading to the home of Barak, he paused, waiting in the shadows, searching. There was no one passing by as he scanned the laneway and surrounding homes, looking for anyone who might be watching the door to Barak's house from a window. He quickly and quietly slipped through the laneway, then down the familiar worn steps. After the traditional signal the door unbolted for him to enter.

Atara was greeted wholeheartedly by his comrades with the noise around the table quickly resuming. The scene was reminiscent of the evenings before, only not everyone was back from their day's excursions. The first question on Atara's mind was for his two brothers. Had anyone heard word? No one at the table had any information, so he decided tomorrow he would visit other Zealot groups scattered throughout the city to see if anyone had any information of their safe arrival back to the Galilee.

Benjamin and Ezra were assigned to raise capital for expenses and food from those sympathetic with their cause. They were not always successful, but this had been a good week for fundraising. With all the pilgrims arriving, and with the Passover's generosity extended to them, they had done quite well. Dinner this night was fresh fish with vegetables. After Simeon said the blessing, everyone partook. Pomegranates, dates and oranges filled the center of the table to be enjoyed by all. Barak had no family, so he was very pleased when this group of religious misfits told him they had acquired a lamb for Passover they would all share together two nights from now.

The talk of the day divided between what recent atrocities the Romans had perpetrated on the Israelites, and reports of the Nazarene on the Temple Mount. As word was shared about both, lively debates followed. There was a unified interest when Atara mentioned that Shira and he followed Jesus up the mountain after the Temple court to listen to more of what he had to say. After initial whistles and teasing about his new "friend," they settled down to listen to the accounts of what Jesus said.

When Atara finished sharing, fresh debating immediately arose among the group, but there seemed to be a general disbelief that this man could be the messiah. His lack of action against the Romans followed by his attack on their own people seemed proof of this. Atara was dismayed, as deep within he still felt there was more at play than just the story of a mad, false prophet.

With the arrival of Uri and Mordechai the debates really livened up. By the end of the evening, the talk became more of the Roman subversion than that of a messiah. So the evening went.

Atara eventually retreated to a place of rest, and shortly after putting his head down he was quickly gone from this world.

On opening his eyes Atara beheld a face. Not a face he recognized, or could ever be recognized, but the face of every man. He could see pain and suffering, blood on the brow and anguish in the eyes. In the background the sky, if it was sky, as it looked more like the heavens, was turning ominously dark. He heard a voice reaching out to him: *"I have come into this world as light, so that no one who believes in me should stay in darkness! Whoever believes in me does not believe in me only, but in the one who sent me."*[28] Suddenly a great light appeared. The face of every man pulled away into the light and vanished. Atara awoke, bolting upright, sweat pouring from his forehead and palms.

He looked around the room, but saw all the men were asleep. It was the middle of the night. He had been dreaming. 'What did it mean? It was so vivid, so real!' He remembered these were the words Jesus spoke today on the mountainside. 'Was this just a dream? Or was this a vision of something to come?' Atara felt the words penetrate deep into his soul as he played them over and over in his mind. Light, darkness, he who believes ... This dream would haunt him in the days to come.

He fell back into a deep sleep as quickly as he had awakened.

---

[28] John 12:46 & 44

Chapter 18

WEDNESDAY: NISSAN 13 / APRIL 9TH

Morning came too early for Atara. As the other men rose to prepare for prayers, Atara groaned, rolling over, hoping to squeeze just a few more precious moments of sleep in before getting up. He did eventually rise, quickly catching up with the rest of the men when they were ready to recite the morning prayers.

Atara knew it was important that the men leave the house early, right after prayers. Too much traffic coming and going from this tiny apartment in a crowded neighborhood would attract attention that might possibly be reported to the Romans. They paid for this type of information, so no one outside of the group of Zealots could be trusted. The streets were not busy at sunrise, but very soon afterward this part of the city would bustle with activity.

While the others prepared to leave, Atara was feeling the weariness from all the events and emotions of the past few days. He thought he would lie down, just for a few moments, as the others left. They exited the house as singles, or in twos, at staggered intervals. Within the hour they were gone. So was Atara. It was midday when he finally awoke.

He quickly prepared himself to leave, eager to find out what had happened to his brothers. He felt a little guilty for having slept all that time, but knew he needed it.

Once ready he peered out the door into the alleyway. Because of the late hour, the laneway was now packed with passersby and merchants moving their wares. Atara wondered how he could slip out unnoticed with such traffic.

Within a few moments a donkey pulling a heavily loaded cartload up the alley lost some of its cargo. All eyes briefly went in that direction. Atara took the opportunity to stealthily bound up the few steps, disappearing anonymously into the crowd.

The priority for today was to find word of his brothers. It worried him that they might not have made it out of the city. He only had the one vague report telling him they were on their way to the Galilee. His first stop would be at a Zealot safe house in the north end of Jerusalem. It took him quite a while to work his way out of the valley, mostly taking the smaller alleys and lanes to avoid any inspection or confrontation.

Several times he managed to get turned around so badly that he found himself back where he had been. It was a labyrinth. The city had evolved around the three mountain peaks that constitute Jerusalem. At one point he found himself in the middle of a busy market section where he had never been before. With Passover arriving tomorrow the market was absolutely jammed with shoppers purchasing their spices, breads and fresh vegetables. He slowly pushed through the static crowds, but after one block decided this was much too slow. The maze of side alleys might prove to be a faster route.

Thinking he had finally arrived close to the safe house, he obtained his bearings by looking toward the Antonia Fortress that towered above all else. The fortress attached to the northern side of the Temple Mount housing the garrisons of Roman troops that controlled the city. He would avoid getting too close, but could use it as a navigation guide. From that point it would just take him a few minutes to arrive at the safe house. Nearer his destination he slowed his pace, sensing danger.

Atara stayed in the deep shadow of a small lane for a moment, checking the surroundings. He then carefully worked his way into a position near a crossroad where the entrance to the safe house could be viewed.

Roman guards were in front of the building.

He quickly pulled back into the shadows, the vision etched into his mind. Two guards at the entrance to the apartment, two walking the laneway out in front. 'The Romans had discovered this lair, but what was the fate of the Zealots? Had the Romans arrested them all? Was this because of a spy among them?' Atara's mind reeled, but one thing was for sure. He needed to remove himself from this place, putting distance between himself and the soldiers before they spotted him.

In a panic Atara backed into the alley he had come from, then rounded the corner to the next laneway, pausing to think. Once again he felt like prey, with the Roman noose becoming rapidly tighter.

The anguish of being hunted by those he hated so much permeated him, drenching him in sweat. He had to think clearly. He knew of another safe house that was not too far. Closer to the west wall, it was still in the general area of the north section, or what is known as the Mishneh Quarter. It only took him a few minutes to arrive near this safe house, and again, he decided to be very cautious with his approach.

Atara took a position inside a local bakery where he could see the entrance clearly. He could not see any soldiers in the vicinity. After waiting a while, he decided to walk by for a closer look. As he passed by he would glance sideways in each direction to see if the apartment was under surveillance. After waiting on the other side, then a second pass-by, he decided it appeared to be safe enough to approach the entrance cautiously.

The coded knock was given, but no response. The door remained shut and from within there was no sound. He nervously stood for a minute, then two. Atara knew he was very exposed standing here. People pushed and jostled their way around him in the lane, unaware of his turmoil.

Sensing he was being watched, he cast his eyes upward to a window above, spying a shadowy figure behind a curtain. The curtain fluttered slightly as the figure withdrew. Soon Atara heard the bolt slide open. The door opened a crack and the person within, after recognizing him, allowed him in.

Inside about 20 Zealots all sat quietly. Their fear of Roman invaders faded when they realized it was Atara.

"Thank God," one of them said.

Atara took a deep breath as well because he too had feared he might be walking into a trap. "I've just come from the other house. It has been taken by Roman soldiers!" Looking around the room he quickly realized half those present were from the raided house.

"We know," came the response as one of the men stepped forward to embrace him. It was Simeon. "Only a handful of men were in the apartment when the Romans raided. Their guard," he said, heartily slapping one man on the back, "Avi's grandmother, saw them coming down the lane from her window! They all managed to escape out the back and through the rooftops!"

"I'm glad no one was captured or hurt," responded Atara. "Any word on my brothers?"

A fellow sitting at the table spoke up. "I have heard from a good friend that they gave refuge to your brothers outside the city when they first left. Just yesterday word returned to us they are making their way back to the Galilee. Their faces had become too recognizable here in the city, making it risky for them to stay here any longer."

Good news for Atara, such a great sense of relief. Although he would miss their presence here, he knew it would be safer for them in the north.

Talk resumed, and of course the topic was of the Roman raid. The men realized they had lost a safe house and that the owner of the house would not be able to return. The Romans would now seal off the house, placing it under the authority of Rome. Details as to where the others would stay now, or how they would find a new safe house to replace the old, were part of the discussions. But the main topic was, "How did they know?" Once again, carelessness on their part, a spy on the street who tipped the Romans off, or someone on the inside … one of them?

Atara stayed for a while, listening to the discussions. Without a clear leader in the group, the heated talk ranged from animated debate to personal accusations shouted across the table.

Soon he felt he needed to move on. As he was preparing to leave, he interrupted the deliberations to ask if anyone could tell him where the house of Joseph of Arimathea was located.

"Joseph of Arimathea? The rich man?" Joseph of Arimathea was a very successful grain merchant, quite possibly the richest man in Jerusalem and a member of the Sanhedrin. "Why would you want to see him?"

Atara sensed the suspicions of the group as all eyes focused on him. He decided being truthful would be the best way to handle this, regardless of the consequences.

"I would like to have an audience with him regarding this Jesus of Nazareth," he stated calmly.

The reaction was as he expected. Most of the men scoffed at this idea. "What would he know about the Nazarene?" "Why are you bothering with that man?" "He is not helping our cause!"

Atara assured them he was merely searching for information about Jesus and would not mention his ties to the Zealots without clearing that with them first. In the end they gave him the location of Joseph's residence and the directions to get there. Atara thanked them all for the help and wishing them well, was on his way.

Chapter 19

As Atara expected Joseph of Arimathea lived in the Upper City, not too far from the home of Nicodemus. Working his way through the streets once again, Atara headed south, this time toward the Upper City quarter.

The sun was now getting low, so he hastened his pace and attempted to stay on the course he had been provided. While walking he reflected on the words Jesus had spoken only yesterday. So much had taken place in the past few hours that it seemed like ages ago. At both safe houses he asked around to see if anybody knew where Jesus would be today, but no one did. Benjamin offered the only information. He had discovered that Jesus and his disciples were on the other side of the Mount of Olives in Bethany, but added other people were claiming he was staying on the slopes of the Mount of Olives in an olive grove.

Atara realized he had no idea what it was he was going to say or ask Joseph of Arimathea when he arrived, or even if the man would be there. Questions started to pour through his mind as he continued walking, but only two really stood out in his mind: 'Who is this Jesus of Nazareth? And what knowledge do you have from inside the Sanhedrin?'

He snapped out of his thoughts when he recognized he was just one block from Shira's home. Atara stood for a moment and wondered what she would be doing now. 'Would she be sitting in the courtyard garden by the pond? What would she be wearing or thinking right about now?' Atara felt a powerful pull in that direction. He would much rather travel the short distance up the familiar, narrow alley to knock on her door than continue to see an important man he had never met. But he had to find out what the council was plotting, so he turned toward the home of Joseph of Arimathea and proceeded on his way, leaving the alleyway behind.

Just three small cross alleys later, Atara stood before what he thought might well be the largest home in Jerusalem, outside the palaces. A great stone wall surrounded the house, which was mysteriously invisible from the street, until someone arrived directly in front of an ornate steel gate protecting the entrance.

Inside that gate the beautiful front garden and home came into full view. The garden had marble flooring which shimmered under the late sun, bathing the courtyard in its warmth. Roses, bougainvillea, geraniums and orange trees lined the walls of the court, providing swaths of color on all sides. But it was the house that stood apart. It was large, three stories tall, with imposing marble columns supporting the stone canopy high above the carved wooden entrance doors. The home was constructed of local quarried stone that glowed a radiant golden in the evening sun. It was this Jerusalem stone which provided Jerusalem the reputation of a city of gold when the sun began to set, or arise, from behind the surrounding mountains.

Atara stood transfixed. Who was he to enter such a place unannounced? For a moment he almost turned on his heel to run back to Shira's garden, but he could not. He had to talk with Joseph. He had to know.

He approached the gate. Just inside sat the gatekeeper in a small stone kiosk. Atara took a breath, announcing in his most official-sounding voice, "I am Atara BenJosiah and I would like to have an audience with Joseph of Arimathea."

The older man looked him over suspiciously. 'What business would a young, and obviously poor, pup like this have with a great man like my master?' However, he had been instructed earlier to say, "The rabbi is expecting you today, young sir. Please proceed to the front door and there the servant will look after you."

This elegant response surprised Atara. He wasn't sure how to respond, other than simply thanking the guard and entering when beckoned. From inside the walls the courtyard was even more spectacular, filled with color and life everywhere he looked. He ascended the wide terraced stairs to the stately front door to knock. A male servant opened the door and greeted him. He was a very tall man with a dark complexion, dark hair and even darker deep-set eyes. An imposing man that could easily strike fear into any passerby on a nightly walk. But beneath the exterior, a warm, comforting smile put Atara at ease as the servant presented himself pleasantly as Samuel.

Atara replied by introducing himself, then was invited inside and guided to a small sitting room to the left. The center hallway entrance he passed through was grand with a polished marble floor of pale green and a magnificent stairway curving its way to a second-story balcony. Once inside the room to the left, Atara was instructed to take a seat on the large, vivid red cushions lining the walls on the floor. There were beautiful, immense tapestries of scenes around Jerusalem draping the walls. In the corners pedestals displaying what appeared to Atara to be valuable pottery stood precariously, demonstrating the absence of any young children.

Atara had never seen anything like this, certainly not in Sidon. His father's estate was large, but nothing on this scale. He was somewhat awestruck with the grandeur.

As he sat down Samuel addressed him. "The master has been at the Temple in meetings today and will be home shortly. I have been instructed to make you comfortable. Is there anything I can provide for you? A drink perhaps?"

Not wanting to be an imposition, Atara's first inclination was to refuse the offer, though on reflection he realized he had nothing to drink since leaving the safe house at noontime. He nodded and Samuel slid away to fetch some refreshments. Atara leaned back into the comfort of the scarlet cushions, the feeling of tiredness finally coming on him. When the servant returned with a tray of cool water and dates, Atara jolted awake. He was resolved not to fall asleep while waiting for his meeting.

The time passed, the sun had now set. Atara had paced the room numerous times, reclined now and then, and spent the rest of the time looking out the window into the garden. Waiting is not a game young men play well, so he found himself pacing the floor in front of the window once again. He had just sat down when at last he heard footsteps and voices coming from the main hall. He bolted to his feet.

Within seconds a man entered the room introducing himself warmly as Joseph. "I have been expecting a visit from you, my young friend. Nicodemus has spoken highly of you."

This took Atara somewhat aback as he could not imagine Nicodemus was anything but suspicious of him, especially regarding Shira.

Joseph was approaching his senior years, not too tall and in generally good shape, although a little plump from his brilliant success. His long beard was more gray than dark, making his rotund face appear very friendly. The clothing was of prime quality, clearly marking him a man who had made a fortune for himself in trade. He would undoubtedly prove to be astute in their conversations.

Atara bowed his head in respect saying, "It is a pleasure to meet you. My name is Atara BenJosiah. I have many questions about the man Jesus and was hoping you might be willing to answer some of these."

"Please, my friend, will you dine with me? We can discuss the situation over a good meal. I apologize for making you wait, but I just returned from a closed council meeting that was very stressful."

The tight lines in Joseph's face revealed the deep concern he was feeling. He immediately beckoned Atara to follow him across the hall into a room used for dining. It seemed to Atara much too large for just two people. The table was low to the ground with the same scarlet cushions in the sitting room surrounding the table. It was the tradition in wealthy homes to dine relaxing in a reclined position while being served, so Atara was instructed to sit. Before he could say anything, the food was already being served by Samuel with another attendant they called Chaim. They both whisked in and out of the room about their business. When Atara attempted to begin a discussion Joseph put his finger to his lips, indicating silence was required for the moment.

Once they were dining alone, Joseph asked Atara, "What is your interest in this Jesus?"

Atara wasn't sure how to answer such a forward question. What was his interest? It had only been three days since he had seen Jesus for the first time and only five days since meeting Shira. Atara was a Zealot, not sure how this man from the Galilee fit in as a possible messiah to the Jews. It conflicted him, torn between his feelings and his ideals. The words Jesus had spoken, the power of the man through his compassion for others, and his dynamic actions of the past few days had left a strong impact on him. One he could not explain.

Answering Joseph honestly he replied, "I'm not sure, sir. I'm a Zealot and I believe God has chosen us Jews to protect His word, the Torah, to worship the one true God. As a Zealot, I believe this should be done by force, if necessary. At this time in our history of great oppression and Roman interference, it would seem necessary. We've been looking for the messiah for ages now and I believe the climax is at hand. I've thought Jesus could be the messiah we've been searching for."

"And now what do you believe?"

"Well, again, I'm not sure. If I follow my intellect, I would have to say he doesn't appear to be the kingly messiah we have been looking for. Yet, when I hear his words, something stirs inside me I don't understand. He heals, casts out demons, has compassion, yet lives modestly. On the other side he criticizes our way of faith and the very way we have traditionally lived. He storms the Temple, not the Romans, like a man of war, then speaks about his fate as a gentle Lamb of God? How can someone possibly understand?"

Joseph sat back for a moment from his food, methodically pushing his plate away.

He scrutinized Atara intensely, rubbing his graying beard with contemplation. Finally he looked directly at Atara. "Atara, I will tell you what I know. I first met this man from the Galilee two years ago when he was in Jerusalem. Nicodemus had spoken with me after his first encounter with Jesus. I decided then to search the man out to speak with him myself. The words he spoke to me stirred my soul, very similar to what you felt, the likes of which I never experienced before.

"We are a people governed by our Laws and Temple traditions. I have felt for a long time something has gone badly wrong. Every year the corruption of the Temple seems to become worse with the internal politics more harsh. We on the Sanhedrin do nothing as long as we profit. Many Pharisees have left to become members of the Essenes, renouncing the current practises of the Temple priests. The Romans mock us, brutalize our people, defile the one true God while we are powerless to do anything. What Jesus said so very simply to me was we have lost our love for God, becoming hardened, indifferent to our people – that we need to have the Law written on our hearts!

"This resonated with me deeply, so I began to think a great deal about it after we met. Jesus has said the way to God is through love, and God so loves us that He would send His Son to us for salvation! But I am afraid we lost our way. You look to the solution as a Zealot to remove the Romans from the land, but is it not possible the Romans are here because we turned from the love of God Himself? We have replaced the Almighty with our Laws and traditions? The true solution is to repent, turn to God."

Joseph looked at Atara to see if he was following, then continued. "I have followed his movements and teachings with great interest after that first meeting through my servants' reports. However impressed I was, there was an obstacle I knew would have to be overcome before I could even begin to believe this man was the true messiah. He must accurately fulfill the prophesies of the messiah! In particular, God brought me to Daniel 9 in the Torah, a long-accepted messianic prophecy that has been contentiously debated these past few years. Are you familiar with it?"

"Yes, we were taught Daniel 9 in yeshiva. Much of the hope for the messiah to come in this troublesome time is based on Daniel 9. Most rabbis agree Daniel 9 is a prophecy that sets out a specific time the messiah will come to the Jewish nation.

"When the angel Gabriel spoke to Daniel, he used a cryptic way of presenting the timeframe for the coming of the messiah that has caused much debate these past few decades among the learned. We know the decree first given by King Cyrus of Persia after he took Babylon would allow the Jews to return home after their exile. This was in the Hebrew year of 3223, almost 500 years ago.

"When the mathematical calculations are worked out from that decree, most rabbis have concluded the messiah should arrive at some time during this generation! For some calculations the time has already passed, but for the majority of theories the time is soon to come for the messiah. Gabriel prophesied it would be seven sevens appointed to Jerusalem. We take this to be years. Sevens in plural was another way of saying 70 in the Torah, so seven times 70 is 490 years. He also said the anointed one, the messiah, would come and be put to death after 69 weeks of sevens (actually seven sevens and 62 sevens), which is 483 years.

"What a perfect time it would be for the messiah! We are under such deep oppression from the Romans with their pagan gods and cruelty! We know the time is close at hand, but many dates have been proposed, so there is much confusion around this."

"Well spoken, young man! Now, please listen carefully to what I've discovered. I needed to find an answer to this mystery to confirm what my heart was telling me, so I delved into research of the scriptures. You are correct. The angel Gabriel was prophesying that the messiah would be cut off, or put to death, 483 years after the decree. But which decree?

"The decree by Cyrus in 3223 was the first, but not the final decree. After Cyrus the following kings of Persia changed their minds over a period of a number of years several times, but according to the Torah in Ezra 7, the final and most complete decree came in the year 3316 on the first day of Nissan from the king of Persia Artaxerxes, commanding the Israelites to return home and rebuild Jerusalem. I believe this to be the starting point for the prophesy.

"The next and largest obstacle is the years. Between the Hebrew, Gregorian and Julian calendars currently in use, with their varied methods of calculating years, it all gets very complicated. But what if we don't use years and instead we use days? A biblical year is different from the others. It does not account for discrepancies like leap years, deficient years, or jubilees that make up the balance of days from season to season. A biblical year is 360 days. We also consider it a prophetic year. If we use the biblical year for the time span of the 483 years, it will multiply to 173,880 days. Quite a number!

"However, this is where the real difficulty comes. Our own Hebrew calendar has many yearly corrections to make it work, so to calculate the days from Nissan 1, 3316, one has to painstakingly work through each year to do a running calculation of the days. I began this arduous task and spent a great deal of time on this over the past year. It was only two weeks ago when I had finished my sums, an extraordinary new date appeared before me!"

"What was it?" Atara was leaning forward with anticipation.

"Nissan 10, 3792."[29]

"That's last Shabbat! The day Jesus entered Jerusalem! How is it possible?" exclaimed Atara. He was astounded at this new revelation.

"It is possible with God," Joseph replied calmly. "For two weeks I did not know exactly what this would mean. Last Sunday, Nissan 10, I awoke with such anticipation for the day ahead, wondering what would happen. If I was correct, then it would be revealed on that day, as the angel Gabriel had prophesied so many years ago, that the messiah would come. I proceeded to the Temple for prayers where I stayed for most of the day, praying God would open my eyes to the truth. Finally, after much prayer, I heard the noise of crowds shouting hosannahs outside. I went running to the balcony to see what was happening. The minute I saw Jesus arriving on this 10th day of Nissan, on a donkey, as King David had done for his own coronation centuries before, I knew the truth."

"What are you saying?" Atara needed to hear the answer.

"I now believe, in fact I know, that this Jesus, born in Bethlehem, descendant of David, is the messiah!"

There was a pause, both men contemplating what had just been spoken. The impact of this revelation hit Atara as profoundly as it had Joseph only a few days earlier.

Eventually Joseph broke the silence, speaking in a very hushed tone. "Atara, you are the only person I have shared my newfound belief with. I might be putting my life on the line by doing so, but I believe you are sincere. God has shown me you have an important role to play in the days to come."

Atara didn't know what to say. 'So much trust from a total stranger, a man with influence with so much to lose? What purpose would God possibly have with me? A Zealot, a man on the run, full of hatred and suspicion!'

"There is more to consider." Joseph looked squarely at him while proceeding with great conviction. "The prophecy in Daniel 9 from Gabriel clearly states after the 69 sevens, or 483 years, the anointed one, the messiah, will be cut off, or interpreted as put to death. I am afraid of what is about to happen. I do not fully understand God's intention here now that this has been revealed, but it does seem very clear that the path ahead will be a very dark one. I fear it might even be at our own hands.

"How could we? Yet we've ignored and killed almost every messenger of God since the beginning of time. Are our hearts so hardened now that we could also put to death our own messiah?"

[29] The Coming Prince by Sir Robert Anderson (Trumpet Press, 1957, 2014).

Rather shocked by Joseph's willingness to reveal himself, Atara questioned, "If you believe him to be the messiah, then why the secrecy? Is that what he would want?"

"No, it is not," Joseph responded quietly with an air of humility. "All of this time I have kept my thoughts of him in secret because I was afraid. Afraid of what others would say, afraid of losing my possessions, afraid of losing my position in society. God has made it quite clear to me now I must be willing to give back all He has given me to find the Kingdom of Heaven. It is undoubtedly a mighty price for someone like me to pay, but I am beginning to understand the words of Jesus. For now, as it turns out, being with council privileges I can have some say on what is to be done. I feel I must remain there for now in secret for that purpose. I am afraid there are some troublesome days ahead, my friend."

"What have you heard?"

"I believe Nicodemus has told you the Sanhedrin council has rejected Jesus' words and admonitions. They are incensed by his teaching and his brazenness! The majority see Jesus' attacks on them as an offense. They want him gone, labeled a blasphemer.

"They are much too proud, usurping their authority while still tied to the Roman command. They will do anything to protect themselves, much as I painfully admit I have done in the past. The council and priests can't see through their own sins to truly examine what Jesus is saying, and repent of their actions."

Joseph paused for a moment, reflecting on the situation and what he was about to reveal to Atara. "They are calling for the death penalty. Nicodemus has been shut out of the council meetings now because they know he is sympathetic toward Jesus. But I am still able to participate in the meetings."

"On what grounds? What crime has he committed they could demand the death penalty for?"

"Today," Joseph continued, "it was revealed just two hours ago at the meeting I have come from that they wish to have Jesus tried for blasphemy before the Passover is over. Caiaphas is consumed with his anger toward Jesus and will not let it lie. One of Jesus' disciples, a man named Judas, has been in contact with the Temple, agreeing to betray Jesus by leading them to him. They've given this Judas 30 pieces of silver to do so." Here Joseph paused, lowering his eyes, his face reflecting a great deal of heaviness from the weight of such knowledge.

Atara was alarmed. "Why would one of his disciples betray him? Have they not spent the past three years with him, witnessing the miracles and learning from him? How could someone turn on his own rabbi and friend!"

"I was dismayed when I first heard the council was to meet with this disciple. At first I thought he had come only for the money. A betrayer for pay. However, when I observed his tortured face on receiving the payment, I am not sure that was his motive. It could be he has fallen into some disagreement with the other disciples. Or possibly he no longer believes what Jesus is saying or that he is even the messiah. Perhaps over the past few days with Jesus' attacks on the Temple and the religious leaders, he has come to believe he needs to protect our customs, and is under the delusion he is the one chosen to do this.

"Jesus did prophesy that the Temple would be destroyed and every stone thrown down within this generation. Perhaps he feels he can stop this from happening and that it is his duty. But I sensed fear in this Judas. I think he sees the conflict coming to a crisis that will end in much suffering for Jesus and the disciples, and he is afraid of what lies ahead. It is possible the only way he sees escape for himself is to align himself with the larger force by betraying his leader. We will never know what his motivation is. It could be one or all of these reasons combined. Of one thing I am certain. He will very much regret his decision!"

"Wait!" The thoughts were racing through Atara's mind at lightning speed. "Why would they do that? Surely they know the messianic scriptures? Zechariah 11:12: 'So they paid me 30 pieces of silver.' Why would they choose an amount of blood money that would fulfill the prophesies?"

"They know," said Joseph. "In their arrogance they chose that specific amount as an insult to Jesus. Since they believe he is an imposter, a false prophet, I suppose they are cynically mocking him. The irony is that if Jesus is the messiah, which I now believe to be true, then the prophesy is being fulfilled by their very own deeds!

"There are other prophesies," Joseph continued. "In Psalm 41:9 and 55:12–14 it is clear the messiah will be betrayed by a friend."

"Can't they see that?"

"I'm afraid they are blinded by their pride, their anger. It is a very difficult political balance with the Romans. But there is still much more hidden here – with a deeper meaning." Joseph continued. "Are you familiar with Numbers 3:44–48?"

"The Redemption of the Son?"

"Yes, the *Pidyon ha Ben* in Hebrew. As you are aware, all firstborn sons of Israel belong to the Temple ministry. Because the population birth far exceeds that which is necessary for the Temple, it has become the custom for fathers to bring their firstborn sons to the Temple and pay a redemption fee. They are to redeem, or buy back, their sons from the Temple with silver, and the silver goes into the Temple treasury. When the priests gave this Judas his 30 pieces of silver from the treasury, for the first time in our history the Temple will buy back one that was redeemed, purchasing his life! If Jesus is the messiah, they will in effect have now purchased the firstborn Son of God! Even more than that, when a father pays this fee, he is procuring the release of his son from Temple ministry. Therefore, it stands to reason when the Temple priests pay for Jesus, they will be purchasing him back into the sacred Temple ministry! The Son of God will assume His priestly role!"

"How could this be happening? How could all these things be falling into place like this?"

"They simply are," reflected Joseph. "No human hand could orchestrate this. I believe in the days to come you will see how this all fits together. It is only by the Hand of God these things can come about. Jesus has talked much about sacrifice and it seems clear to me that the Son of God must fulfill not only the prophecies of the messiah, but also the Temple ordinances for sacrifice as he assumes the priesthood."

"I will warn him," replied Atara. "I will find them and warn them not to return."

"I have already sent word to them, but I believe Jesus has no intention of heeding it. He is here to fulfill his Father's will. And it has begun."

"But there must be something we can do!"

"Pray. Pray for God's will to be carried forth. Pray our people will believe and repent. I don't know what the next few days hold, but it is no coincidence it is happening this Passover. The time has been ordained since the beginning of time."

"What should I do?"

"Follow him. Learn what you can with an open heart. Examine the scriptures, be certain that what you learn is reflected in them. There can be no contradiction, Atara. As for me," said Joseph, "I will do the same. I will also try to find out as much as I can within the Sanhedrin and Temple, and do my best to be a voice for the messiah. Yet, I believe my days in the council are numbered as I will have to make my loyalties known very soon. I feel there is much danger ahead."

With that said Joseph indicated it was time for him to retire. They had finished a magnificent meal Atara had hardly even tasted, he had been listening so intensely to Joseph. Atara was escorted to the door, Joseph telling him to return anytime he had questions and the staff would allow him in safely.

On the front steps the older man paused to place his hand on Atara's head, pronouncing a blessing over him. Atara headed out into the dark street once again.

Chapter 20

WEDNESDAY AFTER SUNSET: NISSAN 14 / APRIL 9TH

Atara headed silently down the wide street away from Joseph's home. While walking, he marveled at the majestic oil lamps that lit his way in this affluent neighborhood. He realized it was now the beginning of Nissan 14, the day according to the Book of Exodus that the lambs would be slaughtered at twilight in preparation for the Passover meal.

His thoughts were of Shira and her lamb, wondering what she might be doing right now. He was very near to the home of Nicodemus and when he was passing by the small alley leading to the back gate, he turned.

Standing outside the familiar wooden door, he felt torn. 'Should I knock to see if Shira is in the garden? No, I should go to the front door and speak to Nicodemus first. What if I'm refused? I was just there last night, and it wasn't exactly a stellar introduction to her father.'

Atara paced back and forth in turmoil. He wanted to tell Shira everything that had happened in his day, but truth be told, it was simply that he wanted to see her once again. To sit, spend time talking with her, to listen to her comforting words. He raised his hand against the door handle at one point, poised for action, then retreated. 'Tomorrow. That would be best.' He turned to continue down the alley.

Atara felt very much alone. He chose a path similar to the one he had traveled the previous night over the rooftops. At one point he sat for a while in a secluded spot, the words of Joseph running through his mind. So many questions. 'Why did this stranger confided in me, putting his career and life on the line? What would happen if Jesus is betrayed? Would he use this occasion to gain political leverage and unite the Jewish nation? Would an army rise up to defend him, taking on the Romans?' His thoughts didn't make sense or fit the messages he had heard Jesus speak.

The words sacrifice and lamb kept running through his mind, but he couldn't understand how it all fit together. He could feel the tension within as he wrestled with these questions. But above all he was questioning his purpose at this critical time. For the first time in his life, he prayed, really prayed. Not the prayers recited three times every day, but he truly spoke to God. When he did a peace came over him as he sat up on the roof under the heavens. Somehow he knew God would show him the way.

After a while, Atara decided he needed to move on, so he continued his way back to the home of Barak the potter in the Lower City. He worked his way by dropping down on the rooftops until a block later it was necessary to descend to the street level to cross. It was a wide street and after carefully checking he began to walk out into the open.

Without warning, two Roman sentries rounded the intersection one block further away. When they spotted Atara crossing the middle of the street, they yelled, "Halt!" Atara assumed they were going to make a random check of a young man out alone, but if they had his name as a wanted man when they checked his identification, he would be arrested. Arrest meant sentenced to prison, the ships' galleys (a sure death sentence) or crucifixion. Atara thought back to the blood on his dagger. He had no idea what he had done. 'Did I kill that soldier or just mildly wound him? Am I a murderer?

With limited time to think, Atara decided rather than bolt and give way to immediate pursuit, he should keep his calm and continue to walk the few steps to the other side of the road into a narrow alley, acting as if he had not heard them. Then run for his life.

When he did not stop, the soldiers shouted louder, but Atara was now already entering the alley. Immediately he bolted at full speed when completely out of sight. Sensing this, the Romans began to chase, but it had given Atara the extra head start he required. As he ran, without missing a beat, he leaned over and pulled off one sandal when his foot was raised up, followed by the other. His footsteps were now silent. He passed one small lane to his side, but continued. He anticipated the soldiers would have to waste time checking this laneway first, giving him more time to get away.

Coming to the second laneway, he made his move and swung right, disappearing just before the soldiers turned off the main street. He didn't get far up the laneway, however, before he discovered it was a dead end. Panic set in. He was trapped with high walls on each side. A few doors beckoned him. 'Should I break the silence and knock on one? Would the occupants let me in? That would surely alert the Romans who would respond immediately, searching each house, being merciless to anyone found harboring a criminal. No. That wouldn't be right.'

Then he noticed it. A narrow wooden gate right in the corner of the dead end. Quickly he moved toward the gate, then spotted a set of stairs leading upward. He gently opened it, making certain it made no noise, closed it behind him, then silently glided up the stairs. The route took him upward through a couple of courtyards, up another flight of stairs leading to the rooftop. Scanning around, he could see a drop ahead to the adjacent roof of no more than 6 feet, so he hurtled toward it, dropping out of sight.

Leaning against the wall, panting for breath, Atara realized that if he ran any farther, his motions could be spotted by other Roman sentries on the rooftops if he was out in the open, so he clung tight to the wall. He prayed he had eluded his pursuers. When the soldiers entered the second laneway and saw it as a dead end, they quickly moved on, foiled in their pursuit.

Atara waited a while before continuing. When he felt it might be safe he crossed the rooftops, descending slowly, keeping to the shadows so not to attract any attention. It didn't take long to reach the home of Barak. When Atara arrived he approached with extreme caution for fear the Romans had discovered this safe house as well.

No one was passing by the apartment due to the curfew and all looked normal as he scanned the nearby windows, so he proceeded down to the door. He listened with his ear to the door for a moment. Hearing the lowered voices of his comrades, he knocked and as the door opened, he slipped into safety.

The atmosphere in the chamber was different from anytime before. There were three new men sitting around who Atara identified from the safe house that had been raided. 'Was one of these men the traitor? Or was it one of them?' After quick greetings he sat at the table where the discussions returned to where they were before he had arrived.

In intense, but hushed voices, the group was heatedly debating the day's events. Some believed there were spies within, as all eyes were roaming throughout the room in search of the guilty. Others argued they were being careless, and Roman spies, Jewish traitors in the neighborhoods were to blame. "We must be more vigilant!" they demanded.

The debates continued for some time, but with no resolve they eventually shifted to the news from the Antonia Fortress.

Word from inside was that it was possible Jesus Barabbas could be the prisoner the Romans might release on Passover. This was a Roman tradition. They demonstrated goodwill every year to the people by selecting one prisoner for clemency. The people would gather in the governor's court to discover who would be released. Sometimes the Romans offered a choice, so supporters of various prisoners would be sure to be there. The Zealots were organizing themselves to be there early with as many as they could muster, to make sure the support for Barabbas was there. It was imperative to them he be released.

Planning went on for hours, but to Atara's disappointment there was no talk of Jesus. It seemed on this day Jesus was not on the minds of these men. At one point he felt the urge to blurt out the news he had received from Joseph about the betrayal, but at once realized he would be breaking confidence with Joseph. This should not be spoken of. After a while, when the talk was waning, Atara found his place against the wall and fell asleep.

Before him Atara saw a lamb. A perfect lamb with no blemishes, pure white. The lamb was standing in front of the blood-smeared Temple altar. Behind this altar was the massive curtain that covers the Holy of Holies, the dwelling place of God's presence. The thick curtain which was of finely woven threads colored scarlet, blue and purple towered over 40 feet high. Woven into the veil were two large golden cherubim with flaming swords. They guarded the Holy of Holies so that no man should pass. With one single leap the lamb went up on the altar and lay down. Many hands appeared and killed it. They were the hands of all men. The hands of priests, Roman officials, soldiers, common people, the hands of everyone. Atara cried, "No!" and all disappeared. He turned away. Then in front of him was the lamb curled up with a mighty lion who said to him, *"Blessed are the pure in heart, for they will see God. Blessed are those who are persecuted because of righteousness, for theirs is the Kingdom of heaven."* Then the lion looked right at Atara and saying, *"It is finished,"* vanished.

Atara awoke once again in a cold sweat. He never had dreams before and was confused. He knew he was being shown something, but couldn't make sense of it. He lay awake for a while amid the cacophony of snoring, trying to find an explanation – some meaning to the dream. But he soon fell back to sleep, overcome by exhaustion.

Chapter 21

THURSDAY MORNING: NISSAN 14 / APRIL 10TH

This was a special day. At the end of this 14th day of Nissan, before sunset, the Passover lamb would be slaughtered in preparation for their Passover supper.

The men woke before sunrise and were eagerly getting ready for prayers and for the day ahead. Each man was assigned a job to attend to. Some were to do the market, some the food preparation (but not Avi, he was a terrible cook), others the roasting of the lamb. Only unleavened bread could be eaten for the next seven days, so a team was appointed to clean every speck of leavened bread that had to be removed from the house. Uri and Mordechai were chosen to co-ordinate the other Zealots throughout Jerusalem to be at Pilot's court on Passover morning. This was for public support in case Barabbas was to be selected for release. Atara was given the task of acquiring the unleavened bread, for which he was happy, as it would free him of the confines of the tiny apartment.

When it was time for prayers, the men donned their tallits and entered into the Sh'ma. *"Hear, O Israel: The Lord our God, the Lord is one. Love the Lord your God with all your heart and with all your soul and with all your strength."* After reciting this, the words of Jesus came to Atara as he added to himself, *'Love your neighbor as yourself.'*

Thoughts of last night came to Atara's mind as he prayed, "Father, help me to understand, help me be righteous in the days to come. Abba, I wish to serve you, show me the path I must follow." The dream flashed through his mind: *"Blessed are the pure in heart, for they will see God."* 'Who can be pure in heart? Who can look on God? We have the Law of Moses to guide us, the Temple for sacrifices when we fail to atone for our sins, but the curtain separates us. If God were to look on us, we would be destroyed because of our sins, for who can stand in the glory of God! There is a veil between us. How can I become pure enough of heart to look on the perfect and righteous face of God? Father in heaven, help me understand.'

With prayers over the men eventually went on their way to fulfill their duty for the day. It was easy to perceive the excitement of the coming Passover in each man, this extraordinary day of redemption for the Jewish nation. However, there was an undertone of tension in these times. Each man had to watch with diligence, being very cautious as the Roman soldiers were constantly on the hunt for Zealots. With the raid yesterday, no one knew what information the Romans had.

Atara waited to talk with Simeon. When the opportunity arose, he asked if he might take a little extra money from the clay pot, not just for the unleavened bread, but also for Naomi and her children. Simeon nodded, Atara scooped up the required coins and with the excitement of the day ahead was out the door.

Without his usual caution he bound up the stairs, stopping dead in his tracks at the top. The laneway was already packed with locals and pilgrims pushing from each direction to pass through. He had to wait a moment to enter the surge of people. Once he had, he was carried away like a bottle in an ocean current.

This was the busiest day of the year in Jerusalem. All the 600,000 residents and perhaps close to 2 million pilgrims would all be making preparations today for their Passover feast. Shopping to be done, houses to be cleaned, families to move around to their Passover locations, then before sunset of this day, Nissan 14, the lambs would all be slain at the Temple. Added to this mass of people were the numerous additional cohorts of Romans soldiers brought in to control the Passover crowds.

At the end of the lane people slowly merged onto the broader street that led northward up through the Lower City to the market area. Once onto the main street, the sea of bodies ground to such a slow pace that Atara had to just shuffle his feet to move along. After about half an hour, Atara had made very limited progress and was becoming impatient. Pushing was pointless. From time to time a scuffle would break out between men who'd had enough. He knew all the streets ahead would be crowded like this, so he thought if he was able to find a way up to the rooftops that would be faster. It would not be as easy as coming down from the Upper City, as there would be many places where he would have to find a way up from one roof to the next if there were no stairs or ladders.

Atara saw an entrance ahead with a stairway leading upward and decided to try it. The narrow stairs were worn and very old, leading past three or four tiny apartments on the way up.

When he reached the top into the sunshine, the scene differed completely from what he had seen any other time he had been walking the rooftops. It was busy. Laundry hanging above every home, women working, children running about in play, people walking and many soldiers standing above the streets with watchful eyes. It seemed that with the streets being so impassable, the other half of Jerusalem had headed for the rooftops.

Atara began his journey northward, finding he just needed to follow others who knew the way. Rooftop to rooftop, stairs, ladders, even with vision blocked, pushing his way through laundry waving in the gentle breeze, all he had to do was follow the crowd. After considerable progress through the Lower City, the rooftops ran out as the open area of the Hippodrome approached. He had made good time this way, but with only busy streets ahead those that had chosen this path found themselves in a lengthy line, waiting to descend a small stairwell to the mayhem below. This took a long time, but everyone was friendly and in good spirits on this day before Passover.

The sun was at a 10 a.m. position in the blue sky, shining brightly with occasional pure white clouds floating freely overhead on this beautiful day. The warm April temperatures were very pleasant. The talk among the travelers was not of the Romans or a messiah, but of family and friends. It was Passover.

When Atara finally managed to return to ground level, it was still jammed with people even though the streets around the Hippodrome were much wider. Here there were many open court areas to accommodate the enormous crowds that came for the chariot races and gladiator combat. Years before the Romans had cleared this part of the city of homes, displacing many people to build the Hippodrome, which was for Roman culture, not for the Jews. For this week it housed garrisons of soldiers brought in to control the Passover crowds. Because it was a more open area the traffic moved slightly faster than on the narrow streets, so Atara was able to push his way further north toward the market area. Arriving by the Hippodrome, he noticed the heavy presence of Roman sentries and tried to avoid coming too close.

Eventually he made his way past the Hippodrome, continuing to work his way northward. He thought if he stayed close to the Temple wall, that route might be the least traveled, which turned out to be a good decision that saved a bit of time. Once past the Temple, the market lay ahead in the Mishneh Quarter of the city. The market was a labyrinth of lanes and alleys that had evolved over the years in this older part of the city. Vendor after vendor filled them with their wares, which even on the slowest of days would be busy. Atara thought back with gratitude to only five days ago when he had been fleeing the Romans only to be saved by the fishmonger and merchants around.

Today, you could hardly move, and to make matters worse the market would be closing in the early afternoon for Passover. Without pushing through you would be at a standstill. There was a lane for meat products where blood would trickle down the center gutter built into the cobblestones. Meats and animal parts hung from the stalls, leaving a pungent smell and fresh fodder for the countless flies. In the next alley where the spices were sold the exotic aromas of cinnamon, cumin and thyme filled the air. There were countless aisles of vegetables, breads, clothing, household wares and alluring fabrics from other nations. This was the Jerusalem market.

After what seemed an infinite time of jostling and bumping, Atara finally reached the first vendor who still had the required unleavened bread for Passover. He resolved this area was as far as he would go. It took massive endurance on his part just to remain until he was finally standing in front of the counter to place his order. Once accomplished, he slung the great sack of provisions over his shoulder, continuing to purchase some fresh vegetables and perhaps a piece of lamb for Naomi.

It was just after noon when his task was completed. It was now time to make his way back down toward the Lower City.

Atara retraced his steps out of the market, but realized he would have to avoid the Temple altogether. The sacrificing of the lambs would begin very soon, creating a massive traffic jam at all entrances to the Temple Mount.

Throughout the afternoon families would bring their lambs into the Temple grounds where the throats would be slit and a sprinkling of blood taken into the Temple as the blood sacrifice.

He decided it would be best to travel west, away from the Temple, before heading south to the Lower City, then back eastward to follow the city wall downward. The plan worked well as he used a combination of streets and roof-tops, but it still took over two hours to make a trip that would normally only take about 15 minutes. Finally arriving by the city wall south of the Temple Mount, he began the trip downward toward the Lower City. The heavy pack he was carrying and the heat of the afternoon sun was taking its toll on him, so as he passed by the port in the wall where he had sat only a few days ago, he decided to climb up into it and rest for a while.

Sitting in this little enclave, he peered out through the narrow opening into the Kidron Valley and up the Mount of Olives. Such a beautiful day ... so many people. From this vantage point high above the valley they looked like tiny ants busying themselves as they prepared for the Passover. Doves flew far below, looking like tiny specks as they darted to and fro. Turning to view the city inside the wall, he could examine the entire south end of Jerusalem as it descended into the valley. To the right, if he leaned out a bit, the Temple Mount towered high above everything else. The only visible gate to the Temple was the Huldah Gate with a sea of humanity coming and going with their lambs.

The words Jesus had spoken two days ago came to Atara: *Jerusalem, Jerusalem, you who kill the prophets and stone those sent to you, how often I have longed to gather your children together, as her chicks under her wings, and you are not willing. For I tell you, you will not see me again until you say, "Blessed is he who comes in the name of the Lord."* Atara meditated on this as he looked out over Jerusalem. 'How right he was. After Jesus had done so much, healed, taught and cared for the people, where were they now? Thousands on thousands had worshiped him as the messiah only last Sunday. Today, it's just like every other Passover in Jerusalem.

'Jesus had sat with multitudes on Monday and Tuesday after clearing out the Temple court. But where are the followers now? And where is he?' *"You will not see me again until you say 'Blessed is he who comes in the name of the Lord."* 'Where will Jesus and his disciples be celebrating Passover tonight? Will I ever see him again? Or does he mean only those who follow him can truly see who he is?' Atara had few answers to his own questions. His mind was in turmoil.

Frustrated, he said to himself, 'Why bother with this? Why does it weigh on my mind so much, and with no answers? It would be so much easier to simply return to my Zealot friends to take up arms!' As soon as he thought this, he knew he could not. Atara needed to understand who this Jesus really was, what his own part in this would be.

His thoughts went back to his dream of last night. It played over and over in his mind, the dream was so real. He had never seen the Temple curtain before. Only the priests were allowed into that section of the Temple. 'How did I know what it looked like?'

Atara pondered on this for a while. 'I've always been taught sin was simply the breaking of God's Laws. That the curtain represented a wall, a barrier, God put between Himself and us as punishment, and that final judgment was based on us adhering to the Law.

'But does it go deeper? What if the wall is there to protect us as a result of us accepting thoughts or behaviors that are not in God's nature?

'When mankind chose to accept the knowledge of good and *evil,* we accepted behavior that is not in God's character. Evil can't stand in the presence of God. So it would follow then, that in the Temple if anyone enters behind the curtain with sin they would be slain, not because of God's wrath, but because the imperfect nature of sin would wither away in the presence of the perfect creator. The imperfect in the presence of the perfect can't survive by the very nature of it, just as darkness can't remain in light.

'If sin is ungodlike behavior that can't exist in the presence of God, and the curtain represents the barrier between us, then what is to be done? Sacrifice is how we're forgiven for our sins before God and the purity of the unblemished lamb will atone for those sins. Why did this lamb of my dream, this lamb which appeared purer than all others, leap up to the altar on its own?

'Jesus had referred to himself as the *"Lamb of God."* Does this mean he's planning to sacrifice himself willingly to break this barrier of sin? Joseph had indicated this when he said he had warned Jesus, but Jesus ignored him. Jesus also said, *"You are going to have the light just a little while longer."* What good would it do, another man dying, just another prophet being stoned to death by an unbelieving crowd? And what of the sacrifices? We, as a nation, have been sacrificing for atonement for generations, millennia, but what has that changed?

'Jesus is right, our hearts are hard. We go through the motions of sacrifice, over and over, but nothing has changed!' Atara just couldn't understand how this all fit together.

'A lion and a lamb lying together?' But it was his final words that really penetrated deep into Atara's soul. *"It is finished."* 'Does it mean the final sacrifice? What then of the Temple?'

Frustrated he had more questions than answers, Atara decided it was best to move on.

He picked up his shopping, climbed down from the wall port, continuing along the city's east wall toward the valley and Pool of Siloam. Before he reached the pool, which was bound to be extremely busy, he headed westward into the Lower City toward the home of Barak. It took quite a while to cover the short distance, but the masses were now thinning out as people were already arriving home with their slain lambs to prepare their Passover meals. When he arrived at the safe house, Atara took the normal precautions to enter.

Once inside, Benjamin immediately cornered him. "So how was the market? It sure took a long time. Did you get the unleavened bread?"

"Packed. I've spent most of the day pushing my way through the crowds!" He threw the unleavened bread firmly onto the table.

"I could really use some help here preparing the meal!" replied Benjamin, standing at the counter up to his elbows in vegetables, hoping to rope Atara in.

"Uh, sure, I won't be long." But before Benjamin knew it, Atara was back out the door. The sun was low and he was anxious to continue, delivering the food to Naomi and the children.

Chapter 22

The apartment of Naomi was not far from the home of Barak. It didn't take Atara long to find his way through the maze of alleys and busy lanes in this poorer neighborhood. People were already gathering in the streets to prepare their lambs for the Passover dinner, which would occur after the sunset.

Many of the families in this area of Jerusalem could not afford their own lamb, so they would purchase one lamb between several families, roasting it together, giving the air of communal spirit evident to Atara as he wove his way between the families and children playing. On occasion he would see a young child embracing their lamb that had not yet been taken to the Temple, speaking gentle words to it with full awareness of what was to come.

Eager to watch the surprise on Naomi's face, he enthusiastically entered through the archway leading to the stairs, bounding up the three flights quickly, even with the payload of groceries on his back. Standing in front of the door, he caught his breath and knocked. The door opened wide. To his surprise it was Shira.

"Atara? What are you doing here?"

Totally taken aback with this reversal of surprise he muttered, "Well … I … uh … I brought some food for Passover," as his face turned a little red. He, of course, had been thinking of Shira throughout the day. The shock of her standing before him caught him more than a little off-guard. Shira looked radiant as she stood in the light of the door, pleased to see him.

"Come on in. This is so thoughtful of you!" she replied with a wide smile.

Atara stepped closely past Shira into the small room, instantly greeted by the children as they affectionately ran to him, wrapping their thin arms around his legs. Atara scooped the youngest up as if he was his own, turning to greet Naomi. "I don't mean to disturb," he said looking back to Shira, "but I thought with Passover today perhaps a little extra would help."

After a couple of tickles and laughs, he put the youngster down, shifting the bundle of goods from his back to the table. They all gathered around to watch what would unfold. When Atara opened the linen pack, the bundle of food toppled onto the table. There were "ahhs" from all those standing around. He had purchased unleavened bread, carrots, avocados, a large slice of squash, oranges and a couple of pomegranates. But it was the lamb that drew the biggest reaction as he unfolded the wrapping to reveal the modest piece of meat. Naomi turned to Atara with a slight flush to her cheeks and tears welling in her eyes, giving Atara a huge hug filled with appreciation.

Atara wasn't used to this amount of feminine attention. He had grown up in a household of boys, so he just stood there awkwardly, a bit short of words.

To the rescue Shira stepped in. "What a wonderful thing you have done, Atara! With all of this food, plus the little that I have brought, they will have a wonderful Passover. I have brought some herbs for their grandmother. She is not doing well and Naomi has been so worried about her."

Atara looked over to the tiny bed against the wall, seeing how drawn out and lifeless Grandmother's face was. 'What a burden for this young woman, yet she so selflessly put these others ahead of herself.'

For the next hour, the children found about a thousand ways to make Atara into a climbing tree or wild wrestling beast. It had been a long time since Atara had allowed his guard to relax a bit. This time with the children took him to a blissful world apart from his own. Sensing the ruckus they were making was inhibiting the preparation of the newly acquired bounty, Atara offered to take the children to the rooftop to play for a while.

They all left the apartment, the children leading him by the hand through a narrow lane to a stairway that ascended to the roof. Up the stairs they bound, Atara right behind, bursting out onto the rooftop. The sun had now set behind the buildings, bathing the roof in the blue tones of twilight. 'In another hour the sun will set behind the mountains. Then I will have to head back to the safe house to be there for Passover.' He watched the children play with a small ball. He wished he could stay here for Passover, but knew that would not be the right thing to do. Not for a bachelor and a widow.

After a while Shira appeared from the stairwell. She came over to Atara and sat on the roof beside him to watch the children play.

"Does your father know you're here today?" Atara questioned.

"Yes, I did ask him. I don't even have to sneak out dressed in disguise anymore! He is expecting me back very soon, though, for our Passover meal. My brothers will arrive shortly, some cousins as well. I'll have to leave, so I came up to say goodbye. You have made Naomi very happy. In fact, I have never seen her this happy before. Thank you, Atara."

"I have been so blessed just to witness the smiles on the faces of these children," he responded. Not able to figure out of what else to say on the subject, he decided a diversion was necessary. "I visited Joseph of Arimathea yesterday. I was surprised he would receive a person like me. He was so open and honest speaking with me."

"He is a good man, Atara. I have known him most of my life. You can trust him."

"He put his trust in me! A perfect stranger!" It was clear to Shira from the tone of Atara's voice that he could not comprehend how someone as influential as Joseph of Arimathea could put his full trust in a young, unknown Zealot.

"Joseph is a good judge of people. I believe he feels God has a plan for you to fulfill."

"I do too," confided Atara for the first time. "Even though I don't understand it, I keep thinking somehow there is a part for me to play in this. When I listened to Jesus, the words he spoke penetrated deep into my mind, spirit and heart, much more so than the rebellious talk of the Zealots. That seems trivial by comparison." He paused for a moment and then somberly confided in her, "Joseph informed me that one of the disciples will betray Jesus."

"He has told Father that as well. The Sanhedrin want to place Jesus on trial for blasphemy. I don't know how they could ever succeed with that! You heard him at the Temple. Every question they attempted to trick him with he answered with ease. I expect it would be very difficult for them to sentence him if there was to be a fair trial, as they are no match for his knowledge and wisdom. He sees right through their traps. Father is worried it won't be a legal trial though, that Caiaphas will select only those he knows are not sympathetic to Jesus." Then Shira added, "I've heard they are waiting until the festivals are over to attempt an arrest."

"There is more to tell you," said Atara. "I had a dream last night ... and the night before."

"Dreams?" asked Shira. "What were they about?"

As Atara related the dreams, she sat listening wide-eyed. Both almost forgot about the children as they tumbled around blissfully on that beautiful holiday afternoon. Fortunately, they were quite good at entertaining themselves.

After Atara had finished speaking, he glanced at the children to ensure they were safe, then continued. "The dreams speak of sacrifice, that is clear. I believe the man in the first dream that vanishes into light might be Jesus, the messiah. In the second dream the lamb is the sacrifice for atonement of sin. The lamb leaping to the altar might mean the sacrifice is a willing one, that would fit some things

Jesus has said. I don't understand the Temple curtain, nor the lion and the lamb lying together. That has me confused! What does this all mean, and why me?"

Shira thought for a moment. "Remember when we talked on Sunday night? Yes, it seems so long ago as so much has happened these past few days. We talked of the messianic prophesies of one messiah that showed the character of a warrior king and the other of a sacrificing servant. Perhaps the lion and the lamb are one and the same. Perhaps the messiah is both. Perhaps Jesus is both lion and lamb, and that is what the dream means?"

Atara could see what Shira was saying was possible. But Jesus as a lion? As a sacrifice? He could not see this, not yet, maybe not ever. He sat quietly for a moment, reflecting on her words.

"Goodness!" exclaimed Shira as they both snapped out of the conversation. "Look at the time! The sun has already disappeared below the city rooftops and it will be dusk soon. I have to be home to help with the Passover preparations and greet everyone!"

"Can I walk you home?" This was more than a suggestion, as Atara was genuinely concerned for her safe return.

"No, I'll be fine. If I leave now, I'll easily be home before the sun completely sets. It's more dangerous for you to be seen moving through the city." Shira noticed the concern on Atara's face and added with emphasis, "I'll be fine!"

Instinctively, Atara knew better than to argue. She had made her mind up and that was that. He so much wanted to be with her, to spend more time talking about the messiah. But he knew she would be alright. After quickly gathering up the three playful little ones, then returning them to the apartment, Shira said her goodbyes, gave her hugs, hastily exiting down the flight of stairs. Atara's heart ached to see her again as he watched her disappear into the street.

He decided to stay a little longer to help Naomi with the children as she prepared the meal. He knew he should not linger too long. A man leaving the home of a poor woman would immediately start gossip, or indeed worse, but felt it was not yet time to leave. He left the door wide open after Shira was gone to avoid neighborly suspicion. He sat on the floor with the children, fashioning an ingenious little game out of a couple of stones and sticks, which they all played for some time.

Every once in a while Naomi would look up from her work to ask Atara a question. Where was he from? Family? Where was he staying? But she never asked how he had met Shira. She already knew. And she also knew how Shira felt about him, but kept it in her heart.

A little more time passed by. Finally, Atara knew he had stayed much too long and it was time to leave. He gathered all three children into his arms, squeezing as hard as they could stand, giggling and squirming. Wishing them all a wonderful Passover, Atara went through the tiny apartment's door and vanished down the stairwell into the street below.

The sun had now set and the streets were empty. 'It's now Nissan 15. Passover.'

Chapter 23

THURSDAY EVENING, PASSOVER: NISSAN 15 / APRIL 10TH

Darkness rapidly descended on the streets of Jerusalem. They became eerily empty as the entire city had retreated indoors to cook for the Passover Seder, as was required in the Torah. Atara could smell the aroma of the wood fireplaces burning in homes, the lamb roasting slowly over the coals.

The city was very dark now as the full moon had not yet risen. There were few oil lamps in this poorer area of the Lower City to light the way, leaving the deep city streets void of light, the only slight illumination coming from the windows of homes lining the street. While Atara walked the paved stones seemed to stick to his sandals. It took him a while to realize the street floor was covered with blood from the preparation of so many lambs.

Inside the homes families assembled together in the warmth of their fires and fellowship. Outside on the streets there was a silent aura of death.

Atara paused for a moment, imagining he was outside the homes of the Israelites in Egypt many centuries before. It was on that night the destroyer[30] traveled over the land, killing the firstborn of all those who did not have the blood of the lamb on their doorpost, passing over those who had the covering of God, thereby redeeming their firstborn sons.

He shivered as a cool breeze blew gently over his neck. Atara knew he was late returning to the home of Barak, so he hastened his pace.

Suddenly, a familiar sound. He halted to listen.

Footsteps. Not of the regular passersby, but the rhythmic step of those in unison, metal clinking in step. Atara pulled back into a deep doorway as they came closer. Within seconds, a contubernium of eight soldiers marched past his lane and disappeared. The footsteps faded away and then abruptly came to a halt. The house! A sense of panic came over Atara as he realized they had stopped near the home of Barak. While trying to think of what action he should take, a shofar sounded. The wail of the ram's horn from high above was the warning call.

---

[30] Exodus 12:23; Hebrews 11:28. Some translations: Angel of Death

At sunset every night now, the Zealots placed a guard on a nearby rooftop to watch for Romans, therefore warning the rebels inside of danger. Clearly, there was danger at this moment.

Atara knew it would be futile to rush forward, so he came out of his shadows, locating nearby stairs that would lead up to the roofs. He bolted upward two steps at a time and within seconds had found his way past apartments, stairs and alleys to the roof. He had become a little disoriented, climbing upward with walls all around, so when he reached the top he had to turn to the city to get his bearings. The Kidron Valley lay ahead just after the city walls. He knew then he was headed in the right direction, so he advanced cautiously to the edge. Once at the precipice the scene unfolded before him.

Atara could see three patrols of Romans had descended on the apartment quickly from different directions. At once they used a battering ram, gaining entrance to round up the Zealots. They must have learned, figured Atara, that all the men would be present for Passover, deciding to lay siege in a rapid raid. 'A traitor! There has to be a traitor in our midst!' There was the sound of fighting inside and he was there just long enough to see Ezra, who must have been on guard to sound the alarm, dash across one roof, dropping to another out of sight. Atara realized he was in danger. The Romans would have heard the shofar sound, sending men immediately up to the rooftops to find the perpetrator. They would be on their way now.

He turned and ran up a small set of stairs onto another roof, again up stairs with a quick turn to the right where he spotted a stairwell heading downward. Thinking he would be exposed on the roof, he decided the best option would be to descend the stairs to lose any pursuing soldiers in the maze of streets below. It was a move of good fortune, for just as he had disappeared down that shaft of stairs, soldiers arrived on the rooftop from another, the one he had been on seconds before.

After passing several lanes, making as many turns, Atara decided it would be best to slow down and continue with much more stealth, now that he had some distance between him and the Romans. He listened for footsteps, but none were audible nearby.

As he stood in the shadows, he could hear the voices of those inside the nearby home. It was the quiet voices of Passover. "*Blessed art thou, Lord our God, Master of the Universe who has kept us alive and sustained us and has brought us to this special time.*" Atara stood for a moment, wishing so much to be with his family. 'Why, Lord, do we have to suffer so much? Why are we persecuted?' He knew it was not safe for him there and potentially dangerous for anyone he might contact.

The Zealots had agreed in advance in the event of a raid those who escaped would meet at the Pool of Siloam. He began by turning southward, working his way down the streets toward the Pool of Siloam, which was at the southeast corner of the Lower City. He would have to circle around the area of the home of Barak, giving it a wide birth, to arrive at this destination. A few streets over he could hear the occasional shout of soldiers as they gave orders for the search. That was when he realized some Zealots from the house must have escaped. It would mean the Romans had begun searching street to street. Nowhere in this sector would he be safe. Atara decided it was too risky to attempt to meet at the pool. It was too close to the safe house and they would surely search the entire area. With voices approaching nearer, he turned facing northwest, advancing swiftly, but silently, up the incline toward the Upper City.

At first he had convinced himself he would travel to the home of Nicodemus for safety, but abruptly changed his mind. 'Why would I subject Nicodemus and Shira to the troubles I faced as a Zealot? But then, where would I go? '

Suddenly, he became aware of movement. He ducked into the darkness of a lower stairwell, waiting. Within a few seconds a dark figure appeared, walking cautiously in the shadows against the wall on the far side. Atara strained to look. It was Ezra.

"Over here," he said, trying to project a whispered message only Ezra would hear. Ezra froze in his tracks. Atara, understanding his fear added, "It's me, Atara."

Relief filled Ezra's face, then he cautiously crossed over to Atara's refuge. They both sat on the stairs in the shadows, silently scanning both directions to be certain they had not been spotted.

Atara leaned close to Ezra. "I saw," he said forlornly. "I was just returning when I heard your shofar warning. I climbed up to the rooftops and saw you there, and the Romans breaking the door down. I realized they would start searching, so I ran."

"As did I," responded Ezra. "As soon as the first contubernium came around the corner I blew the horn, but they came so fast!" There was still a wild look of panic in Ezra's eyes. "Atara, we can't continue to another safe house. Someone has betrayed us! I am certain there will be more raids!"

"I'm sure you're right. My first instinct was to go to the Pool of Siloam, as we had agreed, but it would be too dangerous to go there with the Romans searching the streets. I assume some escaped?"

"I ran into one man from the other cell, he had escaped," replied Ezra, a little calmer. "He told me that some men escaped through the back two windows when the shofar blew. The rest stayed to fight, so I don't know what has happened to them. Simeon was one who stayed to fight, he told me that. Apparently, Uri and Mordechai had not returned yet. They were going to stay with friends elsewhere, as will I now. With the streets being so empty, it will be easy for soldiers to spot anyone crossing intersections. We must be very vigilant."

"Benjamin?"

"I don't know. I didn't see him and the others didn't mention his name."

This concerned Atara as Benjamin was his closest friend. He thought of asking Ezra if they should travel together. It was clear though, that two moving together would be much more dangerous than one. He didn't want to endanger his friend. "Shalom be with you," Atara said looking at Ezra.

"And with you, Atara." Ezra disappeared down the lane.

Atara felt alone once again. A notion came to him as he slid out of his hiding place to continue up the lane. He would go to his favorite place of meditation on the wall, the secluded port. He felt strangely drawn in that direction, as if he knew it would be safe. The approach would have to be carefully executed so as not to be seen, but once he was in the alcove, he would be safe.

Working his way east first, Atara then headed north, up the slope of the City of David toward the wall. He was now nearing the Temple, but made certain he stayed in the smaller lanes and alleys to avoid soldiers, each time crossing a street or lane, being extremely cautious. In several places sentries were stationed nearby where he needed to cross, forcing him to wait until their heads would momentarily turn in another direction, then bolt silently across the lane. After some time he had come close to the eastern city wall near the port. It seemed all was quiet in the area. Soldiers atop the wall were unseen, but they must be there. Making a quick dash he made it to the base of the narrow steps in the wall that would deliver him to his tiny sanctuary. Atara ascended the precarious steps to the top. If he was spotted here, there would be no escape, nowhere to run. "Oh Lord," he whispered. "Please protect me." Seconds later he was sitting securely, hidden from the world.

From his position high above the City of David, he was able to see for miles. Small lights were glowing dim in the urban windows throughout the city as the Passover Seder was coming to a close. Searching southwest toward the Lower City, he could see the torches of Roman soldiers still hunting their prey. If he turned to look out of the port, the view of the Mount of Olives and Kidron

Valley were outside the walls, clearly radiant in the light of the full moon that had just revealed itself over the Mount of Olives.

Atara curled himself up as he sat with his arms wrapped around his knees. For the first time he felt the cool of the nighttime air. Thinking of his close encounter, he shivered. 'Why did I escape? By what fortune did I arrive later than I'd expected, being saved from arrest? What forces were at play here this strange Passover night?'

Atara looked over Jerusalem, imagining the Lord passing over the households of the Jews in Egypt so many years ago, providing salvation for all those with the blood of a lamb on their doorpost.

With much emotion Atara silently cried out, "Oh God, reveal yourself to me! Please, I don't understand what I'm supposed to do! I thought I knew You, Lord, your Laws, your Torah. But I am beginning to see that my heart is hard, angry, full of hatred. I have been looking to violence in your name as justification. Is it possible that I am no more than a murderer? Tonight I have run in fear from helping my comrades! Please forgive me." The words of Jesus rang over and over in his mind: '*You must be born again.*' 'What does this mean and how?' Then clearly more words: '*Whoever believes in me does not believe in me only, but in the one who sent me.*'

As Atara sat in his tiny enclave, meditating on these words, his head slowly nodding until sleep overtook him.

Chapter 24

THURSDAY NIGHT, NEAR 11 P.M.: NISSAN 15 / APRIL 10TH

In a panic Atara ran away as fast as he was able. Down the deserted laneway into a staircase that descended into darkness. Soldiers pursuing close behind and gaining. The lead soldier bellowed, "Stop!" Atara was then jolted from his sleep.

Sweat covered his brow. It took a few bewildered moments for him to fully awaken and gain his bearings. He was curled up in his protected port, inside the wall of Jerusalem, safe. It was late at night.

Looking out over the city, the full moon had risen since he had fallen asleep, but it was not yet midnight. He reflected on his escape from the Romans. Although he was thankful, he felt very solitary in his stone tower. It was Passover. He should be with family, friends, celebrating the redemption of the Israelites.

Atara thought of Shira. It had only been a week ago that they had first met. 'Am I just fooling myself? The daughter of a wealthy and powerful man, what would I have to offer her father for her hand? I'm just a young Zealot, hiding from the Romans like a coward!'

He looked out of the port in contemplation. Movement on the slopes caught his eye. About a third of the way up the Mount of Olives there appeared a procession of lamp lights. He tried to see clearly the other side of the valley through the night air. 'Soldiers! Have they hunted us down into the olive groves? Is this another cell of Zealots?' There was no way of knowing from this distance. All he could do was watch helplessly to see if his comrades were to be arrested.

He saw there was some kind of commotion or altercation after they stopped. It lasted only a few moments. Certainly it was nothing like a fight the rebels would put up if the Romans had found them in the open like that. After a short time the trail of soldiers began their descent back down the Mount of Olives, looking very much like they had found what they were after. At this great distance it was difficult to see exactly what was happening from Atara's vantage point, even under the light of the full moon. They had a few torches to light their way, but not enough to light the scene for him to see.

As the procession reached the bottom of the mountain, it turned south along the footpath into the Kidron Valley. Atara noticed there was no formation to the group. Within a few minutes they were close enough that he could see there was no Roman uniform. 'These aren't soldiers, just a large mob up to something!' Atara felt relief as it meant this was not an arrest of Zealots. From his tower high above the valley, the procession became clearer as it moved closer to the bottom of the wall. When a lick of flame from a torch threw light on a figure in the middle, he had the answer.

'The arrest! Joseph was correct! Jesus is being betrayed! But why at night? It is against our Temple Laws to hold court at night.'

A wave of despondency overtook him in his darkness. This man, who promised to be the messiah, taken by a traitor in the dark! Atara felt more cowardly now than ever. He sat in his secluded safety, not only hiding in fear from the Romans, but also unable to help this man who had penetrated his soul so deeply these past few days. Anger at this injustice rose up within him. As it did his sense of helplessness began to fade. 'I must do something! I can't just sit here and hide!'

Atara looked down at the arresting party, now in the valley directly below his position. He decided to follow them. Perhaps there might be some way he could help.

Scanning the direction they were traveling, it seemed they might be headed for the same path Shira and he had been on Monday, taking them into the city through the Water Gate by the Pool of Siloam.

Atara knew exiting the city at the gates would be a poor choice as the Roman sentries would be on high alert this Passover night. With few crowds on the streets it would be impossible to travel through gates unnoticed. But if he waited until the procession had passed through the gate, it would be easier to attach himself once they were in the streets of Jerusalem. All he would have to do is wait near the gate on the inside, slipping into the procession of men after they passed through. It would be dangerous though because the Water Gate is close to the home of Barak, and the Romans would still be hunting down any Zealots that had escaped the raid earlier.

Atara had made his mind up that this would be his plan, regardless of the danger. He took one last look down the valley at Jesus being led away. Moving into the open he abandoned his place of security and solitude. Once down the narrow stairs, and in the wall's shadow, he was about to begin his descent to the Lower City of David when he felt a strange sensation that this was wrong. He paused in those shadows, confused, alone, then closed his eyes.

"Father," he prayed. "Show me the way."

He then realized, by providence as he would later come to understand, that if they were taking Jesus to the high priest or Sanhedrin, they wouldn't choose to enter at the bottom of the city, risking any crowds that might come out to protest. After all, it was only five days ago that Jesus was welcomed into Jerusalem by hundreds of thousands as the messiah! No, they would stay outside the city walls, climbing the road up to Mount Zion, entering as near as possible to the home of Caiaphas.

This would be a much safer route for Atara. He would cross west through the middle of the city, completely avoiding the Roman searches currently underway in the Lower City. It would also avoid entering, or exiting, any of the city gates. He promptly set out to begin a night that would be etched into his mind for eternity.

Atara made good progress as he crossed Jerusalem with much haste. Mostly he stayed with the route he had used a number of times over the past few days. The majority of the route was using the rooftops, climbing from one roof to another, always upward toward the goal of Mount Zion. Often there would be a short set of steps from one roof to the next, sometimes a creaky old wooden ladder, and occasionally he would have to find a foothold to hoist himself up to the next rooftop.

The only obstacle he could not overcome was when he would come across a gap with a street below, at which point there were always stairs somewhere to be found leading down to the street level. This occurred less frequently than you would expect because many of the lanes in this part of the city had long ago been covered over. When standing on the roof you wouldn't even know there was a street below you, other than the telltale rows of small skylights which followed the streets, allowing daylight to enter.

A few times he had to cover some distance on the ground. These were the most dangerous times. At most street intersections a number of Roman sentries would be standing by a small fire keeping guard. Fortunately, with it being such a quiet night, this worked in his favor as the soldiers seemed to be very relaxed, paying little attention to their duties.

When Atara reached the edge of Mount Zion, on which the Upper City and Essene Quarters are built, the homes for the more affluent were large single dwellings, often with garden spaces between. There were no more rooftops to travel over, so he proceeded at ground level. By his calculations he had moved very quickly and would be well ahead of the arresting mob. They had a much longer route to travel around the wall outside the city and would not be moving as fast as Atara had. It was getting close to midnight now.

'I wonder if Nicodemus knows? Surely he would want to. Perhaps he could intervene. He's a representative of the Sanhedrin! Atara decided he had time to pass by Nicodemus' home as it was only a few blocks away. It was a risk he needed to take.

Arriving there, this time at the front of the house, Atara marveled at its beauty and size. There were lights on inside. Seeing that, he quickly approached the front door and knocked, perhaps too anxiously as it echoed throughout the neighborhood.

The door opened and Nicodemus himself stood in the doorframe. "Atara!" he exclaimed. "How did you?…" Then observing the distress on his face, "Never mind, please come in quickly."

The hallway was not as large as Joseph of Arimathea's, but it was built with the same beautiful marble and attention to detail. A grand staircase went straight to a balcony on the second floor with vaulted ceilings that felt like they reached as high as the Temple walls. Filling the center of the floor was a large mosaic of tiles depicting the 12 tribes of Israel with the gems of the high priest's breastplate surrounding them.

Nicodemus showed Atara to a room on the left. It was a stunning space with cushions and tapestry of light blue with golden highlights. Oil lamps had been placed in an alcove on each wall, bathing the room in a warm light that seemed to dance in unison. Sitting on a large cushion near the center was Shira.

When Atara entered the room, Shira quickly rose to her feet saying, "Have you heard? They have arrested Jesus and are taking him to Caiaphas for trial!"

"I saw," said Atara. "I was in a place on the eastern wall when I saw them arrest him on the Mount of Olives. I believe it was in the Garden of Gethsemane. I wanted to follow, but I knew it would be too dangerous for me to leave the city, so I came this way. Somehow I felt this is where they would be bringing him, so I decided to come here first." He went on for a few minutes explaining the events of the night as both Shira and her father listened.

"You were correct in your assessment," said Nicodemus. "Joseph was here a few moments ago to tell us. Select members of the Sanhedrin and Temple priests were notified and instructed to come to the home of Caiaphas, the high priest. I, of course, was not invited as he intends only to have those present that agree with his judgment. That is all we know at this moment. It would seem that you have more information than we do!"

"But it is against our Laws to have a trial by night with hand-picked judges," protested Atara. "And on a high holiday as well! Surely the council will see through his corrupt actions and wait for a proper trial!"

"I do not believe so," replied Nicodemus. "There is much contempt toward Jesus within the council. There are just a few of us who do not agree, so they have excluded us. Joseph is the only one that I know of that might still have some influence, but he will pay a very dear price if he opposes Caiaphas."

"I need to go. They should be arriving at the Zion Gate soon and I would like to find out what is going to happen."

"You will save time by going directly to the house of the high priest, Caiaphas. That is where they will be taking Jesus."

"Father," interjected Shira. "I'd like to go with Atara."

Before Nicodemus could object she added, "He'll be in danger if he goes by himself, but no one would dare question the daughter of a member of the Sanhedrin! I need to see as well. I need to find out what will happen or if there is anything we can do."

Nicodemus knew his daughter. There would be a lengthy argument if he disagreed with her, one that in the end he would most likely lose. It was dangerous, no doubt about that, but Nicodemus also wanted to know what was about to happen. He reluctantly agreed to let her go.

"Be sure the both of you stay close together. Atara, I expect you to look after Shira and not take any risks that might endanger her. She is my only daughter."

Chapter 25

Shira quickly found a shawl she could use for a covering, then was ready to leave. With no further words, she gave Nicodemus a big appreciative hug, turning to Atara for their exit.

As the two young people descended the front stairs, nervous and with great apprehension, the chilly night dampness penetrated deep into their skin, sending shivers up their spines. They moved through the gate into the moonlit emptiness of the street. Atara found it hard to think it was still the Passover night as so much had transpired over the past few hours. It was midnight when death rolled over Egypt like a fog, killing the firstborn of those without the blood of the lamb on their doorposts.

Lights remained on in many of the houses as people were finishing their family times together, preparing to retire for the night. For Atara and Shira though, the night was just beginning.

Caiaphas' house was only three blocks from the home of Nicodemus. It would take them only minutes to reach. As they neared the house, they spotted the arresting crowd approaching from the direction of the Mount Zion Gate. Both ducked into an archway of a large home across the street, hiding in the shadows, watching.

The small procession moved forward in silence. It was now clear to Atara that they were not Romans, but made up of a mixture of Temple guards and servants, most likely those of Caiaphas himself. The gates swung wide as they advanced into the courtyard. The guards prevented one man, who had been following with the procession, from entering. Another man from the crowd inside returned to speak to the guards, who then permitted him to enter. Atara thought he recognized this fellow, also another one, as those who had been with Jesus before. From where they stood Atara and Shira could see straight into the courtyard, watching as a few of the guards took the bound Jesus directly into the house while the rest remained outside.

"We should go into the courtyard to find out what they're going to do," said Shira.

Atara was just about to tell her they would never get past the guard, but by the time he opened his mouth to speak, she was already out of the shadows, coaxing him forward.

Very uncertain about this move, but not wanting to leave Shira alone, he complied by stepping forward. As they approached the gate, two guards moved forward to block their path.

"I am the daughter of Nicodemus," is all she had to say. The guards stepped back, allowing them through.

To Atara the house was not a home, more of a palace on a slightly smaller scale. 'It's enormous.' Being the official residence of the high priest, it was a model of grandeur. Steps leading up to the house were as wide as Nicodemus' entire house with large marble pillars upholding a luxurious balcony surrounded by marble railing. Three stories of hand-hewn Jerusalem stone made it very imposing. Gold plating glistened around the balcony and facia radiated in the moonlight. Large windows filled the frame, every one lit from within, exposing the affluence of each room. The courtyard appeared to Atara several times larger than that of Joseph of Arimathea. On the left side there were gardens with bushes, vines, orange trees and flora of all kinds with a marble path leading to a large, beautifully carved fountain in the center. On their right a series of stalls lined the wall that Atara assumed would keep the horses of visiting guests.

"I saw Jesus taken directly inside by the guards," Atara said to Shira. "What are they planning?"

Near the center of the court a makeshift fire had been lit. The remainder of the entourage that brought Jesus here now settled into the area around the fire. A few other people began arriving, going directly into the house.

"Sanhedrin members," Shira whispered to Atara, assuming he wouldn't recognize them.

This would be a recurring sight for the next hour as selected members of the Sanhedrin that had been summoned by Caiaphas arrived in the night. The Sanhedrin was composed of priests, judges and treasury officials from both Pharisee and Sadducee positions. They were all prominent, successful citizens of Israel. But this night not everyone would be present.

Shira and Atara moved closer to the area of the fire where they sat on a nearby bench. She leaned close and whispered, "Isn't that one of the disciples we saw with Jesus on Tuesday? Perhaps if we talk with him, we can learn more."

"When we arrived I thought there were two men that looked like disciples of Jesus. One of them seemed to help the other enter past the guards, like he knew his way around. I wonder if that is the disciple who betrayed Jesus. But I think this one here looks like the fellow we saw when we followed Jesus up the Mount of Olives," Atara responded. "If he is a disciple, he would certainly have to be the bravest of them all to have come here. Look around. It appears all the other disciples have abandoned Jesus!" as he gestured with his hands around the court. "They were on the high ground on the Mount of Olives. It should have been easy to defend themselves against this group, escaping into the dark!"

He began to expand more about how they could have escaped, or how the disciples could have quickly raided the party in the dark on the way back to Jerusalem, when they noticed a servant girl approach the man.

"You also were with the Nazarene, Jesus!" she said, coming out of the house with water for the crowd.

But the man denied it saying, "I neither know nor understand what you are talking about!"[31]

The girl went about her business, glancing back suspiciously.

The initial talk around the center of the courtyard was of the arrest. Atara and Shira learned that one disciple had resisted arrest. He apparently had, or obtained, a sword. Striking out to kill, he only managed to cut the ear off one of Caiaphas' servants. Jesus reprimanded the disciple, then picking up the ear he put it back in place, healing the man. In the dark the men could not identify the perpetrator with all the confusion, so he escaped. Their focus was capturing Jesus once the betrayer identified him. The talk was more of the healing, though. "By what sorcery or trickery does he do this?" one guard asked. A debate followed with the majority around the fire believing there had to be some kind of magic at play.

"Why can't they see?" Atara said to Shira. "Jesus gave himself up willingly! He healed an enemy! Why can they not see the good in this man? This kind of goodness can only come from God!"

Then it hit him.

"My dream! In my second dream the lamb leapt up to the altar on its own. It went willingly!"

"Then this is how Jesus intends it to be," responded Shira. "But perhaps God will intervene now as he did with Abraham and Isaac. Let's hope!" They sat quietly for some time pondering this thought, trying to imagine what lay ahead.

By this time the crowd in the court had swelled. As members from the Sanhedrin arrived, most would have servants with them instructed to wait outside

---

[31] Mark 14:67–68

in the courtyard where there was much speculation about what was happening behind those doors. Clearly, from the tone of this crowd, there was little support for Jesus. After an hour went by, the crowd increased to a size where the entire court was full of servants and Temple guards. At one point a large group of Temple guards arrived, setting up positions by the stables, perhaps in anticipation of trouble. It was quite evident most of these midnight guests were not happy about being here on this Passover night.

Another servant girl thought she recognized the mysterious man by the fire. She looked directly at him, turning to those around with her finger pointed saying, "This fellow was with Jesus of Nazareth!"

All heads turned to the stranger, but he defied them all by responding, "I do not know the man!"[32]

Atara and Shira looked at each other. They both were sure this man was one of the disciples. "I'm not sure what I would do in his position," Atara confessed to Shira. "This crowd could turn on a man, stoning him to death in seconds!"

What they did not know was that it was this very disciple who wielded the sword in the attempt to kill the Temple guard. If he was recognized by any of those present, it would mean certain arrest and likely execution.

The gloomy night dragged on. After the initial gossip subsided, it was simply a time of waiting to see what would happen next. Would he be released? The time went by slowly until it was just before sunrise. The official sunrise would be around 5 a.m., well before the sun would rise to be visible above the Mount of Olives. It had been a very uncomfortable few hours for all those present. The cool, damp, mountain air and the hard stone had taken its toll on everyone. Atara looked at Shira. Seeing her shiver he drew himself nearer to her, wrapping his arm around her back to keep her warm. She looked up for a second, then leaned against him with her head against his shoulder.

With the hint of twilight arriving, the crowd stirred. A servant who had come in later was standing nearer the fire to warm himself. He looked directly at the man who previously denied knowing Jesus. "Certainly this fellow was also with him, for he is Galilean!" he exclaimed to the entire assembly.

"Man, I don't know what you're talking about!"[33]

The rooster crowed with the arrival of dawn. The lone figure rose with his head down, walking through the crowd to the exit.

Moments later the other man, the one who had spoken to the guards earlier, came rushing out of the house looking very distressed and angry. "That is the

[32] Matthew 26:71–72
[33] Luke 22:59–60

second man that had come in with the arresting party. I am sure he was one of the disciples as well, most likely the traitor!" Atara said to Shira and she nodded. "Look, he has just stormed through this crowd, leaving the courtyard! What's happening?"

Within a few minutes Jesus, surrounded by Temple guards, appeared on the steps. He was being led bound and tethered through the crowd into the courtyard. As they passed close by Shira gasped, "They have beaten him!" Atara could see the blood trickling down the side of Jesus' head with severe bruising on his cheeks. As he was being marshaled away by the guards through the gate, he remained silent.

Atara and Shira were about to follow when someone grabbed Atara firmly by the arm. Alarmed, he spun swiftly with his fist closed, ready to meet his arrester. It was Joseph! Shira turned when she saw him, falling into his arms in tears.

"What has happened? Where are they taking him? They have beaten him!"

Joseph comforted her for a brief moment, then pulling away to look into her face said, "They are taking him to Pilate. We can't talk here, child. Let us quickly return to your father's house where I will explain what has happened. There is nothing we can do here, but the time is short."

Sanhedrin members were now coming out of Caiaphas' house. Most began heading in the direction Jesus had been led.

The trio hurried back to the home of Nicodemus, taking only minutes to arrive there. It was obvious to both Atara and Shira that Joseph was not in a frame of mind to talk.

His brow was furrowed and his quick pace fierce. This was the countenance of a man showing pain and anger combined. When they arrived Nicodemus was inside the sitting room, waiting for word.

Chapter 26

Nicodemus had not slept. Most of the night since Shira left he had paced the floor with worry. Worry for Shira, Jesus and for the events that were about to unfold.

Food and drink awaited the returning group as they entered. Nicodemus motioned for the three to partake as he prepared the soft cushions around the table for them. It had been a long night for everyone, but especially for Atara who had now been out all night and had not eaten since yesterday morning. As he reclined on a cushion, sinking low into the fine silk, he could feel the temptation to close his eyes and drift away. But he could not.

As soon as they settled in, Nicodemus looked at Joseph, who had remained silent to this point. "What is the news?" he asked, anxiously awaiting a reply.

All three leaned forward with anticipation.

"Bad, very bad," said Joseph in a hushed tone. "They beat him and condemned him to death."

They all gasped at this revelation. This was news they were hoping not to hear.

"All they need now is Pilate's endorsement to crucify him."

"But," Atara interjected, "is it not illegal by Roman law for Jews to sentence a man to death? Was tonight's trial not illegal by Jewish Laws as well?"

"Patience, my young friend," replied Joseph. "You are correct that the Romans do not allow us to condemn a man to death. That is why they are taking Jesus to Pilate. But even so, when has that stopped us? Do we not still stone those who break our Laws behind the Romans' backs? What has become of us!

"Regardless, let me tell you what occurred tonight throughout these early hours. We must be quick, as I believe the events will move rapidly now Caiaphas has resolved to have this over with before Shabbat. One of my servants has gone to Herod's Palace to find out what is developing next. When there is news, he will report back here immediately."

Joseph continued, "I received a summons to go to the home of Caiaphas just before midnight. I took my servant Chaim with me and we entered Caiaphas' house as was requested. Chaim remained in the hallway. As you know, the house is enormous. The grand hall in the center was set up to seat many people, which is where those that were summoned waited. I was not told in advance why I was called in. It wasn't until I was there and heard they had arrested Jesus that I became fully aware of our purpose there. I had no time to prepare.

"They brought Jesus in, bound in ropes, moving directly past us to the back half of the mansion. As you know Annas, who is Caiaphas' father-in-law, was the former high priest before the Romans appointed Caiaphas. It is complicated because technically, by our Laws, Annas would still be the high priest, as it is a lifetime appointment, but the Romans favored Caiaphas. It was by his bribes and political maneuvering they finally appointed him to the position of high priest."

Joseph looked at Atara to be sure he was following. Atara nodded so Joseph continued. "When they passed by with Jesus, Caiaphas indicated to us we should come with him. Only a handful of Sanhedrin members had arrived by that time, so those of us that were there went in. They led us back to the quarters of Annas for a pretrial. Once there, Annas began to question Jesus to determine the charges that should be laid against him. Jesus stood silent through the long interrogation until Annas was completely exasperated. He said nothing in his own defense. Then, looking directly at Annas, Jesus said, *I have spoken openly to the world. I always taught in synagogues or at the Temple where all the Jews come together. I said nothing in secret. Why question me? Ask those who heard me. Surely they know what I have said.*[34]

"With that Annas became extremely angry. A Temple guard moved in, struck Jesus in the face hard saying, 'Is this the way you answer the high priest?' Standing back upright after the blow, Jesus answered the man. *'If I said something wrong, testify as to what is wrong. But if I spoke the truth, why did you strike me?'*[35]

"It was all I could do to restrain myself, even at my age! It happened so fast. How could we treat a man this way who had done no wrong? It was to get worse, however.

"The guards once again grabbed hold of Jesus by force. They removed him from the room at Annas' command to take him back to Caiaphas, who was waiting in a small courtyard to the side. We were still a relatively small group of hand-picked members. I am not sure how I ended up included in this group, as many in the Sanhedrin were aware of my sympathies toward Jesus. I believe it was by God's hand that I was notified.

---

[34] John 18:20–21

[35] John 18:23

"When Jesus was taken to stand before Caiaphas and the other chief priests, he turned and looked right at me. It was a look I will never forget as long as I live. I realized then I was not to interfere, that this was his choice, his mission. I am uncertain I will be able to live with myself after what I have witnessed for the past few hours. Not being able to do a thing!" Joseph's voice choked as he paused, looking down. It was apparent he could not finish.

"Jesus wanted a witness," interjected Nicodemus. "You have nothing to be ashamed of. He needed you there so the world would know. You are possibly the only person who will honestly document what is happening behind those closed doors at this mockery of a trial!"

It took a moment for Joseph to compose himself, then he continued. "Caiaphas and the chief priests began to question Jesus, looking for a charge that would stand up in trial. They brought witness after witness in to testify. But it was a sham! Their testimonies didn't even agree, it was obvious they were false testimonies. Lies! Jesus remained silent to all of it."

Psalm 27:12 came to Atara's mind. He blurted out, *"Do not turn me over to the want of my foes, for false witness will rise up against me, spouting malicious accusations."*

"And also Isaiah 53:7," said Nicodemus quietly. *"He was oppressed and afflicted, yet he did not open his mouth; he was led like a lamb to the slaughter, and as a sheep before its shearers is silent, so he did not open his mouth."*

"He knows," added Atara, recalling his dreams of the nights before. "He knows and is willing to sacrifice himself. But will God save him?"

"We do not yet know," answered Joseph. "But let me continue. Caiaphas was also becoming very frustrated and angry. There was so much tension in the room, it felt like the darkness of the abyss itself. After two witnesses came forward, testifying Jesus said he would tear down the Temple made by human hands, and in three days would build another, there was an uproar in the room. Jesus still remained silent.

"Finally, Caiaphas asked Jesus directly, *'Are you the Messiah, the Son of the Blessed one?'*

"'I am,' said Jesus. *'And you will see the Son of Man sitting at the right hand of the Mighty One and coming on the clouds of heaven!'*[36]

"Caiaphas was furious this man standing before him would use the unspeakable name of God, the name 'I am' God spoke to Moses in Exodus 3:14. Tearing his own clothes and crying, 'Blasphemy!' he struck out, hitting Jesus on the head. Many of the others followed his lead, weighing in, spitting at him and striking

---

[36] Mark 14:62

him with considerable force. I am ashamed of our actions as a nation. I am ashamed that I did nothing."

"Wait!" Atara interjected. "Caiaphas struck Jesus on the head? Put his hand on his head?"

"Yes," responded Joseph patiently as all eyes turned toward Atara.

"Shira and I have been talking and we believe that if Jesus is the messiah, then the events that unfold should obey God's ordinances."

"Continue," said Nicodemus.

"Do you see? On Yom Kippur, the Day of Atonement for our sins, there is a sacrifice to be offered for all the sins, for all the people. On that day the high priest will lay his hands on the head of the sacrifice and confess the sins of the people, transferring their sins to the sacrifice! If Jesus is THE sacrificial lamb, then the high priest would have to place his hands on Jesus' head! John the Baptist ordained Jesus as a priest, the Temple purchased Jesus back into the priesthood, and now the high priest has laid his hand on Jesus' head as THE sacrificial lamb, transfering the sins of all! He would be taking our sins on himself!"

After reflecting for a moment, Joseph replied, "Well done, young man. You seem to know your scriptures very well. Now let us continue. Time is brief as I expect the Roman governor will be ready to see Jesus soon.

"It was now drawing close to sunrise. Jesus was to be brought before the whole Sanhedrin in the Great Hall. I believe they were waiting for everyone to be present. Also waiting until the sun provided some daylight, as it is against our Laws to condemn a man in the nighttime. When I say everyone, I realized some were missing because no word had been sent out to those who are known sympathizers of Jesus, such as Nicodemus here.

"Caiaphas, the chief priests and elders all took their place at the front of this mock trial. They brought Jesus before them, bloody and bruised. The Temple guards had beaten him further after we had left the room. Caiaphas already had what he wanted, the evidence against Jesus that he needed. He brought the witnesses back into the Grand Hall for each to give their testimonies. The Sanhedrin was becoming increasingly hostile.

"Finally, Caiaphas asked Jesus again, *'If you are the Messiah, tell us.'*

"His answer was, *'If I tell you, you will not believe me, and if I asked you, you would not answer. But from now on, the Son of Man will be seated at the right hand of the mighty God.'* [37] The whole Sanhedrin erupted in anger at this statement, shouting at him.

---

[37] Luke 22:67–69

"Sensing victory, Caiaphas held up his hands to quiet the council and asked one final question. 'Are you then the Son of God?'

"To which Jesus replied, *'I am.'*

"Everyone in the Great Hall shook their fists and tore their robes shouting, 'Blasphemy! Death!' They crowded around Jesus, pushing and shoving, but more than that I could not see. I am certain they abused him further.

"During this horrible scene of chaos and anger I saw a man approach Caiaphas to the side. They argued. It was Judas, the man who had agreed to betray Jesus. After a moment of fierce gesturing with the purse of silver in his hand, he stormed out in anger. After that the guards led Jesus bound out into the courtyard. It is Caiaphas' plan to take Jesus to Pilate to have him sentenced to crucifixion. The Sanhedrin members followed. That is when I came out and saw you two standing by the fire."

"It breaks my heart that they beat him so badly and then put him through that sham of a trial," said Shira.

Atara took her hand. "It's what he is prepared for, I think. Trying to do God's will is never easy.'"

It was not yet 6 a.m. when Chaim returned with news that Pilate was prepared to try Jesus soon. The four immediately rose from their place of comfort to leave, including Nicodemus. Shira looked at her father with surprise.

"I will come as well," Nicodemus said to her. "I will not be missed here. I am sure your brothers will sleep late this morning. They have shown no interest in this matter. In fact, they have taken a very harsh point of view about Jesus I believe will cause much division in our family. But we will deal with that later. For now we must hurry!"

The four, Atara, Shira, Nicodemus and Joseph, headed out into the still, moist air of the cool twilight morning, disappearing through the gate into the streets.

Chapter 27

FRIDAY MORNING 6 A.M.: NISSAN 15 / APRIL 11TH

The foursome hurried along the empty streets of the Upper City. The households of Jerusalem were stirring as they arose in preparation for morning prayers. This was a day of celebration, a day of redemption. It was Passover. It was to be a day of families, walks through the parks, playing with the children and reflecting on God's deliverance from oppression.

It took only minutes to arrive at the palace of Herod. The palace was in the northwest corner of the Upper City, near Nicodemus' home. On its west side it was adjacent to the Jaffa Gate, which opened toward the main road leading to the coast. Built with Jerusalem stone, the palace was an immense structure that filled an entire city block. Beautifully trimmed with marble and gold, it was extravagant with many rooms, courtyards and stables. Herod the Great was a builder, his palace paid tribute to his aspirations. However, Herod Antipas, his son, who was sitting on the throne, was a cruel, shallow man. Only two years earlier he had John the Baptist beheaded here in this palace, presenting the head to his wife. This palace was also where the three magi visited Herod the Great, which resulted in the decree to kill all the newborn babies of Bethlehem at that time.

Normally Herod Antipas would not be in this palace, as he preferred others his father had built outside Jerusalem. But this is Passover, so he returned to Jerusalem for the holiday, as he did each year.

Pontius Pilate, Roman governor of Judea, normally resided in Caesarea by the coast, but also traveled to Jerusalem each Passover to oversee the huge influx of pilgrims to make certain Roman law and order was kept. He did not like the austere surroundings of the Antonia Fortress near the Temple where his troops were stationed, but preferred to stay in the opulence of the east wing in the palace, which he had claimed as his own. Herod had little to say about it, being nothing more than a puppet king of the Romans.

As they approached the palace, they saw that inside the main gate the large courtyard was already full of people, with more arriving at the same time as they were. It was the Roman soldiers that caught Atara's attention. Dozens of soldiers lined the street walls around the outside of the palace, fully armed and standing at the ready. There were also guards on the gates, watching as people entered.

Atara was sure he would be safe with Nicodemus and Joseph, but the sight of all the soldiers made him uneasy. As they passed through the gate unquestioned, Atara could now see the entire courtyard was surrounded with troops inside the walls. In front of the palace, two full contuberniums of soldiers stood at the ready by the base of the stairs.

This courtyard was much larger than that of the high priest. It was also more functional than the high priest's court. There was no provision for gardens, only the stone floor, with a series of stables for horses and chariots off to one side. 'The gardens were probably private, inside the interior of the palace structure,' thought Atara. In front of them was an enormous double staircase winding its way from both sides up toward the center door, which was ornately carved and plated with gold. Jutting out from the front into the courtyard, at the top of the stairs, was a large balcony high above. Stone railings and massive columns supporting the canopy lined the front. By this time the balcony was full of Sanhedrin members shuffling around, waiting for Pilate.

Atara scrutinized the crowd on the ground. "It looks like mostly supporters of the Sanhedrin, priests, guards and family," he turned saying to Shira. "I'll bet they spread the word only among those who oppose Jesus. They have all come to make sure he will be sentenced."

Joseph nodded. "From the start, this has been an unjust and illegal trial! I will leave you all now and enter the palace with the rest of the Sanhedrin to see if there is anything that can be done to make this right. I will return when I am able."

He slipped away through the crowds and climbed the colossal staircase. When he arrived at the top, he joined the other Sanhedrin members on the balcony, waiting.

Atara turned and that is when he saw him. Uri! Then he remembered the Zealots had been hoping Jesus Barabbas would be the one Pilate would choose to release this Passover. They had been spreading word among Zealots to be here this early morning to show support for his release. Atara quickly scanned the court and noticed many faces he recognized in the crowd. Excusing himself from Shira and Nicodemus, he made his way over to the back wall to Uri.

"Atara!" Uri exclaimed as he turned to face him.

The next thing Atara felt was the impact of a fist connecting hard on his cheekbone, excruciating pain, and his body being pushed hard against the nearby wall.

"Tell me, my friend, how much are they paying you for your treason?" Uri held him tight to the wall with Mordechai now standing at his side. Atara could feel the sharp point of steel being pressed into his ribs.

"I had nothing to do with it!" Atara pleaded, reeling from the blow. "I was just returning to the house when Ezra blew the warning shofar. I climbed to a rooftop to see what was happening when I saw the raid and then I ran."

Mordechai pressed tight against Atara adding, "What reason can you give that I should not put this dagger into you as we stand here?" Atara felt the steel point in his ribs, gently piercing.

"Because he is with us!" Uri and Mordechai both spun their heads, finding Nicodemus and Shira standing right by them. Nicodemus staring directly at Uri, penetrating. Shira stood by, wide-eyed with shock.

"This boy is a traitor!" Uri exclaimed. He recognized who Nicodemus was, but was not sure how to react to a member of the Sanhedrin.

"No, he most certainly is not," Nicodemus replied calmly. "Atara would not have betrayed you, for it is not in his nature. I will vouch for him. He is here to witness the fate of Jesus of Nazareth, that is all."

Both men, Uri and Mordechai, realized they could not take any action with so many witnesses close at hand. Deep within they also knew Atara was not likely the betrayer for he had not been with the rebels in Jerusalem long enough to know the inner operations.

Uri leaned in close to Atara's ear and whispered, "Yeshiva boy, do you think with your high and mighty friends you are better than us? Are you full of pride, playing at being a Zealot with your first kill? Well, it wasn't you! It was Mordechai's knife that killed that Roman soldier, not yours! But the Romans still have your name, we made sure of that!" Uri spat on the cobbled stone, releasing Atara saying, "You can keep your Jesus of Nazareth. We are looking for a man who will lead us against the Romans, not a man who talks of forgiveness. We are here for Barabbas, a real leader of men!" With that said both men pushed their way back into the crowd.

"Very nice associates you have, my friend," nodded Nicodemus.

"Most of the Zealots are good men," defended Atara. "But these two are Sicarii, some of the more militant. They're bound to find the traitor in the midst. I'm very lucky they didn't use the dagger first." He lifted his hand to his face, feeling the sting of the blow, then to his side to examine the slight damage of the dagger. More importantly, he was relieved at the news he had not killed anyone. He knew at that moment the life of a Zealot was not for him, not anymore.

Shira stood by his side in silence. She was shaking. She looked up to the large bruise forming on Atara's cheek.

The crowd was becoming very thick now. It wasn't long before they saw Joseph descending the staircase from the balcony entrance, shaking his head. The trio made their way through the mass closer to the stairs, meeting Joseph at the bottom.

"What has happened?" asked Nicodemus.

"They brought Jesus before Pilate to question him. The Sanhedrin refused to enter the palace where Pilate, a Gentile, was residing. Pilate had to go to the balcony door to question Jesus where Caiaphas and members of the Sanhedrin were shouting accusations against him. Pilate had to subdue the crowd to even ask questions of Jesus.

"But Jesus would not reply other than to the one question: 'Are you the King of the Jews?'

"Jesus responded by only saying, '*You have said so.*[38]

"It is clear to me that Pilate does not want to get involved in this Jewish problem, so he was attempting to put it all back on the Sanhedrin, who were demanding the death penalty of crucifixion. When Pilate learned Jesus was from the Galilee, Herod's jurisdiction, he saw a way he could deflect the problem. Pilate announced he would send Jesus to Herod for him to decide what to do. So there is still hope!

"There is one more thing of interest. Just as I was leaving the balcony I overheard Pilate speaking to one of the guards. He asked the guard which prisoner they had brought to be released as a token of goodwill for Passover. The soldier responded it was a man they arrested for simple theft of food for his family. Pilate mused on that for a moment and then said, 'That won't do. Who is the worst criminal that we have in our prison at this moment?' 'Barabbas, the rebel,' was the soldier's reply, to which Pilate responded slyly, 'Then send word to the fortress to bring him here immediately. Let's see what the Jewish leaders do with that if it comes down to a choice!' Would the Sanhedrin dare let loose an enemy of Rome, a murderer?

"I must go now as they are moving Jesus to the west section of the palace where Herod will see him soon."

Nicodemus nodded to Joseph, wishing him God's blessing. Joseph hurried back up the stairs to the palace.

It was not yet 7 a.m. when Joseph emerged almost an hour later, descending the stairs once again. All the other members of the Sanhedrin that had been

---

[38] Matthew 27:11

present at Caiaphas' house filed into the courtyard while the chief priests lined the stairs up to the balcony. Joseph quickly found Nicodemus, Shira and Atara.

"Herod just played with him like a toy!"

It was obvious to the three Joseph was very distraught.

"Jesus said nothing the whole time. Herod plied him with questions and tried to goad him into performing miracles. When Jesus would not speak or perform miracles, Herod became angry and had him dressed in one of his palace robes, mocking and ridiculing him. Then his soldiers beat Jesus violently about the head and body, mocking him as a king. I am afraid I couldn't watch any more and left. The whole affair was futile. They are bringing Jesus back to Pilate now."

Joseph had just spoken these words when Pilate came out onto the large terrace overlooking the courtyard. He raised his hands to silence the multitude. *"You brought me this man as one who was inciting the people to rebellion. I have examined him in your presence and have found no basis for your charges against him. Neither has Herod, for he sent him back to us; as you can see, he has done nothing to deserve death. Therefore, I will punish him and then release him."*[39]

Atara hoped this would be the end of the trial, but the crowd, stirred up by the priests who mingled about them, began to chant *"Crucify him! Crucify him!"* It started as a murmur, but within seconds had spread throughout the courtyard, echoing off the walls as thunder. Pilate tried to quiet the crowd, appealing to them, but they kept chanting *"Crucify!"*

Atara could not believe what he was hearing! Jews crying to Romans for crucifixion, a Roman tool of death for one of their own!

Pilate, now afraid of the crowd, went back into the house where Jesus was waiting with the guards. *"Where do you come from?"* he asked Jesus. *"Do you refuse to speak with me? Don't you realize I have power to either free you or to crucify you?"*

Jesus responded, *"You would have no power over me if it were not given to you from above."*[40]

Pilate turned in frustration, motioning to the guards to follow, bringing Jesus out onto the terrace.

Shira gasped when she saw him. "They have beaten him again!" she cried. Atara felt his own bruised cheek and thought of how much more pain Jesus must be in. Jesus stood silently before the mob who were mocking him.

At his signal Pilate had Barabbas brought up to the balcony.

---

[39] Luke 23:14–16

[40] John 19:9–11

The large number of Zealots in the midst went crazy, cheering and shouting, "Barabbas! Barabbas!" Atara realized immediately what would happen next. Pilate was trying to escape sentencing Jesus by using the custom of releasing a prisoner on Passover. He would give the people the choice in an attempt to exonerate himself! He was gambling that the religious authorities would not choose a violent man like Barabbas.

"There is still hope!" Atara exclaimed. "I think Pilate will choose between the two prisoners. He will have to choose Jesus, who has been no threat to Rome!"

Pilate held up his hands once again. When the crowd quieted down he proclaimed with a loud voice, *"Which of these two do you want me to release to you? Jesus of Nazareth or Jesus Barabbas?"*[41]

What transpired next happened so fast that Nicodemus, Joseph, Shira and Atara had no time to have any effect on the crowd whatsoever. They cried out for Jesus, but their voices were immediately drowned out by all the others. This was the very moment the Zealots had been waiting for. They shouted, "Barabbas! Barabbas!" loud and clear, over and over. They moved through the crowd, egging others on, as the cries grew louder. The priests did likewise, although for completely different motives. The chants of "Barabbas! Give us Barabbas!" filled the courtyard.

At this, Pilate motioned to the guards to remove Barabbas' shackles and release him. The Zealots within the crowd cheered, gathering around Barabbas when he descended the stairs. Pilate then turned to the courtyard and asked, *"What shall I do then with Jesus, who is called the messiah?"*[42]

"Crucify him! Crucify him!" chanted the now bloodthirsty mob, over and over.

Shira began to cry uncontrollably. She could take no more. The crowd pressed in all around her, chanting in unison. She held tight to Atara, weeping.

What happened next astonished Atara. Pilate took a basin of water, then washed his hands, declaring his innocence of this sentence. He commanded that Jesus be moved off the balcony immediately to be lashed by the Roman soldiers, then taken to be crucified outside the city walls.

When Atara witnessed this a deep anger tore through his body. "Who is this man? This Roman politician, to exonerate himself of this injustice? Washing his hands of this doesn't absolve him one bit from what he has just decreed. We're all guilty of this judgment! Jew and Gentile, we have all made a mockery of justice, performing an act of evil this night because of the wickedness of our hearts!"

[41] Matthew 27:21
[42] Matthew 27:22

Bolting for the gate Atara grabbed Shira by the hand. He could no longer stay within these walls. Once outside he tore around the corner, dragging Shira until she pleaded for him to stop. Halting abruptly, Atara turned toward the wall, pounding his fist hard into the weathered stone. For the first time he could remember since the death of his father, he broke into tears. Shira leaned into him and wept with him. There they stood this Passover morning, arm in arm, grieving Jesus, having never imagined such terrible forces would be at play that night, forces far beyond their understanding.

In a few moments Nicodemus and Joseph had caught up with them. Shira looked at her father through her tears and pleaded, "Why, Father? Why is this happening to such a good man? A man I believed was the messiah?"

"Child," he replied endearingly, "it is not over yet. I believe in him. There is much more we can learn from Jesus. He has purposely turned himself over to be subjected to this horror. I believe we should stand by him."

Nicodemus' words were a great comfort. She began to feel at peace as she moved from Atara to embrace her father.

Atara agreed with Nicodemus. There was definitely more to this. Everything that had happened seemed to be divinely ordained, against all odds.

"The names," said Atara, struggling to overcome his emotions. "Did you notice the names?"

"What do you mean?" questioned Joseph.

"Who do we believe Jesus is? The messiah, the Son of God. You have heard him say that, have you not, Joseph?"

"Yes I have, just today he made that statement. And I have heard that he has said that many times before."

"Exactly," said Atara. "The Son of God, The Son of the Father. The name Barabbas, Bar Abba, means the son of the father. So this morning we had two men standing before the priests, Jesus (of Nazareth), the Son of the Father and Jesus (Barabbas) the son of the father, and we know the name Jesus means salvation. Today the Son of God stands beside the Son of Adam." Atara had the attention of all three now as his voice became more intense. "Look, if Jesus has come to us as a sacrifice for the forgiveness of our sins, then there had to be two."

"Two? Why two?" asked Shira.

"It's about the Temple! At Yom Kippur, the Day of Atonement, when the yearly sacrifice is made for the sins of the people according to Leviticus, the priest is presented with two identical sacrifices. One will be selected to die for the sins of the people and the other will be released. Today two men, both sons of Adam, but one also the Son of God, stood before us, identical in name, but completely opposite in character. Pilate presented the choice to the people, and they, not the high priest, selected Jesus, The Son of God, to die for their sins. Barabbas was set free. The sacrifice for Yom Kippur has to be pure and flawless, and out of the two they choose Jesus! But also, the one released, the one we call the scapegoat of Yom Kippur, should have been flawless as well, without sin, so the priests could transfer the sins of the people on him. He was not! Barabbas therefore can't be the scapegoat, for he is a violent man, a Zealot. For the first time, the sacrifice and the scapegoat are becoming one as Jesus takes on the role of both. Jesus is the last and final sacrifice for mankind. How impossible is that! How is this anything but the Hand of God at work! And even more, we are Barabbas! Like Barabbas Jesus will die in our place to free us from our sins. We are all the sons of Adam, those with sin. I don't understand how this works yet, but what is unfolding here today is incredible!"

Nicodemus and Joseph looked at each other in amazement. Nicodemus had only known this boy for a few days and already he could see God working in him. 'What was to lie ahead for this young man?'

The crowds were pouring out of the palace court now that the spectacle was over.

"What will happen next?" asked Shira through her tears.

"Pilate has ordered that Jesus be handed over to the soldiers to be lashed," Nicodemus answered. That was all he wished to say to Shira. The lash was 40 strands of leather impregnated with razor-sharp bones that would cut through skin like knives. Nicodemus knew that many times men did not survive the lashing. This was to be the third time this night Jesus would be mocked and savagely beaten.

It was almost 8 a.m. The sun was showing above the tops of the buildings, bathing the streets in light. Atara felt a wave of exhaustion briefly pass over him, just as word was going around the street that Jesus would make the walk to be executed very soon.

By now the priests had already vacated the palace courtyard. The trials had moved quickly for them to be at the Temple before 9 a.m. The first sacrifice of the day would be made then and the Temple opened for daily sacrifices.

It was Passover morning. Jerusalem was waking.

Chapter 28

The spectators began swarming out of the palace gate. As the crowd diminished, the Zealots were anxious to get out of the sight of Roman soldiers before any of them could be identified. Barabbas was freed, they therefore had no other interest in this Jesus or attending his crucifixion.

The judges, servants and members of the Sanhedrin were also in a hurry to arrive home. This was Passover. They had been summoned in the middle of the night for this trial and had very little concern for what was about to happen now to this man they viewed as a blasphemer, a false prophet. The priests had already left, rushing over to the Temple to prepare for the daily sacrifices.

Within a short time, there were only a handful of curious bystanders milling around the palace entrance.

Once the grounds of the palace were empty, Atara heard the familiar unified sound of sandals slapping the hard stone from within the courtyard. Moments later the first contubernium of eight armed soldiers appeared, marching through the gate, a matching ensemble following behind with Jesus in the center.

A wave of shock and horror came over the four as they witnessed Jesus stumble through the gate under the weight of a heavy cross. He had been beaten further, badly. The soldiers had replaced the purple robe he was forced to wear in mockery with his white tunic, which was soaked in his own blood from the severe lashings. Blood poured down his forehead from a crown of thorns pushed hard into place, opening large wounds in his scalp. The bruises on his face and arms were swelling to the point where his face would soon be unrecognizable. On his shoulder was the heavy cross he would be nailed to after being forced to carry it to the place of execution. There were two soldiers on each side with whips and truncheons to ensure his compliance.

As Jesus passed Atara he momentarily glanced over, looking Atara directly in the eyes. Atara saw the face. The face in his dream. It was the blood-soaked face that had faded into the light. Atara was beginning to understand. Jesus was going to sacrifice himself for all humanity. The Lamb of God was being led to the slaughter as a sacrifice for sin. Atara hoped he was wrong. He prayed this messiah, the Son of God, would throw off this cross and command his oppressors leave.

Shira sobbed uncontrollably on her father's shoulder as the procession passed by.

Atara vividly remembered his own lashings. The deep cuts into his own back that had left deep scars paled in comparison to these wounds of Jesus.

The four followed silently as the column of soldiers began the journey through the streets, pushing Jesus forward. Other onlookers also fell in behind, still others lined the street as he passed. There were some who wept, some who were only curious. Many who had stayed vented their anger at this imposter. "Blasphemer!"

The cobbled road to Jaffa Gate in front of the palace was wide and lush with the vibrant flowers of bougainvillea hanging from the walls. With the palace on one side and the homes of the wealthy on the other, it was easily one of the most beautiful streets in Jerusalem. But today it was smeared with blood, the blood of lambs.

The bystanders beginning to arrive shouted jeers, hurling insults at Jesus as he passed. Word quickly spread on the streets that this was Jesus of Nazareth, the self-proclaimed messiah. Atara could not believe that many of these same people had greeted Jesus with shouts of hosannahs and praises just five days ago, welcoming him into Jerusalem as the messiah. They now mocked him in their disappointment and anger.

The distance to the city gate was very short, roughly the length of the palace, which would normally take a man walking quickly mere minutes to arrive. But this procession was slow. It stopped several times as the Romans on each side of Jesus beat and whipped him whenever he stumbled under the heavy load, forcing him to continue. By the time they reached the busy city gate, the crowds had thickened, making the passage even slower.

The din of the taunts grew louder. When they stopped once again, just before passing through the gate, Atara could see that Jesus had stumbled, falling to the ground, weak and unable to uphold the weight of the heavy cross. The Romans at his side appeared to recognize he was so badly beaten that he would not be able to carry the cross any further. So near the gate they pulled a traveler from the crowd, conscripting him to shoulder the cross to the execution site. They pulled Jesus up to his feet and the procession continued slowly through the gate to outside the city as they prodded him on.

It was at this time Atara realized where they were taking Jesus to be crucified. There was a quarry just outside the city walls where many crucifixions took place. It was known as Golgotha, the place of the skull. Behind the quarry was a cliff that had acquired its name from the impression of a skull worn into its rock face. At the bottom of this cliff there was an old quarry pit where bodies from previous crucifixions lay twisted and intertwined. They were covered in lime to prevent the spread of disease, awaiting to be taken away for burning, but the thick flies and stench of death hung in the air. It was a scornful place, sitting at the two crossroads leading into the city where all passersby would witness the crucifixions. It was not far.

Outside the wall Atara noticed a small group of women weeping as they followed beside Jesus. He had seen them before at the Temple. At one point, while Jesus limped along, he spoke to one of the women. Atara wondered who they were.

As they approached the crucifixion site, Atara looked ahead to the area of Golgotha. It was difficult to see past the crowds of jeering travelers and spectators who had been pushed aside by the Roman soldiers to let the procession through, but Atara saw another group was just arriving at the site ahead of them from the opposite direction. 'More crucifixions,' thought Atara. Shira looked terrified now as they continued to pass by the hostile onlookers. She drew close between Nicodemus and Atara.

Reaching Golgotha, they stopped by the side of the road while the procession descended into the shallow quarry where the crucifixions were to take place.

"Benjamin and Simeon!" Atara gasped as he recognized the two others that would be crucified today. 'Not Benjamin!' he thought. 'He is a kind man and doesn't deserve a death like this!' He saw the lashes and bleeding on their backs as they lowered their crosses to the ground. They too had been badly beaten. The deep realization that this could have been him came over Atara like a wave of fear and shame.

"Do you know these men?" asked Shira.

"Yes," replied Atara in a low voice. "The Romans must have captured them in the raid last night. Simeon is a hardened fighter, but Benjamin, he's my friend. Just a good man in the wrong place."

It had only been half an hour since they had left the palace. Many soldiers surrounded the quarry on guard while a handful worked on the crosses with expertise, quickly preparing for the three crucifixions. They stripped Jesus down to his undergarments, throwing aside the bloodied robes, opening the wounds as they did. The skin on his back was shredded, exposing raw flesh and bone underneath. When they laid him on the cross, preparing the nails that would soon penetrate his hands and feet, Shira wailed in anguish, burrowing her face into her father's chest. Amid the dominant jeers and taunts of the bystanders, there were faint cries from those few present who loved him.

When the hammer came down on the head of that first nail, tearing through his wrist, Jesus groaned with agony. At that exact moment the crowds surrounding the scene went completely silent as a shofar was faintly heard in the distance.

It was 9 a.m. The first sacrifice of the day was being made in the Temple.

Most passersby quickly moved on. Nailing a person on a cross is a horrible thing to witness, even for those with a lust for blood. As the steel was being driven in, Jesus wracked with pain. Atara, Shira, Nicodemus and Joseph could not watch and all bowed their heads in prayer. Along the roadside others who knew him did the same. One of the women Atara had seen talking with Jesus as he was leaving the city fainted by the side of the road. The other women knelt beside her, holding her in their arms.

Once the nails were driven in place, the Romans lifted the cross high, plunging the main timber into a deep hole that had been the site of many crucifixions. With a hard jolt tearing at Jesus' hands and feet, it hit bottom. He hung there, awaiting death.

It was then time for the other two. Simeon fought with all his might, taking many soldiers to hold him down. But in the end it was futile, as eventually he hung beside Jesus. Benjamin wrestled with his captors as well, but it was his disparaging screams as the nails penetrated that would haunt Atara forever.

The scene was set. All three hung on their crosses by the roadside, Jesus in the center, the two rebels, one on each side, wrenching in distress. The Romans had placed an inscription prepared by Pilate himself atop the cross of Jesus which translated proclaimed: *"Jesus of Nazareth, The King of the Jews."*[43] The soldiers stood guard.

Jesus lifted his head briefly, and looking at the soldiers said between struggled breaths, *"Father, forgive them, for they do not know what they are doing."*[44]

The four moved off the road, sitting down on the slope by its side. They were not more than 100 feet from the cross, yet they felt so helpless.

"Zechariah 12:10," recited Joseph. *"And I will pour out on the House of David and the inhabitants of Jerusalem a spirit of grace and supplication. They will look on me, the one they have pierced, and they will mourn for him as one mourns for an only child."*

---

[43] John 19:19

[44] Luke 23:34

They sat quietly for a while, each attempting to grasp all that had transpired since last night. It had all occurred so fast.

All the while, the three that hung before them labored for each breath.

Passersby would hurl insults. Word of the crucifixion had spread throughout the city by this time, so now it was not just travelers, but those who would come to gawk at the spectacle.

"He saved others, let him save himself, if he is God's messiah, the Chosen one!"

"You who are going to destroy the Temple and build it in three days, save yourself!"

"Come down from the cross if you are the Son of God!"

Off to the side, Atara saw that the soldiers had taken Jesus' blood-soaked robes and were throwing dice to see who would take them.

"*Psalms 22:16–18: A pack of villains encircles me; they pierce my hands and my feet. All my bones are on display; people stare and gloat over me. They divide my clothes among them and cast lots for my garments,*" recounted Nicodemus. "This psalm was written centuries before crucifixion was a method of execution!"

The morning pressed on. Constant mocking pervaded the background noise as the crowd would swell for a time and then ebb. Yet not all who arrived were there to mock him. Some would reverently take a place to sit and pray for a brief time, but would move on quickly for fear of persecution.

Atara could see the anguish in Simeon as he hung there. He began to join in mocking Jesus in his anger, as others had done. He hurled insults at Jesus, taunting him to save himself, both of them, if he was truly the messiah. Benjamin looked up from his pain, shouting at Simeon, knowing they had both killed the night before during the raid. "*Don't you fear God? We are punished justly, for we are getting what our deeds deserve. But this man has done nothing wrong!*"[45]

Appealing to Jesus Benjamin said in anguish, "*Jesus, remember me when you come into your Kingdom.*"

Jesus looked to Benjamin and responded, "*Truly I tell you, today you will be with me in paradise.*"[46]

Atara heard this from where he sat. Tears welled in his eyes as he looked at his friend suffering on the cross. 'Is that all it takes? One word from Jesus and all is forgiven? How is that possible?' There was still so much Atara did not understand. He then thought of Isaiah 53:*12: '(He) was numbered with the transgres-*

---

[45] Luke 23:40–41
[46] Luke 23:43

sors. For he bore the sins of many and made intercession for the transgressors.' Many prophesies of old were coming true today.

The morning went by so very slowly. Shira and Atara sat beside each other, mostly in silence, ignoring the insults of those from the road. Nicodemus and Joseph were sitting nearby, occasionally conversing with each other, but were for the most part also silent. For what could be said at a time such as this? There was still a tiny sliver of hope within that God would somehow intervene, correcting this gross injustice. Jesus would simply come down from the cross with all his wounds healed, or like Abraham, a substitute sacrifice would appear to save the Son of God. But it was not to be.

It was a highly transient crowd. Even the few priests and Temple guards who had followed were gone now. The people who came to mock Jesus seemed to grow tired of the scene quickly and would move on. Others who had heard in Jerusalem about the crucifixion of a messiah ventured out to see the spectacle, but they too lost interest, quickly returning to the city.

Atara noticed a few small groups gathered by the roadside nervously, watching for only minutes, then fading into the roadside traffic. He surmised these were believers in Jesus who were afraid to be identified by the Romans or Sanhedrin as followers.

There were, though, a few lone individuals scattered around the site who did not leave, but were solemnly sitting vigil. They did not move on like most others or seem concerned about the presence of the soldiers. Wondering who they were, Atara arose from his place, first approaching a young man sitting nearby.

Atara asked him, "Why do you stay here while others are afraid?"

"Sir, I was blind from birth and Jesus healed me. I now can see! I must be here to show my love for him and my gratitude."

Atara continued to move about to speak with the others.

"I was a leper. I am here because Jesus healed me."

"I was possessed by demons and had no control over my life. Jesus cast them away and now I am free!"

"I was lame and now I walk. I praise God every day for this man that I believe to be the messiah!"

"I was deaf and dumb until I met Jesus. He healed me of my afflictions. I want the world to know."

So it went on as Atara went about greeting those that stayed. When he returned to sit with Shira, he related to her what these people had said. "Jesus has given them so much, they are not afraid to be here."

Just before noontime, the women who had been with the procession earlier that morning stood to speak to the soldiers, who allowed them to approach the cross near the base. There was a man with them Atara recognized as one of the disciples. Not the same one who had fled the courtyard last night, but Atara had seen him with Jesus on the Mount of Olives. The women wept. The disciple held the one Atara had seen talking with Jesus.

Between labored breaths Jesus said to her, *"Woman, here is your son,"* and to the disciple he said, *"Here is your mother."*[47]

Atara realized this must be Jesus' mother. He looked at Shira. It was clear she too had understood as the tears welled in her eyes once again. She was thinking of the unfathomable pain a mother would feel as her child hung tortured on this cross.

At noon the sky became very dark. Dense clouds appeared, causing the sun to vanish. These were clouds even blacker than you would see during a winter storm, but there was no rain or wind. Just darkness. The clouds stood still, bringing a clammy calm to the scene.

"Amos 8:9," quoted Atara. " *'In that day,' declares the Sovereign Lord, 'I will make the sun go down at noon and darken the earth in broad daylight.'*"

"Here we sit on Mount Moriah," Atara said to Shira. "The mountain where God told Abraham to take his son to offer him for sacrifice. Because of Abraham's obedience God saved Isaac by providing a ram for sacrifice. Now we sit many centuries later, bearing witness to God offering His son for our sins because of Abraham's willingness. The ram God provided Abraham was a full-grown male lamb caught in thickets and thorns. Look at the crown of thorns on Jesus' head. God has provided once again. Remember, on that first day we met, you told me something that Jesus said. I haven't forgotten. It has played over and over in my mind since: *'Just as Moses lifted up the snake in the wilderness, so the Son of Man must be lifted up, that everyone who believes might have eternal life in* Him.' It's coming true today and it's overwhelming!"

Shira leaned closer to him, feeling the chill of the dark sky. The taunts and jeers lessened as the sky grew even darker, foreshadowing the ominous events that would soon unfold.

Nicodemus and Joseph came to them to speak. "Shira, Joseph and I need to prepare for the burial. Joseph has agreed to have Jesus buried in his tomb, at great risk to himself. We will be going to speak with Pilate, asking for permission to take the body to Joseph's private tomb, which is nearby. We will be stopping by the house first. I think you should come with us."

---

[47] John 19:26–27

Shira looked at Atara, then back to the cross. Jesus was struggling terribly with every breath. He had been beaten so badly about his head and body that the loss of blood within and without had left him extremely weak. "Father," she replied, "I need to be here. I want to stay with Atara until you return for Jesus."

He looked once again through the eyes of a father at his daughter, who now seemed so much older than she did just a few days ago. Nicodemus nodded gently, turning to Joseph to leave. It was now about 1 p.m.

As Shira and Atara sat close together on the quarried rocks beside the road, the realization finally began to sink in that Jesus would die. They were determined to be there to the end, both frequently bowing their heads in prayer, asking God for mercy. The time passed very slowly and the sky grew even darker. When the time was approaching 3 p.m. Atara had never seen a daytime this dark. It was like late twilight, perfectly still with no wind or rain.

All three figures on their crosses were laboring heavily for each breath. Jesus was far worse off than the other two. His chest heaved with every breath now. Each one seemed impossible as he would attempt to push his body up enough on those nail-driven feet to gasp a slight bit of air before collapsing down again. Death on a cross comes from suffocation. Jesus' strength was giving way. Clearly he could not endure much more.

"*I am thirsty,*"[48] he uttered quietly between breaths.

One of the guards took a sponge and soaked it in a jar of wine vinegar. Planting it securely on a long spear, he held it up to Jesus' mouth. Minutes later Jesus cried out, "*My God! My God! Why have you forsaken me?*"[49]

This shocked Shira, looking to Atara for an answer. Atara knew. "If Jesus is now taking the sins of the world on himself, he'll be separated from God. Forsaken, alone. The Son of God would be God forsaken for us, buying our salvation. It's like God Himself being torn apart. I don't understand how this is possible or how he'll be redeemed, but God must have a plan!"

Shira nodded and added, "Jesus said in three days he would rebuild the Temple. I believe we'll have an answer to that soon."

Just as that was spoken, the shofar blew again far off in the distance. It was 3 p.m., and in the Temple the final sacrifice of a lamb on this Passover was to be made for the sins of the people. Jesus cried out with one last breath as he made a final push upward for air. "*It is finished... Father, into your hands I commit my spirit!*"[50]

---

[48] John 19:28
[49] Matthew 27:46
[50] John 19:30; Luke 23:46

At that exact moment the sky grew as dark as night and the earth shook violently beneath their feet. The few spectators that were left screamed, falling to the ground as the earth rolled and pitched beneath them. The three crosses rocked in their foundations, nails tearing at the flesh of the surviving Zealots as the wooden beams swayed, causing them to cry out in agony. Atara held Shira close, both weeping uncontrollably as Jesus' body hung lifeless. It was over.

After regaining his balance, the guard standing closest to the cross was heard saying, *"Surely he was the Son of God!"*[51]

---

[51] Matthew 27:54

FRIDAY AFTER 3 P.M.: NISSAN 15 / APRIL 11TH

No one moved for some time after the earthquake. Neither soldier nor spectator. The ground remained still, time hanging in the air, waiting for the next moment. Eventually the clouds began to disperse, allowing a single beam of light to fall on the gruesome scene.

People began to pick themselves up and after a while continued on their journeys down the road while the soldiers went back about their business. "Just an earthquake," they would say. "A coincidence." But Atara and Shira knew better. The show was over, and it wasn't long before there were only a handful of spectators left, along with the soldiers.

The soldiers had been instructed that these crucifixions were to be over by the end of the day before the Jewish Shabbat was to begin. Simeon and Benjamin were struggling to breathe, but it was clear they would suffer a long time yet. As Atara looked on, his heart was breaking. He felt powerless. He realized he could have met the same fate.

To finish this, one soldier took a large club and went over to Simeon, swinging hard to break his legs to mercifully end his suffering. His body slumped downward. He next moved over to Benjamin, doing the same. Shira turned her face into Atara's shoulder, feeling nauseous at bones cracking. It would not be long until they would suffocate, having no way to push themselves up for air. They both hung there, gasping for breath.

The soldier moved over to Jesus to examine him. Believing him to be dead, the soldier placed his club down and did not break Jesus' legs. However, to ensure that he was (for his own sake) and to offer proof, he took his spear, piercing Jesus' side, bringing a sudden flow of blood and water. Evidence he was indeed dead.

Both Shira and Atara were exhausted. Jesus hung mutilated and lifeless on the cross with the others on each side nearing death. They sat there speechless, arms around each other, trying to understand why.

Moments later the majority of the soldiers were getting ready to leave. The two Zealots had died, so there was no reason to stay. They would leave a couple of soldiers to guard Jesus' body, as they had been instructed to do. But as for the

Zealots, even though the soldiers had instructions to remove the bodies, there was no one there to claim them, so their bodies would hang there for days as an example of Roman might and justice to those passing by.

Shira and Atara stood to move around as they realized it was probably after 4 p.m. Shabbat would commence soon. They had been sitting on the hard quarried rocks for most of the day and were feeling the pain. There was no sign yet of Nicodemus and Joseph.

The only other people left were a small group of women who knew Jesus. The disciple had left them there after Jesus died.

"Did you notice," Atara said to Shira, "Jesus died at the exact moment the shofar blew and the sacrifice was being performed in the Temple?"

"I did," she responded, "and it certainly was no coincidence. Everything we've seen over the past few days has been beyond all earthly possibility. I'm exhausted and sad right now, but I know in my heart this is part of God's plan. But I wish he hadn't suffered so much!"

"Me too." Atara thought for a moment, then added, "His death happened so quickly at the end. I didn't have a chance to say anything at the time, but there were so many more messianic prophesies that were fulfilled. The wine vinegar, no broken bones of the sacrifice, his side being pierced, they were all prophesies I remember from yeshiva. Even the crown of thorns the soldiers put on his head to mock him as a king. It goes back to the Garden of Eden. In Genesis 3:18 God cursed the ground to bear thorns and thistles after the fall of man. The thorns pierced him and wounded him, and he was rejected. When that crown of thorns was placed on his head today, he became a king, the King of Thorns, the King of the Curse. Jesus willingly took that curse of sin on himself!"

Shira immediately picked up on what he was saying. "A crown represents authority, meaning the King of the Curse would have authority over it. He has come to break the curse and give redemption! The soldiers didn't know when they placed that crown on his head that they were fulfilling prophesy!"

"Yes," replied Atara. "It's written in Isaiah 53:

'Surely he took up our pain and bore our suffering, yet we considered him punished by God, stricken by him and afflicted. But he was pierced for our transgressions, he was crushed for our iniquities; the punishment that brought us peace was on him and by his wounds we are healed.

We all, like sheep, have gone astray, each of us has turned to our own way; and the Lord has laid on him the iniquity of us all. He was oppressed and afflicted, yet he did not open his mouth; he was led like a lamb to the slaughter, and as a sheep before its shearers is silent, so he did not open his mouth. By oppression and judgment he was taken away. Yet who of his generation protested? For he was cut off from the land of the living; for the transgression of my people he was punished ...

Because he poured out his life unto death, and was numbered with the transgressors. For he bore the sin of many, and made intercession for the transgressors."'

Shira looked at Atara with astonishment. "How do you do that?"

"Do what?"

"Remember scripture so well?"

"It was taught to us in yeshiva. It seems when I read something I can remember it. It's a gift God has given me. We should go over and speak with the women," he said to divert the attention from himself.

Shira agreed. They walked the short distance to where the mother of Jesus sat quietly on the hard ground with the other women.

"My name is Atara," he said, approaching the women. "This is Shira, daughter of Nicodemus."

When her name was mentioned, there was a nod of approval. They had seen the two with Nicodemus and Joseph, so they knew they were friends.

Shira sat on the ground beside the mother of Jesus. She so badly wanted to say something kind to her, but could not find the words. Shira began weeping. "I am Mary," the woman said, barely holding back her own tears. "Mother of Jesus." She reached out and held Shira in her arms. The two were silent as they rocked together in their grief.

Atara had few words as he knelt down beside them. He simply said, "I'm sorry," but could not force any more words without breaking down himself. 'How can a mother lose her child in such a way and be witness to it?' When he rose he drew in a deep breath, clenching his teeth to hold back the tears. One of the other women came up to him to speak.

"I am Mary Magdalene," she said. "We don't know what to do now. John has left us to see if he can find the other disciples, but what are we to do with Jesus? We do not even know if the Romans will give him to us for burial. Last night the other disciples scattered, fearing for their lives, most of them to Bethany. We have no one to help. Shabbat will be arriving very soon and we do not want to leave Jesus here like this!"

"Nicodemus and Joseph of Arimathea will return soon," replied Atara. "Joseph has a tomb nearby that he has offered for burial. They have gone to seek permission from Pilate to remove the body."

On hearing this, Mary, the mother of Jesus, looked up from her embrace with Shira, nodding appreciation.

It was close to 4:30 p.m. when Nicodemus and Joseph returned. They moved hastily down the road with two of Joseph's servants carrying heavy bags full of linens and perfumes for burial. When they arrived they stopped only for a moment to survey the scene. Three crosses with lifeless bodies hanging limp.

Joseph said to Atara, "We must move quickly. Shabbat is nearly on us. It took us quite a while to get the permission from Pilate to remove the body. He wanted proof Jesus had died, so we had to wait for a messenger to arrive with the news."

Nicodemus and Joseph went over to the women, introducing themselves and offering their condolences. Joseph told them of his plan to move Jesus to his own tomb in his private gardens, which was only a few hundred feet away, and that they must move swiftly as Shabbat was near. Mary Magdalene said they would follow to the grave site, but added they had no linens or spices for burial. Once they saw where Jesus was to be buried, they would have to hurry to be back in Bethany before Shabbat. She mentioned to Joseph they would like to return on Sunday morning to prepare Jesus' body properly.

"I will have my men return on Sunday morning," responded Joseph to their plan. "They will open the tomb for you so you might have your time with him. For now, Nicodemus has brought linens, myrrh and aloes, so we will do what we can today, but we must move quickly."

Joseph descended down the rocky slope to the quarry with his servants. When the guards saw them approach, they stood at attention, blocking the way. No one was to touch this man without authority. As he neared the soldiers, Joseph produced the written order from Pilate to release the body of Jesus of Nazareth to them. After reading the signed declaration, the two soldiers relaxed, and surprisingly offered to help lower the cross to remove the nails. One was the soldier who believed he truly was the Son of God.

It was a struggle for the two servants, Atara and the two guards to lower the heavy cross with the lifeless body. Atara suspected the soldiers would normally just let the body tumble to the ground, but today something quite different occurred as the soldiers helped to gently lower the cross with the respect Jesus deserved. As the cross lay on the earth, the small group of men stood united in silence as they viewed the broken, bruised and blood-stained body of Jesus.

Standing over the torn, lifeless body, Atara thought, 'What if he is not the messiah? Just an ordinary man? That this is the end of it?' Atara had not been this close to Jesus before. He stood staring at the body that lay before him, so broken and void of life. But in his heart he knew there was more to this. He knew, had known, from the very beginning only a week ago, that somehow he had a role to play, that this man lying before him was sent by God. He just knew.

The soldiers bent over the body, removing the nails with a metal pry. Joseph's servants readied the large piece of linen, then when the limp body was free from the cross, they gently moved Jesus onto the sheet. Joseph and Nicodemus took a corner together, while Atara, Chaim and Samuel took a corner each, all together lifting the body to begin the walk.

Thankfully, it wasn't far to Joseph's garden, which was situated almost next to the quarry, normally taking only about ten minutes to make the walk. However, it was strenuous for the men, especially at the beginning when they had to cross the ragged rocks of the quarry up to the road, as Jesus was not a small man. The women followed as the men struggled to make their way along the road until they finally arrived at the garden gate.

A great wall had been built around the garden along the roadside for privacy. The iron gate stood tall in front of them. Atara was on the front corner of the sling, so he reached out with one hand to pull on the gate, allowing it to swing open with ease.

On entering the garden he was astonished at its beauty, size and opulence. Joseph was indeed a very wealthy man. This private garden had been a personal project of his over the years. The tomb cut into the cliff behind, which was not yet in view, had been added as an afterthought because he loved to frequent the garden often for peace and solitude. He had decided not long ago that he would like to be buried here, so the tomb had been freshly cut into the rocks.

From the entrance three separate stone paths diverged, cut through sculpted rock, creating a terrain of varied elevations that were beautifully endowed with flowers and bushes of all species. Pure white lilies, multicolored roses and pink cyclamen lined the paths with large orange and grapefruit trees bursting with fruit overhead for shade. As they made their way down the center path, red flowering pomegranate trees came into view by the central pond. The water's banks were lined with gardens of crocus and lavender. Tall carved stone columns with arches overhead surrounded the pond from which vibrant purple bougainvillea hung. It truly was a magnificent garden.

'Isaiah 53:9,' Atara thought as he took in the bountiful fragrances of the surroundings, *'and with the rich in his death.'* They passed by the central pond with

Jesus' body, heading toward the back of the garden where the tomb now came into view. Near the entrance, which was a ragged cut hole through which they had to stoop to enter, was a stone bench. When they arrived, they lowered the body carefully onto the bench, resting for a moment. The women approached Joseph, thanking him for the generosity of donating his personal tomb in this beautiful garden, and for his devotion. Mary Magdalene stepped forward to tell Joseph they must leave now to return Mary, the mother of Jesus, back to friends in Bethany. She reminded him they would return on Sunday morning to finish preparing the body, if he would have help there to remove the great stone.

Shira had been walking with Mary, mother of Jesus, holding her all the way from Golgotha to the garden. She now gave Mary a final warm embrace, then the women went on their way. They would not make it back to Bethany before Shabbat.

"We have less than an hour until Shabbat," said Nicodemus. "Let us wash and wrap the body as best we can for now." They all went to work. Joseph sent Chaim and Samuel to the garden well to bring water for washing while Nicodemus began to unpack the linens and supplies they had brought.

When they uncovered Jesus' body, they were all, once again, shocked at the amount of abuse. The servants returned with water, then Joseph instructed them to return to the garden gates to keep watch.

The four remaining took the water and cloths, beginning carefully to wash the body down with the aloe to cleanse it. Shira gently and tearfully bathed the blood-caked face of Jesus as the men began to work on his body. There was a lot of damage, and as they cleansed the body they would gently place the torn flesh back into position, so when the women came on Sunday they would not be so horrified by the sight of his wounds.

"*And by his wounds we are healed.*" Atara said softly as he washed the blood out of the deep gashes. "How can we humans be so brutal, so evil? But I've been just as guilty. I was willing to take up arms. Jesus taught this is not the way."

Shira stopped for a moment, looking over the still body. "He looks so drawn with the loss of blood and so pale in death." She closed her eyes. "I want to remember the robust carpenter, laughing with the children on his knee. The strong man that single-handedly cleared the entire Temple grounds!"

After washing the body thoroughly, they applied a copious amount of the expensive perfumed myrrh Nicodemus had brought as an offering. Soon the task was done. Jesus' body was wrapped in temporary linens ready to be taken into the tomb.

Joseph called for Chaim and Samuel to return. The five men moved the body of Jesus through the small opening, placing him into the position that was cut into the stone for Joseph. After they stooped back out of the doorway, the next task was to roll the massive stone into place. It was enormous, carved round, about the height of a tall man. It was then placed into a trough cut into the ground like a track, so when it was moved it would roll easily into place. 'Who would have known,' thought Joseph, 'how this tomb would be used.'

An initial shoulder to the stone made them realize this was no easy task. Shira wouldn't let her father and Joseph participate in this due to their age, so Joseph recalled his servants to help Atara, knowing more manpower was needed. But it still wouldn't budge, even for three men. Atara found a large beam nearby workers must have been using. He suggested that if he pried, and the other two pushed, they might be able to close the entrance. Slowly the massive stone began to move, grinding its way along the rock track. Every few inches Atara would reposition the beam against the trough ledge, then they would thrust with all their weight again. When the stone finally rolled into place, they were exhausted.

Shabbat was now on them. The walk back to the home of Nicodemus was a silent one. Atara and Shira traveled side by side. While entering the gate of Jerusalem, she put her arm through his, where she remained very close.

Nissan 15, the 6th day of this week, was finished.

Passover was over.

Chapter 30

FRIDAY EVENING, SHABBAT: NISSAN 16 / APRIL 11TH

The streets of Jerusalem seemed eerily empty once they entered the city through the Jaffa Gate. The Romans anticipated trouble this Passover day, both because of the crucifixion of Jesus and the possible retaliation from the Zealots for the previous night's raids. The streets were heavily patrolled. It was late twilight with very few venturing out.

Approaching the home of Nicodemus, Atara suddenly realized he had nowhere to go. So much had developed since last night's raid that at no time did he think ahead to where he would be staying now. After a brief discussion with the others, it was agreed it would not be a good idea for him to stay with Nicodemus and Shira as her brothers would be home until the end of Shabbat.

Throughout the past week, Nicodemus noticed the boys were becoming increasingly opposed to the claims of Jesus being the messiah. Nicodemus felt it would be safer if Atara stayed with Joseph. Joseph, of course, was very hospitable, welcoming Atara wholeheartedly. Agreeing they would like to talk again, they decided it would be best to wait until after Shabbat, tomorrow night, when Nicodemus' boys had left for their yeshiva.

The short walk back to the house of Joseph was a quiet one. For Atara, the weight of the day's events was finally sinking in. The past 24 hours seemed like a lifetime of experiences condensed into a tiny fraction of time, passing by in a split second. Yet, while they were at Golgotha sitting vigil with Jesus on the cross, time stood still.

It took only minutes to reach Joseph's home. When they arrived Joseph directed Chaim and Samuel to let the other staff know of their arrival, then attend to food and rest for themselves.

The earthquake that struck in the afternoon had terrified everybody in the house. That initial panic still lingered. The darkness and shaking earth traumatized the whole of Jerusalem. Afterward, the staff carefully checked the house for damage. Joseph listened as they reported the details and that the beautiful ceramic pottery Atara had seen on display in the sitting room were all broken, but that was the extent of the damage.

Dinner was already prepared for them, so they moved directly into the dining area. Normally Joseph would relish good, vibrant company at the table, with wonderful and challenging conversations, but tonight was a time for quiet reflection. When the food arrived, Atara realized he had not eaten for two days. The dinner was magnificent – broiled chicken with vegetables and herbs. But even now he was not hungry. Joseph offered the Shabbat blessings and the two men sat quietly, grieving, both picking at their plates every so often.

Joseph finally broke the silence. "We have much to talk about, my young friend. However, I believe we are both exhausted, both physically and emotionally, after the events that have unfolded today. I do not know why God has chosen you and I, Atara, but I do believe He has a purpose which is yet to be revealed. I wish to thank you for your faithfulness and the strength you have shown this day, while all others have disappeared into hiding. May God richly bless you and prepare you for what lies ahead. Now, my friend, we should retire for the night and refresh."

Atara was speechless. He saw himself as a dropped-out yeshiva student, a failed Zealot, a prisoner and a coward. He had been confused, uncertain of life, full of hatred. But since meeting Shira, and hearing the words of Jesus, so much had changed. Although he did not fully grasp everything that had occurred these past days, the spirit within him testified Joseph was correct, that God did have a plan for him. Atara nodded with gratitude, then both retired for the night.

Great detail could be given about the mansion of Joseph. The walk through the halls, with all their antiquity and art, or about the beautiful room he was given to sleep in. But the truth is that Atara saw very little, only the sight of a large, soft bed, something he had not slept on in over three years.

When he awoke the sun had reached high into the sky.

Chapter 31

It did not go so well in the home of Nicodemus.

Judah and Avi had returned home, as expected. Both brothers were furious that Shira and Nicodemus were mixed up with this radical – this blasphemer! From the minute they walked through the door, the arguments and accusations began.

"Do you have any idea," shouted Judah, with the appropriate hand gestures, "of what is being said around the yeshiva and Temple? You are a supporter of this Jesus? He is DEAD! What kind of messiah was that!"

Avi added, with as much emphasis, but perhaps with a little less anger, "At the yeshiva they are saying you are a follower of this false messiah and that all of his disciples should be put to death as well! They are accusing us!"

"I am sorry that you have been subjected to so much anger, and that you feel this way," replied Nicodemus. "I do not wish to put any of you in danger!"

"Well, you have," retorted Judah. "We knew that you had been listening to him, that you had sympathies, but to believe he is the messiah! Is it not proof enough now that he was hung on a cross?"

"No!" interjected Shira forcefully. "It's not finished yet! Did you not see or hear what happened today? The sky, the earthquake, all at the time of his death!"

"Coincidence," the brothers both agreed.

"But you weren't there! You didn't witness it! Jesus IS the messiah. He WILL be coming back! I'm sure of it!"

"If you think he can break out of that tomb like he said he would, you can think again," Judah snarled in a tone that surprised everyone. "Caiaphas has heard of the disciples' plans to steal the body, so he has had Pilate inspect the tomb and seal it with the imperial seal, posting guards to make sure! Let's see how your messiah deals with that! And, speaking of the tomb, when did Joseph of Arimathea get involved in this? Apparently that was a surprise to everyone on the Sanhedrin! And to give up his personal grave?"

"We should be ashamed of ourselves!" Shira scolded furiously. "We, the people of God, the ones who represent a powerful and loving God, we KILL all those

He sends us. Are we so bound up in our Laws we've forgotten how to love, or who God truly is? I think we love only ourselves in our pride and righteousness! God sent Jesus to us, we mocked him, brutally beat him and crucified him. We're all guilty of this injustice!"

"There is no injustice here! They gave him a trial and found him guilty!"

"Not a trial, a disgrace! You were not there to see how unjust it was!"

"How could you do this to us! Avi and I are top yeshiva students with a promising future! Now we are to be associated with a family that believes in false prophets, one who would, by his own admission, tear down the Temple of God! How could you!"

At this point Nicodemus stepped between them. Tempers flared, brothers and sister facing off against one another. With the little respect the brothers had left for their father, the argument did cease when Nicodemus raised his hand.

"Children," he spoke firmly, but softly. "It is clear we have different opinions and experiences on this matter. Let us forgive each other for harsh words spoken." He looked directly at each of his children, then continued. "Shira and I will take some food, then we will retire for rest. We can discuss this further in the morning."

Storming off together the boys glanced backward in contempt as they left the room.

Nicodemus looked at Shira after they were out of sight. "They do not yet understand, Shira. We will have to be patient with them and love them."

There would be no family Shabbat dinner this night. The two of them went into the kitchen where there was food waiting, but neither could eat much. Saying goodnight to each other, Shira came to her father, wrapping her arms around him, weeping. What they had shared this day was completely beyond belief or explanation. Shira mourned for the messiah she had grown to love.

The images of the day played over and over in her mind until, after two days with no sleep, Shira finally drifted off into a restless slumber, no tears left. The night passed and it was well into the morning before she awoke.

Chapter 32

SATURDAY EVENING: NISSAN 17 / APRIL 12TH

Atara was so exhausted, he did not rise until almost noon. He could not remember the last time he had been so comfortable in his sleep on the large bed in Joseph's home. But his spirit grieved. He could not understand how, in one brief week, he had come so close to Jesus. Even now, after his death, Atara strangely felt the presence of the messiah more. Still, he could not help mourning.

Watching any man suffer such a cruel death would leave deep scars, but to believe he was the Son of God, an innocent brought to the slaughter, cut even deeper. Then to be the only ones left behind to care for the body as all others hid in fear. Atara still felt the pain of washing the wounds of this man he had never met.

His thoughts went to Benjamin and Simeon. *"Today you will be with me in paradise,"* Jesus had declared to Benjamin. This gave Atara great peace as Benjamin was his only close friend. But how was this conceivable?

After dressing, Atara went looking for Joseph, eventually finding him in prayer in his study. Not wishing to disturb him, he quietly retreated. Atara then searched the house, finding a quiet place to sit in the room where he had first met with Joseph only a mere three days ago. He began to ruminate on all the incredible events that had related to the scriptures over the past few days. As he put the scriptures together, arranging the events with them, a sense of excitement boosted his spirit, providing him great peace and joy.

For Shira, the day brought great challenges as the two brothers continued to forcefully express their disdain for her and their father's belief. At one point they clearly warned Nicodemus they had heard there would be persecutions and trials ahead for any of the followers of the Nazarene. They told Nicodemus he should not say any more publicly on the matter, for his own good, and the good of the family. Apparently, Caiaphas was already setting up a force to hunt these radicals down, putting an end to this talk of the messiah or of any threats to the Temple.

Shira would not quarrel with them any further. She was mourning. It was simply too much for her to engage with them. However, it was what she overheard at one point that really captured her attention.

She had gone down to pray in her private place in the garden, the secret place hidden out of view where she and Atara had met, when she overheard her brothers talking by the pond. They were arguing about the events of yesterday, about what they had discovered. Avi was convinced something beyond the norm had occurred and was worried they were trying to overlook the obvious. The earthquake, the sky, the Temple curtain.

'The Temple curtain?' Shira thought, as she strained her ears to hear more.

"It was nothing," insisted Judah, impatient with Avi. "Just a coincidence that happened because of the earthquake. It is all quite explainable to a rational mind."

"But how would it be feasible for the Temple curtain to rip from top to bottom? There was no other damage to the Temple. The curtain is as thick as a man's hand! How could it possibly rip right in two on its own?"

"It had to be the earthquake. No man would be able to tear the curtain from top to bottom, right in two," Judah retorted. He was obviously not pleased with the challenge Avi posed, so he swung around and left, Avi following close behind.

Shira thought about it for a while, then left the garden to find her father, to let him know what the boys had said. On receiving the news, Nicodemus sent one of his servants to call on some friends in the Sanhedrin, to find further information on what had taken place in the Temple yesterday.

Atara and Joseph's afternoon had been very quiet, a time for each of them for personal reflection. As evening approached with the setting sun, Shabbat was over and it was time to walk to the home of Nicodemus, as they had arranged.

On their walk, there were still many people on the streets milling about until the Roman curfew came into effect, while the gossip on the street was clearly still about the extraordinary events of yesterday, and the Nazarene.

When Joseph and Atara arrived at the house, they found Nicodemus and Shira waiting for them in the front room with refreshments. After greeting one another they settled into the cushions with their wine and Passover matzo bread. Everyone was hesitant to speak at first, for no one knew exactly what to say, the events of the previous day were so inconceivable that any discussion seemed impossible.

Joseph finally opened the conversations by wisely asking Nicodemus how his sons were dealing with this. He knew since Nicodemus's initial meeting with Jesus the boys had not been very accepting of Jesus, or their father's willingness to speak with him. Joseph was concerned for Nicodemus. He also was aware that the yeshiva the boys were attending was openly opposed to Jesus' words.

"Not well, Joseph. In fact, most of last night and today was filled with arguments, self-concern, even veiled threats. We must pray their eyes will be opened to the truth very soon as my heart grieves for them."

"Father, tell Joseph what I overheard the boys saying."

"Ah, that," replied Nicodemus, pausing for a moment. "Have you heard news of what happened in the Temple yesterday?"

Both men shook their heads with Joseph adding, "It has been a very quiet day for Atara and I. We have heard no news from outside."

"Shira overheard the boys talking about the Temple curtain, before the Holy of Holies. They were saying it had been torn in two. She overheard them quarreling with each other how that would be possible."

Joseph and Atara were completely astonished. They were both well aware of the significance of the Temple curtain. They leaned forward to engage in discussion, but before they could ask any questions, Nicodemus held up his hand, requesting they listen.

"There is more. Not only did it tear in two, but the reports were it tore from top to bottom. When Shira brought this news to me, I immediately sent one of my faithful servants to ask of some in the Sanhedrin, ones I would still consider my friends. My servant returned only a short time ago, confirming the news, with additional information. At exactly 3 p.m. yesterday, when the earth shook, the massive curtain was ripped in two from top to bottom. There were priests in front of the altar, making the last sacrifice of the day at that exact time. From their position while preparing the sacrifice, they would easily be able to see the curtain through to the Holy Place. When the earthquake hit, there was a deafening sound of the thick curtain tearing. As soon as the priests saw it begin to tear they wisely looked away and fled, leaving the sacrifice behind. To look into the Holy of Holies, the presence of God on earth, would mean immediate death if you harbor sin, which all men do."

"The curtain that separates God from man, or rather from the sin of man, ripped open at the exact moment the final sacrifice of the day was being performed?" At this point Atara could not contain his excitement any longer. "When the last sacrifice before Shabbat, the last sacrifice of the Passover day, was being offered? The last sacrifice of this day is for the common sins of all people! This year, the day also falls on Passover, which signifies redemption, freedom! Then yesterday the curtain is torn in two, from top to bottom! Only God would be able to rip it from top to bottom! No human hand or earthquake could execute that!"

A small smile came across Nicodemus' face. It was the first time Atara had seen a look of contentment on him. "Yes, no human hand. I've been thinking on this since the news was confirmed. You are certainly correct. This Temple sacrifice did represent the forgiveness of sins and redemption. It occurred at the exact moment yesterday when Jesus breathed his last breath saying, 'It is finished.' Jesus became the final sacrifice!"

"My dream!" Atara exclaimed as he suddenly recalled it. "I didn't understand what it meant at the time, but now I can see. In my dream, after the lamb leapt onto the altar, it was sacrificed, then suddenly the curtain disappeared. It was either opened or removed. It was the final act. The curtain represents the separation between God and mankind. If the curtain was removed, then we would have access to God as we once did at the time of creation. But the curtain is there as a protection for us. We can't look at or approach God because of our sin, as we have been separated from Him. He is holy and pure.

"If this is the final sacrifice of the lamb, and he took all our sins on himself in death, then the curtain can now be opened. Jesus has provided a way for us to walk with God once again! We only have to believe in him. Perhaps when he died yesterday, the Holy Spirit of God, or perhaps even Jesus himself, ripped through the Temple curtain, opening the way! In my dream, after the curtain, the veil between us and God disappeared, I saw the lamb curled up with the lion! I see now that Jesus was fulfilling all messianic prophesies of the sacrificial, redeeming lamb, and the mighty king at the same time!"

"But we have the Temple sacrifices now for our forgiveness, our Law for righteousness," Joseph replied, posed more as a question while thinking this through. "Why not just keep those ordinances and traditions while having a messiah to rule?"

"That is what Jesus has been trying to tell us all along! It hasn't worked! Shira pointed that out to me. You've heard him yourself this past week. He has told us the Law has hardened our hearts, that the sacrifices we make have become a hollow ritual. We continue to sin, but act like we are pure. We've killed every prophet God has sent us with a message to turn our hearts to him. We have refused to listen. All this means that God has sent His son, to us, to die as the final sacrifice, so we can be forgiven for our sins once and for all time. He has made the most incredible act of love possible. He has sacrificed His only Son!

Shira sat with her mouth wide open. Nicodemus and Joseph both leaned back into their cushions, thinking.

"I believe you are correct, my young friend," said Joseph. "Jesus did indeed willingly die yesterday as a sacrifice for our sins. As we saw, all the Temple ordinances were fulfilled, against incredible odds. His death came at the exact time of the final sacrifice during the Passover. He is the Lamb of God, born in Bethlehem and sacrificed on Mount Moriah."

"Not to mention," added Nicodemus, "that also against all odds he has fulfilled all the prophesies we have been able to find concerning the messiah."

"It's about love!" interjected Shira, daring to interrupt the conversation of the men, but she could not contain her emotions any longer. "It's about love. We have lost our love for God. We love the Law, our rituals, but we have turned our backs on really loving God. Jesus repeatedly quoted the Sh'ma, '*Love the Lord your God with all your heart,*' then added, '*Love your neighbor as yourself*'. God has heard our prayers. He has sent His son to show us love, the true love of sacrifice, the love of a Father. I have sat all day wondering how God could possibly have stood by yesterday, watching His own son endure so much suffering at the hands of men. I realize now that's the point! God loves us so much, He sent His son, who He loves, as a sacrifice to die for our sins! Father, do you recall the first time Jesus visited our house? He said, '*The Son of Man must be lifted up, that everyone who believes might have eternal life in Him!*' He was telling us he would be sacrificed on a cross and that all we have to do is believe in him for eternal life!"

Nicodemus was pleased as he listened to his daughter speak these words. He only wished the boys could hear this and open their hearts.

"Benjamin!" blurted out Atara as Shira finished. "That is what he said to Benjamin yesterday as he hung on the cross beside him! When Benjamin stood up to Simeon, Jesus said to him, '*Today you will be with me in paradise.*' Benjamin had been listening to Jesus before and was sympathetic. He must've realized Jesus is the messiah. Jesus was forgiving him, offering him eternal life!"

All four sat for a few moments, digesting the significance of all that had been said. If all this was true, as they believed it to be, then the world would never be the same from this point.

They spent time examining the prophesies more, bringing the Torah out to confirm them with what they had witnessed. As the evening continued they debated the accuracy of what they had just discussed, to be certain it was correct. At one point in the conversations, the subject of the disciples came up.

"I don't understand," questioned Shira, "why all the disciples ran away yesterday. We even witnessed the one called Peter (I learned his name from the women) deny Jesus and run out of the courtyard!"

"I understand all too well," admitted Atara. "That very night I ran from the Romans, not remaining to help my friends in need. I should've stayed to fight. It would've been a noble gesture, but in the end I probably would've ended up beside Simeon and Benjamin. Not one Zealot came out to be with them yesterday as they were crucified. Their bodies might even still be hanging there. I have been feeling a lot of guilt over this, but it seems that isn't what God has planned for me right now. It must have been very confusing for the disciples to see Jesus arrested. They probably expected a messiah that would come conquering as a king. I know I did."

"But they knew Jesus so well. They had been with him for the past several years. Surely they could have stayed by him?" said Shira.

"Think of this. How much harder would it be if you had known Jesus personally for the past three years? Every day, day after day, meals, travels, bathings, every detail of his life."

Atara paused for a moment. "I have a confession. Yesterday when we were cleansing the body it all seemed so, well, earthly. Jesus was a man, just as I am, not a celestial being radiating light or floating in the air supernaturally. It was just a man's body, frail, bruised and broken. While I was applying the aloe, I thought, 'How is this possible? How could this physical being be the Son of God?'

But you see, that's exactly the point. Jesus came just as us, in human form. How much harder would it be if you had been with him for the past years, to change your view of him from an earthly messiah to the Son of God? I believe they need time to think and pray this through. God has a plan. Just as I'm alive to testify today, the disciples are alive now to spread the word."

This seemed to satisfy Shira. They all talked about the humanness of Jesus, trying to understand how he could be divine at the same time. In the end they all admitted it was very difficult to understand, at this time, but believed they would know more in the days to come.

Joseph brought up a new point he had been thinking about. "Something I realized today was the significance of the day Jesus died."

The others looked at him.

"We have talked about how providential it was that Jesus was crucified on Passover, the day of redemption, freedom from slavery. That the sacrifice of the lamb and the blood on the doorpost was a foreshadowing of the sacrifice the messiah would make. But there is more mystery hidden here."

"What is it?" asked Atara.

"It was not just by chance Passover fell on a Friday this particular year. Friday is the sixth day of the week. And what does that represent in the Torah? The day of man, the day God created man. On that day God gave man life. But mankind fell into sin and was separated from God. On this past sixth day (Friday), God has offered eternal life, redemption for us to return and be with Him. Not only was he sacrificed on Passover, but also the sixth day, the day of man."

Once again they had more to think about and process. It was all so overwhelming. However, there was one topic that had not yet been discussed.

Until now, they had avoided talking about what would happen next. They were all aware Jesus had talked about being raised up. Was this to be raised from the dead? Spiritually, physically or metaphorically? When and how? They knew Jesus had referred to "three days" at various times, but no one seemed to be willing to speculate on this. Perhaps because of a lack of faith, or uncertainty, on their part. But they all embraced hope.

They did all agree though, that Nicodemus offered the most plausible explanation for the moment. "There must be a resurrection. If Jesus sacrificially died to take on himself the sins of all men who accept him, then he will now be bearing the burden of our sins. He is the Son of God. God cannot be with sin. So either Jesus will be separated from God forever, which does not seem likely as he has said, '*I and the Father are one,*' or he will rise again, defeating death itself, leaving those sins where they belong, in the pit of hell!

"I believe that is what he was telling me two years ago when we first met, when he said to me then, '*You must be born again.*' He will be defeating death itself once and for all. If we believe in him, we too will defeat death. Not death here on earth, but the death that separates us from God, from eternity. From this death to our sins, we will be born again. Like your young friend Benjamin, our sins will be taken on Jesus and we can stand before the Throne of God in forgiveness!"

The room was silent for a while as each one tried to understand what Nicodemus had just said. 'He truly is a wise man,' thought Atara.

"Father, do you believe he will rise from the grave tomorrow?" asked Shira.

"We shall see soon enough."

The evening had long ago turned into night and it was now very late. Soft cushions beckoned to each, reminding them of their weariness. Discussion became more practical, to the particulars of tomorrow.

Atara and Shira were anxious to visit the tomb in the morning to see if the women needed any assistance, and what might happen. Joseph reminded them he would be sending his servants Chaim and Samuel to help with the stone, provided the Romans would allow entry. Shira pressed Nicodemus to take her with him as well to the tomb. However, both Joseph and Nicodemus said they were feeling their age, so in the end Nicodemus agreed to let Shira go, with of course a stern warning to Atara to watch over her.

The final subject of the night was of the dangers that lay ahead. Nicodemus shared the news Caiaphas has not been satisfied just with the death of Jesus. He had placed the soldiers at the tomb, sealing it and standing guard. It might not even be possible in the morning to complete the burial. Also, according to his sons, Caiaphas was planning to find, prosecute and imprison any believers left in Jerusalem.

Atara assured him he was not known by any members of the Sanhedrin and although the Romans were looking for him, as long as he was with one of them, the Romans would not likely take any action. However, Atara was concerned about Joseph and Nicodemus, who were both now known to be followers of Jesus.

Joseph felt it would be some time yet, because of his wealth and position, before the Sanhedrin would dare to turn on him or Nicodemus. But persecution would come in the near future.

Nicodemus added this had caused much division in his own family, so much so that the two boys might even turn him in if they do not have a change of heart. In the end, both men agreed they would begin preparations to move out of Jerusalem if it became necessary, Joseph to his large estate in Arimathea, nearer to the coast, Nicodemus and Shira to the coastal town of Jaffa on the Mediterranean Sea. Atara indicated he would like to find the disciples to learn more.

With nighttime again on them, they decided Atara could stay the night in a guest room, as he and Shira wanted to be at the tomb by sunrise. After saying a blessing over the small group, Joseph headed out the door to return home.

It was just a matter now of waiting until tomorrow, a day for which both Atara and Shira felt so much hope.

Chapter 33

SUNDAY MORNING: NISSAN 17 / APRIL 13TH

Atara was wakened by a sudden jolt. The earth shook violently from below, and for a few seconds the bed danced across the tiled floor as Atara held on.

When it was over, he jumped from his bed to see if anyone had been hurt or if there had been any damage. Shira and Nicodemus were also startled from their sleep, both running out from their rooms into the hall where all three met. The house was abuzz with activity as the servants immediately rushed into the main section of the house from their quarters.

Affirming no one was injured, Nicodemus sent the servants on a search throughout the house and grounds to check for damage. Shira went to the end of the hall, then pulling a drape back they saw it was barely light outside. Early morning twilight, the time when the sun was just rising in the Judean hills behind the Mount of Olives, but had not yet touched down in Jerusalem.

"Well," sighed a tired Nicodemus, "we are already up now. Once the staff have looked over the premises, I will have them prepare a breakfast for you two. I imagine you are both anxious to go to the tomb."

"I wonder if the earthquake had anything to do with Jesus?" Atara questioned. They all nodded, indicating they had the same thought. They hurriedly returned to their bedrooms to prepare for the day.

Their breakfast was a quiet one. It was just Atara and Shira. Nicodemus had returned to his room after his morning prayers. Both were deep in thought, wondering what this day would reveal when they arrived at the Garden Tomb. Neither really ate much. The sun was above the Mount of Olives now, spreading its warmth across the city this April morning.

Joseph was sending Chaim and Samuel to help roll back the stone, hoping the three men would be enough to move the great mass, and that the Romans would allow them to. When they arrived, Atara, Shira, Chaim and Samuel were ready to leave.

The streets were still quiet on this early morning of the first day of the week. They passed only a few men returning from their prayers on their way out to the garden. Even Jaffa Gate was very quiet where Roman soldiers standing guard had very few people to deal with. They traveled straight through the gate without questions asked, but Atara did notice the Roman sentries had taken a man aside who was entering Jerusalem. They were checking his identification.

It was only a short walk to Joseph's garden, one they had made just two days before when following Jesus to his crucifixion. Walking past the place of Golgotha, the bodies of Simeon and Benjamin still hung lifeless on their crosses, a reminder to all those passing not to defy Roman rule. Atara stopped for a moment, looking up at his friend, feeling the tears rising in his chest. Shira put her hand on his arm, letting him know she too felt his pain. The anger was boiling below the tears, but today would stay where it was. They turned and headed for the garden.

Arriving at the garden they entered through the iron gate, once again making their way down the center path to the pond, where they saw Mary Magdalene quietly sitting, looking out over the water, deep in thought. When she heard them approach, she looked up. At first Atara thought they had startled her, but as soon as she saw them she broke into a beaming smile, rushing toward them, almost dancing off the ground with joy. Taking them by their hands, she exclaimed,

"He is risen!"

Atara and Shira just stopped in their tracks and looked at each other, stunned, then bolted down the path toward the tomb to see for themselves. The two stood dumbfounded before the tomb where they had so carefully placed the body of Jesus on Friday. The massive stone had been rolled away! With hesitation, Atara inched forward toward the entrance and peered in. There was no body! The cold tomb was empty. Just the linens they had wrapped Him in remained.

Shira leaned in beside him and gasped, "He's gone! How is this possible?"

They stood outside, looking at each other, questions firing so rapidly that words were simply not there. Chaim and Samuel had caught up and were now staring into the opened, empty tomb with broad smiles on their faces, for both were believers.

Finally Atara said, "Chaim, both of you should return to tell Joseph and Nicodemus the news." Nodding, the two men left immediately, anxious to spread the news of the risen Messiah. "We should go talk with Mary," Atara continued. "Maybe she knows what happened."

As they turned, they saw her coming down the path to join them. She was euphoric, so anxious to tell her story that the words at first were tripping over each other. Atara took her by the arm, motioning for all three to sit on a nearby stone bench.

"Now," said Atara. "Tell us what happened this morning, from the beginning."

She began by taking a deep breath. "There were five of us. We had been staying in Bethany, so we needed to leave early for the long walk. We were nearing the garden entrance when the earthquake arrived at sunrise. We stumbled and dropped our burial packages as the earth moved beneath our feet, but we held onto each other tightly so no one fell or was hurt. When the earthquake finished, we started to pick up our bags again to continue.

"It was then we witnessed two Roman soldiers fleeing at full flight out of the garden, running away from the city! The penalty for desertion of post is death, so I am sure it will be a while before the Romans find out.

"We were afraid of what we might find that would frighten hardened soldiers like that, so we moved forward cautiously. When we arrived close enough to the tomb, we could see the large stone had been pushed aside! Being uncertain of what we would find, I said to the others that I would run to tell Peter and John, who are both staying at a home in the city not far from here. I wanted to tell them to come to the tomb right away to see what had happened.

"Peter and John were already awake after the earthquake and had finished morning prayers just as I arrived. When I told them what we had seen, they took off for the tomb before I could finish speaking. I couldn't keep up with them!

"When I finally arrived here, much after them, they had already seen inside the empty tomb for themselves. They both greeted me excitedly in the middle of the garden with 'He is risen!' The linens that you had placed Him in were lying there, with no body in them!

"Peter told me that just before I had arrived, the other women had left to return to Bethany to tell the other disciples and followers of Jesus the news. Peter said the women told him that when they approached the tomb, they were greeted by two angels. '*He is not here, He is risen!*'[52] the angels declared! They were instructed by the angles to go tell the disciples in Bethany. Before the women left the tomb, they told Peter and John that Jesus Himself appeared in the garden and spoke to them!"

Mary paused for a moment to gather her emotions, tears falling softly down her cheeks, before being able to continue.

---

[52] Luke 24:6

"Peter and John waited for me," she continued once she regained her composure. "And after they had shared what the other women had witnessed, they said they were ready to leave as well. They told me I should go with them, but I said that I wished to stay for a while.

"After Peter and John left, I began walking through the garden toward the tomb. I needed to see the tomb for myself, but I was nervous and frightened. I began to cry as I remembered Jesus after you laid Him out on this bench to prepare His body, the way He looked, so broken and bloodied.

"After waiting a few minutes, I finally gathered enough courage to peer into the tomb. When I entered there were the two angels in white, one sitting at the place where His head had rested and the other at His feet! One angel asked me why I was crying! I said it was because I didn't understand who had taken my Lord away, or where He was. At that point I was weeping so hard and afraid that I backed away from the tomb in tears. As I turned away I saw a man standing on this path.

"He said to me, '*Woman, why are you crying? Who is it you are looking for?*[53]

"I thought he was the gardener through my tears and I answered saying, 'Sir, if you have carried him away, tell me where you have put Him, and I will get Him!'[54]

"The gardener said, '*Mary!*'

"Then I knew it was Jesus! I ran to Him, but He would not let me hold Him saying, '*Do not hold onto me, for I have not yet ascended to the Father. Go instead to my brothers and tell them, "I am ascending to my Father and your Father, to my God and your God."*'[55]

She began weeping uncontrollably. Shira held her, both now shedding tears of joy and happiness, fusing into one.

Atara was so stunned, he just sat in silence, trying to comprehend the miraculous events that had just occurred.

They all sat for a while, surrounded with vivid purple bougainvillea vines that clung tightly to the high garden wall. Pink oleander bushes lined the path with colorful flower beds, full of white lilies in bloom and sweet-scented rose bushes. The Garden Tomb had come to life with the arrival of the warm sun this April morning. Birds filled the trees and bushes with their songs, squirrels scurried around, gathering up the almonds that had fallen from the trees. Life was returning to this place of death.

---

[53] John 20:15
[54] John 20:15
[55] John 20:17

Everything they had been feeling was now turning to pure joy at the realization that Jesus had risen. Tears turned to laughter with the knowledge Jesus was indeed the Messiah. That He was alive! 'Nicodemus was right,' thought Atara. 'Jesus has defeated death and sin!' This was a new era for mankind, where sins can be forgiven because of the unimaginable gift God has given! His own Son, who they witnessed dying on the cross, was alive!

The three talked excitedly. They listened while Mary told them of her past. How Jesus had accepted her so lovingly with all of her sins, when no one else would, and of her great love for Him.

Shira teared up, never hearing anything like this before. Living such a protected, perfect life, she had never really met someone like Mary, a troubled woman who had been scorned and abused by most. Shira felt the shame of her past thoughts. She embraced Mary one more time and simply said to her, "I'm so sorry." Mary understood.

Mary knew she needed to return to Bethany to be with the others. Before she left Atara mentioned he would really like to find the disciples to learn more.

"I can tell you where Peter and John are staying. Perhaps the others will be coming back to Jerusalem when they hear the news." She gave the directions to a home in the north end of Jerusalem, near the market, where the disciples could be found.

It was well into the morning when they parted company. Atara and Shira sat back down close together. They were not ready to leave this beautiful garden that had become so full of miracle and hope. As they sat on the same bench Jesus had been laid on, the two sat in silence until almost noon, reflecting on the events of the past three days.

"It's all about the garden," Atara finally said quietly.

"What"

"The garden. It's all about the garden. That's the mystery of it!"

Shira just looked at him blankly.

"It's about Genesis, about coming back to the Father."

She still wasn't understanding. He continued. "We know from our studies of the Torah that in Genesis on the first day of creation, the first day of the week, God created the earth and heavens, but the earth was in darkness. Then God said, 'Let there be light.' But it was not until the fourth day that God created the sun and the moon. We have always assumed the light of the first day was the Messiah. Here we sit now, on the first day of the week, *yom rishon*, when the Messiah has risen. He died on the sixth day, the day man was created, then He rose on the first day at sunrise, the same day God gave the earth light over the darkness. Don't you see? He came to give light over darkness to mankind! Jesus often referred to Himself as the Light. We didn't understand what He meant then, but I believe it's clear now. He is the light of the world! Where there is light there is no darkness!"

"And all things have come together on these past few days!" responded Shira, now beginning to understand where Atara was going with this.

"Again, it's all about the garden in creation. Why did God create us?"

"To walk and commune with Him. For us to walk with God in the garden, to be with God. We could because there was no sin."

"Exactly, that's what the heart of God yearns for. Yet mankind was disobedient by choosing sin, the knowledge of good and *evil,* and had to be cast out, separated from God. Sin can't be in God's presence, so we were shut out of the garden, out of His presence. Two armed cherubim were posted at the entrance to the garden to prevent the return of any man with sin from approaching the Tree of Life. Over the millennia God has tried so hard to bring us back. He has sent us the prophets and kings, given us His Word, the Torah, sent the flood to begin again, yet we still fail to live without sin. When the Temple curtain was torn in two on Friday, do you know what was woven into it?"

"Two cherubim."

"When we talked last night, we realized the significance of the curtain being torn apart. The wall, or veil, that separated man from God was opened once again. The two huge cherubim woven into the curtain split apart, allowing man to enter God's presence, back to the garden, through the sacrifice of His Son! The *final* sacrifice for sin was made. Jesus took our sins to the depths, defeating death itself! We can now enter His presence approaching the Tree of Life, or eternal life, by accepting the gift of salvation God has provided for us. Jesus has paid the price! The veil and the cherubim have been removed. What did the women say was in the tomb today?"

"Two angels."

"Perhaps they were the two angels, or cherubim, that brought Him back to us!" Atara thought aloud. «We've been separated from walking with God in the Garden of Eden and Jesus was buried in a garden tomb. When He revealed Himself to Mary, he came as a ... ?"

"Gardener! She thought He was a gardener! God brought mankind into the Garden of Eden on the sixth day, and on the sixth day He was brought to a garden tomb!" exclaimed Shira, picking up on what Atara was saying. "The garden is a place of life, the tomb is a place of death. God brought us into this world in a garden of life. We brought God's Son into a garden tomb of death. But it's in this garden He has risen today, conquering death, leading us back to the garden of life, eternally to be with Him! It's about the great love God has for us and His desire to once again be united with us.

"None of these can be called coincidences anymore. God's plan here is incredible and perfect. I imagine we're only grasping at a fraction of the reality behind all of this."

It was now close to noon. Shira and Atara suddenly realized Nicodemus might be alarmed by the length of time they had been away. The full glory of the garden surrounded them in the bright sunlight. Neither wanted to leave. Atara looked at Shira. They had been through so much together the past few days. He admired her strength, her conviction. She had never wavered once in her belief in Jesus, and he would not be sitting here today if it had not been for her convictions.

Atara gently put his arm around her to draw her nearer. She came willingly as she leaned into his shoulder and closed her eyes. They sat for a time longer, neither wanting to move, for this garden had now become a place of life and joy. The tomb before them was empty and defeated.

Knowing they would have to leave soon, Atara looked down at Shira one last time. As she looked back up to him, for a fleeting moment their lips touched. It was only for the briefest of seconds, but to Atara it felt like time stood still. His heart was pounding. They both blushed as they looked shyly toward the ground, each knowing how they felt about the other.

The only thing Atara could think to say, very reluctantly, was, "Shira, I promised your father I would respect you. Please forgive me if I've taken advantage of that."

Shira simply nodded, avoiding his eyes in case she gave away her true feelings for him. "Father will be getting worried so we should leave now."

They rose from the stone bench to walk through Joseph's beautiful garden, hand in hand, eyes now finally open to the surrounding splendor. Shutting the gate behind them, the reality of Jerusalem confronted them as they looked up to the massive city wall running beside the bustling road.

Chapter 34

Off in the distance they could see Roman soldiers coming down the dusty road toward the garden. The hair on the back of Atara's neck stood up. "What if they saw us coming out? Do you think these are the replacement guards that are coming here?"

"The patrol is still far enough away," replied Shira. "I don't think that they have noticed us yet. Perhaps we should hide behind these bushes until they pass by to be sure."

To the side of the road, not too far from the entrance of the garden, thick oleander bushes had grown tall, covering the wall. Atara and Shira tucked themselves in behind, her arm in his, waiting. As the soldiers neared, peering out from between the branches, Atara's face suddenly blanched a ghostly white. Shira could feel his arm muscles tense tightly as his entire body went rigid while he stared ahead, pressing hard against the wall behind him, not breathing.

"Gallus!" he whispered in disbelief.

Instinctively, Shira knew something was seriously wrong. She held Atara's arm firmly as she began to feel him straining forward, ready to leap through the bushes, pulling him back.

It was a large patrol of 12 soldiers with Centurion Gallus at their head, looking as loathsome as Atara remembered. The patrol stopped at the garden gate, opened it and entered.

Atara just stared ahead, perspiration running down his face.

"What's wrong? Who was that?" Shira whispered, gently holding him.

After a moment Atara finally took a breath. "It's Gallus. The man who murdered my father and imprisoned me."

Shira gasped. She could feel the pain, fear and rage running through his veins as she wrapped her arms around him. "We need to move from here. Get away as far as we can!"

"No," responded Atara quietly. Then after a moment, "They might be coming back out as soon as they discover the tomb is empty. If Gallus sees me, he'll recognize me. We must stay well hidden until they're gone."

The warmth of Shira close by his side, her gentle cradling of his arm while firmly stroking his hand had brought him back to be with her. But so much pain was flashing through his mind as he saw the images of his father falling by the sword of Gallus, the icy darkness of the lonely cell. The face of Gallus that had haunted his many nights.

"Atara, I'm here with you. God has brought us this far, the Messiah has just risen! I'm sure God will protect us now."

"You're right. He is risen, that's what's important now. We'll wait until they come out to decide what we should do next."

Shouts and orders could be heard from inside Joseph's garden. It wasn't long before the patrol emerged, Gallus at the head, looking furious. Atara looked away as he clenched his teeth, trying desperately not to react, not making any sound that would cause the soldiers to discover them. But the patrol marched quickly past them back toward the Jaffa Gate, with no notice of the two hidden behind the oleander bush. In minutes the soldiers were out of sight.

"Pilate must have by now heard rumors of Jesus' resurrection, which is why he sent the soldiers. God must be really watching over us because that was a close call!"

They ignored the stares and critical glances of those on the road passing by, at two young lovers emerging from the bushes. They would not be bothered, as it would be clear to anyone passing that Shira was of a distinct class, just by the refinement of her clothing and the way in which she carried herself. They brushed themselves off and began walking back toward the city gate.

After a short distance, once again passing the crucifixion site, the entrance to Jaffa Gate came into view. As they neared the gate Atara stopped abruptly, pulling Shira to the roadside away from other travelers.

"They are checking people entering the city," Atara whispered. "Look, they just stopped another one to check their identification."

"You have yours, don't you?"

"Yes, but Uri said the Romans have my name as a wanted man for that insurrection a week ago. I don't know if he was speaking the truth, but there is a traitor in our midst, so none of us are sure what the Romans know. If I'm questioned by the sentries and they have my name, I'll be taken to jail, or worse. Also if Gallus has remained anywhere near the entrance, I'm sure he'd recognize me."

They watched the gate for a while, watching almost everyone being stopped by the sentries to be searched. "I'll stay with you until we can figure out what to do or until the searches stop!"

Atara would not agree. It was too dangerous for her. "You can go back through that gate with no problem. Your father is expecting you and we've been gone a long time. He'll no doubt be worrying about you. You must leave me. Anyway, I know of another way into the city for later tonight, and I'd like to find the disciples, if possible."

"I won't leave you!"

"You have to."

In the end Shira, being concerned her father would be worrying about her, agreed to return home alone.

She leaned over to give Atara a light kiss on the cheek. Turning, she then walked right up to the Jaffa Gate sentries as if she owned the entire city, passing right through with the sentries not daring to stop or question her.

Once on the inside, the false air of superiority left her as she glanced over her shoulder toward Atara, who was looking gravely concerned.

SUNDAY LATE EVENING: NISSAN 17 APRIL / 13TH

As Atara watched Shira disappear into the city from his position off in the distance by the roadside, he was overcome with a strange feeling, different from anything he had ever experienced. It was a yearning from deep within to be with her, to be near her, just being in her presence made his heart beat a little faster. But at the same time, with the one he cared about most vanishing into the city streets, and his most feared enemy close at hand, he still sensed the presence of God comforting him.

'Odd,' he thought, knowing he was a wanted man with nowhere to go, 'I should be extremely anxious and afraid right now. I should be full of hatred toward Gallus for what he's done, yet the peace of God has descended over me. I know He has brought me safe this far for a purpose.

'He is risen!' echoed in his mind over and over. 'He is risen!'

Unimaginable joy and awe overcame him as he thought about the incredible events of the morning. 'Risen from the grave. Risen from death! How amazing, how impossible!' He was there to bear witness with his own eyes.

Atara took one last look at the Jaffa Gate, then turning back in the direction of the Garden Tomb, began his journey. His trip would take him east, all the way around the outside of the city walls on the north side of Jerusalem to the Kidron Valley. He would then follow the valley down to the Gihon Spring, where he and Shira had sat talking almost a week ago after listening to Jesus on the Mount of Olives. Simeon had told him of another way into the city, but it was dangerous.

The Gihon Spring feeds into the long tunnel and was built in the time of King Hezekiah to bring water into Jerusalem. It ends up pouring fresh spring water into the Pool of Siloam at the lower end of the City of David.

Simeon told Atara that although the entrance to the tunnel through the spring is built over for protection, if you went under the water at the stone wall, within seconds the current would pull you through a narrow opening into the tunnel. You then simply follow the 1,500-or-so-foot tunnel to the Pool of Siloam. There were two obstacles though. The first was to get into the water undetected. There was a guard who lived at the spring who made his living collecting money from travelers and locals for fresh water. Atara would have to wait until dark, then quietly slip by him undetected. The second obstacle was at the other end where the iron gate positioned at the Pool of Siloam sealed off the tunnel. Simeon told Atara that the pins for the gate were badly rusted, but that the Zealots had filed off the ends so they could be easily removed. The gate was heavy, but one man would be able to manage it, if he was careful. He also told Atara if he ever had to use the tunnel, to be sure he replaced the gate and pins so his actions would be undetected. They needed the tunnel to be useful for others in the future.

For the third time that morning, Atara had to pass his friends Benjamin and Simeon still hanging on their crosses. The sun was hot now and the crows had landed on their perches. Atara shuddered, turning away when one of the crows went to work. His stomach turned and he felt slightly dizzy. Giving a silent prayer of thanks for his friend as he passed his body, his eyes averted, he left the scene. But as he proceeded past Joseph's garden, his spirit lifted as he couldn't help but smile thinking of Jesus' words to Benjamin: *'Truly I tell you, today you will be with me in paradise.'* Now He has risen!

Atara headed around the city in the direction of the Damascus Gate. Worried that because he was a single traveler on the road he might be stopped and questioned by Roman soldiers, he decided to catch up with a cluster of Passover pilgrims leaving Jerusalem for the north lands. He started conversing with them as they walked together to attach himself to the group for safety.

In the short walk around to the Damascus Gate, Atara had enthusiastically shared the incredible events of the morning at the Garden Tomb. He had given them sound reason why Jesus of Nazareth, who they had heard of as they had come from the north, was indeed the Messiah!

Arriving at the Damascus Gate, the pilgrims turned to head north. Atara wished them God's blessing as they parted ways, then continued onward.

During the day the area outside the Damascus Gate was filled with numerous daytime vendors who set up their stalls. Fresh fish, produce, wares, colorful fabrics and livestock all lined the roads around the gate. Atara was a little nervous pushing through the market crowds, being careful not to attract any attention from the numerous Roman sentries nearby. Once through the market he headed eastward, which would lead to the Kidron Valley if he followed the city wall. It took less than half an hour to reach the Kidron Valley from the Damascus Gate.

Standing at the same crossroads where he and Shira had stood last week, after following Jesus up the Mount of Olives to listen to Him speak, Atara needed to make a choice. To his right was the cobbled road that led to the Golden Gate, where the wall of Jerusalem towered high above, and behind that stood the Temple. Straight ahead was the path that led down to the Kidron Valley where the Gihon Spring would be found. It was too light out to get close to the spring now, so he decided to turn left on the road, climbing up the Mount of Olives into a position where he could observe the surroundings better. Just a few minutes up the slope, he pulled off to the right, walking through the thick olive groves that lined the mountainside.

Atara realized he had not had anything to drink since leaving Jerusalem in the early morning. With all that happened at the Garden Tomb, they had simply not thought of drinking from the water there. Atara knew he would be dehydrated soon if water was not found. Just as he was thinking this, he spotted an orange tree in the midst of all the olive trees with leftover fruit from the season. He picked a few, thanking God for such a blessing, then peeled the thick skins back to suck the sweet juice. Finding a secluded area on the mountainside, he sat on the grass with the vista of Jerusalem before him.

Atara now had the afternoon to pass before it would be safe to descend into the valley to the Gihon Spring. As he looked over the city, toward the Temple, he began to recall all the events of the past week. He thought of all the Temple ordinances of sacrifice that Jesus fulfilled, of the first time he saw Jesus when He was clearing out the Temple court of merchants, then the time Shira and he had followed Jesus and the disciples up this mountainside. He could hear in his mind all the words Jesus had spoken.

For a while his thoughts went to Shira, and how much he wanted to be with her at this moment. But mostly he thought about the past three days, the incredible events that had transpired. Over and over in his mind, he relived those moments to be sure they had truly occurred. They would be etched into his memory forever. He then realized that close to this very spot was where he saw the Temple guards arrest Jesus in the middle of the night, only three days ago! It all seemed so surreal. Eventually he lay back, then for a brief heartbeat closed his eyes. It was late in the afternoon before laborers returning home from working in the groves woke Atara as they passed nearby.

The sun was low on the horizon, radiating golden beams over the city. From this viewpoint on the Mount of Olives, Jerusalem at sunset was spectacular. Atara was so overwhelmed with emotion knowing that Jesus, the Messiah, had risen, that he began to pray and worship God.

This was something Atara had never experienced before. Not the recited prayers or songs of tradition, but something that was coming from within. The more he worshiped the God of all creation for the love He demonstrated, and the sacrifice He made, the more Atara felt he was standing in the presence of God Himself. It was extraordinary! Atara stood with his hands uplifted to the Holy One. His heart felt as if it would burst with joy and thanksgiving. 'What's happening?' he thought for a brief moment, but resisted the draw of the mind, surrendering his heart to God. He finally opened his eyes. Standing there on the Mount of Olives where Jesus Himself had prayed, the sun vanishing below the horizon and the sky above bathed in an amber glow like a warm blanket over the city of gold, he gave thanks.

As the sun disappeared, twilight washed over the mountainside. Atara thought he would wait a while longer, then head down to be nearer to the Gihon Spring before it was completely dark.

When he began the journey down, he was excited about hopefully meeting the disciples later that night. Atara had so many questions, so much to learn from them. However, he was also full of apprehension about the task ahead. He was not an experienced swimmer and the thought of diving into a deep hole, under the water, in the dark, left him chilled.

Descending the mountain, the closer he came to the spring, the more he began to worry if he could actually do it. When he reached the path that headed southward down into the Kidron Valley, he made the turn, then continued. It was beginning to get dark now, so he found a hiding spot behind some large rocks near the spring where the well was in view.

The man guarding the well had just filled some jugs for a customer and then sat down beside the well. It was evident this man lived here as he had a tent with his possessions nearby. Atara was hoping at some point he would retreat into the tent for the night. Passover was over now and there did not seem to be any other people around, which was in Atara's favor.

When darkness fully arrived Atara worked his way closer to the spring. When he was certain no one was looking, he ran across the last open space until he was crouched behind the low wall that had been built around the spring to create a pool. Every few moments he would peek over the top to see if the guard had moved. The fellow was sitting with a small candle nearby, making it easy to see him, but he had not risen from his seat. The night was dark, with no moon yet, and Atara thought he might even be able to slip over the wall into the pool unnoticed if the guard stayed in his chair. Fortunately, he didn't have to try.

At one point the man got up and entered his tent. Atara could hear some rustling around, sounding like the guard might be preparing food for himself. 'I might not have much time.' Atara stealthily slipped over the edge of the wall, sliding into the cold spring water without a sound. He could not be seen now that he was inside the pool unless someone approached close to the spring walls, looking down. But regardless, he knew he had to move quickly.

Atara made his way over to the far side of the spring, facing the great wall of Jerusalem. Chest deep, he felt the strong pull of the current tugging on his legs and feet underneath. When he stood facing the stone wall, he knew that under the water the spring flowed into the tunnel. But could he make it? The water was now forcefully pulling at his legs, straining to draw him into the abyss.

It was dark. Atara had no way of knowing what was on the other side, if indeed there was one. It was only what Simeon had described to him. He looked straight down into the black. Memories of the many days of darkness in his tiny cell flashed through his mind, releasing a flood of emotions. He wasn't sure he could do this. If the tunnel went too far before opening up, he might drown.

He stood there in the chill of the water hesitating, mesmerized by the swirling, black current. Then a cough! Suddenly Atara was alerted to the sound of the guard emerging from his tent.

No time to think! With one deep breath he dove down under the water. The current immediately grabbed him, sucking him in and tumbling him around into the darkness, pulling him forward.

Within a few seconds his head popped above the water, the current rapidly dragging him along a narrow corridor. In the absolute black of the tunnel, he floundered to find which way was up. Several times he tumbled over and over until he finally dug his heels into some uneven rock, enabling him to struggle to his feet, gravity guiding the way. The water here seemed only thigh deep. He found that once standing, the strong current was manageable. It was, however, pitch black.

Atara had never been in blackness like this before. Not in prison, nor in the Midras tunnels. Stretching his arms out he felt the cold walls on each side, realizing now the tunnel was very narrow. Reaching up he could not touch the tall ceiling above, so he had no idea of its height. He began to inch his way through the rapidly flowing water in the darkness, moving his feet slowly over the uneven floor beneath while using his hands against the walls to keep his balance. After a few moments he felt more at ease navigating the tunnel, so he slightly increased the pace.

Several times, when the ground dropped down, or a ledge protruded, he would trip and fall into the water. The current was strong when he was not standing. Each time he fell it would turn him over and over until he was able to right himself, then anchor his feet again. More than once he could feel the hard rock against an elbow or knee, knowing there would be some bruises to show for his mistakes. In some places the water was only knee deep, but moving fast. In others it was up to his waist, making it difficult to judge his footing.

Continuing to grope his way along the tunnel, time stood still. In this place void of light, all reference to reality had vanished. It was a world unto itself.

Atara stopped for a moment. He moved his head around, trying to see something, anything, but he could not. Only cold and dampness engulfed him, rushing water echoing off the stone walls in this extended tomb.

'I wonder what happened to Jesus after He died?' Atara thought. 'Nicodemus had suggested that to rid the world of sin and to break the bonds of death, Jesus would have to go to the pit of hell itself! How many times worse would that be than being here in this gloomy catacomb? What suffering did He face, even after death? What battle with Satan would've taken place? What pain did Jesus endure, taking all our sins on Himself?' Atara shuddered at the thought.

Deciding he needed to keep moving to not be overcome by the cold pressing in on him, he continued forward. There was still quite a distance to cover before he would finally emerge from the rock.

After stumbling and groping some more, he finally saw a hint of light up ahead. Of course, it was night out, so it was dark enough in itself, but the faint glow from the city lamps filtering through the air, reflecting off the walls, gave just enough light that Atara could make out the entrance of the tunnel ahead and the iron gate of his prison.

Atara stealthily moved through the water to the bars, looking through them into the Pool of Siloam where the water flowed more gently. He had to be certain no one would see him emerge. The pool was long and narrow, large steps lining the walls into it. The courtyard was surrounded by high walls that enclosed the entire area with only one entrance at the far end.

When Atara was certain there was no one present, he gripped the bars with both hands and attempted to lift the gate. He was testing to see how much play there was on the hinges and judge its weight. The gate was heavy for sure and very tight. Atara fumbled around to one side, looking to find the hinges. Sliding his hand down into the water, he found the lock that held the gate secure. He moved to the other side, reaching to the top. He could feel the upper hinge and the pin that secured it. Anxious to attempt pulling the pin out, Atara lifted the weight of the gate with one hand with all his strength, then reached up with the other to the hinge pin.

Suddenly, he felt strongly this was wrong. He eased off on the gate, then stood back to think. 'If I pull out the top pin first, I won't be able to steady the door in place while I remove the bottom pin.'

He moved back into position, but this time reached deep down underwater to the bottom pin. When he lifted the weight off the hinge, the pin pulled out easily. The gate was wobbly now, but it stayed upright. Atara knew the next step was critical. If he was not able to hold the gate after pulling the top pin out, it would swivel around uncontrollably to the lock side, making a thunderous clatter. For certain there would be soldiers nearby who would hear. He reached up to the top hinge, pushed up on the gate with all his strength, pulling the pin out.

The hinge gave way with the gate leaning heavily against his body. After palming the pin, he slowly inched forward, the gate pressing hard against him. It was pivoting precariously on the lock. When he was out he let the gate down for a moment, gathering his breath to look around. Thankfully, the pool was empty of people at this time of night. Seeing there was no cause for alarm, Atara moved around to the outside of the gate. Lifting as hard as he was able, he moved it back through the water to its position on the hinges. Replacing the pins he was now totally free of this unholy catacomb as he climbed out of the pool.

The cool night air caused him to shiver. In reality, it was a beautiful April evening, but emerging from the long, cold tunnel, soaking wet, he was chilled through to his bones. He had not thought this far ahead, so was not sure what to do next.

Finally he decided the dripping wet clothes would have to be removed, then wrung them out to remove as much water as possible. He could not travel through the city soaking wet, drawing attention to himself. His clothing was a light material, so it wrung out well. Once he had dressed, he made his way to the other end of the pool to the exit.

Moving cautiously along the wall, he approached the wide arched doorway, then froze at the voices. Peering around the corner he saw two sentries stationed at the entrance. 'Simeon never said it was guarded!' He felt trapped.

Fortunately, they were guarding the entrance to the pool. They were not expecting someone to be inside attempting to come out. He retreated back into the pool area, looking for another way. It was a blessing that the iron gate to the tunnel had made no noise or he would be in chains by now. Atara stopped for a moment, realizing it was no premonition that prevented him from unhinging that gate incorrectly. It was the quiet voice of God watching over him. He gave thanks to the Lord for His merciful protection and asked Him to reveal a path out of this place.

Then he saw it. An ancient bougainvillea vine that ran up the wall at the far end.

From the position the soldiers occupied, outside the pool courtyard on the far corner, he calculated they would not likely be able to see anyone drop down from the wall on the other side. But he couldn't be certain. He found a stone lying nearby, picked it up, then made the climb to the top of the wall using the vine. At the crest he paused, scanning ahead for any danger. Turning back, he threw the stone as far as he could to the other side of the pool, where it landed with a thud that echoed around all four walls. The two sentries came rushing into the pool area as Atara dropped to the ground on the other side, to the empty street below.

Atara estimated it was at least 9 p.m. by now. It had taken over two hours from the time he entered the water at the well to come this far. He was still obviously wet, but the adrenaline now pumping through his veins was keeping him warm. This was familiar territory. He thought the best approach was to use the rooftops as much as possible at this time of night. The only dangerous place to cross was the wide open street that led past the Hippodrome. When there, he had to wait a while until he was absolutely certain no one was about or watching before he crossed. Once past that obstacle, he was back on the rooftops heading to the north end of the city where he hoped to find the disciples.

Just before he headed across the market area, Atara paused for a moment, turning back as he felt drawn to look over Jerusalem from this high vantage point. The Temple to his left, Mount Zion on his right, and ahead of him the City of David descending Mount Moriah. It was spectacular as the full moon rose amber over the top of the Mount of Olives. Atara once again could hear the words of Jesus, *'Jerusalem Jerusalem, you who kill the prophets and stoned those sent to you, how often I have longed to gather your children together.'* Atara stood still for a moment longer, then quickly turned toward his destination, disappearing across the rooftops.

When Atara arrived in the crowded north area of the city, he finally stood opposite the door Mary Magdalene had carefully described to him earlier that day. Deciding it would be best to wait and watch for a while, he found a shadowed archway to slip into where he could observe the street. There was the occasional passerby at this late hour, but on the whole it seemed very quiet. After a diligent amount of time, being certain no one was watching, Atara crossed the lane to the door, then softly knocked.

There was no answer.

SUNDAY NIGHT: NISSAN 18 / APRIL 13TH

The heavy wooden door was exposed to the passing lane, offering no protection from prying eyes. This was an older, very crowded area in the north end of Jerusalem, similar in character to the Lower City.

Atara was concerned about making noise that would attract attention from the neighbors. For a few moments he waited, listening, without a response, so he wasn't sure what to do next. Knocking again might attract unwanted scrutiny from the overlooking windows. 'Is this the right home? What if I have made a mistake and the disciples are not here? Perhaps the disciples have left Jerusalem altogether, then what will I do?' All these thoughts raced through his mind, until he finally decided to try knocking one more time a little more forcefully while nervously looking around.

The door resounded with the deep thump of several hard knocks, harder than Atara had intended. He put his ear to the door to listen.

Trying unsuccessfully to keep his voice down to a whisper, he called out against the door, "Mary sent me."

In the quiet lane his voice cut through the peacefulness of the night air like a knife through water. Looking sharply around Atara feared he might have stirred the neighbors. There was a moment of silence until the door abruptly swung open a crack. A large, burly arm suddenly appeared, pulling Atara right off his feet into the small dwelling place, the door immediately slammed shut behind.

"You will wake the whole city like that!" the stocky, bearded man exclaimed.

Atara regained his balance, looking directly into the face of the man he had seen in the palace court on Thursday night. He quickly surveyed the room. Standing close around him were several men. Behind them he could see more men were sitting by a table. Atara could feel all eyes on him, scrutinizing him. He recognized one of the men standing close by as John, the man he had seen with the women on Friday. Realizing he was indeed in the right place, he relaxed and addressed the men.

"Mary gave me directions where to find you. My name is Atara."

This little bit of information made everyone in the room relax. The burly man still holding onto Atara released his grip, smothering him in a huge bear hug. This was not what Atara was expecting and he became a bit flustered for words.

"We've been expecting you," the burly man said as he held Atara by the shoulders, looking right at him. "He said you would be arriving!"

"Who said?" was all Atara could think to respond, rather confused by the whole scenario.

"Why, Jesus!" he answered with an enormous grin erupting across his entire face. "He just left! He has been here for most of the evening, talking and eating with us! He is risen!"

"He knew I, uh, how…?"

Seeing Atara stumble for words, the entire room broke into joyous laughter. The burly man bellowed a heartfelt laugh and put his arm around Atara's shoulder, leading him into the room.

"I am Peter," he said. "And these are His disciples. And you are … soaking wet? We will have to hear this story!" The men laughed all the more.

Atara smiled at everyone in the room as Peter began to introduce him to all that were present. He started with John, who was standing beside him. Atara turned to John saying, "I saw you at Golgotha with the women. I heard what He said to you. You were very brave and faithful to Jesus by being there."

"You as well, my young friend! It seems that you have been popping up everywhere the past few days!" replied John, placing his hands on Atara's shoulders with brotherly love.

Before Atara could respond Peter took him around the room to complete the introductions to all the others. Atara could not understand how they could all be so welcoming, so caring. They didn't even know him! When he stood before Simon, who he recognized as the Zealot he had spoken with on the Mount of Olives, the man stood, embracing Atara in a zealous hug.

After the introductions were over and Atara was seated at the table, he anxiously asked the question he had been waiting for the opportunity to ask. "He was here?"

It was John who spoke up. "We were just eating our dinner after the sun went down when He appeared. When I say appeared, that is what I mean! I am ashamed to admit that we have all been cowering in fear the past few days since the arrest, even bolting the doors after the others arrived from Bethany. Then He appeared! The door bolted! He was just suddenly in the room with us!

"Jesus embraced us all, showing us His hands and feet where the nails had pierced. We were so stunned, we didn't know whether to weep or dance with joy!

"For the next two hours, until just before you arrived, we talked with Him, listening to all He had to say. When we asked about the past three days, because we were too afraid to be with Him, He said that a young man named Atara would be arriving soon. That man could tell us everything! And here you are!

"He also revealed to us that He is sending us out as the Father had sent Him. Before He left He breathed on each one of us saying, 'Receive the Holy Spirit.' Then He was gone! Just as He had come! We all were filled with a new joy, a sense of hope and confidence that none of us have ever experienced!"

"Jesus appeared to me and one of the others earlier as well," interjected Simon. "We had already left Jerusalem to travel to Emmaus this morning, so we had not heard the news of Jesus' resurrection. On the way there Jesus met us on the road. It was odd because we didn't recognize Him at first, but after talking for a while it was like the veil was lifted from our eyes and it was Him! After He left us we ran the whole 7 miles back to Jerusalem as fast as we could to tell the others. When we arrived, He was here!"

Atara wanted to hear more. He wanted to know what Jesus had said to them and what it was like to be in His presence. But before he could ask the multitude of questions forming in his mind, Peter was already addressing him. "Now, Atara, Jesus told us you would be able to tell us what has happened these past few days while we have been hiding. And perhaps" (he added with some jest) "why you are so wet!"

Peter then moved Atara through the room of smiling men, awaiting anxiously to hear what he had to say, by the fireplace so he could dry out while speaking. Others brought him some food and drink, deducing by the looks of him that he had not eaten in a while.

Until well into the early hours of the next morning, Atara related the whole story as he had experienced it. He spoke of Shira, Nicodemus and Joseph, how they had met and his involvement with the Zealots.

At one point the mood was lightened a bit when he unintentionally hinted of his feelings for Shira while describing her courage and wisdom over the past week. Once the taunts and whistles died down (after all, they were Galileans), he was able to continue.

He shared the impressions he had on seeing Jesus for the first time on the Temple Mount, then the day after when he and Shira followed Him up the Mount of Olives.

However, it was when he recounted the events of Passover up until this time that he truly had the attention of all. There were times in his narration that many of the men were holding back tears as Atara described in detail the suffering Jesus experienced. He was sure many of the men were grappling with the guilt they felt at abandoning Him in His time of need. When he mentioned he saw Peter in the palace court that night, wanting to approach him, Peter's head bowed in humility.

"Not my finest hour," said Peter solemnly. "I am ashamed that I did not stand up to be counted with my Savior. At the Passover supper Jesus even warned me I would deny Him three times that very night. I should have been a witness, not a coward. Even worse, I tried to kill a Temple Guard when they came to arrest Him! Three years of listening to His teachings and I still didn't understand his message of loving even our enemies."

"You were brave enough to stay with Him until the courtyard! I saw that you risked your life to be there for Him. But God has other plans for you, Peter," encouraged Atara. "I'm a coward. I ran from helping my friends when they needed me that very same night. Two of them hung on the crosses on each side of Jesus the next morning! Perhaps I could've fought to save them when the Romans raided us. That's what I was trained to do. Until the night of the trials I thought I had murdered a Roman soldier I fought with. But in a way I was responsible as others came to do what I couldn't. I'll have to live with that as well, but I believe now God has a different purpose for me."

"And He is forgiving," added Peter quietly. "If there is one thing that I have learned from Jesus, it is about forgiveness. I have a tendency to act first and think later."

The other men all nodded, restraining their smirks.

"And it is a good thing your skills with the sword need some improvement!" chided Simon, the only trained fighter among them, as he slapped Peter on the back to lighten the room, causing an all-out roar of laughter among the men.

The accounting of the resurrection was brief as the disciples had heard the testimonies of the women earlier. Atara continued, sharing the thoughts of the past events he, Nicodemus, Joseph and Shira had discussed over the past few days. Thoughts concerning the fulfillment of prophesies and the compliance with the sacrificial ordinances of the Temple. The men all voiced their approval as he spoke, encouraging him.

One thing that was very clear through the whole dialogue was that Jesus, the Messiah, had risen from the dead. The talk always came back to that.

They unanimously accepted that they did not yet fully understand everything, but they knew Jesus would be unveiling more to them soon. When He breathed the Holy Spirit on them, the disciples acknowledged they felt as if their eyes had been opened and the truth could now be fully revealed.

Atara was not sure he understood. The past week had been all about facts, events and emotions. He knew what he knew to be true, he had seen with his own eyes. But where did that leave him with God? He still harbored much hatred and anger against the Romans. He did not feel clean, nor free of sin. Atara confessed this to the group.

"Before Jesus left tonight," offered John, "He anointed us with the power to forgive sins. Are you ready to have your sins forgiven?"

"Yes, I am now."

"Do you believe that Jesus is the Messiah, the Son of God?"

"Yes, I do believe! With all of my heart, I believe!"

The disciples gathered around Atara and placed their hands on him. John spoke. "Atara, do you ask Jesus, the Messiah, the Son of the living God to forgive you of all your sins?"

With his head bowed in prayer, Atara spoke to the Savior. "Yes, Lord, please forgive me and cleanse me of all my sins, my hatred of others and my pride. Please give me a new life in you!"

"Will you follow Him as a disciple?"

"Yes, I surrender my life to Jesus." And surrender he did. As Atara exhaled he felt the old life vanish. When he took a deep breath, it was as if the Spirit of God came over him, filling him with a new life.

At that moment a wave of peace came over him he had never before experienced. He felt forgiven, free of guilt, like a new creation. The burden of all his sins and past wrongs had been lifted off and removed. He was cleansed in the powerful and enduring love of God.

And then it hit him as he cried out, "Born again! This is what Jesus meant by 'You must be born again'!"

The room erupted into cheers and whoops as the 11 men embraced Atara, slapping him on the back, singing a joyous baritone song of thanksgiving. And to his own surprise and delight, Atara joined in. The men did not care if the whole of Jerusalem was awakened this night, their joy was so full. Jesus was alive and had returned to them from the grave in power and glory! Now they celebrated a new life, a new creation in Jesus, the Messiah!

He is risen!

Chapter 37

MONDAY: NISSAN 18 / APRIL 14TH

The sun had risen well into the sky by the time Atara eventually awoke. Most of the disciples had finished their morning prayers and were going about the business of preparing for the day.

James and Matthew were sitting off to the side still in prayer, Peter and Andrew were preparing food while John, Simon and the others were studying scriptures. Two of the men had already left the house to find needed supplies. Thomas, Atara was later told, had not made it back to Jerusalem the night before, but was on his way.

When Atara was finally awake, Peter and Andrew chided him for sleeping so late, but it was all done in a brotherly spirit. Atara stretched, painfully feeling the aftermath of sleeping on a stone floor. Trying to rub the sleep from his eyes, he rose and stumbled to the washbasin in the corner of the room to rid his face of sleep. His first thought was of bathing, but then remembered he had quite a long bath the night before in the tunnel. It seemed like such a distant memory already.

Once refreshed he looked after the small fire for cooking. Afterward he went over to Peter and Andrew to help with the food, noticing they seemed quite sad compared to the day before. Talking of last night, and asking how he felt today, Peter and Andrew then turned the conversation back to their original discussion of the news they had just received.

"Poor soul," said Peter sadly. "I don't know if we will ever understand what made him decide to betray Jesus."

Andrew answered, "It would be so easy to be angry with him. In fact, I confess that I had held onto hatred for Judas for what he did. But, now more than ever, I understand forgiveness is the way of God. I have forgiven Judas. Now that he has taken his own life, I can't imagine how much sorrow he must have felt when he realized the impact of what he had done. Do you think he believed it would result in His crucifixion?"

"We will never know," said Peter.

The talk went on to other topics, mostly related to the events of the past few days. Many times the disciples would refer to the words Jesus had spoken.

Atara would listen, intensely absorbing and trying to understand what they were saying. They had spent three years listening to Him teach. He had mere days, not even hours really. So much to learn.

Throughout the day that small house in the middle of north Jerusalem was the scene of many people coming and going. Believers in Jesus were coming to hear the news and listen to the disciples teach. 'Other believers!' Atara marveled. 'There are more!' When he questioned Peter about this, he was told there were many more out there, and that it was their calling to share the news of the Messiah with people. At one point the tiny house was so full that barely anyone could move while John was teaching. He was summarizing the resurrection of Jesus and what that would mean to each person in the room. Songs of worship arose spontaneously from time to time with people bowing in prayer after John spoke. They were asking for forgiveness of sins and accepting Jesus as their Lord and Messiah. Everyone who came into the room that day made that life-altering choice.

Cautions were being taken by those entering, but something had changed. The disciples were no longer bound by fear. As they spoke Atara was surprised at how clearly they were presenting the message of the risen Messiah.

It was late in the afternoon when he took a few moments to reflect on the day. Far too much had happened over this past week. The teachings today were a lot to grasp, even for a keen mind and memory such as his. Atara knew he should spend some time alone with his Lord to truly absorb all he had experienced. His mind then drifted to Shira. 'I miss her. I wish she was here to experience this with me. We've shared so much together this past week. If it wasn't for her courage and understanding, I'd still be full of hatred and anger, fighting alongside the Zealots. I need to go see her.' When the opportunity arose, Atara spoke with Peter and explained his feelings.

"Yes, then you must go to her now, to Nicodemus and Joseph as well, to share the news with them. We will be here for a few more days, God willing, and at that time we will return to the Galilee as Jesus has instructed us."

The Galilee! Atara was eager to see his brothers. To share the good news with them. "Would it be alright if I come with you?"

"Of course," replied Peter. "Now go see your friends. We will talk more when you return. Be cautious, but be bold in Him. May the Lord bless you and watch over you. Please give our blessings to Joseph and Nicodemus and your Shira. He is risen!"

Atara worked his way through the crowd inside to the door. When a quiet moment came, he narrowly opened the door to check, then when no one was looking in his direction, he slipped into the daylight. It was a bright, sunny day and it took a moment for Atara's eyes to adjust. Unlike the night before the little street was now very active with people coming and going about their daily business. He quickly scanned the street for any sign of someone watching, or anything out of place, as he now was not only on the run from the Romans, but from the Sanhedrin as well.

When Atara stepped into the busy street, he was instantly caught up in the flow of traffic heading southward. This would ultimately lead him to the Upper City, to the home of Nicodemus. Atara stayed far to the west side to avoid the Antonia Fortress with all its soldiers and activity. It was only ten days ago he had been with the Zealots in their failed attempt to attack the gates. He wondered where Barabbas was now? Where his fellow former compatriots were?

Being careful to avoid a few sentries, after a short distance Atara entered the busy market area. It was packed with shoppers hunting for their daily bargains, but the Passover crowds were gone now, making it easier for Atara to work his way through. Vendors hailed customers as they passed, making promises of the best merchandise. People paused to bargain, gesturing arms flailing away, expressing their skills of negotiation. The concept of a line was nonexistent as shoulders pushed together, vying for space. On one street the sounds and aromas affronted the senses. On another the amazing colors of silks and cottons dazzled the eyes. Atara slowly made his way through the labyrinth of streets, lanes and alleys, finally emerging at the south end of the market.

Here the streets widened as they approached the Jaffa Gate into the Upper City. Rather than pass Herod's Palace, Atara took a more circular route, very similar to the first day he had run from the Romans. As he left the main street past the Jaffa Gate, he turned down into smaller lanes. After two more turns, he was standing at the end of the alley that led to Shira's garden door.

Atara walked to the door and stopped. He had fully intended to pass by this door and enter by the front of the house. But he stood on the outside of this garden wall, remembering with fondness his first, not so gracious, encounter with her.

Impulsively, he pushed the vines aside to reach out and knock. To his great surprise he could hear a sliding bolt. The door opened ever so cautiously, just a crack, with a reddened pair of eyes peering out.

Chapter 38

"Atara!" Shira exclaimed as she flung the door open, immediately throwing her arms around his neck and burying her head in his chest.

It was obvious she was very upset. Her cheeks were crimson with the tears still running down. He embraced her for a few precious moments, pulling her closer and stroking her hair, then gently guided her back into the garden to close the gate for fear of being noticed. 'Much different,' he thought, 'than the first time when we both landed bottoms up with Shira glaring at me!' Even so, he sensed there was something seriously wrong.

"I'm so glad you're here!" Shira blurted out before anything else could be said. "Father is in the house with Caiaphas and members of the Sanhedrin! They're shouting and threatening him! Father sent me back here as soon as they arrived. I'm so worried about him! I'm afraid the guards will take him away!"

Atara's heart ached as he heard this. At that moment he realized how much he had come to love and respect Nicodemus. Atara took Shira to the stone bench they had sat on many times before and sat beside her with his arm around her in comfort.

"Shira, we need to pray. We need to ask the Lord to intervene and protect your father."

Pray? This was not something she had been taught to do on the impromptu. Prayers were always recited. They usually only invoked a blessing or thanks.' What was Atara suggesting?'

He could see the confusion in her eyes. "Jesus is alive. He will hear our prayers, petitioning them to the Father. I know He loves Nicodemus. He will hear us and answer our prayers."

'Who is this man? Is this the boy who tackled me a week ago, running in fear?' She looked up at him, completely lost for words, and simply nodded.

Then they prayed, the two of them on that stone bench pouring out their hearts to God, that He would spare Nicodemus. Atara first, but then as Shira saw his example, she shyly began. As she prayed, the Spirit of God moved her. For the first time in her life, she truly spoke with the Father. They prayed, back and forth, each of them petitioning the God of Creation, through the authority of His Son who sacrificed His life out of love, that Nicodemus would be safe from harm.

After they had been praying for a while, there was a moment of quiet where they both reflected. Atara said, "Shira, I have learned from the disciples that all we have to do is ask for forgiveness of our sins and they will be forgiven. If we believe in Jesus as the Son of God, the Messiah, and follow Him, we will be born again of spirit, not flesh. John said today…"

"John?" She looked at him, so many questions whirling behind her tired eyes.

"I'll explain later, but yes, the disciple John who we saw at the cross said, '*For God so loved the world that he gave his one and only Son, that whoever believes in him shall not perish but have eternal life. For God did not send his Son into the world to condemn the world, but to save the world through Him.*'[56] Do you see? This is what Jesus meant when He first spoke to your father saying, '*You must be born again.*'"

And Shira did see. It was as if she had believed all along in her heart Jesus was the Messiah. Even over the past few days she hadn't lost faith, but she also sensed there was still something inside, blocking the way.

"Would you pray with me, Shira? Ask God for forgiveness and proclaim your faith."

Shira's eyes lit up. She was so ready for this moment, she just had not known what to do. Atara led her through the prayer, just as John had done with him the night before, and Shira became born anew in spirit. When she looked up at Atara he thought her eyes would explode, they were so large and full of joy. She wrapped her arms around him in a quick embrace, flew to her feet and threw her arms into the air in worship.

Shira felt the warm embrace of a Savior envelop her, a Messiah, as she stood with her eyes closed, worshiping the God of Creation who loved her enough to die for her on that wretched cross. She reminisced of sitting on the ground only three days ago, wiping the blood from His beaten face. Now He had risen and overcome death!

Atara marveled at God's Spirit, the Holy Spirit, at work. After a while Shira sat back down and prayed with Atara, thanking God for all He had done. She knew her father was going to be safe.

But the questions! Shira could hardly get them out fast enough. They poured out in a jumbled mix about Atara's last 24 hours since they parted. "Where have

---

[56] John 3:16–17

you been? How did you get there? What was it like?" She had questions about Jesus. "Did you see Him? What did He say? What were the disciples like?"

Atara could only laugh as he put his hand up to intervene. "Let's do one question at a time!"

For the next hour he related his story from the time they had last seen each other. He started by telling her how difficult it was to watch her pass through that Roman checkpoint the day before by herself, he was so worried about her safety. Then, how many times he thought of her throughout the day, wishing she was with him.

From there it was the story as it unfolded, with many questions and interruptions, of course, as Shira listened intently to what he had been through. Her palms grew sweaty when Atara described the anxiety of peering into the dark underwater entrance to the tunnel. She was especially excited when he shared of his first meeting with the disciples and that Jesus had been there just before he arrived!

He even mentioned the taunts and whistles from the men, to which she turned a beautiful shade of red. What they really talked about most, though, was what Atara had learned from the disciples about Jesus.

The sun was very low now and the couple could feel its warmth diminish as its light vanished behind city walls. They sat for a moment, hand in hand, quietly reflecting as the subject had evolved into what the future might hold. Neither could imagine what would be next.

Suddenly, Atara became aware of a presence. He swung his head around to find Nicodemus standing by the vines, quietly watching.

"Rabbi!" exclaimed Atara, startled. "We didn't see you!"

He stood to greet Nicodemus, but before Atara was able to say any more, Shira flew off the bench, embracing Nicodemus with all the love of a daughter. "Father, you're here! They haven't taken you away!"

"No, my child. It was very peculiar, though. A while ago the threats had risen to a climax as they were building a case for me to be tried in court. I had almost conceded to the fact that I was to be taken away. It was then that Caiaphas and his cronies simply just ran out of threats and left, leaving me with only a stern warning!"

Shira and Atara looked at each other and smiled. God had answered their prayers!

Her arms were still wrapped around Nicodemus as he placed his hand gently to her cheek saying, "I am sorry I did not come down earlier to find you, but

I was so shaken that I needed to sit and pray for a while after they left, to give thanks to our Lord and Savior for His mercy and salvation."

Shira hugged Nicodemus again to show her father it did not matter, then moved away to stand beside Atara. In a change of demeanor, Nicodemus looked at the two of them, as a father would, with one eyebrow raised slightly at the scene before him. "And what has happened here? I leave you alone for a moment and just like magic, poof! A young man appears?"

Shira knew her father. She saw the slight glint of amusement in his eyes as he was attempting to tease the now tense young man standing beside her.

"I'm sorry, Rabbi," offered Atara. "I was going to enter by the front door, but when I passed by the garden door, I really felt convicted to knock, not even thinking she would actually be here at that moment. When she unbolted the door, I found her in tears. We've been sitting here talking and praying while waiting for news from you."

Nicodemus rubbed his gray whiskers to prolong the agony he saw in Atara, then finally submitted to a truce as he felt the penetrating eyes of his daughter. "Well, Atara, it was a very good thing you did not come to the front door today. You surely would have been questioned, possibly arrested by the Temple guards if you had! It seems that we have all been under God's watchful eye today! Let us all go up to the house where we can talk and be more comfortable."

Shira could feel Atara relax as Nicodemus turned to walk away. She placed her arm into Atara's, following Nicodemus past the pond and up the staircase. Once inside they went through the home to the front room, settling into the cushions. No sooner had they done so when a knock could be heard at the front door, followed by a servant answering it. All three looked at each other with apprehension, but relaxed when they saw it was Joseph.

"Nicodemus, I came as soon as I heard! You are alright? What did Caiaphas say?"

"Come and sit with us, my friend," Nicodemus said as he led Joseph to a seat. "When Caiaphas arrived this afternoon with his guards, and a few members of the Sanhedrin that do his bidding, he was so angry that I believed I was to be arrested immediately.

"They accused me of conspiring with you! Of stealing Jesus' body from the tomb! At first I was ready to rebut, accusing him of condemning the Son of God. But a peace came on me. All I could think of was Jesus saying, '*Love your neighbor as yourself.*'

"Then I heard a voice within my head saying, 'You are standing here as a witness of my great love for all men.' For over an hour Caiaphas and his men tried to find fault. They tried every tactic, making many threats. But I could only answer out of love and concern for them. For each accusation their anger increased until finally Caiaphas stomped out in a fierce anger, totally lost for words! But I am afraid it is not over yet. And what about you, Joseph?"

"I have heard that he was looking for me as well today, so I have made myself scarce! But I am interested in hearing from our young friend here."

"I as well," said Nicodemus turning to Atara. "Shira gave both of us a detailed report of yesterday's miraculous events. Atara, we are eager to hear your accounting of the past day!"

Once again, Atara chronicled the events since yesterday morning. He was concerned at one point that Shira might not be as interested in listening to him for a second time, but whenever he glanced at her to check, she was leaning forward, hanging on every word he spoke. The two men would stop him every so often with questions that would lead into discussions, then back to the narration. When Atara finished they all accepted Nicodemus' offer to have some food and drink brought in to refresh themselves.

The talk of the risen Messiah had lifted their spirits high. For a time while they were communing together, the thoughts of persecution gave way to joy and merriment. As Shira and Atara recounted their first meeting, they all laughed at the absurdity of it. Yet, they could clearly see now that it was the hand of God that brought them together.

"What a sense of humor God must have!" mused Atara.

"Or when Father first found us in the garden after being told you were Cousin Jonathan!" added Shira, to which Nicodemus bellowed in laughter.

Atara went on to describe the feeling of flying into a darkened room by the burly hand of Peter. They laughed together again with his expressive accounting. When the meal and fellowship were over, the four knew the topic would have to return to the reality of the day.

Joseph spoke first on the subject. "We have been so blessed to be a part of this momentous moment in history. I don't know why God chose us to be witness to this, but I would not go back in time to change a thing. Even though the day of the crucifixion and burial brought us all such extreme agony, here we are just a few days later rejoicing!

"However, I have had word from some I know inside the Sanhedrin that I am a marked man. Caiaphas is livid that he invited me into the inner circles of his scheme. He accuses me of betraying his trust. I am sure he believes that I provided the tomb so we could remove the body to make claims of a resurrection. Regardless, I will have to leave Jerusalem for now."

Not a harsh word was spoken within the group. They all knew this to be true. That it would be better for Joseph to leave, at least for a while.

"I will travel to Arimathea tomorrow," he added, "where I can just as easily run my business and share the good news of the Messiah without having to look over my shoulder for Temple guards. You are all welcome anytime."

"I too have grave concerns," replied Nicodemus. "But I do feel that I have enough support in the Sanhedrin that I can fend off any attacks for now, with God's help. And I also believe this is where God wants me to be for a while longer. I have the boys to consider."

Shira was frowning as Nicodemus revealed his intentions to stay. She knew it would be very dangerous for him and was very worried.

"Shira," Nicodemus said, turning to look directly at her, "I am sending you to Jaffa, to our estate there, until I am certain that it is safe here in Jerusalem. I will join you there shortly."

Immediately Shira's back arched, with her leaning forward to voice her strong objections, but Nicodemus put his hand up before she uttered a word. "I understand your objections. You have played a very important part in this moment of history. You have been so brave and wise, but it is time now for you to listen to your father. I could not bear to lose you, knowing I could have prevented it. You will be a light unto Jaffa, spreading the word. I am sure of that!"

Shira's shoulders sank as she realized Nicodemus was right, that he was acting out of his love for her. 'But Jaffa, it's so far away. And what about Atara? When we prayed together today, I felt as one with him. How could I leave now?

The room was quiet as the others allowed Shira a few moments to accept her father's wishes. Joseph broke the awkward silence asking Atara, "And your plans, my young friend?"

Atara too was torn. The news of Shira having to leave hit him hard. He so much wanted to be with her more, sharing this adventure with her at his side, as they had done for so much of the past week. Finally he had to concede that was not God's plan for him, at least for a while. He was convinced God had a path for him he needed to be obedient to. Atara knew he was to spend more time with the disciples, learning the way.

Attempting to lighten spirits, he began with a bit of wry humor. "Well, it seems as if I'll have the Romans and the Sanhedrin both after me now!" The men smiled a bit. Shira did not.

"I've asked the disciples if I can stay on with them. I have so much to learn and so many questions to be answered. Jesus told them they were to be in the

Galilee next week and they have agreed to let me accompany them. Hopefully, I'll find my brothers there as well, to share the good news of the resurrected Messiah with them. I believe strongly God is calling me in this direction. I don't know what my future holds, but I know what I believe is the Truth. That I must share it with others."

The men's heads nodded. Shira remained still.

"Shira," Atara addressed her directly. "I have come to care for you very much. This has been a difficult decision, but we can see each other again, I'm sure of that. With your father's permission I'll visit you in Jaffa as soon as I can."

Nicodemus nodded as Atara glanced over for approval. Shira softened her stance, looked at Atara, then slowly nodded.

It was late now. The group of four, who had been witness to God's incredible plan of redemption as it unfolded, all bowed their heads and prayed together. At the end of the prayers Nicodemus stood, evoking a blessing of God on those in the room, in the name of their Savior.

They said their goodbyes as Atara headed out into the night.

Part III

A.D. 32

Chapter 39

LATE MONDAY AFTERNOON: TAMUZ 9 / JULY 5TH A.D. 32

The humidity and heat were extreme on this particular day in July. The traveler had been following the coastline of the Mediterranean to take advantage of the cool salt breeze from the sea air and the flat plains of sand to travel on.

There were no Roman soldiers patrolling this far off the road, making the way safe for travel. As he walked along the shoreline, his footsteps impressed themselves deeply into the moist sand, leaving a trail behind that ran many miles to the north. The sun was nearing the horizon this late afternoon, painting the sky with golden rays, soon to be melting into the vast ocean water to the west, bringing relief from the oppressive heat.

The Port of Jaffa lay before him. Beautiful white-faced homes on the water's edge reflected the increasing warmth of the amber sun as he approached. Fishermen were hastily returning to port in their colorful boats to arrive just before the encroaching darkness.

By the time the traveler had arrived at the city walls, the sun was touching the water with brilliant shades of fire and the tide had come in, caressing the shoreline with its soft waves.

Jaffa was not a large city compared to Jerusalem, so it did not take long with the help of locals to search out the large home on the water's edge he had come to find. It was dark by the time he reached the front door where he hesitated for a moment. Taking a deep breath, he reached out to knock.

A beautiful young woman opened the door. She was wearing a fine white cotton dress, colorfully embroidered, tied at the waist with a woven dark cord. Her long ebony hair fell over her shoulder, reflecting the warm light from behind within the house, giving her hair a silky appearance that glowed. The traveler gasped at her beauty.

"Atara!" she exclaimed, as she jumped into his arms for a long embrace.

"Blessings of our Lord, the Messiah," he replied, holding her in his arms. "I missed you so much. I have so much to share with you!"

They stood for a moment facing each other, hand in hand.. For that short moment nothing else existed but the two of them together, innocent of the circumstances of the world around them. Atara finally broke the silence when he could no longer contain himself. "You look radiant!"

Shira smiled. She no longer saw the lost, frightened young man who had collided with her through providence only months before, but a confident young man whose eyes were filled with the passion and love of the living Messiah.

"Atara, you must've been walking all day in this heat! Come in and we'll give you something to eat and drink."

As she ushered him into the beautiful home the questions immediately began to pour out. "Where have you come from? What's happening in Jerusalem? Have you been with the disciples? Did you see Him?"

Atara couldn't help but smile now. This was the Shira he knew, the Shira he had come to love. So many questions! "There is so much to tell. We must sit with each other and spend some time together. But I'll answer one question for now. Yes, I met Him."

"I want to hear everything! We have been apart for too long. So much has happened over these past months to talk about. We will have to get you washed up and have something to eat quickly. Others will be arriving soon!"

"Others?"

"Yes. It's very exciting. We have begun a fellowship here in Jaffa. Many are coming to believe in the Messiah as the word is being spread here. We meet together most days in the evenings for a time of teaching and worship. I have set up a ministry to help the poor, spreading the word as we do! It's incredible how God is moving here among the people!"

"Praise be to God! I'm glad to hear He is using you." He knew it would not have been long before Shira would be helping others. "How is your father?"

"Father is doing very well. He seems so much happier now since he arrived from Jerusalem. We were so excited when we heard the news of the Holy Spirit in Jerusalem. All of us gathered together about two weeks ago one evening, praying we too would be filled with the Holy Spirit. It was like a strong breeze from the ocean blowing through the room. Then we were filled with so much joy and thanksgiving, we could barely contain ourselves! Well, we didn't really, we danced and worshiped as we never could have imagined! A few even spoke to others in their mother tongues in languages they didn't know! We have added so many to the fellowship since that day."

Atara embraced her again. "I'm so happy for you. Jesus told us He would be sending His great comforter to us, but we had no idea! It was incredible! We added 3,000 to the fellowship that day!"

"You were there?"

"I'll tell you all about it when we get a chance to talk."

"Father is out delivering some food to a family in great need. He should be back soon. Come."

Shira took Atara into the kitchen near the back of the house where there was food that had been prepared for later. This was a beautiful two-story white stucco house built on the seawall near the outskirts of Jaffa as a winter retreat from the Jerusalem cold. It was not nearly as large as the mansion in Jerusalem, however it made up for it in charm. Atara could see a spacious room adjacent to the kitchen at the back of the house, with large windows overlooking the sea. The walls were lined with cushions and chairs to accommodate the large crowd they were expecting that night. When Atara had filled a plate, they moved into the back room to sit. The cooler evening breeze drifted through the house, refreshing the air. As Atara ate they talked together.

"I've just been to visit Joseph in Arimathea. He is doing very well. Joseph has been busy with the help of a new believer, a Greek doctor by the name of Lucas, chronicling the events of the trial and crucifixion."

"A Gentile believer?"

"Yes, it's amazing! I believe Jesus died for all men, Jew and Gentile. We're all guilty of His death, Roman and Jew. The love of the Messiah was so great that He sacrificed Himself for all mankind.

"The fellowship in Arimathea is adding to the believers in their city as well. Joseph is using his great wealth to help many people in need. He is a changed man. There has been some persecution from the local rabbis, but nothing compared to that in Jerusalem. Always keep the Jerusalem believers in your prayers as it's very difficult there and becoming worse."

Shira nodded.

"Joseph sends his love to you and your father. It was so good to talk with him, recounting the time we had together in Jerusalem. Not so happy at the time, but look at what we know now! Naomi also sends her love."

"Naomi! I've been so worried about her! I had to leave in such a hurry that I wasn't able to provide for her. What has happened?"

"She is fine. The body in Jerusalem is providing for her now. The children are doing well. I see them as often as I can. Shira, Naomi is a believer now!"

Shira's eyes welled with tears. "Thank God for His loving grace! This news is such an answer to prayer!"

Atara continued to tell Shira about the fellowship in Jerusalem. "Persecutions from the Sanhedrin are increasing daily. They have just appointed a team led by a zealous young Pharisee named Saul to find and arrest believers. So far only Peter and John have been arrested, but by God's grace they escaped sentencing with only an order not to preach in the Temple grounds. They went right back out and began preaching! Peter is the man we saw cowering in the palace courtyard that night! God has turned him into a mighty warrior of the Word! I've been appointed by the leaders to look after those in need. We gather our resources together to feed the widows and the poor."

Shira was just about to respond when a deep voice boomed across the kitchen. "Atara!"

It was Nicodemus.

The older man rapidly crossed the kitchen floor with a gait Atara had not seen in him before. As Atara stood Nicodemus planted a huge bear hug on him, just about taking him off his feet.

"Atara, it is so good to see you again. Are you well?"

"Yes, Rabbi. I'm sorry I haven't been able to come sooner. It has been very busy in Jerusalem."

Atara wanted to say more, but at just that moment other believers started to arrive for fellowship together.

Chapter 40

As people arrived they greeted each other with embraces, excitedly sharing the events of their day. There was a great deal of attention paid to Atara when he was introduced as a disciple from Jerusalem. They were all eager to talk with him, to hear the latest news of the Messiah.

After greeting, eating and fellowship in the kitchen, the crowd eventually moved into the back room overlooking the sea. There were about 40 people present – men, women, young and old, all sitting around the room spontaneously entering into worship together. The wonderful harmony of psalms echoed through the room out across the ocean waters, as arms lifted high, worshiping the Almighty God of Creation, His Son and His Spirit.

Every so often someone would give testimony to what God was doing in their life, sharing revelations God had given to them through scriptures or inspiration, good news of how God had provided for the community, or a need they had that the fellowship could take action on either in prayer or deed.

After a while Nicodemus asked Atara if he would speak. Atara nodded. He was more than happy to share with this fellowship. They had all heard of Atara as Nicodemus and Shira had told their accounting of Jesus' crucifixion and resurrection many times, so he felt led to begin where they had left off when they parted ways.

"The night I left you," looking to both Nicodemus and Shira, "I worked my way back past all the Roman checkpoints to the home of the disciples. For the next five days, I helped there in any way I could. There was still a lot of concern someone else might betray them from within the fellowship, so they were very cautious in their dealings. Also, Caiaphas had begun searching out anyone known to believe in Jesus, so the vigilance was warranted.

"Slowly the disciples were connecting with those who had earlier expressed a belief in Jesus as the Messiah. They began to tell others of the resurrection, that Jesus was alive after being crucified to death. They boldly spoke of Jesus' appearances. I studied hard that week, learning much from the disciples, and I'm grateful to God for giving me that opportunity.

"The following Sunday all 11 disciples were gathered together, including Thomas, who had just returned to Jerusalem. He was still skeptical about the physical resurrection of Jesus. He emphatically told the others he would believe Jesus had been resurrected if he not only could see Him, but also touch the wounds for himself. We were just finishing the meal that Sunday when we heard, 'Peace be with you.' Jesus was – standing inside the room where the doors had been tightly bolted shut! My heart jumped! Jesus moved directly to Thomas, holding out His hands saying, *Put your finger here; see my hands. Reach out your hand and put it into my side. Stop doubting and* believe!' He also said something to Thomas I believe is so important to all of us. *'Because you have seen me, you have believed; blessed are those who have not seen and yet believed.'* [57] Jesus was saying to us it is so important to understand that faith comes from the heart, not from what we see."

The room was silent as Atara continued.

"Jesus stayed for the evening, teaching us many things, which I will share later. But for now all I can say is that I was overwhelmed in His presence. This was the man that we," gesturing again toward Shira and Nicodemus, "witnessed hanging on the cross and dying just two weeks earlier. The man whose body we took down from that cross, moved, cleansed wounds and laid in the tomb. I assure you He was very much dead. As Jesus addressed the disciples, I sat to the side of the room, listening with reverence to all He had to say.

"At the end of the evening Jesus stood and approached me. All I could do was fall on my knees and bow before Him. Then He did the most amazing thing. Jesus took me by the arm, bidding me to rise. When I stood, He embraced me without saying a word. It was more that I could bear and I broke down weeping on His shoulder. The room was silent. After a moment, once I regained my composure, Jesus stepped away, looking at me with a smile. He turned back to the disciples, then was gone!"

Atara was tearing up, barely able to speak. He had not mentioned this to anyone outside of the disciples before and was now sharing this for the benefit of Shira and Nicodemus, who had been through so much with him. Shira was in tears as he was speaking, as was Nicodemus. It had brought back such difficult, tragic memories for the three of them.

"He is risen!" came a cry from the fellowship, sensing the pain the three were feeling. "He is risen indeed!" came the multiple responses from the rest as they all affirmed their faith.

---

[57] John 20:26–29

"Indeed," said Atara regaining his composure. "He is the Son of the living God. He has risen! He is very much alive today and forever!

"Jesus had told some of the disciples to go to the Galilee. I had asked if I could travel with them to see my brothers, but I think I really just wanted to stay with them to learn more. We departed the next day, arriving in the Galilee before the Shabbat at the end of the week.

"I found my brothers in Tiberias with other Zealots. It was a good reunion. I had several days to visit with them, so I had ample opportunity to share my story and the gospel message with my brothers, with all the other Zealots there as well. But I have to say they are still full of hatred for the Romans, making the gospel message hard for them to receive, as it was for me. I pray God will touch their hearts as He has done mine.

"Two days later, when I returned to be with the disciples, there was much excitement. That very day a man had just called out to the disciples from the shore of the Galilee while they were out fishing earlier in the morning. They told me they had caught nothing (swore they were out of practise!) when the man called out to them, instructing them to throw their nets into the sea, on the right-hand side of the boat. They admitted to me there was a fair bit of grumbling and discussion. 'Who does this man think he is! What difference would one side of the boat to the other make?' They could've ignored the man, but in the end they agreed with each other to comply. After they cast the net it immediately became so full of fish, it almost capsized the boat! That is when John recognized it was Jesus standing on the shore!

"Later that day Peter came to speak with me. It was because Shira and I had seen him in the palace court the night they arrested Jesus. Peter confided in me what Jesus had said to him. Jesus asked Peter three times if he loved Him. Each time Peter said yes, Jesus said, '*Feed my lambs.* [58] At first Peter was very upset Jesus would even ask him that question. The second time Peter felt very hurt. It wasn't until Jesus said it the third time, Peter understood this was because he had denied Him three times in that courtyard. I think that Jesus, in His lovingkindness, was giving Peter the opportunity to affirm his love. Perhaps this was so Peter would be able to accept Jesus' forgiveness, forgiving himself as well, for not acknowledging his faith in Jesus at that time of crisis. But look, he is now the most bold disciple of them all, risking his life every day, proclaiming the gospel in the Temple court!

"I saw Jesus once while I was in the Galilee. He had already revealed Himself several other times to the disciples. Then one day word went around He would

---

[58] John 21:15–18

be present on the mountain overlooking the Sea of Galilee. Crowds of believers, and nonbelievers, went up that mountain to hear Him speak. In all, there must have been around 500 people present to witness the resurrected Messiah. Jesus came into their midst, teaching forgiveness and salvation for most of the day.

"Before I left the Galilee I was baptized with other new believers," Atara added looking at Shira, knowing she would be pleased.

"I'm so happy for you, Atara. We have been baptizing here in the sea as people have been coming to faith. Father and I were baptized only two weeks ago!"

"God has been so good to us," responded Atara. "We returned to Jerusalem after that day, as He instructed. One day, when the disciples had traveled to Bethany, Jesus appeared to them on the Mount of Olives. He taught and ate with them for a while, then He said to them:

'Do not leave Jerusalem, but wait for the gift my Father promised, which you have heard me speak about. For John baptized with water, but in a few days you will be baptized with the Holy Spirit . . . you will receive power when the Holy Spirit comes on you; and you will be my witnesses in Jerusalem, and in all Judea and Samaria, and to the ends of the earth.[59]

"They say He ascended into heaven, that He was taken up into a cloud. Two angels then stood beside them, telling them that Jesus would return from heaven through the clouds on this mountain, the same way He had left. This occurred on the 40th day since His resurrection.

"The disciples returned to Jerusalem to stay in the same house of the upper room where they had their Passover supper with Jesus. I remained where I was needed, at the house in the north part of the city, organizing help for those in need.

"We were all to gather on the festival day of Pentecost to worship, which was one week later, 50 days since the Passover. As we worshiped a strong wind pushed through the room, filling everyone present with the Holy Spirit. It's hard to describe all that took place. Each of us has tried, but can't yet find the proper words. It looked like fire and wind with languages, swirling all around as each person began to speak in a different language. And the joy! On the streets afterward they thought we were drunk!

"Shira has told me you have experienced the Holy Spirit for yourselves!" Atara looked around the room at the smiling faces, as they could also testify to the same experience.

[59] Acts 1:4–7

"I believe you have heard everyone poured out into the streets, speaking to those from different countries in their own language. Peter stood to address the crowd that had gathered. That day 3,000 people came to know the salvation of the Messiah!

"Now, this was the day of Pentecost, *Shavuot* in Hebrew. It is the festival of the first fruits when the crops are brought to the Temple. But this year it was a day of God's first fruits when the gifts of the Holy Spirit were imparted to His people! Praise to God the Father! But there is more. According to the rabbis it was on this very same day millennia ago that Moses came down from the mountain with the Laws of God, the Ten Commandments. The Israelites had fallen away, constructing a golden calf to worship in sin. That day there were 3,000 slain under the Law. This day of Shavuot, God redeemed 3,000 as He wrote the Law into our hearts, freeing us from the old covenant of the Law!

"When I first met Shira," he was looking into her eyes now and smiling, "she explained to me who this Jesus was, how He might be the expected Messiah. But He was not the type of Messiah I was looking for. I wanted a Messiah that fit my image, a fighting man, a savior with a sword to beat back the Romans, an earthly king to rule.

"But after His entry into Jerusalem on a donkey this last Passover, as a lamb from Bethlehem, I began to think. I thought that if this Messiah is coming to us as a sacrifice for our sins, as Shira was suggesting, that He would have to follow God's own ordinances for the Temple sacrifices and the prophesies of the Torah.

"That is when I started to look for the links – born in the shepherds' fields of Bethlehem, redeemed from the Temple with silver as the firstborn, ordained by John the Baptist a priest of holy lineage, bought back by the priests as a priest with 30 pieces of silver, sacrificed on the sixth day, nailed to the cross at the time of the first Temple sacrifice and died at exactly the time of the final Passover sacrifice for the sins of the people. This all took place on Mount Moriah where Abraham willingly offered his son. Jesus rose on the first day, the day of light. And not by chance, but by God's hand, this all took place on Passover, a time of redemption and salvation from bondage which all centers on the blood of the Passover Lamb, a perfect lamb, with no flaws or broken bones.

"For we Jews, the final act of atonement comes at Yom Kippur, the Day of Atonement, when the sacrifice for all Israel's sin is made. Two sacrifices are presented – one is chosen. When the crowds, not the high priest or Pilate, released Barabbas, Jesus was left to become both the sacrifice and the scapegoat to cleanse and carry our sins. This was to be the last and final sacrifice for the atonement of our sins.

"The high priest had to place his hand on the head of the sacrifice to transfer the sins of the people, which Caiaphas did in brutal anger on Jesus.

"And the prophesies! I began to challenge the events as they unfolded against the messianic prophesies. Slowly they were all revealed to me as fulfilled in Jesus. Too many to examine tonight!

"What I will say is, between the fulfillment of the Temple ordinances and messianic prophesies, I was led to believe Jesus is the Messiah, the Chosen one. The odds of all these falling into place couldn't be by the hand of man. They're not only astronomical, they're impossible!

"Only by God's divine plan could all of this have occurred. But that is not enough. It's not enough to understand in your mind that a Messiah has come. We must surrender ourselves to Him, asking for forgiveness. We must be born again, born anew in His Spirit, believing in our hearts. It's then that we'll experience the saving grace of the risen Messiah!"

There was a moment of silence before one of the members broke into a song of praise followed by others. The evening turned into night, then night turned into early morning. There were many questions for Atara as he shared more of his story with the fellowship. Others shared testimonies and prayer requests as they prayed together. In the early hours, Nicodemus signaled it was time for everyone to go to their homes for some much-needed rest.

When everyone had left, Atara sat down by the ocean window, leaning back with his eyes closed. He could feel the soft breeze of the ocean drift across his face as he breathed in deeply the warm salty air. 'Thank you, Lord, for such goodness, for providing the words.' He worshiped, giving God the glory.

Atara felt a soft rustle beside him and a quiet voice. "I wish I was there. I wish I could've met Him."

"Shira, you have met Him. Yes, Jesus and I stood face to face and it was an experience I'll never forget, but I wouldn't exchange that for having Him live within me! Jesus made it quite clear that those who find Him through faith, without having to place their hands on His scars, will be richly blessed.

"You'll be rewarded for all of your steadfast faithfulness. It is you who has shown me the way to the Messiah. You have bathed His beaten body with your tears. I can't even begin to imagine the love God has for you, or the place in His Kingdom He has prepared for you!"

Shira leaned against Atara as he placed his arm around her. Both were still so very awestruck with all that had happened in their lives, leading them to this point, together, that there were very few words for the moment.

"My children," said Nicodemus, arriving in the room at, of course, the appropriate time fathers have a tendency to do. "I've seen the last of our guests out. I believe it is time to retire for the night. I will show Atara to our guest room and we can talk more in the morning. I have many questions myself for you, young man."

"I don't have much time," confessed Atara. "It was difficult for me to leave Jerusalem with all that is happening. I must begin my trip back the morning after next. I hope you understand, Shira. My heart is torn. I really just want to stay here with you."

With disappointment Shira looked at him with her deep brown eyes, the ones that first captivated him. But she knew the road ahead was to be full of challenges and sacrifices. She simply nodded.

They held each other, Atara gently catching her tears as they slid down her lovely face, then saying goodnight as Nicodemus led him to a comfortable room overlooking the ocean. The rhythmic sound of the waves lapping against the shore would quickly lull him into a perfect sleep.

Chapter 41

TUESDAY MORNING: TAMUZ 10 / JULY 6TH

Atara lay in the soft bed with the gentle sea breeze caressing his face, listening to the harmony of the waves echoing off the break wall. The sun had been up for a while, beaming through the front of the house, but here at the back, by the sea, with the fresh scent of salt air, the morning seemed timeless.

He had not yet heard any voices from within the household and with last night being such a very late night, he resolved it would be best to wait before disturbing Shira or Nicodemus. When Atara finally decided to rise, he moved over to relax by the open window where he began his morning prayers.

Prayer had evolved so much for him over these past few weeks. He still opened with the Sh'ma, and the morning blessings, but after reciting these he entered a time when he was learning to talk with the Lord, one on one. Since the filling of the Holy Spirit, his prayer time would incorporate many petitions for those around him in need, but would always end with a time of worship. During this worship time it was always like that exact moment when Jesus first embraced him. It felt like it had never ended.

He could hear footsteps downstairs. Atara quickly dressed and went down to the kitchen to see who was up. Shira was behind the counter with a small basket of fresh eggs they purchased every morning from a local vendor who came door to door. She plopped a few into the boiling water, smiling at Atara as he entered. Atara came around the counter to give her a quick morning hug, then began to tease her.

"You can cook?"

"Anyone can boil an egg!" She stared at him with fire in her eyes. "Yes, I can also cook!"

"Well, I never would've guessed!"

The closest thing at hand was a discarded eggshell which found itself bouncing off Atara a second later. "Truce!" he conceded, holding up his hands for protection. Atara thought it might be best not to challenge her further this early in the morning.

They both laughed. This tiny bit of playfulness felt so good after the challenges they had faced together. Atara began helping set out some of the food and tableware for the morning meal.

Nicodemus entered the kitchen, greeting them both with a "Good morning."

The eggs were ready, so they all sat down at the table to enjoy the fresh vegetables, figs, dates and eggs. After the blessing was said by Nicodemus, the talk around the table was about the plans for the day. Nicodemus told them he had errands to run and would likely be back sometime mid-afternoon, if all went well. Also, there was to be another meeting tonight where food would be shared once again, so some preparation was necessary.

Shira said she would like to spend as much time with Atara as possible, but had some families she needed to visit in the early afternoon.

"Would you like to come with me?"

"Yes, I would really like that. I'm sure I can help somehow."

"You certainly can! There is much to carry and those strong muscles of yours will be really helpful! We have been distributing food to a few very needy families here in Jaffa. A woman by the name of Tabitha has been helping. She is a new believer, as we all are, with a genuine passion God has given her to help those in need. I don't know what I would do without her! You'll meet her this afternoon when we go out."

By the time they had finished washing up after breakfast, Nicodemus had already left. It was mid-morning. The sun was rising high in the sky, adding to the heat and stifling humidity of this coastal town. Shira excused herself to go upstairs to bathe, while Atara went for a walk down to the beach to try a swim in the Mediterranean Sea.

It was a short distance from the house to the lovely sandy shore, taking Atara only minutes to reach. He escaped the scorching sun by entering the water, slowly walking deeper as the cool, salty liquid rose, whirling around him. It felt so amazing. When up to his chest he laid back, floating in the gentle morning waves that rocked him back and forth like a cradle. He gazed at the sky. 'Perfect.' Weightless and cool with the sun filling his pores while the waves gently massaged his body. After a while he thought he had best get back to the house to see if Shira was ready. Reluctantly, he waded ashore, dried off a bit, then headed back up the sand path to the house.

Shira was finished when Atara entered the back room. She looked just as beautiful today as she had yesterday when answering the door. Her dress today was a simple but finely woven cotton tied tightly at the waist with beautifully embroidered threads of azure enhancing the matching rounded neckline. It was one of her favorite dresses she had put on especially for him. Shira did not dress gaudy, as many young women of the more affluent families did. She always had dressed modestly with very little jewelry. Today was a testament to that.

"You look wonderful," said Atara, trying hard not to gaze for too long.

"I hope I'm not overdressed for our visits," blushed Shira slightly, "but I did want to look my best for you today. We have so little time together."

The two sat talking for a little while longer. It was the first time they had been alone for any length of time since he had arrived. They spoke of more personal feelings, particularly about how each was coping after the traumatic and emotional experiences of the past two months. It was clear to each that their faith was strong, and that God was raising them up in strength and knowledge to minister to others. Shira's unwavering faith had always impressed him, right from the first day he had met her.

Tabitha arrived at noon, and after introductions the three headed out to pick up the supplies needed to make their rounds for the day.

The first three visits were to those in need who lived on the outskirts of Jaffa. Two, to elderly widows living alone, another to a family who had fallen on troublesome times. The walk out of town carrying their wares was extremely hot and humid, which Atara found very oppressive as he was used to the more moderate temperatures of Jerusalem high up in the mountains. The farther they traveled from the breeze of the sea, the more the roads baked under the sun in the quivering heat.

On each delivery, Atara marveled at the compassion both women showed to those in need while sharing the message of the Messiah. He particularly enjoyed the short time visiting the family, playfully occupying the children while the ladies helped and prayed with the parents.

The walk back to Jaffa was much easier as the sun was lower in the sky and their load much lighter. When they arrived at the edge of the city, Tabitha departed for her home to be with her family to prepare for the evening. There were still two more visits remaining, so Shira and Atara continued.

As they approached Jaffa they could see a Roman checkpoint on the road ahead. Shira hesitated, looking at Atara to see what he would do. 'Should they turn around to try a different route, one that would avoid Romans?' Much to her surprise he smiled at her, then took her arm, continuing down the road right through the checkpoint, greeting the soldiers cordially. This happened a second time when they passed a Roman patrol near the port.

After helping the homeless man who begged down by the docks, giving him some needed food and money, they went to the break wall to sit by the sea.

"Atara," Shira said to him once they had settled into a beautiful spot overlooking the Port of Jaffa. "When we passed the Roman soldiers today you didn't even flinch. In fact, I saw you smile at them! What has happened?"

"Forgiveness," Atara answered. "I was so full of hatred, so angry, that I blamed any man wearing a Roman uniform for all my troubles. In fact, though, I wouldn't be here today if not for a Roman centurion named Quintus who helped me escape prison."

Atara began to tell Shira of his past in detail. They had never had the time in Jerusalem to sit and talk like this because the events of that Passover week had unfolded so quickly. She knew very little of his past. He told her how much this port town of Jaffa reminded him of his home in Sidon, his father and his brothers. He detailed the death of his father at the hands of Gallus, his own arrest, the prison, the desperation, then the daring escape carried out by his brothers and Quintus. For over an hour he shared his past experiences and feelings with her.

"I can see God's hand in my life as I look back at it now. As I searched so desperately for Him, bit by bit He answered my prayers, revealing Himself to me, leading me to the Messiah."

"But what about Gallus? The terrible things he did?" asked Shira, remembering Atara's reaction on seeing him at the Garden Tomb.

"That time I saw Gallus in Jerusalem I felt the hatred, fear and anger welling up in me. But the strangest thing happened. As I prayed I could sense the peace of God come over me as we stood together behind those bushes, waiting for him to leave. I have forgiven Gallus. Jesus has taught us we need to forgive those who harm us. Look what He experienced! He came here, the Son of God, to save us from our own sins and we despised Him, mocked and beat Him, then took His life in the most horrible way. Yet, He has come back with open arms and forgiveness to all those who repent and turn to Him! If Jesus can forgive us, how can we not forgive those who wrong us?

My hatred of the Romans, and Gallus, was rooted in fear. In the Messiah I have learned there is nothing to fear, for He is with us always, even in death, as we are resurrected to be with Him."

"The day we first met, I sensed the conflict in you, the fear," confided Shira.

"That day with the Romans pursuing me, thinking I had murdered a man, a young man much like myself who I looked eye to eye as we struggled, I was in turmoil, full of guilt. Thanks to Jesus, I am free now, Shira. Free of fear, free of hatred, guilt, free of the bondage of the Law, free of death itself because I have been born anew in spirit through the Messiah, through His forgiveness! What joy it is to be free in Him! No matter what lies ahead, I know it will be in God's will.

"When the Holy Spirit came on us at Pentecost, all the past worldly emotions of fear and hate were replaced with God's love. It was what Jesus had been saying all along. *'Love the Lord your God with all your soul and with all your mind. This is the first and greatest commandment. And the second is like it: Love your neighbor as yourself.' All the Law and the Prophets hang on these two commandments.'*[60]

"After that night," replied Shira, "the night Jesus was condemned and beaten, I confess that even though Jesus went willingly, I too held onto anger and contempt for our leaders and the Romans, for they both had their hand in the most horrible crime of history. Though, in a way, we all did with our own sins. Since that time God has shown me the same love and forgiveness you have experienced."

"Yes, we have all sinned. Jesus came to bring us back to the Father. That is why we must spread the word of the Messiah," added Atara. "Our people, all people, need to know of God's amazing gift to us through His great sacrifice of the salvation that Jesus has brought."

Shira and Atara sat closely together on the stone break wall overlooking the Mediterranean Sea. The sun was nearing the horizon, beginning the transition to a blazing orange as it prepared to vanish into the night. They both sat silently, side by side, viewing the splendor for some time before deciding they must return home to prepare for the evening.

---

[60] Matthew 22:37–40

Chapter 42

Nicodemus was sitting in the back room by the sea when Shira and Atara entered the house. He had returned only a short while ago, having just enough time to refresh himself before they arrived.

Atara was dripping in sweat. Shira took one look at him, promptly marching him into the kitchen where she handed him a cloth with instructions to rinse off from the basin of water, or no one would sit near him tonight. She excused herself to go upstairs to do the same.

Afterward, all three were sitting in the back room enjoying a cool drink of freshly squeezed orange juice, watching the twilight of golden sky that followed the sun into the sea. The evening breeze had arrived, filling the room with light swirls of current that tickled the back of the neck as they sat and talked.

Finishing their conversations of the afternoon's missions, Nicodemus was still curious about Atara's experience of faith. "Atara, at what point did you know Jesus was the Messiah, the Son of God?"

Atara thought for a moment as Shira leaned forward, anxious to hear. "I suppose there were several steps I had to take to find faith. The first step was to find a rational explanation in my mind. Perhaps it's the yeshiva training in me, or just my cynicism from the years of hardships, but I needed to be able to think this through logically. When it appeared as though Jesus was coming as a sacrifice for sins, I knew all the events would have to fall perfectly into place with the scriptures. They had to. If it didn't unfold according to the scriptures, then He would be just another false prophet. As I searched for the answers, I found that as God revealed them to me, the fulfilled prophesies and Temple ordinances became so overwhelmingly true against any probability and odds, they became compelling. I had no choice but to recognize God's hand. But it was the garden that really brought it all into perspective for me."

"The garden?" asked Nicodemus. "Our garden behind the house?"

At this, both Atara and Shira smiled at each other. Nicodemus had not been present at the Garden Tomb when they had first seen the relevance of this.

"No, sir," Atara said, still smiling. "Although I do see the irony of that, being where Shira and I first met, finding the love we have for each other."

Shira's heart skipped a beat, then began to race. This was the first time Atara had confessed his love for her. She felt it, of course, but hearing it spoken made all the difference.

"Joseph's Garden. It all came down to the Garden Tomb and God's plan for all of us. In the beginning when God created the earth, on the first day He provided the Light of the earth, not the sun or moon, but the light of the Messiah lit the world.

"On the sixth day God created man and woman, placing them in the garden. He created us in His image to walk with Him and commune with Him in a way none of His other creations could. He gave us free will. We could choose to walk with Him in that Garden, or not. Man fell, as we chose the knowledge of good and evil. We could no longer walk with God, or stand in His presence. We could no longer look on His face because of sin in our hearts. God cast us out of that garden, placing two cherubim armed with flaming swords at its entrance to guard the way in, separating us from God.

"We have always viewed that as being the harsh God keeping us out, but perhaps we've been wrong. Jesus has taught us of the love of the Father, so just as darkness can't enter light without being destroyed, we can't enter His perfect presence without being destroyed. The cherubim and curtain are there to protect us because of our sin.

"For the next millennia God tried to bring mankind back to Himself. At one point He could find only one righteous man left in the world and brought the flood to start anew, but sin still prevailed. He brought Abraham, sacrifices, Moses, the Law, kings and prophets, all to bring us back to Him, but we ignored them all, killing most. God offered us redemption through the Temple, and we have turned that into a place of pride, corruption and hardened hearts.

"But God promised a Messiah, one who would bring salvation and freedom for His people. One who would bring us back to the Father, to the Garden! Jesus came, not as we expected, but lowly, born out of wedlock in poverty and with no kingly features.

"Even the prophesies were masked, so only those who would truly seek Him would see. God sent His son as a sacrifice to take our sins on Himself, so we can stand blameless before God and go back into the Garden to be with Him, to commune and walk with Him.

"The Garden was the final piece of the puzzle for me. It was no accident Jesus was taken to a Garden Tomb, or when He appeared to Mary Magdalene as a gardener. It was no accident He died on the sixth day, the day of man, rising in the garden on the first day, the day of the Messiah, the Light of the world! That is when I realized this was all God's plan and He was offering us forgiveness. The incredible thing was He was willing, out of His great love for us, to sacrifice His own Son in the most horrible of deaths, which we can testify to.

"Even more, Jesus carried the burden of the sins of all mankind! Unimaginable! The agony of the cross must have only been an infinitely small fraction of the pain these sins caused Him as He carried all that evil to the pit of hell. Satan declared a victory with His death, but then when Jesus rose again, scarred from the cross, He overcame sin and death forever!

"When the curtain tore in the Temple, the two cherubim woven into the fabric parted, opening the way into the Garden once again. It is a metaphor, but also very real, of us being united with the Father again, free from sin through His love. God is showing us the way!"

After a pause Atara added, "And all we have to do is accept Jesus as the Messiah, God's sacrifice for us."

Nicodemus sat back to process this. After a moment he asked Atara to continue.

"You would think that in the garden the morning of the resurrection that it was the missing body of Jesus and the women's testimonies that would have given me faith. But it wasn't. When we took Jesus' body to the Garden Tomb, all I could see was a man. As we wiped away the blood, I couldn't find the faith I needed to believe this man, flesh and blood, was the Son of God. Even the morning after He arose, while Shira and I sat in the garden, I was trying to process how this could all be. As we talked God revealed to me that He wants us to come back to the Garden, His Garden, to walk with Him again. So much so that He sacrificed His only Son for us so that we can.

"That was the first step for me. I had to find the answers. The next step was when Peter prayed with me. I accepted, no, I surrendered myself to the living Messiah, asking for His forgiveness. That's when I knew in my heart Jesus was the Son of God. That's when I felt the living Messiah within me. The next week when I stood face to face with Jesus, I couldn't say a word. It was as if He who was living within me was standing in front of me! When He embraced me, the warmth and peace of forgiveness came on me. It's impossible to explain in words because it's a decision of the heart and faith.

"The third step was when the Holy Spirit came on me and filled my soul. It was then that I finally *knew*. Again, it's hard to explain with words, but until that time my mind and my heart knew Jesus was the Messiah and that I was forgiven. My sins had been washed away, forgotten, and I was free. But when the Holy Spirit came on us all at Pentecost, my very soul knew. I don't understand it quite yet, but I feel the Holy Spirit connects our very beings, our souls, with God. He fills us with His love and peace. I've been freed from the bitterness and hatred I once held onto. My search has ended. I've been called to testify to others so they might know God's amazing love for each of us! I was a prisoner and a Zealot full of hatred. Now I'm a disciple full of God's love."

Shira exhaled as if she had been holding her breath. "I came to believe in Jesus the first time I heard Him speak," she said. "Father, remember when you invited Him to our home and the two of you spoke? I knew in my heart He was the Messiah. I didn't have the proof, but somehow I just knew. As I watched Atara process the proof in his mind, I understood that is what he needed before he could find faith. We all will find our way to the Lord in our own way. If we're searching, I believe He will reveal Himself to us!"

"God will bless you for your gentle and accepting heart, Shira. If it had not been for your faith, I wouldn't be sitting here today. I guess I was a much more difficult case, full of skepticism and hatred. I thank Jesus that He didn't give up on me. He revealed to me what I needed to see to find faith in Him."

"I do remember the first time Jesus visited us," added Nicodemus. "I too, like Atara, had to be sure all the prophetic signs fit. When we first talked I was taken aback with the message He had for me. But God did not let go. I had to find the answers. As I learned more about Him and studied the prophesies, I came to believe Jesus was the Messiah. It wasn't until after His resurrection though, that I truly surrendered myself to God and my heart was given. And, like Atara, it was when the Holy Spirit came on us that I felt my soul reunited with God in a peace I had never before experienced, despite what we have been through."

People were now beginning to arrive. They had been talking so intensely together that they had completely lost track of time. It didn't seem to matter, as those who arrived came right into the kitchen, preparing the food for everyone.

After the meal the evening continued with songs, prayers, sharing and worship. The focus was on the returning Messiah. After a brief discussion with much hearsay, the fellowship turned their eyes toward Atara for word from the disciples.

"It's true. Jesus spoke to the disciples of the things to come, and His return. He commissioned them, and those of us who are followers, to go out into the world, spreading the good news of His resurrection and the life eternal He is offering to everyone who repents and believes.

"But this also came with a serious warning of the trials ahead. Jesus warned against being deceived by false prophets claiming to be Him, and that nation will rise against nation at the end of times. Even the prophet Daniel spoke of the '*abomination that causes desolation*' in the Temple in the last seven years. We don't understand this all yet, but we do know that He has promised to be with us through all the persecutions saying: '*For I will give you words and wisdom that none of your adversaries will be able to resist or contradict.*'[61]

"His last words to us before ascending to the Father were, '*Surely I am with you always, to the very end of the age.*'[62] We know He will be returning, not as He came to us now, humble, sacrificing Himself for our sins, but in His true greatness. He said to the disciples, '*At that time they will see the Son of Man coming in a cloud with power and great glory!*'[63] We don't know when He'll return, but we're to remain vigilant, ready to stand before our Savior at any moment!"

With arms lifted high all those in the room began worshiping the Lord God of all Creation. Shira stood to be by Atara's side, looking up at the young man she had grown to love with tears in her eyes, in awe of the great work God had done in his life. She slipped her hand into his, high above their heads, united in spirit as they gave praise to God.

'What will happen to us,' she thought, meditating on God's plan for their lives. 'Are we to be together? Is Jesus sending us on separate paths? There are dangerous days ahead for believers, Lord. How can we serve you? Lay our lives down as you have done for us?'

As people took their seats again, the evening progressed with much discussion about the return of Jesus. The meeting went on not as late as the previous night, but it was another wonderful time filled with the presence of the Holy Spirit as they worshiped and prayed together.

When the fellowship was over, Nicodemus promptly hinted to Atara and Shira that he would like to retire for the night, but would wait up in the next room, allowing them some time to talk, adding that they too should follow soon.

The cool night air blew past Atara and Shira as they stood by the open window, overlooking the moonlit sea. The waves collided with the break wall in a hypnotic rhythm that synchronized with each breath as the two stood close together.

"Do you have to leave tomorrow?"

---

[61] Luke 21:15

[62] Matthew 28:20

[63] Luke 21:27

"Yes. I'll be leaving very early, but I've been meaning to ask you something. I'll really miss you and we have great needs in Jerusalem. The other women are very shorthanded and could use the help. Would you come back to Jerusalem to help in the ministry there?"

Shira looked down and thought for a moment. How could she possibly make a choice like this? "In my heart it's what I want. Will you let me to pray tonight before I give you my answer in the morning? I need to be certain it would be God's will for us."

"Of course, and I'll pray too for God's guidance. I love you, Shira. I don't believe I really understood how much until I arrived here for the past two days. Our love for God, and His Son the Messiah, has become such a strong bond for us, we need to know we're in His will."

They held each other closely, and as she raised her eyes to meet his, their lips met and lingered, just for a moment. The young lovers had been through such a profound experience together, one that would ultimately change the course of history. A love for the Son of God bound them so deeply, it went well beyond human understanding.

Chapter 43

WEDNESDAY MORNING: TAMUZ 11 / JULY 7TH

It was early morning when Atara woke after a restless night. He was torn between leaving and lingering longer in Jaffa, but knew he was needed back in Jerusalem.

Reluctantly, he rose to gather his few possessions for the long trip up the mountains back to the disciples. Finished he stood for a moment, looking out over the sea, breathing in the fresh salt air, realizing it might be quite some time before he would be able to see Shira again. With the decision to come to Jaffa, he hadn't realized how strong his feelings were for her, or how difficult it would be to leave her.

Atara spent time in prayer before going downstairs. Entering the kitchen he found her sitting by the window, quietly waiting for him with a breakfast already prepared on the table.

"Good morning," she said, as she rose to embrace him.

"Yes, it's a beautiful morning," he replied, "though I hardly slept last night knowing I must leave you this morning."

«Me too. But I understand the Lord is calling you back to Jerusalem."

"Do you have an answer from the Lord about coming with me?"

Shira hesitated.

"My heart wants to be with you, Atara," Shira finally responded. "But I can't. I feel God has placed me in Jaffa for a purpose at this time and Father needs me to be with him. There is also the new ministry here I have become part of."

"I understand. I respect you for that. I believe God has a specific role for me to play as well and I too want to obey His will, so I must return. I'll miss you so much, but it was selfish of me to ask. It'll become more dangerous in Jerusalem for believers in the coming days as the persecutions intensify. I love you and I pray we will be together again one day, if not here, with Jesus when He returns.

"There is so much to do, so much to bear witness to. I feel the Lord is calling me to testify to our people, to our leaders, about the great gift God has given us. The last words Jesus spoke to the disciples before ascending to heaven were:

"All authority in heaven and on earth has been given to me. Therefore, go and make disciples of all nations, baptizing them in the name of the Father and of the Son and of the Holy Spirit, and teaching them to obey everything I have commanded you. And surely I am with you always, to the very end of the age."[64]

Tears falling now they both sat at the table and prayed together. They prayed for each other, that God would use them according to His will, for the mission ahead. The breakfast was a silent one, each thinking of how much they would miss the other, how much they had experienced together, wondering when they would be together again.

Forcing himself to rise Atara took Shira by the hand as they made their way to the front door. Embracing for their last farewell, and with a kiss that did last forever, Atara then turned to leave.

But before he made three steps, he paused, and turning back to her said, "I almost forgot. The disciples have chosen a new name for me. A new life, a new name. They felt as well a new name would help protect me from the Romans. If you need to send a message to me, use my new name."

"What is it?"

"Well, *Atara* in Hebrew means the crown. Translated into Greek that would be Stephen. They've given me the name Stephen."

---

[64] Matthew 28:18–20

Epilogue

S tephen performed many signs and wonders among the people and was filled with the Holy Spirit. Within a few months he was arrested and brought before the Sanhedrin for preaching the gospel. After a passionate oration, pleading for repentance:

"Look," he said, "I see heaven open and the Son of Man standing at the right hand of God!"

At this they covered their ears and yelling at the top of their voices, they rushed at him, dragged him out of the city and began to stone him. Meanwhile the witnesses laid their coats at the feet of a young man named Saul.

While they were stoning him, Stephen prayed, "Lord Jesus, receive my spirit." Then he fell on his knees and cried out, "Lord, do not hold this sin against them." When he had said this he [died] fell asleep.[65]

And Saul approved of them killing him.

Atara learned to love and found eternal life in his Savior.

---

[65] Acts 7:56–60

Author's Notes

THE CHARACTERS

Jesus, Y'shua in Hebrew

The New Testament. Read the New Testament.

It is always a potential problem trying to introduce the character of Jesus into a play or novel. This is one area I did not take on lightly.

This novel is about coming to faith. Also about the incredible number of biblical prophesies and Temple ordinances Jesus fulfilled in that last week. I attempted to limit the number of direct encounters with the Messiah to avoid having to shape His character into how I see Him. What is written here is my interpretation of the events and how they affected the two young characters. The only words I included from Jesus come directly from scriptures and are footnoted. I simply felt I could not put words into His mouth.

There were two instances where I took the liberty to add an encounter that was not in the scriptures, the first being when Jesus looked at Atara while carrying the cross, and the second when Atara met Jesus at the home of the disciples. All other times Jesus was only observed or listened to by the characters, and I attempted to follow the scriptures accurately.

As far as the burial goes, at this point Jesus' character would not be in question. It was about how those present would have been affected.

I pray you, the reader, understand this.

I also chose not to capitalize *he, him* or *messiah* until after the resurrection in the novel. This would be from the perspective of the characters at the time, reflecting their uncertainty until after the resurrection.

Y'shua in Hebrew means salvation. Atara in Hebrew can be translated as crown. Therefore the title of *The Crown & Salvation* is the story of Stephen and Jesus.

Atara

Who was Stephen? How did he come to faith? When I asked myself these questions, I began to imagine how it might have happened, hence this novel.

We know very little. In Acts 6:8 Luke states he was a man filled with God's grace and power, performing wonders and signs among the people. In Acts 6:5 the disciples selected him to look after the needs of others. He was arrested for continuously and boldly preaching the gospel in the Temple. When brought before the Sanhedrin, Stephen proclaimed the Messiah in a brilliant defense recorded in Acts 7. It so infuriated the council, that he was taken out and stoned to death. Saul of Tarsus, later to be Paul, was present and likely overseeing the execution.

To be perfectly clear, this story of Stephen is fiction – my imagination. It has provided a timeline and story to present the events of the Passover week. Some day, when I meet Stephen, I am really looking forward to hearing his actual testimony!

Shira

Fictional character. We do not know if Nicodemus had any children or was even married. Shira provides a contrast to Atara in how she came to faith. I must confess, she reminds me much of my dear wife of over 50 years Barb, who was so patient with me while I, like Atara, was searching for God many years ago before we were married.

Nicodemus

Only the Gospel of John records Nicodemus, mentioning him three times. First in John 3, a nighttime visit with Jesus when the famous "born again" and "God so loved the world" messages were given. Later, when he defends Jesus in a confrontation with the chief priests and finally after the crucifixion, John mentions Nicodemus was with Joseph to take the body away.

There is a Gospel of Nicodemus, but it has never been canonized as authentic.

All the other references to Nicodemus in this story are fiction. Wife? Children? I believe these might be in the character of the man. I wonder what he was really like?

Joseph of Arimathea

We know from the four gospels he was a wealthy member of council and a secret disciple who asked for the body of Jesus so he could bury Him in his own tomb. We have no information on whether he ever married, but most likely was, as history tells, that members of the Sanhedrin were required to be married.

One question I have often asked myself is 'How do we know what went on inside the trials?' They would have been closed to only those members of the Sanhedrin that were present. Personally I believe Joseph, and perhaps others who secretly believed in the Messiah, recorded those events. I reflected that in this story.

Many stories exist about Joseph, probably some of them are true, many no doubt are not. Legend has it Joseph preached the gospel message all the way to England and later was connected to the mystical stories of the holy grail.

Barabbas

Barabbas literally means the son of the father in Hebrew (bar = son, abba = father). Jesus Barabbas was a Zealot who had taken part in riots and insurrections. Matthew called him a notorious criminal. I attempted to demonstrate the significance of Barabbas in the novel. The symbolism certainly goes very deep.

The question has always been there, though: Why would a Roman governor choose to release a notorious criminal, a murderer, and a Zealot leader at Passover? It just doesn't make any practical sense from a Roman perspective. The case I presented here is my own thinking, but what if Pilate really assumed the priests would never choose Barabbas over Jesus? That he gave them the choice in spite, forcing them to release either an enemy of Rome or enemy of the Temple?

Disciples: Peter, John, Simon the Zealot, Judas and the others.

Someday, I would love to meet these guys! What stories they must have to tell. Any part of this novel where I have them involved is my imagination of what they might have been like. I tried to stay as close to scripture as I could to fit in with the story.

Pilate, Herod, Caiaphas

These leaders are all documented people in the Bible and other history. Some have questioned the authenticity of Pilate, but a discovery in recent years of a limestone inscription in Caesarea, Israel names "Pontius Pilate, prefect of the Roman Province of Judea" from 26 to 36 A.D.

Tabitha

A disciple of the Messiah in the coastal town of Jaffa. She was recorded in Acts 9:32 as a person doing many good works and helping the poor. She fell sick and died, but when Peter arrived he sent everyone out of the room and she was raised back to life.

Lucas (Luke)

The author of the Gospel of Luke and Acts of the Apostles. It is believed Luke was a Greek physician, a Gentile, who came to faith sometime not long after the resurrection of Jesus. He made no claim to being a firsthand witness, but Paul's writings indicate he was there at the time of Paul. He was a writer, recording all he could of the events and words of Jesus' life.

All other characters in this novel are fictional.

THE EVENTS

Palm Sunday

On the 10th day of Nissan every year. What amazes me is that I have spent most of my life in churches and the only thing I have personally ever heard from the pulpit of what the Church calls Palm Sunday is the triumphant entrance of Jesus into the Temple. As amazing as that is, it is so much more. I hope the chapter on the bringing in the lambs sheds light on the wonderful mystery of Nissan 10.

Passover

The book is about the significance of the Passover week. Hopefully, this story demonstrates that. But there is still much more significance that can be brought to light. For example, in the novel I could not work the Passover, or Last Supper, directly into the plot as I had no characters that could be present there.

I urge you to look into the Passover supper to learn about the significance it represents.

The Trials

Jesus went through an incredible gauntlet of six trials, all over a span of only a few hours. They are well recorded in the four gospels, each from the perspective of the writer, none of whom were actually there. The information they received must have come from an inside source. Joseph, Nicodemus and other secret believers are the most likely sources. Perhaps even others who came to be believers long after the resurrection.

For the novel I chose Joseph as the prime source of information and wove the story around that. Again, this is my interpretation of the trials. Read the scriptures and decide for yourself how this all took place.

One thing I would like to point out is how the Christian Church has pointed fingers at the Jewish people for the death of Christ over the past centuries, often in an attempt to absolve Gentiles to the point of harboring deep anti-Semitism. There is no doubt the Jewish leadership had become very corrupt. But were the occupying Romans, Gentiles, much better? They were a brutal regime, an occupying force with little mercy and pagan beliefs. The historian Josephus records that when the Romans destroyed Jerusalem in 70 A.D., they slaughtered 1.1 million people, most of whom were peaceful citizens and unarmed. A genocide of horrific proportions. Bodies piled so high on the Temple Mount, he described how when a new body was thrown on top it slid all the way down the Temple stairs. Over 100,000 were taken into slavery, only to die as fodder for gladiators or powering the navy's galleys. During the time of Jesus, crucifixion was a daily sight in Jerusalem.

Did the act of Pilate washing his hands absolve him from his actions? Can we say we are not responsible, and then go out and do evil acts. In fact, he was very much responsible for agreeing to have Jesus beaten and crucified despite washing his hands of it.

What a very unique moment in history where the death of the Messiah would incorporate the hands of both Gentile and Jew.

As in Atara's fictional dream, all of us who have sinned are responsible for the death of the Messiah.

The Crucifixion

Crucifixion is one of the most cruel methods of execution used by the Romans and is meant to strike fear into all who witness them.

Most traditional Christian scenes have the crucifixion taking place at a very high point, on top of a hill. I personally don't believe that is where the Romans would have placed it. The crucifixions were very common and meant to be a deterrent. They were usually held right by the roadside where everyone passing by would witness them, not likely at a high point to glorify those who were being crucified. So I placed the crucifixion site at the bottom in a rock quarry near the road.

This looks surprisingly like the cliff just outside the Garden Tomb in Jerusalem today. Regardless of how we envision it, the fact remains Jesus was crucified.

How many people were present? Who stayed for the entire time? Again, we have only a few snippets of information in the scriptures.

I added the section of many healed or touched by Jesus for effect. It is not in the scriptures, but if you had been healed by Jesus, would you not have gone to the cross to bear witness to what He had done for you?

The Burial

I always wondered who took the broken body of Jesus away for burial. Scriptures record Joseph and Nicodemus, but these two men were most likely older and would have required help. Servants? Household members? Not the disciples. It was clear they had scattered in fear. Who then?

For this story I have Stephen, Shira and the two servants helping. It is just my imagination, but what would it have been like? Could you imagine yourself in this situation? How difficult would it be to believe the broken body in front of you was the Son of the Living God?

Please understand for this story it is my personal interpretation. But put yourself in the midst of that week and think about how you would have reacted. Would it have been like Stephen or Shira?

The disciples are another matter. We know John was there with Jesus' mother Mary. With regard to the others, we have no information. Were they there and it is just not recorded? Or had they scattered in fear?

The Resurrection and Garden Tomb

Have you ever read the four gospels' accounts of the resurrection morning? Each one seems so different with Mary, Jesus' mother, Mary Magdalene, Peter, John, the other women, angels, Jesus and a different experience for each? I have given one interpretation, which shows how it could have all taken place seamlessly. It is just speculation on my part, an effort to put it together into a cohesive story.

Each gospel author told the story from their perspective, making it look like they might not agree, but it is simply that each told the story of one person and not the others. When you put it all together it paints a harmonious, beautiful picture of those who visited the garden that morning.

The fact the four gospels recorded it was a garden tomb and that Jesus appeared as a gardener was no accident. Every word in scripture has so much depth and meaning behind it!

Easter

Why do we still celebrate the Resurrection at a time called Easter? Clearly this all took place over Passover, and I believe it would be much more meaningful if we were to celebrate it then. Of course, it would be less convenient, not always falling on a weekend, but still.

No matter, though. What really is important is that Jesus fulfilled the will of His Heavenly Father and rose from the grave!

Daniel 9:20–25

The Coming Prince by Sir Robert Anderson

Daniel 9 is an incredible prophetic word brought to Daniel 500 years before the time of Jesus. By all accounts it places the arrival of the Anointed One or the Messiah around the time of Jesus.

A British man by the name of Sir Robert Anderson attempted to unravel the mystery behind Daniel 9. He was a scholar, lawyer, and author who was assistant director of Scotland Yard for many years. He spent several years working out Daniel 9 and concluded with the information I have provided in the novel – that the prophesy points to the date of Nissan 10, 32 A.D. that Jesus entered Jerusalem as the Messiah. Read his works and see what you think.

The book is *The Coming Prince* by Sir Robert Anderson, first published in 1957 and still available, most recently by Trumpet Press, 2014.

In the Daniel prophesy the final week of sevens, or the last seven years, is still to come, with the culmination of the return of the Messiah.

DATES AND TIMES

We know for certain Jesus was crucified at Passover. Passover is on the 15th day of Nissan, on a full moon, always.

It is not clear when exactly Jesus died or was resurrected. There were three calendars in use at the time, which can cause much confusion – Gregorian, Julian and Hebrew.

Not enough records have survived to, at this time, accurately date the last week of the Messiah definitively. To add to the confusion, year dates were not recorded as they are today until hundreds of years later. For example, in 100 A.D. they would not be calling that 100 A.D. because it wasn't until over 200 years later the birth of the Messiah was used as a pivot point for A.D./B.C.

In question is the year and on which days. Most scholars agree it would be between the years of 28 A.D. and 34 A.D., with the most popular year being 30 A.D., which churches have held to for a long time.

In recent years the leaning has been more to 32 A.D. In Luke 3:1 it states John baptized Jesus in the 15th year of Tiberius Caesar. Records show Caesar was in power from 14 A.D. Therefore, according to Luke, Jesus began His ministry in the year 29 A.D. (14 + 15). It is generally held Jesus' ministry was a little over three years, in which case it would be likely that the last week of the Messiah would be in 32 A.D. at Passover.

The days are another problem. Luke makes it clear in Luke 22:7 that the Last Supper was a Passover supper, and in Luke 23:54 Joseph of Arimathea took the body to prepare just before the Sabbath, which would place the crucifixion day on a Friday.

There is a lot of discussion over this one because of confusion over holiday sabbaths with many arguing for a Wednesday date. What adds to the complication is that Hebrew days start on the evening before, which is why I carefully placed dates and times at the beginning of each chapter.

The most traditional approach is Jesus was crucified on a Friday, so that is what I used for this novel.

MAPS AND PLACES

Every year the Israelis dig up more archaeological information, so this is an ever-changing subject.

I've used a map structure similar to those in common biblical use, but one thing to note is I used the modern names for the two main gates of Jerusalem – the Jaffa and Damascus gates because they are so familiar to many people. The gates were originally called Gennath Gate and Fish Gate. Today the Damascus Gate, or Fish Gate, is farther north than it was in biblical times when the city walls were expanded during the Byzantine era.

Recent archaeological discoveries have determined Herod's Palace was adjacent to the entrance of Jaffa Gate. The current thinking is that Pilate would have stayed at this palace when in Jerusalem. This works much better with the time frame given in the gospels. If Jesus had been taken back and forth between the Antonia Fortress, Herod's Palace and the high priests, it would have involved a lot of very quick moving around over lengthy distances. If it had happened similar to what is laid out in this novel, then a very compact area was involved, even to the crucifixion site. I make no claims this is absolutely correct, but it would seem likely given the information we have today.

The site of the crucifixion and burial were outside the city walls. But again, the walls were expanded centuries after the event, leaving the sites inside the current city walls.

Queen Helena of Rome selected a site 300 years after the Messiah and built the Church of the Holy Sepulchre on it. Again, the most likely spot of the crucifixion. Unfortunately, this location has been so overbuilt throughout the centuries, it is impossible to get a genuine sense of the sites as they would have been at the time of Jesus.

The more recent discovery of Gordon's Tomb, or the Garden Tomb north of the city, is another possibility that has been beautifully restored. Right beside the Garden Tomb are the cliffs which have the markings of a skull worn into the face. A beautiful and compelling location. It would be a lengthy walk to this location from the center of the city, so for the novel I chose to use the traditional site where the Church of the Holy Sepulchre sits, making the distance traveled in those few hours of the trial and crucifixion very short.

FINAL WORD

I encourage you, if you have not yet met the Messiah, reach out to Him. He will answer. That simple act will change your life forever.

If you are anything like I was, then you will identify with Atara in this novel. Before you can let your guard down enough to step out in faith, you will need to be able to justify taking that step in your mind. Throughout this novel I have attempted to show the incredible detail God laid out in His plan for salvation. From the prophetic words hundreds of years prior, to the intricacies of the Temple ordinances. The odds of all these randomly occurring at one point in history is virtually impossible. God laid out a beautiful plan for salvation right from the beginning of time, and all that is required of us is to turn back to Him. As the disciple John has written:

> "For God so loved the world that He gave His one and only Son, that whoever believes in Him shall not perish, but have eternal life. For God did not send His Son into the world to condemn the world, but to save the world through Him."[66]

Jesus is our advocate and our salvation. Seek Him. He is waiting to welcome you.

---

[66] John 3:16–17

Acknowledgements

Completing a work such as *The Crown and Salvation* cannot go without special acknowledgement of all those who have participated in this journey with me.

First, I would like to thank our heavenly Father for His guidance through this delicate subject. I do not take weaving a fictional story of faith through the factual Passover week of Christ lightly, and I cannot tell you how many times I was emotionally overtaken while writing. Any credit and glory go to God.

For all those around me who participated, you have my thanks. To my wife, who was very patient and helpful throughout the process, and those friends who helped by reading the early manuscripts and offering their feedback. To Dustin and Shawna, for their encouragement and help. This is the result of all that effort.

I also offer a special thanks to Messianic believers who have brought new insight to the life of Y'shua through their Jewish heritage. I recommend the writings of Jonathan Cahn for those who wish to learn more.

The hard work and personal interest of my editor, Janet, was very much appreciated, making the story so much more readable. I also thank young Melanie for her wonderful sketches.

Lastly, I would like to thank you, the reader, and pray that this story has deepened your faith and understanding of the Bible.

About the Author

Neil Fox is a retired professor and past coordinator of the Creative Photography program at Humber College in Toronto. He currently resides in Orillia, Ontario with his wife Barbara. Over the years, Neil has been involved in many business ventures, exhibits, and innovative projects, including the writing of numerous manuals for course material. A believer since 1971, Neil and his family spent several years in Jerusalem through the mid-1980s, learning and photographing the land. His passion for the wealth of biblical information that has been revealed in recent years through Messianic believers is reflected in this work.

www.ingramcontent.com/pod-product-compliance
Lightning Source LLC
Chambersburg PA
CBHW070220030726
47505CB00006B/1743